PRAISE FOR JON COURTENAY GRIMWOOD
AND HIS NOVELS

'Fascinating and compelling . . . A story which has as much to do with today's world as the world of the future. Crime is commonplace and life is cheap, but the human spirit is alive and well and refusing to submit' *BIRMINGHAM EVENING MAIL*

'A definite breath of fresh air for a science fiction genre long overdue for reinvention' *SFX*

'William Gibson meets Quentin Tarantino . . .' *NEW WOMAN*

'A virtuoso head-on collision between futur-noir cyberSurgery and blasphemous ghoulish antiquity – in full detail' Colin Greenland, best-selling author of TAKE BACK PLENTY

'Grimwood has so much energy and such a talent he carries you along relentlessly, like a crazed hijacker' *LOCUS*

'Grimwood unravels for us a dangerous future: transformed by new technology, but riven by religious intolerance, fascism, cruelty and greed . . . a future-shock blizzard' Stephen Baxter, best-selling author of THE TIME SHIPS and winner of the Philip K. Dick Award

'Grimwood assembles a cast of strong, mainly female characters in a pacy journey, interspersed with awesome descriptions of cybertechnology' *MIXMAG*

'Jon Courtenay Grimwood eats hard-boiled punk SF for breakfast . . . with soldiers' *MATRIX* (British SF Association)

'Violent, passionate and thoroughly seedy, Lucifer's Dragon makes for a cracking good read.' *ODYSSEY*

'A multi-layered thriller in which the exotic, tech-saturated setting is as beguiling as the plot. Firmly in the Gibson and Sterling tradition, but much more than a mere imitator, Grimwood spurs cyberpunk one step on. The narrative steams with galvanising inventiveness.'   *TIME OUT*

'. . . sex, violence, real-seeming computer games (the Lucifer's Dragon of the title), corrupt mega-corporations, genetically-altered humans in street gangs . . . Lucifer's Dragon is publicised as 'Cybershock' – and shocking it certainly is.'   *VECTOR*

'Grimwood's Napoleonic alternate history gives him a jump cut to a future that could be ours sooner than we'd like to think . . . You'd need a heart of stone not to laugh.' Ken MacLeod, best-selling author of THE STAR FRACTION

Other books by Jon Courtenay Grimwood

neoAddix

Lucifer's Dragon

About the author . . .

Born in Malta and christened in the upturned bell of a ship, Jon Courtenay Grimwood grew up in Britain, the Far East and Scandinavia. He currently works as a freelance journalist and lives in North London. He writes for a number of newspapers and magazines, including the *Guardian* and *SFX*.

Jon is also the author of *neoAddix* and *Lucifer's Dragon* and has just finished writing his fourth novel, *redRobe*.

The *reMix* website is at http://www.hardcopy.demon.co.uk

reMix

Jon Courtenay Grimwood

LONDON · SYDNEY · NEW YORK · TOKYO · SINGAPORE · TORONTO

www.earthlight.co.uk

First published in Great Britain by Earthlight, 1999
An imprint of Simon & Schuster UK Ltd
A Viacom Company

1 3 5 7 9 10 8 6 4 2

Simon & Schuster UK Ltd
Africa House
64-78 Kingsway
London WC2 6AH

Simon & Schuster Australia
Sydney

A CIP catalogue record for this book is available
from the British Library

ISBN 0-671-02222-9

Typeset in Melior by Palimpsest Book Production Limited,
Polmont, Stirlingshire
Printed and bound in Great Britain by
Caledonian International
Book Manufacturing, Glasgow

For Sam, with thanks. I owe you big time. And for Jammer, who'd rather be in Spain at Finestrat or beating hell out of some games machine . . .

'There are no innocent bystanders . . . What are they doing there in the first place?'

W.S. Burroughs

Chapter One

Aim to please, Shoot to kill

'Save the world, leave the planet . . .'

'Yeah, right,' thought LizAlec, stuffing her hands deeper in her pockets.

As a piece of logic it sucked. But then, the poster was there to sell lottery tickets, not win a Nobel prize for intelligence. Not that LizAlec would have been seen dead wasting $15 on an odds-off chance of blasting into space as the new Eve. Inflation or not, $15 still bought half a twist of crystal rage, which was exactly what LizAlec needed just then.

It was New Year's Day and LizAlec was having a mare.

No one else getting off the budget shuttle gave the poster any thought, but it still kept on chanting Brother Michael's slogan at any visitor near enough to set off its sensors, which was everyone approaching Customs. The hologram was fly-posted to a pillar in the Arrivals Hall, and the hall was busy 24/7.

Brother Michael and Sister Aaron . . . Rumour said Sister Aaron was just another West Coast chick-with-a-dick until she met Brother Michael, the man who did what other ex-cons only dreamed of – burnt down the penitentiary at Rikers Island.

Now Sister Aaron was rumoured to be in cryo, somewhere between Earth and Luna, while Eden was rebuilt around her. It took money to build a ring-colony – even a small one – and that meant donations. Tax-free and with the promise not just of salvation but of a chance in the lottery. A chance to float off into deep space, surrounded by trees, animals and fresh air . . . not to mention some shit-for-brains who happened to be the other lucky winner.

LizAlec was already palming a gold HKS credit card by the time she reached the Kodak vidbooth, her fingers doing that come-down amphetamine dance that cuts in just before you get the full shakes. One call home to Mummy to say sorry was all it would take, but the fuck she would. This one was for Fixx, to remind the bastard what he was missing. Three weeks she'd been back in Paris with him all over her like a rash and then not even a goodbye call . . .

LizAlec came out of the booth buttoning her school shirt, cotton blazer slung sloppily over one thin shoulder. Her deep violet eyes flicked over the hired bodyguard, and her *WeGuard* looked hurriedly away as LizAlec fumbled with pearl buttons, hunching her shoulders as she slipped a black tippet round her neck and knotted it neatly, like the regulations at St Lucius demanded.

It was time to go find Ms Gwyneth.

A year from now, if LizAlec wanted to, she'd be able to recall everything around her, from that crying brat with the McDonald's soyburger to the cheap chrome façade of the franchised sushi bar.

LizAlec shook her head, trying to wipe it of images. Most people summoned up scents, tastes or emotions to pluck memories from the brain's limbic system. LizAlec recorded images only, eidetic-style. Cold clear images, perfect scans. No feelings to her memories, certainly no accompanying sounds or smells.

Not now. Not for a long time.

The chances of her e-vid ever reaching Fixx were almost zero, but at least she'd tried. The address she'd called was a drop box for his fan club; knowing Fixx, something cheap and automated, run out of a derelict basement in Bastille. She'd done what she could to make sure it got past her mother, used heavyweight crypt, forked out for a new coms card because her own was bound to be on a filter list. She'd even paid extra to bounce a back-up off a different orbital re-mailer.

What else could she do? LizAlec already knew the answer to that. Niet, Nothing, Nada . . . Chances were, Lady Clare would still have her message intercepted and wiped clean by some web-bot, but then, that was just her mother for you. LizAlec buttoned her blue blazer and sunk her hands deep into trouser pockets, pushing down until the cloth was pulled tight across her hips.

Up ahead was Luna Customs – two droids and a token human – not that getting checked was necessary. Without even knowing it, LizAlec had already been stripped, recorded, every cavity scanned by m/wave cameras as she stepped onto and off the shuttle. All she need do now was pass through the barrier and go find the prissy Ms Gwyneth.

Except it wasn't just Ms Gwyneth who was waiting. With the headmistress was a geeky little Chinese girl clutching a metal flower. That was who LizAlec was going to be sharing her room with and sending Anchee along was meant to make LizAlec feel at home. Instead it just made her feel sick.

'Fuck it,' LizAlec muttered hoarsely, pushing her way through the Customs booth. Her voice had that cut-glass quality that says *money* no matter what language is used. But even LizAlec's accent couldn't disguise the fact she'd been crying for most of the flight, pretty much from blast off to landing. And the fact she was wired to hell probably didn't help either.

'Fuck it, fuck it, fuck it . . .'

In front of her, Anchee frowned while Ms Gwyneth pretended not to hear. Not that it made any difference to LizAlec. What were the Sisters of St Lucius going to do? Tell her mother?

As if LizAlec would care.

Expel her?

If only . . . But they wouldn't. She'd already tried. LizAlec wanted out but it just wasn't going to happen.

'It's not going to happen, is it?' LizAlec demanded loudly, staring at Ms Gwyneth. The woman was staring back like LizAlec was a freak. Actually, LizAlec realized, everyone was staring.

LizAlec looked for her *WeGuard*, noted he'd freeze-framed in mid-stride and finally saw what had grabbed everyone's attention. Though it wasn't actually the man in the Mickey Mouse mask that Anchee, Ms Gwyneth and her *WeGuard* were watching: it was what he held in his hand.

Rainbow-chrome barrel. A laser sight half as long as the barrel, riveted to the top. An enormous enamel cartouche braised to its ivory handle, the crest something triple-hatted, papal.

Stolen or fake, LizAlec decided.

It was an old-model ten-shot Heckler and Koch, retrofitted for the new lock-on slugs. Okay for some Parisian street gang, if they weren't too choosy, but the Papal States were better armed than that. Besides, what quarrel could Pope Joan have with a schoolgirl in transit on the moon?

St Lucius Academy was single-sex, classically structured and – as of now – based in its own full-gravity O'Neill colony. It also now kept a facility on the moon for low-gravity sports, a roofed-over crater 300 klicks from Chrysler City, 800 klicks from Fracture and a full 100 klicks from the nearest male human, guaranteed. No wonder her mother loved it. Christ, it had to be the only school in existence that still taught in Latin.

The laser bead was moving now, dropping down LizAlec's school shirt, ticking off the fussy pearl buttons one by one. And then the red dot began to move up again, until LizAlec could no longer see it. But it wasn't hard to guess where it was now. Not if the expression on her *WeGuard*'s sweat-beaded face was anything to go by. Resting neatly on her forehead, probably. So she looked like some fifteen-to-a-room dothead from the projects out beyond Cluny.

'Shit.' LizAlec sucked at her teeth in disgust. First Fixx, then her mother. And now just to wind things up, it looked like she was about to get slotted by some B-movie psycho in a plastic mouse-mask. What a perfect bloody start to the New Year.

'You going to shoot, or not?' LizAlec asked. She smiled sweetly at the man, watching the glint of his eyes through the idiot mask hiding his face. The whole Arrivals Hall was holding its breath, LizAlec knew that. It was what she was counting on. She had one eye on the frozen crowd, one on the security vids busy recording everything that went down.

'Please, no . . .' The tiny Chinese girl, Anchee, stepped forward only to stop dead as the muzzle of the man's automatic rammed against her mouth in a cold ceramic kiss. Three years of priceless orthodontics went straight down the drain. LizAlec didn't even blink.

'Well?' LizAlec's voice carried easily over the head of the silent crowd. She didn't want her mother to miss a single dramatic moment. Come to that, she didn't want her to miss how useless her locally hired *WeGuard* was either.

'You going to do something about this?' LizAlec said to her frozen-faced black bodyguard. Very slowly, the man shook his head.

Typical.

'Get on with it, then,' LizAlec told the man in the mouse-mask and stepped back, giving him space. She counted off the time in fractions, the way she used to do back when she was a kid. He was furious, she knew that. And this wasn't how hits were meant to go, she knew that, too. But LizAlec didn't care.

For three whole seconds, it almost seemed like the mouse-man might actually blast a little smart slug straight through her head. But then the gun's muzzle swept over the frozen crowd and the man fell back on the words he'd been practising earlier, while he was still waiting for LizAlec's Boeing to land.

'Get down and stay down . . .'

His words were digital, issuing from a kid's translation box. The kind Toys 'R' Us piled high and sold cheap from wire baskets near the door. At least, that was the last place LizAlec had seen one, at the kiddie boutique right after you came through Sonic Cleaning & Immigration.

LizAlec looked around at the Arrivals Hall. Everyone but her and the frozen bodyguard were busy falling to their knees, like they'd got instant religion – just add fear.

LizAlec felt like asking Anchee what she thought of the blue mosaic on the floor, but now didn't seem a good time. Anchee was face down on the tiles, sobbing. And from what LizAlec could see of the hand held to Anchee's mouth, the only colour Anchee could see was red.

So, instead, LizAlec made do with looking at Mickey's long brown coat. Close up the coat wasn't as stupid as it looked. Inappropriate, yes. A style insult, undoubtedly. But stupid . . . ? No coat that combined a flame-proof, heat-dispersing outer layer with an anti-shrapnel, spider's-silk lining could be called stupid.

Maybe the *WeGuard* at her side wasn't really a gutless waste of money at all. Maybe the man just recognized a true professional when he met one. For a second LizAlec was tempted to give her bodyguard the benefit of the doubt, but then decided not to bother.

'You,' said the man, pointing at LizAlec. 'Come with me.'

LizAlec thought about it for all of one second, and then shook her head, heavy black curls briefly brushing her ears. Her decision was to cost someone their life, but LizAlec was still a full fifteen seconds away from knowing that.

'If you don't move,' said the man, taking a step towards her, 'I *will* shoot you.' His words were dangerously quiet. Casually he brought the automatic up level with LizAlec's face. And behind her, LizAlec's *WeGuard* chose that moment to make his play. Fat fingers reaching for a 50,000-volt taser velcroed to his wide leather belt.

It was a brave move but a seriously stupid one.

LizAlec caught the flash but didn't see the .38 ceramic rip through the bodyguard's Kevlar-lined black shirt, opening a black hole over his heart that grew fist-sized by the time the slug exploded out of his back, showering fragments of spine and shredded lung over the stunned crowd.

Sweet Jesus.

Everyone started screaming at once, but it was Anchee that LizAlec immediately noticed. The tiny Chinese girl was up on her knees screaming so hard no sound came out of her bloodied mouth. 'It's okay,' LizAlec said harshly, crouching down beside the girl. 'Hey, it's okay.' It wasn't. LizAlec knew that: she'd been there.

Desperately, LizAlec stroked the other girl's hair. Which wasn't LizAlec's style at all, but she was too shocked to remember that. And besides, she was too busy trying to wipe Anchee's mouth clean of blood and fragments of tooth without letting Anchee know what she was doing.

LizAlec was still wiping red spittle from Anchee's lips when the Chinese girl blacked out in LizAlec's arms, her silver flower clattering to the floor. Without thinking, LizAlec grabbed it and waves of darkness immediately swept in over her like someone had just invented the code.

The last thing LizAlec remembered before the man hoisted her onto his shoulder was that Anchee's silver flower closed itself up and slid over her bloodied fingers, until it locked itself around the outside of LizAlec's wrist. And then the void came in, amphetamine-fast and twice as unforgiving.

Medical droids carried Anchee to the St Lucius skimmer on a MediSoft stretcher, the Chinese girl's mouth wide open with shock, blood and spittle dribbling down her once perfect face.

It was classic trauma, announced the stretcher cheerfully, and Ms Gwyneth winced. Classic trauma was almost guaranteed to develop into full-blown post-trauma and cases of PTS got schools like St Lucius sued for billions. Not least because Anchee had been sent to school precisely to keep her away from such incidents.

That Lady Elizabeth Alexandra Fabio had been abducted was a disaster . . . poor child. By the time they reached the shuttle, Ms Gwyneth had finally trained herself to think of LizAlec as *poor child*, though it didn't come naturally, not after hearing about the little brat's temper tantrums on the flight out.

But, to be brutal about it, Lady Elizabeth's disappearance wasn't the disaster it could have been, or even would have been, only three months back . . . Paris would fall to the Reich, that much was now commonly accepted. And when it did, it would take the whole ossified Napoleonic empire with it, LizAlec's mother and all.

It was what had happened to Anchee that terrified Ms Gwyneth. Quite simply, if this was handled wrongly, it might mean the end of the school. St Lucius was in the business of education, not moral judgement. The school made it a point of principle not to enquire how parents came by their money. But Ms Gwyneth had heard rumours about Anchee's father, dark unpleasant rumours. And Ms Gwyneth made a point of listening to rumour: one always heard so much of the truth . . .

She would have to make contingency plans.

She did.

It took thirty-five per cent of St Lucius's capital reserve to have ten per cent of Planetside's m/wave surveillance cameras wiped by a freak bot that somehow bypassed all standard cut-outs and affected only the vids covering what took place in the Arrivals Hall. The old Cray bioAI put in place specifically to see that kind of thing didn't happen didn't turn a hair. It had been corrupted years back, and now spent most of its time watching reruns of *SpaceHospital: The Final Years.*

Chapter 2

Walk/Don't Walk

Even Lars thought of himself as *the ratboy*. Though the fact was that Lars had only ever been one-third of the ratboy, but the newsfeeds didn't know that. They thought *the ratboy* was one psychotic little scavenger camped out in the heating ducts and service tunnels of Planetside Arrivals. But the feeds were wrong about that, as they were wrong about most things. *Psychotic*, yes. *Scavenger*, ditto. It was *little* that was way off target.

The ratboy was famous. You could buy tri-Ds at tourist booths in both Arrivals and Departures. Lars had one, stapled to the wall of his bunker – in fact he was looking at it now. The picture showed a thin blond boy with spiky hair crouched near a vidbooth. It didn't look anything like him at all.

For a start, his hair was dark brown and flopped round his head as if it had been crudely hacked off with a molywire knife, which it had. His brown eyes bulged from a face wide enough to look square. Add heavy lower canines and a protruding lower jaw and even Lars could work out that when it came to looks he'd been dealt a lousy hand. Unfortunately, luck hadn't bothered to add intelligence or a sunny disposition to make up a counterweight.

He was the last third of the rat-boy left. Causley had been the first to buy it, caught in a blow-out, breath vacuum-sucked from his body in an airlock accident. That was what happened if you used tunnels reserved for tourist luggage. Which had left Lars and Ben, except Ben came up with a raid on LunaWorld: Ben was always coming up with shit like that.

Usually he had the sense not go through with it, but not this time.

Somewhere between Planetside Arrivals and LunaWorld, Ben lanced the bolts off a service hatch and slid down into the rough-hewn tunnel below. The tunnel was unlit, slung along its black walls with long snake-loops of obsolete optic fibre. The prints of crêpe soles in the dust said some guy had been there before them. But this was Luna, no dust shifted unless it was made to. It could have been a hundred years since the tracks were made, or it might have been that morning.

Lars had slid down behind Ben, protesting. He'd still been protesting when a suited-up, distant *WeGuard* kicked Ben's leg out from under him with a burst of ceramic. It wouldn't have happened if Lars had been doing his job, but he'd been too busy sulking to read off the infrared. That was how Ben got caught.

The 'fight' lasted all of three seconds, which was how long it took the guard to rip open Ben's lungs with another burst. Sucking chest wounds are rough enough when there's air around. Remove the oxygen and add in a near-vacuum and Ben never stood a chance. Roughly 350 million alveoli ruptured like exploding bubblepak and the inside of Ben's lungs turned to foaming red sponge.

Lars was in there and rolling across the floor towards Ben before he realized what he was doing. Slugs hit the rock face around him but nothing landed. Ignoring Ben's frenzied thrashing, Lars dragged him down the tunnel, away from the guard.

As soon as Lars could, he took a tiny side tunnel, pulling Ben after him, levering off a hatch to drop down another level, tossing Ben down ahead of him. As soon as Lars felt safe, he stopped and reached into the pocket of his bubble suit for a lightstick. Twisting the precious tube, Lars saw by its bioluminescnence that Ben was already neatly vacuum-packed. The void had pulled the air out of Ben's face bubble, sucking it down his throat and out of his ruptured lungs, sealing the mask to Ben's face.

Blue eyes were open and stark behind the soft clear Kevlar. It was way too late to take Ben to a hospital, even if Lars had had credit to pay the fees. Shit happens and then some idiot in a uniform wants you to fill out the forms. That wasn't the way Ben and Lars worked.

Reaching into his other pocket, Lars pulled out his molywire knife and did what he'd always promised Ben he'd do, if it came to it. But first he tied Ben off at the neck, just under the other boy's chin, so the vacuum didn't get any more of Ben's blood. Lars didn't know if that made sense or not, it just seemed like a good idea.

Ben's head came away clean, molywire slicing through vertebrae, gristle, veins and arteries. It wasn't effortless, but it was still a lot easier than Lars was expecting. And when he looked at the severed neck, Lars was proud that the cut was clean, the edges of the jugular and subclavian veins all neatly sheared. Only the voice box was damaged and that wasn't serious – at least, Lars hoped it wasn't.

He wrapped the head tight in cloth cut from Ben's suit and knotted it at the corners. Not ideal, but Lars figured it would have to do, at least until he could manage something better. Only something better never turned up, so Ben's head was still wrapped in tattered Kevlar. But these days Lars kept the bundle in an ice bucket, which was what he called the Matsui coldbox he'd lifted from some tourist's luggage.

Somewhere at the back of Lars's mind the inconvenient fact that extops were meant to be kept in liquid nitrogen kept trying to break through: chilled down to something like minus 192. Well, tough. A coldbox had to be better than nothing, didn't it? And besides, when Lars got money, he was going to book Ben into the best cryo facility that the moon could produce . . .

Lars had known he was at the bottom of the food chain, long before he even knew what a food chain was. When he was five, a fat Russian tourist with heavy fists told Lars that was where he belonged. Back then, Lars had figured it meant he was always going to be the last one in the children's home to get fed. Which made sense: he always was.

These days Lars fed himself, which was just as well, as there was no one else to do it. Sixteen was the cut-off point for getting the social; after that you were on your own. When he wasn't ransacking other people's luggage, Lars lived in the tunnels. Used to be lots of people lived in the tunnels under Planetside Arrivals, but they'd been hosed out five years before in the last really big clean-up. That was how Lars was able to get himself a space.

Not that surviving in Planetside was easy. There were airlocks, of course, and not just between Arrivals and the outlying crater cities. Even inside Arrivals the main streets had bomb-mesh security doors, laser-cut steel with recessed titanium deadlocks. But Lars made a point of finding out each week's codes for the service tunnels, and then trading them for food. People might not want to live in the warrens anymore, but the tunnels still made the best route from A to Z, especially if you didn't want any of the letters in the middle to know you'd been past. And a lot of low-end LunaWorld kitchen staff didn't.

After the big clean-out, most of the old tunnel-dwellers had ended up in Fracture, but then Fracture was 2500 square miles of rock and mud-walled houses thrown up by the CasAdobe virus and they were welcome to it. He'd stick with the five square miles of franchise-heaving, LunaWorld-owned Arrivals Hall.

In the beginning there was LunaWorld, then Chrysler and finally Fracture. After that, the O'Neills took over. Who needed one-sixth G on the surface when they could have full gravity for nothing in an O'Neill? By the time a minor pressure glitch blew a fifteen-mile crack into the 2500-square-mile ceiling that glass spiders had spun across the crater mouth at what became known as Fracture, five other crater cities had been announced. But Fracture finished the building boom.

It didn't matter that an emergency contingent of Microsoft's code police had stripped out the glitch and clean-coded the pressure program inside twelve hours. It didn't even matter that if the roof had blown – and there would have been warning – it would have blown up and outwards, not dumped the water baffle directly on the heads of the crater's inhabitants. All of whom owned pressure suits anyway.

That wasn't how the investors, customers and real estate agents saw it. They didn't see that the water baffle was there to drop radiation down to safe levels, that it was a miracle of equivalence that kept the precious water safely between two vast sheets of glass and roofed in an entire crater. They just saw themselves spending each day looking nervously up at a broken sky. Fracture went out of fashion bigtime.

But all that was long after LunaWorld was built. Back then, it was the Malays who put the lines of credit in place, Beijing who supplied most of the surface work force. While the Americans provided sandrats and franchise holders to fill the cavernous space of Planetside Arrivals once it was dug into the rock and domed over. It was an old idea, sinking a base into the surface and then roofing it: most of the US Antarctic bases had been built like that for years.

Lars knew none of this, of course. All he knew was that his great-grandfather had come from New Jersey, freighted out on ready cash and promises of a better life, back in the days when the Moon was still a frontier. Now the frontier had moved out to Mars and until last month LunaWorld was a trailer-park trash substitute for SonyCorp's new GinzaGold orbital.

But now there were new flights every day. The Hyatts were full. Bars that hadn't seen a non-package tourist in thirty years were busy hiring out beds to the highest bidder. Something big was going down: the only problem for Lars was that he didn't know what. His bunker was too deep for him to be able to splice into a newsfeed, otherwise he'd have wired Ben up permanent, instead of having to find a socket every now and then, when the readout showed Ben's battery pack was getting low.

He'd seen something interesting today, though. A scowling Earth kid grabbed from a shocked crowd, a *WeGuard* killed, guns firing. It was more excitement than Lars had seen in . . . he didn't know how long. Since Ben died, probably.

Patting Ben's ice bucket affectionately, Lars used its top to cut himself a huge slice of Jarlsburg. The Norwegian cheese was stale, but Lars didn't mind. It tasted good enough to him. Besides, it was free. He'd lifted if off a cargo hand who'd scooped it from the luggage of some flax-haired Scandinavian refugee.

In a minute, he'd take a shit behind a pillar in a dead-end tunnel that ran off the downshaft, then he'd come back and wank to the soft glow of a holoporn slab he'd stolen years before. Lars knew each of the girls and all of their moves by heart, but it did for him. That done, he'd probably sleep. It wasn't a perfect life but it would do.

All the same, he wished he had a newsfeed . . .

Chapter 3

Still Life (but only just . . .)

Passion was back – a new body and a new haircut – miked-up with a subvocal throat bead, standing in the middle of a pile of concrete rubble. It was forty years since she'd given up presenting a show for CySat and only eighteen months since she'd come back on air – syndicated to every major newsfeed.

She was in Tbilisi now, dressed in combat fatigues, the backgound carefully chosen to match her stark words. She spoke, as only Passion still could, straight to the vid, no script, no rehearsals, no retakes . . .

'Three hundred innocent Georgians, mostly women and small children, caught in the biggest skyscraper crash since the virus escaped.'

Red hair and the ends of her purple scarf flapping wildly in the January wind, Passion pointed behind her, to where the crushed and broken husk of a snow-covered tenement block stood chopped off like the stump of a rotten tree. Just in case the audience didn't make an immediate connection, the camera lingered on the half-eaten carcass of a Russian tank, chewed down to its ceramic tracks and surrounded by the now familiar circle of dark grey ash.

It wasn't ash, of course. It was what you got left with when a nanetic virus had finished chewing its way through weapons-grade steel. And the tank hadn't been in front of the collapsed building when Passion arrived, any more than the rubble had been arranged in artistic heaps. The tank had been several hundred paces away, kitty-corner to the intersection where it had first started to rot. But Passion wasn't interested in the small-code stuff, never had been, she was there to present the overall programme in a way it could be understood.

It had taken gold to get eight suspicious Georgian soldiers to lug the ceramic tracks to the exact position Passion wanted, and the grey residue was soot mixed with flour. Snow had covered the real ash hours before. But Passion wasn't worried: it was a real tank, really eaten, in front of a ferroconcrete block that had really collapsed, killing real people. She'd just brought the elements together.

'Bayer-Rochelle, SkB, Imperial Impirical, all are rumoured to be working on a 'dote. But what if that is not enough? What then? Who knows how much longer this plague will rage? Who knows if it can even be stopped?' Signing off with a long, serious gaze to the camera, Passion clicked her fingers and the tiny Aerospatiale 182 retracted its lens and flew into her hand. From there Passion downloaded the data to her belt, uploaded it to a local low-level ComSat and smiled. One of these days the virus was going to get into her camera, but until then . . .

Job done and done well. Twisting her head to ease the tension in her neck, Passion tucked the little camera into a canvas pouch on her belt and palmed a packet of Lucky Strike. Half a morning into the New Year and she'd already blown her resolution, just like always. Zero tar, low carcinogenic content, smart filter – and they still whacked up her health premiums. Still, that was CySat's problem, and given what the network had to pay out on a hack who insisted on being on site in person, rather than sending in a drone and then doing a voice-over, the cigs probably made little difference.

Besides, Passion was a full director of CySat nV, not just the US franchise. She held a neoVenetian passport, with full diplomatic immunity, so she could afford to indulge herself.

Passion flicked open an antique Zippo, inscribed *101st Airborne – Summer of Love*. It fired up first time. Passion prided herself on the small touches, and that brass lighter was one of her best. Of course, it needed fuel but Tbilisi had plenty of that, from wooden barrels of crude to bottles of petrol. And not a single functioning 4x4 anywhere in the country.

Which was why Passion had come down the mountains on a horse, balanced on the spavined back of an eighteen-year-old chestnut nag, which still cost CySat more than a new Seraphim four-track would have done had anyone still been bothering to grow them. Passion knew from neoVenetian intelligence – which took feeds from almost everyone else – that Honda and Ford were both busy trying to finalize code for an all-ceramic vehicle. The problem was, it could be months, maybe even longer, before the all-ceramics hit the market. And until they did, Eastern Europe, the North African littoral and most of Imperial Turkey had reverted to the era of the nag and carriage.

It wasn't until you stopped to think how much of the world's infrastructure relied on steel that the extent of the Azerbaijani catastrophe became obvious. That building behind her went down because it was polycrete thrown up around a standard ferric matrix. Let a nanetic virus reach part of a ferric frame and the building, any building, was eaten up from inside.

And the big problem – at least, Passion had been told it was the big problem – was that the building looked perfectly healthy until the ferroconcrete crumbled. Small wonder the police were failing to get Tbilisi's project dwellers to move. Not that there was anywhere for them to go, except out into the ever-falling snow.

Sighing heavily, Passion ground the butt of her Lucky Strike under one boot heel and reached for a canvas bag. It contained goat's cheese, rye bread and a flask of real coffee. High-grown Colombian, delivered by CySat's diplomatic pouch, flown into Tbilisi just before the wind changed and the virus struck.

The woman chewed an edge off the hard bread while pouring herself half a mug of the hot thick liquid from an antique silver Alessi flask, inhaling the coffee's rich earth tones over the distinctive sourdough smell of the rye bread. It was too hot to drink but Passion drank it anyway, following it with a second cup.

Nothing like it . . . Well, apart from raw sex, crystal meth and the thrill of discovering an unknown painting by Andy Warhol. And sad to admit, even Passion felt she was getting a bit too old for those these days. Too old for the harsh reality of combat reporting as well, if she was honest. All the same, Passion was glad she'd insisted on getting back in front of the camera, even if the little Aerospatiale was hers and CySat had only agreed to the trip because Passion was too senior, too stroppy and too famous to stop. Passion sighed again and began to dribble the dregs of her coffee into the snow at her feet.

'Miss . . .' An old man, walrus moustache and creased face, was watching her, a snot-nosed toddler tucked under his arm, struggling silently. *Shit* . . . It was obvious what the man wanted: the dregs of Passion's cup. Passion didn't know whether to be cross not to have thought of it herself, or ashamed to admit the idea of charity embarrassed her.

Either way, Passion knew she couldn't refuse. Not the remains of her coffee or what was left of her rye bread, which was most of it. Handing them over, along with a soft, rancid-smelling goat's cheese she had been saving for later, she looked into the man's tired eyes and accepted what she already knew. That however much older than her the hollow-eyed, distraught man looked, he was years, decades, maybe even a century younger than Passion.

'So hate yourself,' Passion thought bitterly, reaching for her belt. And some days Passion did, but she still did what she was going to do. Pulling the little satellite camera from her pouch, Passion threw the Aerospatiale lightly into the air where it whirred like a mechanical wasp before flying to a preset p.o.v. five paces to the front and right of her.

Facts were sacred but human interest was the hook. If you were slumped slobbing on a settee in New Jersey it didn't matter a flying fuck that the virus had started in Uzbekistan as a flawed attempt to stop Chinese tanks in their tracks. In fact, statistically you were unlikely to know what a *telimar* mechanism was, never mind caring about the fact that the cut-off mechanism had failed in ten per cent of Uzbek created nanites, forcing them to feed on whatever ferric metal the prevailing wind allowed them to find.

'*And so a military weapon designed to last no longer than twelve hours is spreading westwards towards central Europe, leaving heartbreak in its trail. Heartbreak like the tragedy of this old man whose three dead sons still lie in the rubble behind me . . .*'

Passion had no idea whether or not that was strictly true. But all the same, there would be a core of reality to it. You only had to look into the man's grey eyes to see the grief. It wasn't an easy sight and Passion hoped she'd never get used to it, but somewhere inside herself she was afraid that she already had.

If there had been a plane out of Tbilisi, she'd have bought it, at whatever cost. But it was three days since Tbilisi airport had been functioning. Like it or not, Passion was trapped on the wrong side of the virus. Word was, the infection would reach Odessa within twelve hours, Paris within five days.

No one knew if it would reach the US but – like Luna – Congress was in the process of closing down its borders, and setting up a strict sonic-cleansing process for anyone so rich or famous they absolutely couldn't be turned away. But Passion had a feeling that wasn't going to work, not least because it was impossible to legislate against the wind or birds and insects. Not that the White House wouldn't at least try. A heart of gold the President might have, not to mention skin like Teflon, but his brain was pure marshmallow.

No, Passion was stuck with her camera and a beltful of Louis Napoleon gold dollars. It was time she got used to the idea. Holding out her hand to retrieve her little silver camera, Passion pocketed it and straightened up, walking away without once looking back at the bitter-eyed man and child, or the crumpled building behind her.

Chapter 4

Sour Times

Lars tracked LizAlec from the Arrivals Hall out to the Edge and then topside as the kidnappers buggied out for fifteen miles over the dust wastes of a small sea. The kidnappers had gone topside, Lars had gone under, running the disused service tunnels between Planetside and Fracture. Some habits were too hard to break.

To get to Planetside's Edge, he jumped a mail drone when it wasn't looking, dropping down onto it from a tunnel above. The delivery drone hadn't liked that. In fact, its opening response had been, 'Get off my back now or I'll fry your balls.' Which wasn't an idle threat. All mail delivery drones had zap capabilities to discourage pilferers. But, in the end, Lars had argued it into submission. Though from the ease with which the drone gave up, Lars got the feeling it was glad of the company.

But that was way back. Now he was tubed in with the Big Black all around him, trying to ignore the cold and the lack of oxygen. By pressing his back against one side of the shaft and keeping his legs pushed out straight, Lars could move up the steep bore-hole without too much effort. It didn't matter that a thin line of monofilament dropped away into the vacuum below – the weight of Ben's ice bucket wasn't enough to upset his balance. Luna gravity was a sixth of that on Earth – not that Lars knew what standard gravity felt like, or ever would.

He'd been conceived, podded and brought up on the moon and it showed in his bones, in the onset of incipient osteoporosis, in the brittleness of their matrices and the pronounced lack of calcium. Lars looked fat-faced because his endocrine system was fucked over by the lack of light, gravity and basic health care. His muscles too were undeveloped by earth standards, but pot-belly or not Lars could still move more gracefully than any tourist. As for climbing, he wasn't *Ratboy* for nothing. No vent was too steep, no optix tunnel too cold, dark or low to keep him out.

All the same, he hated working beyond the Edge. It was off-code as far as Lars was concerned. He was strictly a Planetside creature. It wasn't just that the off-Edge blackness meant he burnt up precious lightsticks, or even that the fierce cold could strip warmth from a human body as surely as dropping it in liquid nitrogen. It was having to rely on an o/lung.

Even wearing his precious bubble suit, the rough-hewn wall was sharp against his back, where it pressed against black Kevlar mesh. So sharp, Lars felt sure it would snag. But that didn't make him anxious. What scared him shitless, was the thought of getting his o/lung caught against an outcrop of rock in the darkness, ripping it out of his side to leave a gaping hole.

Sandrats only had one lung. To keep things simple, most sandrats were born with a right lung only, on the left the cavity space was hollow. It was a standard week five foetal modification, carried out when the gecko-sized embryo was still pretty plastic in biotek terms. Partly it was a straight DNA rewrite, but mostly it was microsurgery. You couldn't put the blood/oxygen exchange in until after the birth, though.

Getting him lunged-up at birth was about the only good thing his Ma had done for Lars. Sure it was a primitive model, thrift-store cheap, a basic oxygen/CO2 swap that took its top-up straight from a metal o/lung strapped to Lars's left side, but it worked and that meant Lars could roam the airless, lifeless mail tunnels that most lowlives avoided. That was the basis of being a good scavenger, getting to places others couldn't reach.

It meant he could stash stuff too, well away from the *WeGuard* goons and LunaWorld security. And it let Lars drop out of sight every time the heat got too much: but it also meant Lars went through any vacuum with a bottle strapped to his side, ever-present, vulnerable. Ready for a rip-out.

Lars didn't know anyone that had happened to. Come to that, Lars wasn't sure *anyone* knew someone it had happened too, but it got talked about all the time in the simBars out on the Edge. It was one of those Cheshire-cat memes. It came, it went . . . and then it came back again. A half-decent memetecist would have had a field day.

'Ten metres, maybe twenty . . .' Lars was talking to himself again. It might be an unknown tunnel to Lars – hell, even he didn't usually travel this far out – but there was an opening somewhere above him. An entry into Fracture. He could *feel* it. A shape of silence in the static of his head. There was a real difference in shapes between being in air and running a vacuum. A vacuum felt more internal, like fuzz, less firm. With air, Lars got definite shapes inside his head. Without air, it was just a gut feeling.

Just how hearing objects worked Lars didn't know, but it did. Pulling on the thin wire, Lars began to haul up Ben's ice bucket. He didn't want the monofilament snagging when he crawled over the lip into the branch tunnel up ahead. The bucket came up slowly, the length of monofilament telling Lars how far he'd already climbed. Only what Lars saw first was an orange flicker, like a glowbug rising up through the darkness.

'Shit, Ben,' said Lars, when he spotted the diode's warning. 'I'm sorry, man.' The bucket needed feeding. If Lars didn't get it power real soon that diode was going to turn to red, and after that to black. It had never got to black before, ever – though it got to red once, when the whole of Planetside's power grid went down and the authorities cut the ring feed on the Edge to concentrate on keeping the tourists warm and safe. And the diode had got to orange a couple of times before, too . . .

Lars sighed. Okay, more than a couple of times, but it wasn't because he was careless, it was just . . . Splicing into a feed when you were an illegal took stealth, skill or brawn and sometimes Lars was just running too much on empty to make the trade.

'So what do I do now?' Lars asked. But enough of Ben wasn't there to answer, so Lars answered himself.

'Go in after them, of course . . .' What other option was there? She had expensive clothes, which meant she was rich. She'd had her own bodyguard, even if he was a crap *WeGuard*. That meant she was richer still. All his life he had been waiting to meet someone like this, someone who could help him if he helped her.

Ben needed a new body for a start. And – postcards or not – Planetside had a contract out on Lars. Lars didn't really understand that part of it, but Ben had been certain Lars couldn't just go back to being good, even if Lars wanted to, which he didn't.

'Got to 'fess up and pay the man,' was the way Ben told it. Lars didn't see how this was an incentive to be good. But he hadn't told Ben that. Ben was the clever one, except he'd got dead and that hadn't been too clever.

Clambering over the lip, Lars pulled Ben's head up behind him and balanced the ice bucket on the nearest ledge. The new tunnel was narrow and lined with polycrete. Big signs said something in a language he didn't understand. There were even strands of rotting fibre optic strung along its walls, unscavenged.

Lars could feel them up ahead. Three of them. Not that he'd have known the number if he hadn't first felt them back in Planetside where there was air. But then they'd gone for the surface, out towards Fracture, after cracking the security code on a triple airlock. But they'd reached the airlock in a vehicle of sorts, a NASA buggy, and Lars had been able to sense three of them up to then. He'd been riding the chattering mail drone, only stopping his tracking to assure it that yes, he was interested and no, he wasn't bored.

They were near the old US Base at Placid now. Rubble and cracked concrete was all that was left on the surface these days, but once upon a time that rubble had been the US*Endeavour* deep-space observatory until a Chinese combat shuttle flipped its circuits, ripping the concrete roof open like popping the top off a can of beer. Forty died, maybe fifty . . . Lars didn't bother with the figures, it was back in his granddad's time and Lars wasn't big on history.

These days Placid was an official US war grave, off limits to anyone without a permit. Though the number of fat Midwestern combat freaks who were granted a permit was staggering. Usually they turned up in Planetside Arrivals kitted out with real paper maps and those grey military-grade Rom-Readers, dressed up in black jumpsuits with eagle flashes. All equipped to relive a war that lasted three days and started by accident.

'Shitheads': Lars hated them worst of all. They hung around the Edge where they weren't wanted, trying to bum lifts out to Placid and talking flashpoint tactics for a battle they'd never been at. And, worst of all, started fights they couldn't finish when no one wanted to give them free rides.

But that wasn't who this lot were. No, these were professionals, at least the two men were. Like muscle for hire but slicker and richer; better armed too. They were the kind who could afford to do six weeks on, six months off, so their muscles didn't waste. Not Luna-born, but definitely lowGee trained.

The third person was the girl. The pretty one with the strange clothes. Lars wasn't sure how a straight grab like that could be personal, but in the room up ahead the two men had been giving her too hard a time for it to be pure commerce. If the words 'pure' and 'commerce' weren't too big a contradiction.

She swore — they hit her, so she swore again. That had been the pattern right the way down the first tunnel until they hit the airlock. Then she really went ape, until her screams were slapped into silence. Maybe she thought they'd been about to do a half-black on her.

It wouldn't be the first time that had happened to a good-looking tourist, not that prospective customers got to see that in the brochures. You could cabbage anyone if you did it right, toss them out, pull them back. Working body, empty head – it made for cheap spares or cheaper sex if you weren't fussy about emotional feedback. But that wasn't what this was about: Lars had already agreed with himself on that.

No one pulled a rich kid out of a line at Planetside just to cabbage her as soon as they hit the Edge. She was being taken out to Placid for a reason. Lars just couldn't work out what it was, but he would . . . Lars settled down in the tunnel, pushed his ear hard against a cold block of polycrete, squashing his balloon-suit helmet out of shape, and flicked channels in his head, looking for images.

He could wait.

Chapter 5

Internal Exile

'Fuck it.' LizAlec punched her fist against a wall and swore, more from anger than pain. Split knuckles hurt, but not that badly. So LizAlec punched the door instead, harder this time. Its slick metal surface didn't even clang. She'd tried shouting, screaming, even kicking the door but it made no difference.

No one came. Not that LizAlec knew what she was going to do or say if they did. She'd tried, 'What do you want?' But that worked no better than, 'Can't we work this through?' and 'Do you know who I am?'

The door was antique, NASA-made, with some kind of manual handle that had no electronic override. It was also sheet steel laser-bonded onto a titanium frame. There was no need for it to be so strong and there never had been, but the first NASA ground station had been a belt-and-braces affair.

LizAlec bounced her knuckles one final time against its unyielding, cold, unrusting steel and began to cry. Tears trickled slowly down her thin face, smudging what little was left of her Dior mascara.

Laughing Boy and Mickey had stripped her, not just of the stupid, stinking balloon suit that blew up around her like some bulimic rubber doll every time she went through a vacuum, but of her skirt and blazer, even her black socks and buckle shoes. LizAlec wiped her wet nose with the back of a hand and, without thinking, wiped it dry on one bare hip.

God, she'd never thought she'd miss the St Lucius uniform.

But Laughing Boy had tossed her a paper gown, the kind hospitals used, then growled at her to strip. When LizAlec refused, he'd waved a shockblade under her nose and offered to do it himself. She'd almost tripped over her own feet in her hurry to get the navy skirt unbuttoned. Now she stood dressed in a cheap grey gown, small breasts brushing rough paper, her back and thin buttocks exposed to the biting cold. And all she felt, apart from fucking freezing, was contempt for her own cowardice.

Frustration.

Shame.

Impotent fury. LizAlec despised her own fear, hated having stripped to order and loathed herself. But most of all, LizAlec hated the darkness. Holding her split and bleeding knuckles to her lips, LizAlec sucked at the torn skin and didn't know what to do next.

The grab wasn't a set-up, not even a sick gag. It was as real as the salt-taste of blood on her lips and the gown that somehow made her feel more naked than if they'd just stripped her and had done with it. The tall man in the mouse mask wasn't Fixx. When LizAlec asked, he hadn't even heard of Fixx. Nor had the other one, the fat sullen slob with the mullet cut and wraparound n/Vision spex. Neither even recognized the classic *Bach, Strangeness and Quarms*, on which Johann Sebastian jammed with virtuals of Tom Petty, Lou Reed and Goldie. It wasn't right, it wasn't fair and LizAlec was afraid.

Not worried or anxious, but fucking full-on terrified. Fear gripped her throat with hangman's hands, her bowels churned like liquid. She wanted to shit but wasn't yet desperate enough to just dump on the floor. And the bile that pushed up into her mouth refused to turn to vomit, no matter how often LizAlec knelt on the black grit floor, clutched her thin gut and pulled upwards against her diaphragm. Water was what it usually took. Two small glasses of warm water and a finger down her throat.

Something weird was going down. But LizAlec was fucked if she could work out what. If they'd wanted to rape her, they'd have done it already. And rape wouldn't exactly have been a novelty act anyway, LizAlec thought angrily, at least not to her. And it couldn't be the money, because she wasn't the richest. No one at St Lucius came richer than that tiny Chinese girl and the man in the Mickey mask hadn't even bothered to look at Anchee. Shatter her teeth, sure, but that hadn't been personal.

LizAlec was goods, nothing more, but, try as the girl might, she couldn't see how she had any value. She wasn't filthy rich like Anchee, or a princess like Ingrid Bernadotte. She wasn't Kira, there was no CySat copyright on her looks. She wasn't even brilliant like the Aziz twins.

It made no sense. But then, she'd been hanging round with Fixx for the last six months, so she should have been used to that.

Time passed.

She was going to have to get used to that too . . .

She did.

Chapter 6

Our Lady of the Crystals

Biting back tears. How the hell do you bite back your tears, LizAlec wondered crossly to herself, wiping them away with the back of her hand. Laughing Boy had just waddled in to slop her down with a bucket of water. At least, LizAlec hoped it was water: the liquid was certainly cold enough, but she wasn't taking bets. Not that she didn't need it, even she could tell she stank.

And she'd been cold enough before Laughing Boy appeared. In fact, the air was so chilled it burnt her throat as she pulled it into her lungs. LizAlec wasn't sure if the two goons had known in advance that part of this strange wrecked building was still pressurized, or whether they just got lucky, but either way, over the last week keeping her warm hadn't seemed part of their plans . . .

Now one of them was back again, wrestling with the door. The hinges were old, not rusty but thick with grit. Which was how LizAlec knew someone was coming into her cell. All the same, she stayed curled into a little ball in the corner and kept her violet eyes tight shut, even though the stinking cell was way too dark for Mickey or Laughing Boy to see she'd been crying.

Except it wasn't the fat depressive or the man in the plastic mask.

'Lady Elizabeth?' Someone clicked their fingers and for the first time in days light pushed in against her scrunched-up eyes. Without even being aware of it, LizAlec pulled her sodden paper gown more tightly around her.

The new voice was cultured, its accent well-bred Parisian. Lady Elizabeth Alexandra Fabio rolled away from the wall, blinking into the sudden glare. This was no simple lightstick like Laughing Boy's. The new man held a small Braun lamp, the circular kind she'd seen on sale in the Rue de Rivoli. And his clothes were a whole gold card away from those worn by the two goons. Silk jacket padded at the shoulders to give him width, double cuffs kept closed with jade links, an obsidian signet ring circling the little finger of his left hand. Even his black English-made shoes were unscuffed by the dust.

He was tall enough to tower over LizAlec and he was so thin that it looked like someone had just lacquered his bones with skin and missed out the muscle. All of that LizAlec saw, but she missed the small enamel button in his lapel indicating membership of an Order that tithed five per cent of everything he earned and made Opus Dei look liberal. And she missed the discreet contacts that changed his eyes from green to grey.

Crouched back on her heels, bare knees tight together, LizAlec pressed her hands hard against the ground to steady herself and took another look at the man. He was in his early forties, maybe late thirties, with long swept-back hair that was flecked with grey. His face had character enough to pass for experienced, but was not so lined that it was yet old. The twist to his lips was natural, by the look of it. His sneer was practised, but not quite perfect enough to come from a surgeon's lipid-coated scalpel. LizAlec had a nasty feeling she'd seen the man before, and she hadn't liked him then either.

'Lady Elizabeth?' Impatience was what LizAlec heard and what she reacted against.

'It's LizAlec,' she said shortly, pushing herself upright.

'No,' he said, 'it's whatever I want it to be.' And before LizAlec could reply, he caught her left arm and twisted it hard up behind her back until she thought the bones would break. LizAlec could almost feel his eyes rake down her naked spine and buttocks, and then he shoved her forward, bouncing her into a wall.

Shock, LizAlec told herself furiously, scrabbling to her feet and pushing her clenched hands into her eyes to stop fresh tears. That's all it was, shock, not pain. LizAlec reached deep into herself and ripped out what she always held in reserve: utter contempt for anyone who showed emotion, herself included.

'Arsewipe.' She spat the word back without having to think about it, looking the thin man up and down as if he was something she'd just stepped in. The tears were already drying on her cheeks.

'I could hurt you badly,' the man said simply.

'No,' replied LizAlec, refusing to drop her gaze. 'You think you could, but you couldn't.' She held up two thin hands in cold, mocking surrender. 'Not that I want you to try.'

The tall man pursed his thin lips, as if thinking. So it wasn't going the way he intended, well LizAlec was glad about that. He looked like somebody who was too used to getting his own way.

'You know your problem?' The man's voice was dangerously quiet.

LizAlec kicked one heel against the cold wall behind her, then shrugged dismissively. 'You mean, besides getting kidnapped by some fuck-head tailor's dummy?' She watched with icy disdain as the man fought down his urge to slap her; she kept kicking her heel against the wall, waiting for him to tell her to stop. LizAlec was good at disdain: she'd had a lot of practice.

When the man said nothing, LizAlec shrugged again. 'Oh, come on,' she said, 'you can tell me . . .'

'You're too like your mother.' He made it obvious no compliment was intended.

'You know Lady Clare . . . ?' LizAlec stopped herself. Stupid question. With that accent he was bound to have met her. Lady Clare was an Imperial Minister, *aide de camp* to Louis Napoleon, the Prince Imperial, and head of the Third Section. Everyone in Paris who counted for anything knew her mother. Poor bastards.

'Lady Clare?' The amusement in the man's voice should have

warned LizAlec that the balance was shifting again and not in her favour. Though how much further it could shift against her when she was sodden, kidnapped, shuddering with cold and wrapped in a wet hospital gown LizAlec didn't know.

'You think Lady Clare is your mother?'

'Of course she is,' LizAlec answered. There was no 'think' about it. 'You think I'd have anything to do with that bitch if she wasn't?'

'Lady . . . Clare . . . is . . . not . . . your . . . mother.' He left mocking gaps between the words, as if giving LizAlec time for the words to sink in. But they didn't. However hard she tried she couldn't pin any meaning on them except the obvious one. And that wasn't possible.

'Your mother's dead.' The man's eyes were bright, coldly amused. But for the briefest second, there was something else there that might just have been pity, but probably wasn't. It was wiped so fast LizAlec couldn't be sure.

'I'm sorry,' he said, reaching out to touch one hunched shoulder. 'I assumed you knew . . .'

The hell he did.

LizAlec's fist swung towards his elegant face before even she realized what she was doing. But her punch never landed. Instead the tall man twisted fast sideways, swivelling so LizAlec's fist slipped uselessly past his face, throwing her off balance. She didn't fall. She couldn't. Iron fingers gripped her thin wrist and the cell did a half-spin as he flicked her round and slammed her face first into the rough polycrete wall. She stayed upright, but only because the man had her arm twisted halfway up her back.

I'm going to have to stop this, LizAlec thought when the man finally stopped pulling her arm out of its socket and she got her brain back. Casually, callously, he spun the girl round so she could took at him.

'Lady Clare is French,' he said coldly, 'Well bred, European, white . . .' The man laid the list out in front of her. 'You're black.'

LizAlec looked up at him and frowned. No, she wasn't. If anything, she was *café au lait*, like most girls at St Lucius. Like most of the world, really. LizAlec started to shake her head.

'She's pure European,' the man said heavily. 'You're black – how do you think that happened?'

'Maybe she met someone and they *fucked*,' suggested LizAlec. She placed bitter emphasis on her last word. 'Maybe her gynaecologist just mixed me up in a Petri dish. How should I know?'

'Your father wasn't black, Lady Clare isn't black . . .' The iron grip on her wrist tightened further, grinding bones against each other until LizAlec bit her bottom lip but kept silent. Arrogant he might be, and probably psychotic, but it sounded like he held the missing piece to her life, and she wanted to know it. Unless the whole thing was just a mind fuck, which wouldn't have surprised her.

'How do you know my father wasn't *black*?' LizAlec asked. Because if that was all he knew, it was still more than she did. Lady Clare and LizAlec didn't communicate much, not these days, but they'd never talked about her father at all. Not ever, not even back when she was a kid.

'How do you know?' LizAlec demanded crossly.

'Because I know your father,' said the man.

'He sent you.' LizAlec had the words out of her mouth before she could stop them.

The man actually laughed. 'Sent me? I doubt if he even knows you exist. But take it from me, your father's many things, starting with insane, but he's not responsible for the melanin coding in your DNA. That shit's down to Stepping Razor.'

'Razz!'

LizAlec knew Razz. Hell, every retarded Left Bank student and martial arts fetishist knew Razz. Razz was dead but that didn't mean she didn't still live on, naked and oiled in endless adolescent-owned tri-D posters, silver skin glinting, lizard-skin and shark-cartilage shoulder-armour polished to a sheen. She was GoreFest wank material, nothing more. Fixx loved her, no matter how much he pretended to despise everything Razz stood for.

LizAlec looked down at her own thin legs, her narrow shoulders and bony hips. It didn't seem likely. Having Lady Clare for a mother was bad enough. But Razz . . . LizAlec didn't think so. It was like discovering she was related to Ronald-fucking-McDonald.

'Razz?' LizAlec said in disbelief.

The man looked at her, then spat pointedly in the dust. The gesture didn't come naturally, but it made plain his position. 'Get used to it. That silver bitch was your *mother*, you stupid, spoilt, sullen little shit . . .'

There was a long silence, the kind that reaches out and stills everything except the thud of your heart and the roar of blood in your head. Under the silence, LizAlec could hear the low rumble of a distant pump and the slow hiss of an air-recyc.

'So tell me,' said LizAlec. 'Just who did Razz fuck to produce me and where does Lady Clare come into this?'

'Gibson,' the man told her viciously, 'That's who. You're the by-blow of a hired killer and the world's only living god. And now look at you . . .'

Alex Gibson. That didn't sound bad to LizAlec, in fact it sounded pretty good. Okay, Alex Gibson didn't own most of Shanghai like Anchee's dad, but a god? She could live with that . . . LizAlec straightened up and stared at the man. It was a bad mistake.

She was still sneering, staring him in the eyes when the tall Frenchman pulled back his fist and sucker punched her in the gut, dropping LizAlec to her knees. Breath exploded from her lungs as blackness swirled like dark mist in front of her eyes, eating at the edges of the room.

When LizAlec came to, she was curled up on the ground and above her she could hear the man's elegant, contemptuous voice, far away down a long tunnel.

'Stupid little cunt.' Somewhere in the background Laughing Boy grunted. LizAlec hadn't remembered him being there. Maybe he wasn't. Perhaps he was back in a control room somewhere and it was all being captured on i/red camera so the suit could watch it all again for fun, later on. Except that wasn't it. LizAlec had just been out for longer than she remembered.

'Okay,' said the tall man. 'Let's deal with this, shall we?' A hand yanked back her hair, reaching for the nape of her neck. LizAlec tensed as fingers expertly ripped away a tiny circle of plastic skin to reveal a minuscule glass chip, half the size of a rice grain. LizAlec couldn't remember it being fitted, but she felt it being pulled away, blood welling up where tiny electrodes had fed beneath her skin.

'Tracer,' the man said contemptuously, cracking it under his heel. 'Okay,' he said to LizAlec. 'Get up.'

LizAlec didn't.

'Get *up*,' he said crossly and when she still didn't move he crouched down beside her. LizAlec felt hands brush across her small breasts and then she felt his fingers grip nipples that were already upright with cold. But it wasn't cheap sex he was interested in. Grasping her nipples between first finger and thumb, the man yanked LizAlec to her feet.

'I say move, you move,' the man said bluntly. 'Try anything that stupid again and I'll break both your arms. Understand me?' He punctuated the last word with a vicious jab to her kidneys that had LizAlec wimpering with pain.

'Now,' he said. 'Let's get this over, okay?' The man produced a tiny Sony camcorder and tossed it gently into the air, waiting while the machine spun up into a corner to steady itself a hand's breadth below the rough grey 'crete of the ceiling. When it was stable, a single green diode lit at its base and the lens whirred slightly as the camera clicked into fine focus.

'Say something,' the man told the quivering girl.

'Say what?' She had her hands folded tight across the front of her paper gown, clutching her sides in pain.

'Oh . . . That you're fine, unharmed . . .' He smiled coldly, the smile lifting his thin lips at one corner. High cheekbones framed his deep-set eyes and a pointed chin. His face would have been rat-like but the expression was too self-confident. Maybe he was a weasel, thought LizAlec. Wasn't that one social step up from a rat?

'Do it,' the man said, 'And talk direct to the camera.'

LizAlec did. 'I've been kidnapped by two gorillas,' she said coldly, staring straight at the little satellite. 'Sexually molested by a moron . . .' That was all she had time for before a second punch dropped her back to her knees.

She wiped her lips with the back of a hand and spat into the dirt. Sweet from blood and sour from vomit, her mouth was turning into a regular Chinese meal. 'Well,' LizAlec gasped, when she stopped heaving. 'That should convince them everyone's behaving.'

'Jesus,' hissed the man. 'You really *are* a poisonous little shit . . .' He clicked his fingers at Laughing Boy. 'You, hold the bitch still.'

LizAlec felt vice-like fingers tighten on her shoulders and pull her upright. It hurt, but LizAlec reckoned it was still an improvement on the tall man's method. For a second, it looked as if the suit was going to punch her again, but he didn't, which was interesting in itself. LizAlec knew all about deferred gratification. Instead the man dipped his fingers into the side pocket of his immaculate jacket and pulled out a smallish silver ball.

'Do you know what this is?'

LizAlec didn't, but she had a nasty feeling she was about to find out.

'Should I?' she said coldly.

Fingers brushed her cheek making her shiver, and the man smiled. 'You know what?' he said softly.

The girl shook her head.

'Maybe we've all got it wrong,' said the man, sounding amused. 'Maybe culture really is more important than race . . .'

LizAlec just looked blank.

'You're really *very* like Lady Clare. And believe me,' he added quickly, 'that isn't intended as a compliment . . .' He took the silver ball and held it close to LizAlec's face. 'This is an unhatched worm. You *have* heard of bioSemtex?

Of course she had. Semi-intelligent explosive. It was what the Vernacular Front had used in London to take out the orbital ring of high-rise slums, back before she was born. It was what fundamentalists in Megrib had used more recently to blow out the glass-roofed souk at M'Dina, killing thousands.

'Good,' the man said watching her eyes. 'I wouldn't want you to remain ignorant. You,' he nodded at Laughing Boy, dipping his fingers into his pocket again, 'you know how *this* works?'

The fat man nodded and held out one podgy hand. He took a heavy black ring from the tall Frenchman and slipped it onto his own little finger. Then held out his hand for the bioSemtex ball.

'Prime it,' the Frenchman said, and Laughing Boy pressed his black ring into the silver ball's soft surface.

'Try to run away,' said the tall man, keeping his voice so politely matter-of-fact he could have been standing in the crush bar of the Paris Opera discussing Verdi, 'and you'll be . . .'

'Dead?' LizAlec asked, her voice as polite as his, her accent if anything even more polished. She could do that shit if she had to. The tall Frenchman flushed.

One to me, thought LizAlec. He might be psychotic but he was also a raving snob. Which might be useful, if only she could work out how. But LizAlec never got the chance. She was still trying to suss out who might want to kidnap her when the Frenchman made his move, suddenly grabbing her neck with one hand to press his thumb in against an upper vertebra, half paralysing her. His other hand dipped down, pulling the edge of LizAlec's paper gown away from her thin buttocks.

'You just don't learn, do you?' The man nodded over her shoulder at Laughing Boy. 'Do it.'

'No,' LizAlec's voice was almost a howl. But he still understood what she said.

'Oh yes,' the man said softly. 'We've got to get this worm into you somehow. And we can hardly hang it on a chain round your neck, can we?' At her back, LizAlec could feel Laughing Boy begin to push the wriggling worm hard between her buttocks.

LizAlec screamed, hard and long. A real scream this time, one that burnt the air with its noise as she twisted desperately away from Laughing Boy, pulling free from the other man's grip on her neck. Frantically, LizAlec kicked at Laughing Boy's fingers, sending the wriggling worm into the dirt.

'Shit.' Laughing Boy was on his knees now, scrabbling along the cell floor to grab the silver worm which was trying to slither away, collecting a caddis-shell of grit as it went. Wiping the worm against his shirt, Laughing Boy stilled it, watching as the worm flowed back into a liquid silver ball. 'Mouth,' he suggested sullenly. 'Or nose. They're both easier. More effective, too.'

Even LizAlec could see the tall Frenchman didn't like being questioned, but in the end he just shrugged. 'Whatever . . .' And before LizAlec could protest, Laughing Boy had slammed one arm round her neck and had his other hand over her nose and mouth.

'. . . fifteen, sixteen, seventeen, eighteen, nineteen . . .'

LizAlec gulped air as Laughing Boy released his hand on *twenty*, and froze in horror as she felt the worm slither up her nose. She did the obvious, screaming as she clawed desperately at her own face, but it was already too late. The worm was settling inside her, curled up in a sinus cavity.

'500 paces,' the Frenchman said shortly. 'More than that and the worm will crack your head open.' He pointed to the ring nestling around Laughing Boy's little finger. 'As for closing the circuit, touch that with the worm still in your head and . . .' The man paused and ruffled LizAlec's filthy black curls. 'You can kiss all this goodbye.'

LizAlec shuddered. She was still shuddering when the man left her cell, opening the door with a simple touch of his hand to let himself out of her life.

He would kill the girl, of course, once he'd got what he wanted. And then an S3 sweeper would go in to clean up Laughing Boy and Mickey. Lazlo Portea smiled, a grin so wide it almost split his face. The man was pleased with life and with the success of his plan, but most of all he was pleased with himself. All his life he had lived on the edges of real power. Sterling silver to Lady Clare's gold: never quite handsome enough, adept enough or rich enough to catch the eye of the Prince Imperial.

Well, that was going to change. In fact, a lot of things were going to change. Starting with who ruled Paris. If Lady Clare wanted that little half-breed back she'd have to do what Lazlo demanded. And she would. Lazlo knew that. Everyone had a weakness and where Lady Clare Fabio was concerned it was her dangerously sentimental sense of duty.

Paris or that little bitch. It was an impossible choice and with any luck deciding would kill her.

Chapter 7

Ein SchattenKönig

The wolves came down from Scandinavia. Screaming newsfeeds said hunger had driven them in from the wild Asiatic steppes but that was so much cack. There'd been wolves in Hungary and Poland for as long as anyone could remember. Wolves in Latvia and Finland, too. It was only Western Europe that wasn't used to having beasts that slunk like grey shadows through city streets, scavenging for food. And it wasn't hunger that drove the largest pack into Paris: it was the Reich moving westwards again, like a black stain across the map.

Wolf skins made excellent rugs, their bristling tails streamed banner-like from the whip aerials of a hundred APVs, and the hepmann shot them down for sport, with delicately balanced Ruger .722s. And by the time the Azerbaijani virus ate out the springs of the APVs and trashed ninety per cent of the Rugers it was already too late. Paris had been under siege for three days and the wolves had reached the Champs Elysées.

It was a seriously bad move, at least for the wolves. The only thing more dangerous than a hungry wolf is a human in need of food but not yet so weak that hunting is out of the question. In the outskirts the wolves were killed with ceramic gutting knives, rocks and sharpened sticks. And in the centre the animals were butchered with the same crude but effective weapons. They were cooked, not as the exotic delicacy wolf had once been, marinated in Meuse vinegar or grilled with wild chanterelle and shredded truffle as Brillat Saveran recommended, but over open fires and in earth pits, from blind necessity, from increasing hunger.

No deliveries could get through from the surrounding countryside, had the storms left any food in the fields. Half the limited-function Drexie-boxes were already virus-eaten. Without regular power for temperature control or maintenance of pressure, the ceramic monoclonal vats were becoming thick with rancid fermenting protein. It was small wonder the wolves didn't last. Three days without food seems an eternity, until you try five or face the prospect of ten, fifteen . . .

The urban foxes would go too, following dogs and cats into the mouths of the starving. The rats would also go, but not for a week or more: hunger was not yet strong enough to draw them to the surface. It was a crap time to be human but a much worse time to be an animal. That humans were animal too was not a connection that anyone had yet made. But they would.

It was raining, not the light mid-January drizzle Lady Clare Fabio remembered from childhood, but backed-up sheets of black rain that hammered across the city's rooftops like waves of sound, battering everything they touched. It crashed like cannon fire, it drum-rolled on the large cracked slates of the Hotel Sabatini like sticks on the skin of a kettle drum, it . . . Lady Clare didn't know what the rain sounded like.

Rain, probably.

Hard driving rain had been falling for weeks out of a gunmetal sky so dark each day could have been permanently fixed at dusk. Today's storm came from the Atlantic, but that wasn't significant, not now the virus was here. The week before the virus had come in on the wind from Germany, followed by rain that re-drowned the sodden countryside before it hit Paris. There would be no winter crops, nothing useful anyway. And even if there had been, no estate manager – not even Lady Clare's – would be stupid enough to try to run the Reich's blockade.

Not that most Parisians wanted fresh food anyway, Lady Clare thought in disgust, at least, not normally. Back before the Reich hired the Black Hundreds to add Western Europe to what Prussia already possessed and the Parisians developed a sudden taste for anything that wasn't actually rancid, the preferred food texture in the Paris slums had been fried chicken, though ham had been briefly in fashion last summer, except with the Muslims. Lady Clare knew these things. Facts like that passed her desk in digest, amended, annotated memoranda, in lists of supposedly relevant social data. History written as a series of shopping lists.

According to the finest meme-counters the CIA possessed you could define society by analysing what it stuffed down its gullet, not to mention what animals it cried over on *WonderfulWorld*, or which plucky downtrodden loser it rooted for in the *novelas*. Personally Lady Clare didn't buy that. The only way you ever really found out what your people were thinking was to pull a random selection of them in and gut out their heads, literally. A SQUID could do it and often did.

Which was why Lady Clare was not just *aide de camp* to the Prince Imperial but also the longest-lasting head of the Third Section, the French Empire's Directorate of Internal Security. The only bit of government still willing to get its hands dirty in the day-to-day shit of keeping society together. Of course, no one ever put it like that when talking to Lady Clare, but that was how she put it in her own head. She took the shit so that none of it could stick to the Prince Imperial. That was her job: Lady Clare didn't have a problem with it.

Though sometimes she wondered if any of the other Ministers had the slightest idea of what went on inside her. The black demons, the violent dreams, the whole bubbling cauldron hidden behind her immaculate carapace of effortless manners and Dior make-up.

It was Friday, 12th January, at least she thought it was. The sub-stations for the electricity grid were now so virus-ridden that brown-outs were common and regular power was no longer an option. In fact, as of tomorrow or the day after, it looked like power itself might no longer be an option, unless you had your own virus-free generator, which she didn't.

The Napoleonic Empire was falling, crumbling around her like cancerous concrete. In theory it still ruled from Schleswig-Holstein in the north to Gibraltar in southern Spain, from the Brittany coast to the borders of Austro-Hungary. But with a good pair of field glasses Lady Clare could have seen all that really remained from where she stood, if only the rain would stop. And she could count on one hand the number of Ministers who still thought it was a good thing. But, worse yet, Lady Clare no longer knew if she was still one of them.

Standing in the rain on the roof of the Hôtel Sabatini, her priceless house on the Ile St-Louis, Lady Clare stared down over the inner courtyard to the slate-grey swollen waters of the Seine far below. The river was full to the point of bursting its banks. Only hastily piled sandbags held back the water that threatened to swallow her quiet, impossibly expensive street.

To live on the Ile took a *carte blanche*. It helped that Lady Clare was a registered noble, with the tax advantages that conferred: helped, too, that she was a Minister. But neither of those priceless social advantages could hold back the water if it decided to spill over the edge of the sandbags onto the cobbled quay. Rain had soaked through Lady Clare's Dior coat, staining the purple Versace dress below. Her court shoes were ruined, as was the Hermès silk scarf wrapped round her neck. Water ran under the collar of her coat, dripped from black-lacquered fingertips and tumbled from the tiny rat tails of her close-cropped grey hair. But the water running over her cheeks was not rain. Not all of it, anyway.

The head of the French Empire's most feared Directorate was weeping. Looking out at the grey ribbon of the swollen river, staring blankly at where the vast cross-and-double-helix hologram of the Church Geneticist should have been, if only that *arrondissement* had power, Lady Clare let burning tears stream down her frozen face. There was no one to see her misery, and why should she care even if there was? God knew, there was enough horror in the city for even the most hardbitten Minister of the Empire to be crying. Even one rumoured to be more brittle than glass and sharper than diamond.

Lady Clare had worked hard to get that reputation. And even if only a quarter of the things whispered about her were true, she'd still be poison to cross. As it was, they were all true, more or less, except one. The one that said Lady Elizabeth Alexandra Fabio was her illegitimate daughter.

It was strange, Lady Clare thought grimly. The Empire was falling, the Prince Imperial was tucked up in bed with a guardsman, the army of the Reich was sitting twenty klicks away, positioned in a deadly circle around the city – and what really worried Lady Clare was the fate of some spoilt, poisonous little fifteen-year-old. A girl she didn't even like, a girl who, if you'd asked her two weeks ago – Lady Clare was too wet and too cold not to be brutally honest about it – she'd have said she loathed. And now Lady Clare couldn't get that vile message out of her head.

The briefest clip of LizAlec looking at a camera, a scream and then nothing but static snow. There would be a second part to that message soon enough, there had to be. Some impossible demand that Lady Clare was supposed to meet. No one would kill LizAlec before Lady Clare got the rest of the message.

Whoever it was, whatever they wanted, the kidnappers couldn't take the risk that Lady Clare might discover LizAlec was already dead. Not that she was any closer to finding out where the original e-vid had come from. Back before the power went down, she'd accessed the SCIS machine in Brussels, called in favours at MIT and CalTek. Had Light&Magic strip away the e-vid's dropped-in background with its luminous 'Free Luna' graffito sprayed onto a glass wall. And at the end of it she was no closer to having an answer.

Hours of precious AI time had been wasted tracking the e-vid, only for Lady Clare to be told by S3's own machine that the e-vid had been uploaded from her own terminal. The upload and download began and ended at the same terminal, the AI was prepared to guarantee it. Not that the Turing was in a condition to guarantee anything now. All that was back on Monday when the mainframe was still running. Now there wasn't a system anywhere in the city still functioning, or not fully. Maybe one or two stand-alones might still be virus-free.

Lady Clare shrugged, sodden silk shirt sticking to her hunched shoulders, rain dripping between her small breasts to trickle down the flat expanse of her stomach. Lady Clare didn't wear a bra: even at sixty she didn't need it. And as for her gut, it was hard to get fat when you didn't eat. If anorexia was a disease of the troubled teenage years, then Lady Clare's adolescence had been infinitely protracted. Lady Clare knew why, always had done if she was honest, it was just that these days she didn't bother to think about it.

S3's tame psychologists insisted there was a limit to how long any one person could stay angry with their family. But Lady Clare was already well past her hate-by date. And she needed another gratuitous attack of guilt like she needed her father back from the dead.

She'd intercepted LizAlec's mail to Fixx, of course. She'd have found the e-vid anyway when she bothered to check the Web traffic held against his name. But within two hours of LizAlec sending it an S3 semi-Turing had pulled LizAlec out of the traffic, juggling packages and breaking crypt to match the girl's face to a visual template it had been given earlier.

Lady Clare had been shocked, which surprised her. Saddened too, though she'd been getting used to that where LizAlec was concerned. The child looked so young, so terrifyingly defence-less. Sitting there in school uniform in a public vidbooth, over-made-up eyes staring darkly at the camera, white cotton shirt unbuttoned to show small breasts. Part of Lady Clare wanted to know what Fixx would have made of that e-vid had he ever received it.

Maybe it would be worth showing him to find out. As LizAlec

was being driven to Charles de Gaulle to catch her shuttle, members of a Third Section snatch squad were already blowing out the steel door to Fixx's squalid seventh-floor studio in Bastille. The man was safely behind bars before LizAlec's Boeing had even begun its ascent.

Sending LizAlec back to school had been the right decision, Lady Clare didn't doubt that for a minute, and she would do it again if necessary. As the old Breton woman who cleaned Lady Clare's office always said, shit came in threes. And she was right. Take weather from hell, toss in an out-of-control nanetic virus mixed up by some under-age mujahedin and add the black-costumed forces of the Reich, sitting in a circle around Europe's greatest city like bored vultures.

Clare wanted to blame it all on the Germans . . . Of course she did, she was French. But her clinically cold intellectual standards wouldn't let her. She knew the statistics, that was her job. There were nearly as many Frenchmen in that army as there were Prussians, and twice as many Cossacks, come to that. Whichever way you cut the figures, there were three 'foreigners' for every one Prussian.

Elective fascism . . . And why not Lady Clare thought, head down against the driving rain. We've had elective surgery, elective sexuality – what was politics if not elective? The new Reich via Cossack Black Hundreds out of Nazi nostalgia. And who was she to be surprised? If the last century could get nostalgic enough about the little Corsican corporal to allow a Napoleon back on the French throne, who should be shocked that this one got all nostalgic about that little shit corporal from Austro-Hungary?

Section Three existed to ensure the Empire's stability, though most of what it had done over the last twenty years was soft management. From its base at Les Tourelles, the Pool monitored data, meme-checked and spun news stories along with the best. Which wasn't to say it couldn't get down-and-dirty when necessary . . . And it was necessary now, except that 'now' was already too late. Lady Clare had been so busy trying to reach a compromise with the Jihad hackers, she hadn't realized the Azerbaijani virus might rupture European opinion, spilling out decades of resentment, pulling rioting slum crowds onto provincial streets. *La Haine* was reborn as a thousand pirate newsfeeds switched allegiance.

Pro-compromise, pro-Jihad news stories were being quoted back at her, twisted. Her own anti-Reich memes, dropped quietly into the electronic cesspit of rumour, were being taken up as Black Hundred boasts and flung back against her. From Montana to Monaco, the same waves of racist paranoia swept the Web.

The Hundreds were no longer just a Ukrainian problem: the Reich was no longer just history. And standing on the rain-slicked tiles of her own roof, watching France's worst-ever storm rip buildings apart, Lady Clare knew that – at least in part – she was to blame.

Lady Clare made herself look towards the Eiffel Tower then, what was left of it. Millions of tons of steel, billions of rivets, hundreds of years of history eaten away into a brutal metal stump. The virus hadn't even finished its job, it had just aborted suddenly, switching itself off.

When the virus first struck, it looked like the most lethal side effects might be burnt out. But then the eastern edges of the city had begun to crumble, ferroconcrete projects and slum arcologies falling in on themselves. That was when Lady Clare had tried to arrange for the Prince Imperial to be given asylum in the US, for one last AirFrance Boeing to get permission to land at JFK.

Congress hadn't liked the idea.

Not that Lady Clare could blame them. What was the Empire State Building but concrete thrown up around a huge steel grid? And as for the famous Flatiron building . . . At least Paris had some streets made entirely of stone. The Mayor of New York had Columbia run a projection on what would be left of Manhattan if the virus hit. The answer was some rather nice brownstones south of Bleeker Street and a surprising amount of Harlem. It wasn't the answer he wanted to hear.

And he didn't want the Prince Imperial either. Nor did Los Angeles, São Paulo or Bogotá. Lady Clare was last year's model when it came to negotiators, if not the year before that. Washington no longer took her calls: all that remained for her to do was negotiate the surrender of Paris and hope for a civilized exile.

Of course, a week ago the Reich could have bombed the city back into the Stone Age. Or, if they didn't want to trash a historic centre more than was strictly necessary, they could have limited themselves to taking out most of the inhabitants with a low-grade neutron burst. But that was before their planes started to drop out of the sky.

Now they were going to have to fight their way from the Périphérique right into the Place de la Concorde, street by bloody street.

But that wasn't going to happen.

At least, it wasn't going to happen yet. Not if Lady Clare had anything to do with it. She might have fucked up over the Reich, but she was still the person who used the last working Sikorski to fly in as many CySat reporters, Ishies and wannabe warjocks as that 'copter could carry. Nothing happened in Paris that didn't go out over the Web, uploaded from a thousand eyecams, fed unedited into newsfeeds, voiced over by kids with dreams of one day anchoring their own syndicated shows. And it wasn't just the Ishies with their implant modems and in-head wetware cameras who could upload. The professionals were using Cousteau-kit. Rubber-wrapped, shock-resistant, waterproof smartbooks used for diving.

She had every low-level surveillance satellite S3 owned hovering over the city centre, focused in on m/wave and positioned above Notre-Dame, the Tuileries, Sacré-Coeur, l'Arc de Triomphe. Anything that was stone-built and counted as culture.

When it came to moral blackmail, Lady Clare Fabio was in there with the best of them. No one survived that long at the top of the greasy pole without knowing how to keep their balance. And if it wasn't for bloody Elizabeth Alexandra, Lady Clare's balance would have been as rock-fucking-solid as those buildings she was using to blackmail the Reich.

It was a simple enough stand-off. The Reich were self-proclaimed guardians of European culture. For which read *White, Christian, non-Islamic*, Lady Clare thought bitterly. To take Paris by force they'd have to trash some of Europe's most famous buildings, not to mention risk destroying its priceless art collections.

If the Reich did that, it was going to be caught on camera, guaranteed. The whole world was going to watch General Kukovsy go against his own proclaimed aims. Lady Clare shook her head. It came to something, she decided, when the *Mona Lisa* and the *Venus de Milo* were the only things still holding up the Empire.

Chapter 8

Down 2 Zero

Lady Clare's black cloak was too sodden to swirl dramatically in the wind. All it could manage was a sullen flap against her ankles as the cold air howled around her; the huge slate roof was once again dark and slick with rain like a black mirror. Twenty-four hours were gone and the situation was no better.

Lady Clare wanted to jump, to feel the darkness swallow her into its narcotic grip. But she couldn't do it, though the ledge rested right under her sodden feet. Neurotic, self-destructive, vicious . . . She was many things, but gutless had never been one of them. And besides, she never had been able to leave a job undone.

It was time to go. The digits were there, luminous but still almost invisible, counting off just below her rain-soaked skin. The Patek Philippe tattoo was a simple transparent subdermal mesh, powered by electrical resistance in her skin: Lady Clare's one concession to wetware modernity.

She smiled, sadly. Her days were done. Politically, morally, probably genetically she was already a dinosaur. Self-pity was a wasted emotion, the refuge of the weak, the CPU for a victim culture Lady Clare had long ago dismissed out of hand. But it was hard not to feel self-pity now.

'Let Carthage burn,' Lady Clare tossed off the Latin tag as she took one last look out over the roofs of her city. Let her whole life burn down around her. Why should she care? Except that she did, fiercely.

It wasn't any warmer in the attic below, but at least it was marginally more dry, though the air inside the vast roof space still quivered like the inside of a beaten drum and stank with the vinegar smell of wet rot. Once the attic had been full of crumbling furniture, ugly old paintings and fat, worm-like rolls of ancient stained tapestry, but Lady Clare had ordered those to be cleared out the summer before. A pity. Even the tapestries would have burnt better than nothing.

Ditching her Hermès scarf, the woman pulled off her sodden black cloak and bundled it under her arm long before she reached the narrow stairs down to the floor below. By the time Lady Clare reached the carved oakwood cherubs of her bedroom door she'd already unbuttoned her silk shirt. The Versace shoes she discarded just inside, tossing them into an oval bin.

'Shut,' demanded Lady Clare and was surprised when the curtains on the far wall did what they were told. Long, velvet and dark maroon, they draped a huge window glazed in shatter-proof perspex. Its only view now was of the rain-hammered cobbles in the courtyard below. Although on a clear day it was possible to look over the top of the gate and see clear across the river to the polished steel walls of the Institut Bonaparte on the bank beyond. Now the rain made it hard even to see this edge of the river and, even if it hadn't, the Institut was gone, eaten down to a brittle rim like a badly rusted tin can. The higher the iron content the more virulent the viral attack. And the Institut Bonaparte had been walled with pure steel.

Habit made her fold the black Dior skirt and drape it over the back of a Louis XVII chair. Just as habit made her slip her cloak onto an old-fashioned hanger. Too late, of course. There were clothes and then there was haute couture. Smart fabric or not, Dior had never intended that skirt to be worn in the needle's eye of a thunder storm.

All the same, Clare tried to smooth out the skirt's creases before stepping out of her shot-silk slip. That got treated to a hanger, too. And then, stripped naked, Lady Clare stepped into a sonic cubicle, punching the setting up to maximum. It took two seconds to get clean, but she stayed inside the Matsui cubicle for a full half-minute, which was what the cubicle had left in its powerpack.

She knew the definition of obsessive compulsive disorder as well as the next neurotic, but didn't regret burning up all the power at once. It was the sharp edges that gave life its shape. Besides, what was the point of saving the power when the Matsui could be a virus-ridden pile of junk by the next morning? As opposed to an empty-batteried pile of junk, she reminded herself darkly.

Smiling grimly, Lady Clare flicked on a Braun cafemeister, filling her vast bedroom with the dark scent of crushed and hand-roasted Colombian. That too would go pear-shaped soon. Its circuits eaten away or its powerpack drained. Everything was always just a matter of time.

Once this room had belonged to a Prince. It had been his study, but nothing from those days remained in the room to remind Lady Clare of the Prince or Alex Gibson. The oak panelling had long since been ripped out, the stone walls replastered and stippled off-white. One antique chair, one Third Empire rattan and mahogany bed, one vast wardrobe inset with an oval bevelled mirror filled a room that had a ceiling too high to ever know if there were cobwebs or not. Not that there would have been, Lady Clare used mitebots without even thinking about it, sprinkling the tiny nanites through the Hotel Sabatini to eat dirt, dust and crumbs.

Behind her – set either side of the over-carved door – were two oil paintings, striking in their honesty and cruelty. The larger oil was Christian Schad's 1927 *Count d'Anneaucout*, a portrait of a thin man in a black dinner jacket standing between two hatchet-faced women The other showed an anorexically thin woman splayed on a bed in the background while another starvling sat in front of her, sad eyes staring at the floor, one jewelled hand absent-mindedly touching her own shaved vulva. It too was by Schad but painted the following year.

Each one had cost more than even Lady Clare earned in a year. Of course, Lady Clare hadn't needed to buy them. Both had been bribes from a Flemish cocaine dealer ten years before, the year Lady Clare was confirmed as aide to the Prince Imperial. The dealer had bought them on the open market. Sotheby's, probably.

Lady Clare sighed.

In the corner of her room a green diode was flashing quietly. But Lady Clare made herself wait until she'd struggled into a heavy red Kenzo dressing gown. Only then did she sit on the edge of her huge, unshared bed and power up her Toshiba smartbook.

On the screen a small envelope was revolving . . . So they weren't using e-vid, which was interesting in itself, or maybe not. Lady Clare was finding it increasingly hard to recognize what was a significant clue and what wasn't. But then, that was life. As her predecessor as His Highness's *aide de camp* used to point out, jigsaw pieces only had relationships if you knew the picture. Though that probably wasn't why he blew his brains out with an antique Smith & Wesson.

The e-mail was simple, even brutal. The life of Lady Elizabeth Alexandra Fabio would be forfeit unless Lady Clare Fabio voted in favour of an immediate surrender of Paris to the armies of the Reich. So it wasn't money they were after, Lady Clare realized with shock. The kidnappers didn't even want access codes for S3's famous, triple-encrypted orbiting database. Lady Clare had to throw in her lot with the Reich. Nothing else would do.

It was time to summon an official car. Always assuming Les Tourelles had a Renault that was still functioning – and even that wasn't a certainty. But then again, these days what was? Lady Clare opened her vast cupboard and started to take out dry clothes, laying them neatly on the bed.

Chapter 9

Laughing Boy

'If you don't let me out I'm going to . . .'

What? Scream? She'd tried that. Howling obscenities at the polycrete walls until her throat was sore and her voice worn down to a croaking whisper. LizAlec had tried the lot, from dignified silence through shouting to trying to flirt with Laughing Boy. None had been successful – and now she was wired up to the eyeballs with PMS and felt like a Niponshi Zeppelin. Periods and one-sixth G didn't go together at all.

Not that LizAlec knew how long she'd been there: her Circadian rhythms were on shutdown, her melatonin levels down to pitiful, her pituitary on strike . . . It was near impossible to judge time accurately in the dark. LizAlec hadn't realized that before, but it was true.

They weren't watching her. At least, LizAlec didn't think they were. At the start she'd been embarrassed at using the bucket they brought her just in case Mickey or Laughing Boy somehow had her up on screen, but in the end basic need and the ache in her gut won out. That was on the second day, and when Mickey brought her food next time round he'd taken away her soiled bucket without comment.

They didn't talk to her, neither of them ever did. She insulted them, joked at them, pleaded . . . but they might as well have been deaf. She knew just what they were doing, of course: distancing themselves, in case they had to kill her. LizAlec had no idea how she knew that, but she did. Maybe it was something about the way they wouldn't look at her whenever they came into her cell. Though they used the light these days and had done ever since she'd had a visit from the suit.

The sequence would go: blinding light from overhead, clang of door as the outside bolt was flung back and then the sullen thud of feet and the clatter of a tray being slid onto the table. By the time her eyes had adjusted to the brightness, whichever one it was would already be on his way out, slop bucket in hand, while the other stood in the doorway holding a Browning pulse rifle.

'I'm due on tomorrow,' LizAlec shouted at the door. 'Ragging, blood, period. What are you going to do then?' Like they cared. Other girls at St Lucius had taken the implant as advised, but LizAlec had been too bloody-minded. Low-gravity menstruation was unpleasant at the best of times – or so LizAlec had been warned – and stripped virtually naked in a cell wasn't the best of times, or places, not by anybody's standards.

She'd refused the implant, just as she'd later refused in-flight sedatives and the stewardess's offer of an injection for zero-gravity sickness. LizAlec didn't want to be at St Lucius and she'd had no intention of letting anyone forget the fact, especially herself.

But that was then and this was now – and it was time to get a grip. LizAlec was going to escape. That thought was now burned so firmly into her brain she no longer doubted it would happen. Sure, doubt flickered somewhere in her limbic system, but it was mostly unnoticed. Consciousness was happening high up on the surface, fierce feeling tucked into the wet-flannel folds of her cortex as chemical intimations of anger.

Her breathing was steadying now. The last screaming fit was hours behind her – and even howling like a banshee was more balanced than punching the door, even if it couldn't punch back. LizAlec wouldn't let herself let rip like that again; histrionics trashed too much of her dwindling energy. Of course, she could always eat the reprocessed slop that Mickey offered her but every time LizAlec ate their food she dropped into deep sleep.

The first time she'd assumed it was just tiredness, but not the second time or the third.

Not that hunger was all bad. For a start it kept the terror at bay. The way it worked was that LizAlec was so busy trying to ignore the gnawing in her hollow gut that no time was left for all the other discomforts. Of which there were many . . .

Cold, dark and too small – her cell was walled with rough polycrete blocks and roofed with slabs of some shiny black stone she couldn't reach. There were only three ways out of the cell. Well, only three that LizAlec could see in the brief seconds she grabbed each time her eyes adjusted to the light. One was the door, the other two were small air vents just above floor level, both covered with a steel grille and epoxyed to the wall. She'd already broken most of her nails trying to prise away one of the grilles.

Set into the wall at waist height was what might have been a fourth way, but LizAlec was afraid to go too close. Half the time the rusting metal plate radiated a bitter chill that leeched heat from her cell and body, the rest of the time it burned like a heater. The only time she'd tried to touch it, cold had glued her index finger to its edge and she'd lost skin from her fingertip trying to pull herself free.

'Oh shit.' PMS from hell, no way out and she didn't even have Fixx to shout at . . . LizAlec rolled over in the grit and pushed herself to her feet. Three paces to the right, then a wall, turn ninety degrees and then eight paces to the next wall, six paces and a turn. Another eight paces and one more turn would bring her back to the original wall. And another three paces would bring her back to where she started. Now she knew exactly what a lab rat felt like.

Not expecting much, LizAlec pulled at the grille over an air vent. No movement at all. Maybe if she had a blade it might shift. But her slop came on a paper plate with a paper spoon. And anyway a blade would probably just snap on her, knowing her recent luck. What she really needed was explosive. An H&K

eight-shot would be nice, and maybe some molywire, toggled up into a lariat. LizAlec smiled to herself in the dark, surprised to find she suddenly felt better. It had to be all that screaming.

She took another turn round the cell, stepping sideways like a crab in the darkness, reading off the rough walls with her fingertips, Braille-like.

'The door's out,' LizAlec told herself, knowing that was obvious. But then what was obvious was also usually true, or so Fixx reckoned anyway. And judging from the state of her nails it would take more than sheer will to separate the air vents from the wall. BioSemtex probably, if that didn't take out the surrounding polycrete blocks first. Like it or not, it was time she got back to that steel plate . . .

Slipping out of her filthy paper robe, LizAlec scrunched the hospital gown into a tight ball, then changed her mind and uncrumpled it, folding the tattered paper into a neat square. Five layers of cheap paper was not much to keep the heat or the cold at bay but it was all she had to work with, so it would have to do.

Without her robe, LizAlec could suddenly smell herself clearly in the heat that rose from her body. Sweat, fear and shit. Unpleasant and feral. It wasn't pretty. All humans must have smelt like that once, LizAlec reminded herself and then shrugged. So what? That didn't make her like it any better.

Chapter 10

Find a wall/Sit on it . . .

Lady Clare casually flicked at the purple lapel of her velvet jacket, even though she knew it was spotless. She had to do something with her trembling hands and smoking in the Imperial presence was forbidden. As was sitting unasked, interrupting, not paying attention . . .

Coolly casual she could do. Casual and coherent was proving more difficult. The Minister for Internal Affairs sighed, nodded and jotted something meaningless on a leather-bound smartpad in front of her. Affectation, all of it. She'd sooner have been using her Tosh, but a little pad was all tradition allowed her to bring to the vast walnut Council table. Still, at least hers was working. Two of the other pretty little machines had caught the virus overnight and broken up, which was what happened when Finance cut corners and allowed supplies to source their cases from steel rather than the pure silver that tradition demanded.

War or surrender? What could she say?

Lady Clare knew what she was *meant* to say. The e-mail left her in no doubt of that. Paris was to surrender on whatever terms the Reich offered. All of those little Aerospatiale cameras would be left in place, even the Ishies were to be untouched, free to eyecam history in the making. Nothing was to be done to stop the world from seeing the fall of Paris for what it was, a polite and stately diplomatic dance. Scrabbling blind panic would remain hidden.

Hunger ate at Lady Clare's gut, heightened by the three scalding cups of black coffee she'd swallowed before being delivered to the Court of St Cloud. Her face was skull-like, hollow-eyed. It usually was, it was just that most of the time

Lady Clare couldn't recognize the fact. Tapeworms and purging had once been the polite way of getting thin, but no longer. And it was a long time since anyone other than obsessives had actually needed to starve to achieve malnutrition – anyone rich, that was. Simple viral rewiring now speeded up bodily metabolism as efficiently as any old-fashioned drug, and for those nervous souls who didn't like permanent solutions there was always an appropriate, easily prescribed enzyme.

Non-medical genetic manipulation was meant to be forbidden. But Lady Clare couldn't remember how long it was since any of the Ministerial families had obeyed that particular law. If the Third Section had arrested every Minister whose pregnant wife had paid a quiet visit to one of FffC's *G&Stork* clinics there'd be no government left. Even LizAlec . . .

Especially LizAlec. The woman glanced again at her own face, seeing it stare back from a huge Napoleon III looking-glass on the wall opposite. The gilt frame was oversized, vulgar and almost priceless, which made it fit perfectly with the rest of the vast Council chamber. The Bonapartes had always been big on ambition, but the same could never be said for their taste. Red and gold seemed to be the only two colours they knew. And what couldn't be adorned with wreathed Ns – which wasn't much – was covered instead with an endless row of Merovingian bees.

Of the seven people at the table only Count Lazlo Portea was actually ignoring her; the rest were getting in surreptitious glances when they thought Lady Clare wouldn't notice. No one had asked her yet what was wrong, they didn't dare, but the Prince Imperial would when his irritation finally got the better of his impeccable manners. As for being ignored by Lazlo, that wasn't a surprise. It might be five years since the Potsdam Conference, but she still had him by the balls.

He'd thought himself so smart, taking her to his bed while the other junior Ministers sat in the mirrored splendour of the downstairs bar and whispered. But that simple act of sex had ruined his career, as Lady Clare'd intended it to. She would have been forced to promote the man eventually, anyway: then watched, half nervous as he clawed his way over the careers of his friends to the top of the shit heap.

But this way Lazlo was hers. Like it or not – and he loathed it – none of his colleagues distinguished between Lazlo's climb of the ladder and his climb into her bed. In one simple move, Lady Clare had fucked, promoted and politically castrated him. It was small wonder the man hated her.

'Your Highness, gentlemen . . .' Lady Clare settled back into her ornate chair and keyed up the S3 data she'd been working on that morning. It was Saturday: the meeting was an emergency one. She should be keeping the Prince Imperial on message while guiding the others politely but firmly through the Cabinet's limited options. Indicating, without making it too obvious, which one the Third Section felt was expedient. Instead she was politely, discreetly, simply panicking.

Surrender or not? They were waiting on her, as they always had, afraid to commit themselves without her guidance. Lady Clare looked round the table, discounting everyone except the Prince Imperial who sat resplendent at the head of the table in a black silk suit, his snow-white moustache and goatee carefully waxed. He was an old man now, but he'd been born as the Prince Imperial and that was how he would die. There *was* an Emperor, a true Napoleon, but he'd been on ice for a hundred years. At least, his headless cancer-ridden carcass had, wired into a Matsui cryonics tank, chilled and then flash-frozen in liquid nitrogen. His head was orbiting somewhere in a satellite. It wasn't easy keeping a head alive indefinitely, not cheap either. Lady Clare had seen the bills.

Still, dialysis kept the blood glucose levels stable, nutrient IV solutions kept him fed, and pressurized/oxygenated blood kept his severed head alive. What passed for an immune system was boosted with selected lymphocytes. Of course, even without a body, the blood to his head still needed detoxifying, its isotonicity required maintaining and urea had to be removed regularly. The satellite had back-ups to its back-ups – and then there were back-ups to those. Downtime wasn't an option for life support systems, certainly not for the Emperor's.

Imperial France was a lifetime's empire. That was the promise on which the Prince had been elected Emperor and President, and that was what was scripted into the constitution. 'The Empire dies with the Emperor,' ran the last sentence of all. But it would never happen. Or rather, Lady Clare reminded herself, it hadn't happened yet.

Surrender or not . . .

'Do you have an opinion?' It was Lazlo, icily polite, finally deciding to give Lady Clare some of his attention. The woman flushed, half rose in her chair before settling back in confusion. Despite the neatness of her dress and the perfection of her make-up, she knew that for once she wasn't making a good impression. But then, who could, with 100,000 Cossack mercenaries camped around the city?

'Lazlo.' The Prince Imperial spoke only one word but it was reproof enough to make the Minister for Security sit back in his seat, his handsome face frozen into a sullen mask. It was weird, Clare thought, watching His Highness. Fifty years of ruling as a spoilt neurotic and at the first sign of real danger he came off opium, clean break. Just like that. Not one pipe in three weeks, if his surgeon's daily report was to be believed.

'My opinion?' Lady Clare looked around the table, settling her gaze on Lazlo. Whatever the maxim said, there were times when you had to sweat the small stuff and as far as Lady Clare was concerned, that was what Lazlo was. 'My opinion on what?'

'Do we surrender now?' Lazlo asked her coldly. 'Or do we wait for another day, two days, a week . . .'

'Or should we fight?' Field Marshal Lena interrupted loudly and pushed his still-full coffee cup away from him in disgust, slopping dark liquid onto the table's Maltese lace tablecloth. At seventy the man still only had two states, alcohol-induced sleep and full-on, testosterone-fuelled aggression. Lady Clare liked him and so did the Prince Imperial: it was how he survived despite not having been sober for over ten years.

'We can't win.' Lady Clare said firmly. That wasn't her opinion, it was a fact. The army was split down the middle, whatever the field marshal might say. Generals Regis and Dershowitz were arguing among themselves, with Dershowitz having already made tentative overtures to the Reich. And if Field Marshal Lena didn't know that then he should have done. S3 had grabs of Dershowitz's communications. Military crypt was strong, but there was no PGP in use for which the Third Section didn't have a breaker.

'We can't win . . .' The Prince Imperial repeated Lady Clare's words back at her, his smoke-grey eyes watching her face. 'But we could fight?'

Yeah, Lady Clare thought tiredly, *if you want a massacre*. She looked at the old man and wondered if he knew how few soldiers would be willing to die if that was the order he issued. All government worked on the basis that the army was both loyal and stupid, but Lady Clare wasn't sure they were *that* stupid.

Though the Old Guard would die to a man if ordered. Intensive psychometric testing was in place to guarantee that. And the really bizarre thing was that the man they'd die for was truly nondescript. If he hadn't been a Bonaparte, no one would have glanced at him twice. As it was, his face was on every bank draft issued by the *Banque Impériale de Paris*.

And why should he be concerned? Even the Reich wouldn't dare kill the Prince Imperial if he surrendered. He was an old man, revered, all but defeated: not that he'd been that threatening to start with, except as a figurehead. The Reich could afford to offer him safe passage to Zurich. And the Swiss would have him, Lady Clare had no doubt about that, not with the amount of gold his family had salted away in the vaults of Hong Kong Suisse. It was locked in unbreakable trusts, of course. Otherwise Lady Clare would have suggested moving it somewhere safer, like off-planet.

Outside it was still raining, water slicking the dark streets and undermining already corroded concrete, making the sidewalks even more unsafe. She could see the rain as it beat hard against the window, but she couldn't hear it. Triple-glazed, micromesh-laminated polymer, it was designed to keep out more than the sound of a storm.

'My dear?' It was the Prince Imperial this time, his voice polite but insistent. The old man wasn't going to let her sit this one out: she had to commit.

What she wanted to say was *Surrender now, please.* But she couldn't get those words out, no matter how much half of her wanted to. So instead Lady Clare took a deep breath and did what she'd promised herself she wouldn't do: tell the truth, or as much of it as she could manage. 'At the moment surrender isn't our best option. But, even so, fighting might not be wise.'

'Wise?' The elderly man seemed puzzled. 'Why not?'

'Keep the army as your last resort,' suggested Lady Clare and shut her mouth, sitting back in her chair. With luck she could leave it at that.

Luck wasn't with her.

'Because we should save them?'

'No.' Lady Clare said brusquely, meeting the Prince Imperial's gaze. 'Because they can't be trusted.'

The crash of the field marshal's chair tipping backwards was shock enough to still the whole Council Room but − on his feet or not − the field marshal still didn't get a chance to speak. Count Lazlo was in there first, telling them all his version of what it was Lady Clare was trying to say.

'No alternative but eventual surrender then . . .' Fussy, snide, mocking − Lady Clare loathed his voice on instinct, but not as much, Lady Clare suspected, as Lazlo loathed everything about her. Lazlo smiled at Lady Clare, his green eyes watchful but cold. 'At least, I think that's what the Minister for Internal Affairs and National Security is trying to say . . .' He stressed the second part of her title, as if it were her personal fault that Paris was surrounded, its ferroconcrete buildings being eaten away from within.

'No,' Lady Clare said. 'That isn't what I mean at all . . .'

She saw surprise reach Lazlo's eyes, noted too that the young Minister for Finance was suddenly watching her, but what Lady Clare really noticed was hope sparking in the eyes of the Prince Imperial, then just as suddenly dying.

'I won't sacrifice this city.' His voice was calm, undramatic. But for once his habitual politeness was cut with steel.

'I'm not suggesting that,' Clare said shortly. 'The battle computers are down. We have fewer than fifty functioning APVs, almost no working aircraft and hardly any cannon, the virus has seen to that. At best we have fifteen hundred officer-issue Colt ceramics. Hardly enough to fight a war. But then what about the Black Hundreds?' She turned to Lena. 'Are their hovers still functioning? What is the state of their guns? And what of . . .'

'So you vote against surrender?' Lazlo interrupted.

'Wait until I've finished talking,' Lady Clare said sharply and then turned her attention to the field marshal who was sheepishly retaking his seat, trying not to catch her eye. They were all men but her. That was the way the Third Empire worked. She hadn't liked it when she started out, and she didn't like it now. What she liked even less was that she'd managed to change so little in her forty years of serving the Imperial Government.

She was back in control, at least in control of them if not of herself. They were waiting for her now. Her words would carry dangerous weight as they always had done: and until now she'd always liked that feeling. Liked the slight fear that flickered across people's eyes when she appeared.

But this was payback and none of them even knew what she was going through. Paris or LizAlec was a choice Lady Clare couldn't easily make. Not just because the child still thought Lady Clare was her mother, but because it was Lady Clare who gave LizAlec life. Lady Clare had overruled the refusal of the Sorbonne's Ecole de Médecin to release Alex Gibson's frozen sperm. That was sixteen years ago. Three weeks later, having ordered a Web-wide search for details of Razz's clone-insurance policy, she'd had an entire Razz clone quietly lifted from the cryonic vaults of FirstVirtual.

It wasn't the meat Lady Clare wanted, that vat-kept heap of barely living flesh, it was the clone's ovaries. The director at Marne had mixed sperm and ova himself, implanting the resulting cytoplast into Lady Clare in her own bedroom at the Hôtel Sabatini. Nine months later Elizabeth Alexandra was born – no surrogates, no synthetic wombs, no fast-forwarding the period of gestation.

The child Alex and Razz would never have, because one was psychotic and dead and the other was alive and a god, but still insane for all that. Both had been her lovers in their time: not for long, admittedly, and she'd never meant to either of them what they meant to each other. But all the same, she'd had their child. Alone, at night, in that vast bed.

LizAlec or Paris? How could she vote to surrender the capital of the Empire? How could she not vote . . . ? Lady Clare put her head in her hands, pushing knuckles into dark-ringed eye sockets until fractal stars exploded behind her eyes. No tears, not here. Not in front of these people.

Let the Prince Imperial decide.

'I abstain,' Lady Clare said flatly. Ignoring Lena, Count Lazlo and the youthful but fat Minister of Finance, she met the Prince Imperial's sad eyes. Saw the tired old man bow under the weight of another responsibility. Saw the hurt in his face and knew she could never tell him why.

Kidnappers killed their victims in seventy-three per cent of cases: Lady Clare had looked up the figures. The cold probability was that she couldn't save LizAlec whichever way she voted, that there was a twenty-nine per cent likelihood that she was already dead, but that wasn't the point. At least, Lady Clare told herself it wasn't.

Chapter 11

Vacuum Sucks

Suction kept the steel plate attached to the wall. It was true that epoxy clips had been gunned to the polycrete blocks at all four corners, but even Lars could see these were powdery with age, shoddily positioned and barely able to cope with the minimal strain of Luna gravity. No, what kept the steel plate stuck to the wall was suction, pure and simple . . .

Which meant there was atmosphere on the other side of that plate. Not a weak quarter-atmosphere like in the tunnel he was in, but a full half or maybe more. Maybe even the full fucking monty. Hung in a tunnel, feet extended forward and back pressed hard against cold rock, Lars couldn't name the relevant laws of physics, but he knew from experience the basic rules governing grades of vacuum. Staying alive depended on it. And if there was breathable air on the other side of that gap then he wanted to get through. Where there was good air there was usually power and what Lars needed more than anything right now was somewhere to plug in Ben's ice bucket. He also needed to find food and recharge the catalyst for his lung, but they came lower down his list of essentials. And to be honest, he could go a lot longer than a couple of weeks with his metabolism turned down to low.

Lars wasn't letting himself think about the girl, because thinking about her upped his breathing rate and that messed up his metabolism. She was there, though. Every time he touched his fingertips against the metal, he could feel her words, like a low and angry vibration. How that happened, Lars didn't know and didn't care.

He had a bigger problem. Lars was suction-side to the plate which meant he'd have to push *against* the pressure. Even if he could push the plate away from the wall, chances were the escaping atmosphere from the airlock on the other side would slam it straight back, and probably take his hand or fingers with it.

'Right,' said Lars, tugging on Ben's monofilament line. 'Let's scam you that power . . .' The icebox came up sweet and easy from the shaft below. Nothing snagged or caught, and Lars didn't have to clamber back down to help the icebox make the climb. Though the warning diode was still flashing, with a slow and sullen flicker.

'Real soon,' Lars promised. 'Just as soon as we get through this . . .'

In front of him was a hole cut in the side of the tunnel and closed off with a metal plate. Between the black rock of the tunnel and the plate was a single block's thickness of polycrete. Lars pushed hard against the metal, putting all of his weight behind the effort. Even so, he was shocked when the plate shifted slightly under his feet. It was one thing to promise Ben everything would be all right, quite another for the rusted plate to actually move.

'Shit, man . . . We're going do it.' Lars pushed again, hard as he could, and felt the plate slide suddenly sideways.

Baby Blowout. Baby Black.

Whatever was on the other side of that hatch it wasn't an airlock. Lars could feel a sudden blast of decompression as high atmosphere was sucked through the narrow gap to be swallowed by the partial vacuum of his own tunnel. He was crouched in front of the hatch, hot wind whistling past his head as Lars fought to use his foot to slide the hatch back into place, sealing the air loss.

He thought it was hot air he'd felt but Lars wasn't too sure: sometimes his feelings and imagination got bad-wired. Mostly he was fine, but just occasionally he'd grab a burger from a stall and instead of it being hot or sweet with ketchup it would taste blue and tingly. Or he'd stop off at a bar out on the Edge to catch NiFlyz Cadillac Jukebox and instead of notes he'd get different tastes.

'Synaesthesia' wasn't a word Lars knew. But he knew the side effects well enough. Sometimes it was useful, like when he could feel his way up a new rock tunnel by listening to the notes of its surface, watching for the dark tones that indicated danger. Other times it just fucked up his head.

When that happened he'd go surface at Planetside Arrivals and steal a strip of ParaDerm from the shop with the green neon cross in its window. Lars had a thing for ParaDerm. Two stopped his headache, four made him feel warm and eight kicked him into sleep without dreams. Eight was good.

'This time,' said Lars and pushed hard with his foot, dislodging the plate further, wind howling past him so hard it almost blew him down the tunnel like shit off a shovel. Flipping round, Lars jammed his fingers through the hatch and gripped the edge of the plate, trying to shift it. Grit hammered against the mask of his suit and, as Lars tried to ram his shoulders in through the newly opened gap, something soft slammed into the other side of the wall, smashing into his head and partly sealing the gap.

'Shi—' Scrabbling frantically, fingers clawing at laser-cut rock, half stunned, Lars only just kept his balance as colours exploded in front of his eyes, like opening flowers. It took Lars a fraction of a second to realize that the flowers were pain. And when he came to – another fraction of a second after that – he was crouched back in the access shaft, back pushed hard against cold rock, facing the blast of air. His face mask was powdery with ice crystals or dust.

Lars turned, the way a baby turns in the womb, but infinitely faster, with snake-like fluidity. Shuffling his shoulders and hips, bending his thick legs under him until his head was pushed into the narrow opening, Lars flexed his legs hard against the stone shaft behind him and shoved himself forwards, his hands digging into warm flesh.

Not scavenger fat but soft, rich with spare muscle. Fed. Lars couldn't imagine what it was like to have someone just give you food. But this one, she probably couldn't imagine what it was like to scavenge.

On the other side of the wall, LizAlec was screaming, Lars could feel it through his fingertips. Not that he blamed her. If someone had been trying to burrow their hands through his stomach while suction from a blow-out held him flat against a rough wall – hell, he'd have been screaming too.

Hands palm-on to the wall, Earth-strong muscles pushing her aching torso away from the wall, knees ripped raw and bloody, LizAlec fought to unglue her gut from the deadly suction. It wasn't until she felt her body peel free from the hole that she even consciously became aware of Lars fighting past her as the boy slithered swiftly into her tiny cell, one shoulder casually dislocated to let him fit through the gap.

As Lars tumbled onto the ground, LizAlec's cell went from minor decompression back up to a baby blowout, grit being sucked clean off the floor as precious atmosphere howled under the door like air dragged the wrong way down an organ pipe only to be swallowed through the ravenous hatch. It was time to put the cork back in the monkey.

'Help me,' Lars shouted desperately, struggling with the plate as the girl stood there letting heat and oxygen bleed away around her. 'Fucking help me,' Lars shouted, grabbing her shoulder, then ducked as she swung wildly in his direction, wide-eyed with horror, breath streaming from her lungs in a long scream. The girl was blind in the dark, Lars realized with shock. She couldn't see him. Couldn't hear him either come to that.

'Here,' said Lars, ripping aside his bubble mask. He grabbed her wrist, dragging LizAlec's fingers towards the floor. Lars had no doubts she was stronger than him: how could she be otherwise when she'd only recently left Earth gravity? He was smarter though, Lars decided. Otherwise she'd have already plugged the gap on her own.

LizAlec touched the steel plate, felt the strange hand grip her wrist and guessed what she was meant to do. Lifting the plate waist high, she started to position it clumsily over the open hatch. But Lars had other ideas, ones that didn't involve LizAlec losing all her fingers.

Pulling the raised plate out of her hands, Lars threw it hard at the wall and saw the baby black half catch the hatch and hold it. He couldn't have hacked lifting the plate by himself, his legs weren't strong enough, but once it was up off the ground he could manage the rest.

A tiny gap still bled away atmosphere, but it was nothing to the swallowing emptiness of before. Pulling the girl over towards the wall, Lars tried to get her to help him slide the plate shut, but she jerked away from him and tripped, crashing to her knees.

'Jesus fuck.' Lars left her there – shuddering with cold and fear – and grabbed a folded square of paper from the ground, wrapped this round one shaking hand and pushed the steel square back into place himself.

Instant silence broken only by a siren somewhere in the background, its wail rising and falling like the howl of a distant ghost. In total, from when Lars and LizAlec simultaneously – but unknown to each other – began trying to removing the plate, to LizAlec finally sliding it back in place was maybe thirty-five seconds. Thirty-five seconds of oxygen and heat being bled away into a partial vacuum.

It wasn't a Big Black, thirteen seconds of which killed you as surely as a bullet to the head, but it felt like one, at least it did to Lars. LizAlec didn't seem to be feeling anything. She'd toppled sideways and was curled up in the dirt, choking, her mouth open like a dying fish as desperate gulps of air going down met vomit coming back up.

'Oh, fuck it.' Lars kicked her lightly in the diaphragm, which did the trick, bubbles of vomit spewing out on to the floor and then air rasping back down her suddenly cleared throat. He used the few seconds it took the girl to get her breath back to take a good look at her.

It was the first time Lars had seen a naked woman, at least a real live one. All the others had been holoporn projections or spread wide with some flashing pay-by-access Web address strung behind their blonde wigs like a dayglo banner. She was less contoured than he'd have expected a woman to be. Smaller breasts, narrower hips, less of her all round. Her nipples were neat, though, puckered and pulled erect by the chill.

It didn't occur to Lars that the pneumatic porn-babes he lusted after were not just computer-enhanced, they were mostly just not real. Most were vActors, digital flesh pasted over three-dimensional, fully functional raytraced frames. Some were masterpieces of coding, but most were cut-and-paste clones of earlier idoru, updated for changes in taste. Small tails were big again, so were fine all-over pelts and pixie-like ears that folded in on themselves until they looked like vulvas. Furry was massive right now.

This one was way different, and Lars liked the difference. Her skin was smooth and mostly hairless, its shade pink and yellow mixed in with brown, and there were glints of deep red fire in her dark curls. Not that her hair was cropped close like most people's, instead it just tumbled below the back of her neck. Casual and chaotic.

Lars had no idea a cut like that cost more than Planetside was offering for his arrest, but then neither did LizAlec. She'd just palm-printed the make-over against her mother's account at *Gattopardo*.

Stepping over the still-gasping LizAlec, Lars took a quick look at the girl from behind. Her thin body didn't go in much at the waist and her spine could be seen all the way down her back. Her legs were thin and muscled and she had tight buttocks that made Lars swallow hard just from looking. From behind she looked like Ben.

'What name?' Lars asked LizAlec, touching her lightly on the shoulder. LizAlec jumped and scrambled to her feet, arms outstretched in the darkness to keep him away.

'What name?' Lars demanded again, less patiently. Outside her door two men were now shouting at each other and some-where down the corridor a siren was still going banshee. It would keep howling until the air pressure came up normal – that was what it was there for.

Beneath its distant electronic wail Lars could hear someone fumbling at a manual lock on the cell door, metal grating against metal as whoever it was tried to use a key. Which meant the power was down in this sector. Bad news for . . .

Ben.

'Shit . . . Fucking, fucking shit.' Lars punched himself crossly in the head. How could he forget Ben like that? Ben was still out there, stuck in his ice bucket, hanging from a single strand of monofilament on the wrong side of the metal plate. Lars could only think of two ways of getting him back and he didn't like the idea of either of them. Although retracing his steps from Planetside was a tad more attractive than trying to prise off that metal plate and having another battle with the Baby Black.

'Fuck it,' Lars said loudly, 'fuck it, fucking fuck it . . .'

'Who are you? What's happening?' LizAlec's voice was strung to breaking with fear. Lars's accent might make him sound to LizAlec like he was talking English through a mouthful of sand, but she understood well enough that he was swearing. And even she could now hear Laughing Boy and Mickey wrestling with the door.

'It's Ben,' said Lars.

'Ben? Who's Ben? Did my mother send you?' She stumbled slightly over calling Lady Clare her mother but did it anyway: she couldn't get used to thinking of the bitch as anything else, not even in her own head.

'Ben's my friend,' said Lars. 'But he's dead, so I'm looking after him.'

That got LizAlec's attention. 'Dead?'

'I've got his head in an ice bucket,' Lars told her, his voice quiet but matter-of-fact as if he didn't find the idea unusual, which he didn't. The boy was already watching LizAlec's heavy cell door, which had just clicked loudly as four deadlocks finally slid back. It was opening now, and Lars could see the barrel of a rifle poking nervously through the slit . . . Had that door been airtight, the girl would probably be dead, oxygen-starved, lungs ruptured open.

'Down,' Lars whispered, pushing on the girl's shoulder. And when LizAlec stayed standing, Lars kicked her legs rapidly out from under her in one easy sweep and they fell together, Lars's face pushed tight into the back of her neck. One of his arms went under her, the other snaked up over her face, finding her mouth.

'Quiet,' Lars hissed.

LizAlec bit down hard on his filthy glove and Lars punched her in the kidneys, feeling breath explode from her body. She tried to whimper but Lars had his hand too firmly over her mouth.

'Do you want to get dead?' Lars whispered.

LizAlec wasn't sure if Lars meant killed by him or by Laughing Boy or Mickey, whichever one it was had just slowly opened the door. Lars didn't know either. But she shut up and that was all that mattered. At least, it was all that mattered to him.

There was a quick click just outside the door, as if someone was trying and failing to turn on a light, but LizAlec's cell stayed as dark as the corridor outside. The whole of the rifle barrel was in the room now, held waist high by a tall man wearing the cartoon face of a mouse. Mouse-face had frozen in the doorway, sweeping his gun in a hesitant arc above Lars's and LizAlec's heads.

The man was night-blind too, Lars realized. Maybe it was

more common than he thought. Ben had been sightless in the dark, reduced to wearing a strange pair of CK NightRyders taken off a dead *WeGuard*. The CKs made everything glow red in the dark and go fuzzy at the edges. Lars hated them, they gave him a headache.

'Lady Elizabeth Alexandra?' Mickey's voice was worried, as well he might be. Getting paid depended on nothing bad happening to the girl, Count Lazlo had been firm about that. When he said nothing, he meant nothing: not just crap that might leave permanent scars or bruises. Nothing. Losing her to a blow-out was not acceptable practice.

Lars kept his hand tight over the girl's mouth, leaving her enough space to breath through her nose, nothing more.

'Lady Elizabeth?'

Silence.

'She's not answering,' the tall man said sullenly.

Lying face down with some stranger's hand covering her face, LizAlec forced herself to stop panicking and begin to listen. It was Mickey and he was standing in the blackness above her talking into a button mike. He had to be, since Laughing Boy obviously wasn't with him.

'Yeah, right . . .' There was a hiss of static and then the man mumbled agreement to something else. 'Yeah, all we fucking need,' the man said tiredly. 'You go get a lamp and I'll check the floor. No . . . I didn't know this fucking cell was one skin deep to a vacuum.'

He sighed, drumming his fingers against the zytel stock of his Browning. 'Yeah, you're right. What's left of her probably is gumming tight a pressure leak.' He sighed again, heavily. 'Right, yeah. The Boss is going to fucking love this.'

Lars saw Mickey lower the rifle until its barrel pointed towards the floor and then sweep it backwards and forwards in front of him like a blind man with a stick. Mickey was searching for the girl's body, Lars realized, but he wasn't going to find it. Not if Lars could help it. Keeping his fingers tight over LizAlec's mouth, Lars rolled them both out of the way and saw Mickey suddenly freeze at the slight noise, head turned to one side to hear better, eyes flicking snake-like but useless in the dark.

'Don't move,' Mickey ordered. 'Don't even think of it.' He had the rifle up now, waist high again, sweeping the small cell. Not that he could risk opening fire on LizAlec, the man had to be professional enough to know the odds were shit. If the Browning was on ceramic then the frag splinters would probably rip him apart too. And if the rifle was switched to pulse . . . Well, he could risk it but he didn't know which wall bled to the vacuum. Given it wasn't the one with the door in it behind him, he had a one in three chance of getting it wrong.

Party time.

Lars rolled off the girl, hearing her drag in a breath as he pulled his trapped arm roughly from under her, fingers brushing swiftly across one bare breast. Lars's grin lasted just as long as it took LizAlec to scramble to her feet. More than anything, Lars wanted to shout at LizAlec to get out of Mickey's way, but he didn't dare give away his own position low on the floor. Instead he watched helplessly as the sweeping gun touched her side and LizAlec gasped.

'That you?' Relief was written through Mickey's voice. 'You okay?'

'Yeah,' LizAlec said slowly, straightening up. 'I'm still here.' LizAlec touched a hand to her ribs and winced. She tried to wipe grit from her dirt-encrusted face but had to give up. Her fingers were so battered from fighting the vacuum she couldn't manage it. LizAlec didn't know which bit of her hurt the most.

'What happened?' Mickey asked, his question halfway between suspicion and concern. He was reaching forward to touch LizAlec when Lars came up off the floor behind Mickey, wrapping a short length of monofilament around the man's throat, not fixed with a running knot or toggled at the end like a proper garrotte, just fast and tight with the ends wrapped round his own bare hands. Mickey froze, fixed on the edge of panic.

Then combat reflexes cut in as his right fist swept up and back to punch Lars in the face.

Lars grunted but by then Mickey was already gripping his right fist in his left hand and swinging down to drive his elbow hard back into Lars's chest, shattering three ribs. Purples and blacks exploded as the boy dropped his monofilament in shock. Lars saw the man pivot and kick, fresh colours blossoming as the blow caught Lars's shoulder, ripping his upper arm from its joint. Without even thinking about it, the boy hurled himself into the wall, slamming the bone back into its socket. This wasn't what he'd had in mind.

Ducking away from a second kick, Lars rolled backwards in the dark and grabbed his dropped length of monofilament. A yard of molywire would have had the man's head off but Lars had only heard of moly garrottes, he'd never actually used one himself. Looping the monofilament quickly round Mickey's foot, Lars scrambled to his feet and yanked upwards, lifting the man's leg out in front of him. Quick as sin, Lars swivelled sideways and stamped hard into the man's exposed groin without letting go of the monofilament.

Mickey screamed.

Stupid, Lars told himself as the sweating, gasping guard staggered backwards, bouncing into a wall. Stupid. He should have taken out the man's knee, put him on the ground permanently. Hauling high his length of wire, the boy swivelled again. This time, hearing the crunch of a foot pivoting on grit, Mickey dropped his hands to his groin, cupping his balls. Pure instinct.

It was all Lars needed. Slamming his heel into the man's kneecap, Lars ruptured the guard's synovial capsule, shredding cartilage and dislocating one knee. One was enough. Mickey went down with a gasp of pain and never got up again.

Razor-sharp incisors went with the Sandrat genes: it was part of the package. That, and two prominent lower canines that gave the Ratboys their name. It didn't matter to Lars that these were originally gene-coded in to allow tunnellers to tear hard rations, back in the days when payloads were expensive, water even rarer than it was now and clone protein came in dried strips, like some whitecoat version of *biltong*.

Lars used his teeth only when fighting, and then only when desperate. Like now. The first taste he got when he bit into the man's neck was sweat, followed quickly by a darker taste as Lars's mouth filled with warm blood.

Mickey shat himself, bowels opening and a fetid stink filling the tiny cell as surely as the guard's unearthly scream. It was instinct that made Lars hook one yellow canine behind a jugular and rip, incisors chewing at the hot rubbery tube.

Fingers thrust in through Lars's eyes would have stopped the boy in his tracks, but the man was beyond saving, combat training drowned by panic. Frantically, he pushed one hand up to catch Lars's chin – and Mickey ended up helping rip out his own throat as Lars pulled away to avoid Mickey's clutching fingers and tore open the vein as he did.

There was a larger vein somewhere, sunk under thick muscle, and Lars bent his head to find it, chewing raw flesh as he worried his way into the man's open throat. The vein was where Ben had said he'd find it, but biting it open wasn't necessary. The struggling man was almost dead, limbs twitching weakly, his screams swallowed down to low animal-like gurgles of pure horror. Lars rolled off the man and spat, already hunkering back on his heels.

The tiny cell stank of shit and blood.

Over in the corner the girl sat, wide-eyed and moaning, her tightly pulled-up knees wrapped protectively in her own bare arms. Lars shrugged. She was alive and one kidnapper was already dead. He didn't see what the problem was. That looked like a good result to him.

'Shut it,' Lars told her. 'I want to listen . . .' And when she didn't, he pushed himself noisily to his feet. LizAlec was silent before he'd taken two paces so instead Lars went to fetch the rifle.

'*Browning*,' it said on one side, not that Lars could read it. '*Pulse/R model 3.ii. Factored under licence in IslamBeirut.*' There was some other stuff about implied warranties and a DNA-recognition chip was set into the gun's matt-grey zytel butt, but someone had hot-jumped it and taped a h/ware patch into position. Not that Lars knew that: he just saw a cracked silicon square crudely taped over with grey tamperTell.

Pointing the Browning towards the open door, Lars squeezed the trigger, letting loose a ceramic slug. Muzzle flare lit the cell, and in the echoing crash of that single explosion LizAlec saw Lars for the first time. A fat child dressed in a strange white suit that hung round him like someone else's flayed skin. Bolted to his hip was a black metal bottle, its hose feeding straight into his chest. His slack-jawed mouth was coated in red. LizAlec saw Mickey too, sprawled dead on the floor, neck ripped open – and then she put the two nightmarish sights together.

'Sweet Jesus,' LizAlec whispered as she backed herself against the wall, crouched low, hands folded even tighter across her knees. Her night-blind eyes had dilated with shock.

'What *are* you?' LizAlec asked.

'Lars,' said Lars, dropping into a crouch in front of her, rifle cradled in one hand. Part of him was listening to her ragged breathing, watching the way her mouth opened slightly with each little gasp, but most of his mind was tuned to the echoing silence outside. The other guard would come down that corridor, Lars was certain of it. And from the way the corridor had echoed his shot, it was long and straight with no tunnels opening off. Which meant that when the man came it would be down an unlit corridor, straight towards Lars's waiting gun.

Lars grinnned and allowed himself a sly glance between LizAlec's pulled-up ankles. He wanted to touch her there for real, see if it felt how it looked, soft and salt. There would be a signature scent to her, Lars knew that, but for the moment all his senses were buried beneath the stink of the guard's death.

Besides, there would be time enough later and Lars had the

advantage, he knew that. The little rich girl was night-blind, while he could see her face, her small breasts where they flattened against her knees and that hungry darkness between her legs. He could watch LizAlec without her knowing he watched, though she sensed he was near. Lars could tell that by the way she twisted her head, trying to follow his movements.

'Lars who?' LizAlec asked finally.

'Just Lars,' Lars said, keeping his gaze on the empty corridor.

'And my mother didn't send you?'

Lars shook his head, then realized the girl couldn't see him. 'No,' he said. 'No, not your mum.'

'Then it was Fixx!' The girl said suddenly, a grin splitting her face. 'You work for Fixx!' She was nodding to herself as if it was obvious.

'No,' said Lars. 'Not your mum, not Fixx. No one sent me.' He rolled backward in the grit, twisting his legs over his head to pivot on one foot, landing face forward, stretched out, the rifle never even touching the ground. Sandrat style. Even a life as brief as his had its advantages.

He knew the other guard was coming long before Laughing Boy waddled into view. Listening intently to the shuffle of Laughing Boy's crepe soles on the extruded polycrete of the corridor floor, Lars heard the man move carefully through the dark as he swivelled himself round the far corner, wide hips wobbling as he pushed his bulk against the wall, a pistol of some sort held upright, clutched tight in both hands as he crept forward.

Over one eye was a black lens, fed by optic fibre from a box attached to the side of his head by a flyweight boron-fibre Alice band. The thing looked like an expensive version of the NightRyders Ben used to wear.

Lars flipped sideways in the dirt, rolling out of sight. He'd counted on getting off a clean shot, seeing without being seen, but that wasn't going to happen.

'Man coming,' Lars told LizAlec. The girl started to ask some question but Lars hushed her into silence. 'Don't move, don't speak' he said. He could have told LizAlec that he needed her as his decoy, that battered, dirty and naked she was worth more to him than a free shot. But Lars didn't have time and besides he didn't know the words to say it.

So instead he left her there and trusted she wouldn't do anything stupid, like move. Hunched against the far wall, knees pulled up under her chin and genitals displayed, LizAlec was in Laughing Boy's direct line of sight through the open door. If Lars had been that guard, then, scream or no scream, he knew exactly where he'd have been looking. Some instincts were hardwired into the psyche: that's why they were instincts.

Time to get ready. Resting his rifle briefly against the nearest wall, Lars flexed his hands until he heard the bones in his fingers click. Then he swung his head heavily from side to side, trying to release the tension in his neck. According to Ben, rule one of combat was get wired or hang loose, because there was nothing in between. Ben had liked to hang tight but reflex enhancers weren't Lars's style. He'd tried ice once, though, but all it did was burn when it hit the back of his throat and give him a headache and a bad case of the shakes. Ben thought it was hilarious, but then Ben thought lots of weird shit was amusing.

No, Lars liked loose; it was cooler for a start. Any shithead could go round radiating *psycho* but Lars preferred to keep people guessing — is this guy dangerous or not? Is this shit for real? Hefting the Browning up with one hand, Lars swivelled the rifle so its barrel was facing down and took up a position just inside the door. He could hear Laughing Boy's breathing now, heavy and shallow, on the wrong side of nervous . . . Mind you, *he*'d have been brick-shitting if he'd heard a scream like Mickey's coming over his ear bead. The soft shoe shuffle was right outside LizAlec's cell door now.

'Lars . . . ?'

'Shut it,' Lars hissed, as quietly as he could. This wasn't the time to let the guard know there were two of them. In fact there

couldn't have been a worse time for LizAlec to open her mouth
– but it was all right. Laughing Boy was too busy dealing with
his own fear to be paying proper attention.

And then the guard came in. Beretta held high, barrel up,
handle gripped between interlocking fingers, standard stuff.
Laughing Boy's eyes raked to the left, checked that corner and
then he kicked back the door, steel hitting 'crete with a loud
clang. Nothing there. His eyes began to flick rapidly across the
back wall only to stop, as Lars knew they would, when they
reached the naked girl. It was a moment's hesitation only, but
it was all Lars needed.

Stepping quietly out from behind the door frame, he swung
the butt of the late Mickey's Browning hard into the point
where neck met jaw. There was a crack as bone fractured and
then Laughing Boy crashed screaming to his knees. Pushing
the fat man sideways with his foot, Lars aimed his butt at the
uppermost vertebra – where skull joined spine – and slammed
down, snapping Laughing Boy's neck. Instant silence.

'Lars?' LizAlec's voice was high, anxious.

'Still here,' Lars said shortly. He was busy going through
Laughing Boy's jacket pocket. Not that there was much. A cheap
Jap inhaler of some kind, pure oxygen probably. Lars didn't read
Nip – or anything else for that matter. Other than that, there
was a bubble-pack of derms and a transparent lock-knife with
plexiglass handle and zytel blade, the kind of street-punk shit
that was meant not to show up on m/wave surveillance cameras
and always did.

The nightspex were more interesting. The word 'Zeiss' was
laser-etched in blue round the edge of the single lens and the
autofocus mechanism was undamaged, which was pure luck on
Lars's part. For a brief second, Lars considered letting LizAlec
have the spex but then he shook his head. There were advantages
to having her remain night-blind. Like, she wasn't going to be
able to see him coming . . .

As quietly as possible – undoing velcro straps one at a time, rather than ripping them open as he usually did – Lars freed the o/lung bottle from his side and unscrewed its vacuum-proof hose. Dipping one hand into a balloon-suit pocket for the bung, Lars began to undo the front of his balloon suit.

The garment might have been a cheap Korean copy of an outdated NASA model, but it still featured a double seal down the front: the first an outer flap that folded back to reveal two nanetic edges that joined and unjoined as if by magic. Once the suit was off, he'd be able to close off the hole into his ribs, plugging the circular ceramic vent with a replaceable neoprene bung that screwed level with his skin.

Lars shuffled out of the suit as if it was an unwanted skin and stood naked in the blackness of the tiny cell, screwing the plug into his side. Then he got on with doing what he really wanted to do: take a good look at the naked girl. The most obvious difference between himself and LizAlec stuck out in front of him, but there were other, less intrusive differences, and not just that she had neater breasts.

His stomach pushed forward where her gut was flat, and his legs were wasted while hers were still muscled, thicker at the top, getting narrower as they moved down. She still stank, though. In that they were equal.

Briefly, Lars considered dragging the girl out into the passage first, away from the dead bodies, but decided not to bother. He didn't want to make trouble for himself and besides, she looked glued to the spot.

'Lars?' Her face still searched the darkness, scared and anxious. He'd stopped moving, Lars realized. She'd been tracking him by sound and now there was silence, broken only by the thud of some distant air-scrubber.

'You still here?'

'Yeah,' Lars thought, dropping to a crouch, one hand reaching for the transparent lock-knife. He was still here.

The rape didn't go the way Lars planned. To start with, yeah, but not by the end, no way . . . Moving silently in towards

LizAlec, Lars squatted near her feet, not yet touching her, his brown eyes hungrily swallowing the sight of her. He was hungry in a way no holoporn made him hunger, frightened too. His whole body shaking as sweat gathered under his arms and trickled thin and hot down his ribs.

Mostly plans just happened in his head, but this time Lars couldn't suss out where to start: not when he had one knife and a pair of elegant legs to deal with, and only two hands. In the end, he jammed the zytel blade down in the dirt and grabbed LizAlec roughly by the ankles, pulling her towards him so she tipped backwards, and almost split her skull.

'Little fucker!' LizAlec kicked out, the heel of her foot catching Lars on the shoulder, pushing him back onto his bare arse. She kicked again, freeing her other foot, and began to scramble to her feet.

Shock was the first thing Lars felt, then burning anger. His shoulder was numbed down to nothing, flash-frozen by the blow. Still sitting on the ground, he drove his fist into her leg, hard, taking her down. And while she was still protesting, Lars grabbed the knife and held the blade to her throat.

LizAlec froze into utter silence.

'I'm not going to get killed for it,' she said at last.

That was good, Lars nodded to himself in agreement, he didn't want her dead either. With one hand he reached forward and found a wrist, pushing LizAlec's arm up above her head. There wasn't quite room to stretch her out, so Lars let go the wrist and grabbed an ankle instead, jerking her body towards where he was squatting between her legs.

'Okay, okay . . .' LizAlec shuffled her body away from the wall, her words more irritated than scared.

'Good,' said Lars, not sure if he was talking about the action or her. She was beautiful, he knew that. Blind to the night and not the shape he'd expected, but her brown skin was as smooth as glass and her violet eyes were lit from inside with splinters of fire. And as for her breasts . . .

Lars drove the knife into the dirt next to LizAlec's head and reached for a breast, feeling it small and hard beneath his callused fingers. Instinctively, his thumb and finger closed round a nipple and he closed his eyes, tasting its texture, hearing the soft darkness of the puckered circle around it.

Desire exploded in his mind. Not just to taste her, to feel her Earth-hard body crushed beneath his, but to own her totally. To squat forever like a wine-dark memory on the inside of her mind. To hear the full bittersweet symphony of her fear.

Lars sunk his face into her hair and inhaled, nuzzled his mouth below one small breast and bit, tasting sweet blood, ignoring her frantic lurch of protest. Hungrily, Lars uncurled the fingers gripping her nipple and cupped the salt sweetness between her legs, rough fingers curling up through damp hair.

Salt, blood, darkness.

He'd found her.

Found what all the tri-Ds and holoporn couldn't reveal.

Rape. Pure and simple. No excuses. No mitigation. Not that there ever was for terrorism, murder or rape. LizAlec's views on that were fixed firm. It came from having an ex-Chief Imperial Prosecutor for a mother.

She couldn't see Lars but she could hear him, feel and smell him. He stank worse than she did, his fat unwashed body rank with sweat. She could feel him prodding clumsily against her and hear his frantic hunger sour into anger as he missed every time.

LizAlec took a deep breath and let it out slowly, feeling her heart steady. Ignoring Lars as he tensed above her, LizAlec reached up with one hand and found his face, fingers pushing under the badly cut shock of hair to touch his temple.

Lars stopped his struggle, briefly puzzled by her touch. And then fire exploded like lightning inside his head, knocking him from bright light into deepest empty darkness.

LizAlec smiled.

Chapter 12

Wide-eyed & Legless

'Here, put it on.'

The police sergeant gave Fixx back his left arm, which puzzled Fixx since it wasn't two hours since the squat Gascon had been encased in a slop-down, happily beating him to pulp with a short length of rubber hose. Only this time the sergeant was wearing his best uniform, his blue jacket pulled tight over his jutting belly.

'Put it on, you fuckwit.' The sergeant raised his hand and Fixx ducked. Over the past two weeks those five minutes of explosive mid-morning violence had become something of a ritual.

Five minutes wasn't prescribed in any training manual, it was how long it took the man to get out of breath. Ten years ago the Gascon had been able to manage fifteen minutes, and ten years before that he'd been able to keep it going for what seemed like forever.

The fat man sighed and pulled in his gut. Even he'd heard of Freud.

The *Préfecture Imperiale* had more sophisticated pleasures at its disposal, of course, from the effective but tek-crude delights of a Matsui taser to the full cerebral meltdown of a Bayer-Rochelle parasite *SQUID. SQUIDS* were meant for medical use only, but it was obvious even to an illiterate that any machine capable of reading sensations could be reverse-engineered to provide them as well. And Fixx was many things, from a crystal-head to eight years older than he admitted, but tek-illiterate wasn't one of them.

Luckily, the sergeant was the old-fashioned type. Neanderthal.

'Put your fucking arm on.' The man's voice was raw with a breakfast of Gauloises and cheap alcohol. Fixx didn't blame him. The only way he could have hacked the sergeant's job would have been to blunt his edges too.

Sighing heavily, Fixx balanced himself on the hard plastic bed and slotted the stump of his left arm into a shining black prosthetic. The stump had been bleeding ever since the sergeant first ripped Fixx's arm off and putting it back stung badly as prosthetic meshed with bloody flesh.

No, that wasn't the right description. Fixx shook his head, short bleached dreadlocks flicking from side to side like little snakes. Get the words right. Slotting on his arm didn't sting, it hurt like fuck. And it would go on hurting until flesh healed and the nerves in his stump grew back through the chip gate at the hard/wet interface.

There was a gizmo built into his left arm that was meant to deaden any pain, but it didn't work, or if it did and this was it working, then Fixx didn't want to be around when the gizmo hung, as it undoubtedly would. All his limbs had a nasty habit of going belly-up.

Outside might be up two floors and along a corridor, but Fixx still knew it was pouring out there. Thunder crashed off the corridor walls, loud enough to drown out the screams of those in interrogation. Questioning took place each morning from 11:00 to 11:30, and in that half-hour the whole prefecture was a riot of animal howls. By noon the howls were reduced to whimpers that faded to silence. And so it would remain, until 14:00 when it started up again and the sequence was repeated.

'What about my legs?' Fixx demanded.

'What about them?' Pig-like eyes raking contemptuously down Fixx's naked body, stopping at the oozing pink stumps that passed for his thighs. They'd been bleeding too, but then the prosthetics Fixx had chosen back when he was rich weren't meant to be removed. They were the permanent kind, wired into his peripheral nervous system using motor nerves grown straight to Japanese silicon. The best that Chiba could supply.

Not that it was difficult to work out why the pig-eyed bronze had decided to ignore the manufacturer's instructions. Fixx was a renegade Jihad hacker, so violent even the Imans wouldn't have anything to do with him. At least, he was according to the slab they'd thrust in his face, shortly after hot-keying his studio door straight out of its frame and just before some black-booted gendarme kicked him into unconsciousness.

Which was kind of weird, because Fixx had always been too busy f'f'fixxing *hoojChoons* to give squit for politics – moral, sexual or racial. Anyway, he'd hardly been inside long enough to soften up some petty data thief, never mind the hardened Jihad fanatic he apparently was. But then, Fixx knew he was really in there for shitting on someone else's doorstep. If that's what you could call hanging out at the Crash&Burn with the jailbait daughter of some brain-dead policewoman . . .

'Do I get my fucking legs back or not?' Fixx demanded, and was surprised to see the squat man hesitate. The sergeant was scared! Not of him, that was obvious, which meant it had to be his visitor. Fixx began to look interested.

'Someone important?' Despite four years in Paris, the French that Fixx spoke was tourist-crude. LizAlec reckoned the English were incapable of speaking French properly and no matter how many times Fixx explained about being Irish, he was still forced to agree. English, Irish, American – none of them could speak real French, never mind hack a proper fifth *arrondissement* Parisian accent.

'Your boss?' The sergeant said nothing and Fixx grinned. It was the wrong move – or it would have been at any other time. Bulges of neck muscles and knots of vein told Fixx the sergeant wanted to whip out the *exerciser*, but something made the man's hand stop just before it reached his belt.

Blind fear, for real . . . Fixx was impressed. He could imagine few things that could stop the Gascon when he was at play in his own cells: whatever was going down was heavy. And better than that, whoever was about to visit, they obviously had the sergeant by the balls.

'Give me my legs,' suggested Fixx. 'You don't want to get it wrong . . .'

The sergeant actually thought about it, his pug face tipped to one side. And he shook his head, flicked a lighter and went straight ahead, pulling carcinogens into his lungs from an untipped Gauloise.

'Nah,' he said dismissively. 'It only mentions your arm.' Checking a standard-issue Matsui pager inset in his wrist to make double sure he'd got that right, the sergeant nodded to himself and wandered away to check his appearance in a mirror. The uniform was fine but nothing short of a complete remake could have helped his face. Not that Fixx was going to mention it.

Fixx hadn't had that many new faces – in fact, Fixx was the same sex and colour as when he started out, which made him something of a rarity, at least it did in the music business. Though he sure as hell needed a new face now. That was, if he ever got out. Fixx sighed and shuffled on the plastic bed. If he could, he'd have hidden the stumps of his legs, but the cell had no blankets and he couldn't remember when he'd last seen his clothes . . . Fuck it, Fixx smiled grimly. So he was going to have to stand on his dignity: so be it, because it was all he *did* have to stand on.

Heels clicked on the floor outside and someone *knocked*, making the fat Gascon jump. God, Fixx thought to himself as the door swung back, the Neanderthal really was frightened. A tall major with high cheeks, thin lips and sunken eyes entered the room, hook nose wrinkling at the stench of tobacco and the acrid stink that rose from the floor where Fixx had pissed himself earlier after a particularly nasty blow to the kidneys. But, inquisitor's face or not, it wasn't the major who was important. It was the thin, bird-like woman behind him who mattered.

Not that Fixx noticed the woman, not at first. He was too busy eyeing up the Ted Brewer violin clutched in the major's hands. It was an original Gothic, body cut down to a swirl of clear acrylic, Ashworth pickup, Pirastro strings. There were fifteen working models left in the world, and that was his.

Or had been until the préfecture blew out his door.

After seeing what the police had done to his antique 303, the Thereman and his mixing decks, Fixx hadn't dared hope the Ted Brewer was still unbroken. But it was and poking out of the major's pocket was a matching acrylic bow, strung with purple horsehair. The hair was snapped but that didn't matter, the bow itself looked fine.

Lady Clare Fabio walked abruptly into the room, pushing past the major who stammered his apologies for not getting out of her way. Her greying crop was immaculate, her dark Dior lipstick perfectly applied. The only thing that looked out of place were the deep shadows round her eyes, shadows so dark that not even quality make-up could hide them.

No one need have greying hair, enhancers could reverse that as easily as a laser peel could have taken the fine lines from around her blue eyes. Any half-decent hairdresser could have done both.

'My Lady, let me get the man moved. The smell . . .'

Lady Clare shook her head. 'I've smelt worse,' she said abruptly, 'much worse.' She didn't bother to mention it had been many, many years before. Her eyes took in the cell, the basic plastic bed, the lack of sheets and sharp edges, the ceiling's permanent light strip turned up to daylight and inset behind shatter-proof polymer. The place hadn't improved since her time as a junior prosecutor.

Everything was as it always was, including a man sitting broken-nosed and naked on the bed. Briefly Lady Clare wondered on whose orders the gendarmes had stripped him and then remembered they were hers. The man looked different to his official tri-Ds, but then, he would without his legs. His natural height had been 1.78 metres but after his accident in Moscow he'd sued himself and used the insurance to acquire the most expensive prosthetics that money could buy. Back on stage in his new legs, the man now stood 1.88 metres tall – so far as Lady Clare was concerned, that said it all.

As did the fact he could have used limb grafts or, if he was squeamish about accepting cadaver tissue, he could have had limbs clone-grown in less than five months. As it was, it took him that long to get used to his new heavy metal prosthetics. Lady Clare knew, she'd had it checked.

There was little she didn't know about this man's history. And most of it she would have been glad to forget, especially the bits after LizAlec came into the equation. It had been going on for over a year and she hadn't known. Minister for Internal Security, the ultimate head of S3 and she didn't even have a clue until just before Christmas . . . When Lady Clare got the first hint of what was going on, she'd tagged Fixx in her head as a social retard but nothing more, not dangerous to her or LizAlec. Except that wasn't how LizAlec's diary read. It seemed this was the creep LizAlec had chosen as her first lover . . . The kind of shit who could take a fourteen-year-old innocent to his bed without even asking her name.

Not that Lady Clare needed to have that last fact checked; LizAlec had thrown it in her face, on the drive out to the shuttle port at Charles de Gaulle.

Pulling off her black ultrasuede gloves, Lady Clare stalked over to Fixx's narrow bed and stood in front of him, legs apart. Three vicious slaps slammed into his face. *Back, forward, back.* The last blow toppled him sideways into a heap on the bed. Even the sergeant looked shocked.

'Feeling better?' Fixx asked, pushing himself upright. There was blood running from a split in his bottom lip.

Lady Clare shook her head and reached for his right arm, the only limb that wasn't a prosthetic. She wanted to snap it at the elbow and grind the jagged edges against each other but she didn't. Instead Lady Clare made herself step back a pace and let her arms rest at her sides. The man had no idea how difficult that was for her to do.

'Finished?' Fixx asked and shot Lady Clare his most irritating smile. It wasn't the brightest thing he'd ever done. Turning her back on Fixx, Lady Clare reached for a Korean-made ceramic-and-copper taser velcroed to the sergeant's belt. It was Fixx's bad luck that the manufacturers in Seoul had designed it without including steel.

She saw sudden worry fire up in his silver eyes and it was her turn to smile. Where to start depended on what it was you wanted from the victim. Abject terror was easy: from the relative subtlety of the underside of the tongue to the obviousness of exposed testicles, it took a matter of seconds only. There were other places . . . just inside the anus was always effective for humiliation. Eyeballs were good for instant panic. But that wasn't what she wanted.

'Gloves,' she told the major, who made to pass the woman her own discarded pair until he saw her frown. Hastily he reached for the sergeant's heavy pair of mitts and thrust his thin fingers into them, stretching the rubber.

'This isn't necessary,' said Fixx, eyes fixed to her hand. 'Whatever it is, I'll do it . . .'

The unique selling point about the new Korean tasers was that they were pressure-sensitive. The more Lady Clare pressed down on the button, the brighter the spark . . . 'Do what?' Lady Clare demanded. The taser felt light in her hand, pleasingly clinical in its white ceramic finish. She thumbed the button and watched jagged lightning dance from one electrode to the other.

'Do what?'

'Whatever you want,' Fixx said quickly. 'You're S3. First you hurt people, then you sympathize, then they do what you want. A kid I know told me . . .'

'Hold him.' Lady Clare demanded and the major grabbed Fixx by the shoulders.

'Face down . . .' Lady Clare ordered and waited while the major pushed the suddenly struggling Fixx flat on the bed.

Lower spine?

Neck?

Lady Clare ran the taser lightly down his spine, from neck to buttocks, increasing thumb pressure as she went. By the time she reached his lower spine, a gurgling Fixx was bucking under the hiss of sparks, muscles locked rigid with pain across his back. Flecks of froth dotted his lips.

This was the man . . . Lady Clare looked down, seeing the naked buttocks, the broad shoulders, the bloody stumps of his legs, though those wouldn't have been there. *This was the man who . . .*

Oh fuck it. She tossed the taser onto the bed beside Fixx and nodded to the major. On cue, the man stood back, his piano-players having left bruised circles across Fixx's shoulders

'You can go,' Lady Clare told the major and waited for him to tell her it was against regulations. But all the man did was toss rubber gloves onto the bed, nod for the fat sergeant to leave first and click the door quietly behind him. If he had any sense he'd go straight up the concrete stairs and out onto the rain-slicked cobbles of the Ile de la Cité, and then keep going, right to the outskirts where he could buy a new identity and lose himself in the teeming mass that passed for humanity. Then all he had to do was stand and *Seig heil* the Black Hundreds as they came marching in.

But he wouldn't. Loyalty might be bred into the bone, but the *procuraté* didn't choose its bulls for intelligence or intuition. The major would go and read something obscure by Barthes at his club, while the sergeant would camp out upstairs in the NCOs' Mess and drink bad Megrib coffee laced with cheap Normandy *marc* while flicking though frames of holoporn. Always assuming the system wasn't down again.

Lady Clare might not know their names, but she knew how her men thought, even the insignificant ones. When she'd finished, the sergeant would stagger back down and expect to scrape Fixx off the tiled floor with a shovel, because shit shovelling was what the police did these days.

But instead of reaching for the taser to start it all over again, Lady Clare pulled a military hypodermic from her pocket and blasted 50ml of endorphin through the skin of Fixx's neck. Switching the cartridge, she followed the endorphin with 100ml of seratonin and then 200mg of coproximol.

Pain slid away and Fixx suddenly felt both calm and slightly elated, which even he realized was pretty weird, given the discarded taser on the bed and the streaks of vomit drying on his chin. All the same, he didn't let logic get in the way of his relief.

Indecent acts . . . It was odd, thought Lady Clare while looking at Fixx, it was odd the way sometimes the weapon you really needed was the one closest at hand. There were two cases against Fixx that involved indecent acts and only one of them concerned LizAlec. The other one, the earlier one, the really obscene one, involved illegal activity with a computer on the Moon.

'My daughter,' Lady Clare said but got no further.

Fixx nodded. The bitch was who he thought she was. Just a bit further up the greasy pole than LizAlec had led him to believe. 'LizAlec,' he said, 'what about her?'

'Kidnapped,' said Lady Clare, obscurely proud that not a single tremor betrayed the blackness inside her. She might feel old as sin but she wasn't going to demean herself in front of Fixx, at least not more than she already had.

'Where?'

'The Arrivals Hall at Planetside . . .'

'You sent her?' Taser or not, Fixx didn't bother to keep the contempt out of his voice. 'How could you be that fucking stupid?' Shaking his head, Fixx caught sight of the abandoned Ted Brewer violin, and he nodded towards it with his chin. 'And now that's meant to make me want to go after her?'

She could tell him she'd sent LizAlec back to St Lucius for her own safety, because she'd know the Reich would move on Paris as soon as the virus struck, but Lady Clare didn't bother, she didn't believe it herself. Instead Lady Clare wondered if Fixx knew he was seconds away from writing his own suicide note and decided he just didn't care. Either the man was tired of life or she'd pumped in too much coproximol.

'That's what you want, right? You want my help?'

Lady Clare nodded.

Fixx thought about it. In one way she'd come to the right person, and not just because he had a bit of a thing going with LizAlec. Fixx knew all about Planetside. It was where he'd got thrown out of five years before, after he got emotionally too close to a full-Turing AI. Hell, he still owned an apartment there. In Chrysler. Seven vast rooms of art deco steel grown from a cross between Corbusier Lite and Mannerheim. He just couldn't afford to live in them, even if he'd been allowed.

'Have the kidnappers made contact?' Fixx asked her at last.

'No.' Lady Clare lied without thinking about it. Fixx knew nothing of foreign policy and, for all she knew, probably cared even less. Her world wasn't his, thank God. Besides, the situation was difficult enough without letting two separate parts of her life collide.

'But you're worried?'

Lady Clare thought about nodding, then rejected the idea — too many tears were backed up in her eyes for them not to spill down her cheeks if she did.

'For what it's worth, it wasn't me.' Fixx said, but she knew that already

Lady Clare had a question to ask him. No, she had dozens, each darker than the one before. Starting with, *Why my daughter?* What had he got out of corrupting some defenceless kid? She wasn't beautiful or even that rich, just intelligent and too strong-willed for her own good. *Why? Why? Why?* But instead, Lady Clare decided to ask just one question, the question that mattered. The only problem was that Lady Clare didn't know which one it was, never mind how to ask it.

She didn't need to.

'I loved her,' Fixx said baldly and dared her to deny it, to disagree. For a second, sitting there on the stumps of his legs, the steam-driven Samurai, the man who was once Sony's most famous reMixer, looked almost sad. 'Not at first,' he said 'I didn't really know her at first. She was just someone who hung about Schrödinger's Kaff. You know, one of the street kids . . .'

Clare didn't know. She didn't know at all.

'Lady Elizabeth a street kid?'

Lady Clare was so busy being shocked she nearly missed the disbelief that flicked across Fixx's battered face.

LizAlec? *Lady Elizabeth . . . ?*

James Begley, mostly known as Fixx Valmont, stared at Lady Clare Fabio, who stared straight back. He really hadn't known who LizAlec was, Lady Clare realized. Which meant LizAlec hadn't told him. And that said more about LizAlec than it could ever say about Fixx.

Lady Clare sighed. 'You used to meet her at Schrödinger's Kaff?' Stupid question, hadn't he just said he did . . .

Fixx nodded, thinking of their two-up battles against the Dragon and the incongruous glass tent he'd coded her for *Fistful*, patching it onto scrub in the Sierra Madre. Her home, LizAlec had called it, the one she didn't have. Broken home, single-parent syndrome, a mother who was always out at work, he could remember almost everything she told him: if that wasn't love, what was?

'St Lucius,' he said at last. 'She's not there on a scholarship, right?'

Lady Clare thought about the obscenely high fees and tried not to feel hurt. 'No,' she said, 'she's not.'

Fixx was going to tell Lady Clare how LizAlec had followed him from Schrödinger's Kaff to the Crash&Burn one night, hung at a nearby table until he'd had to take notice, but now didn't seem the right moment.

'Right,' said Fixx. 'So where do I come into this?'

'I want LizAlec back. And you get to take this with you, if you still want it.' She held up his Ted Brewer violin.

Of course he did: it was his, for a start. Of course, if the electricity supply died for good then the violin was useless, but Fixx didn't reckon that would happen, not gone forever.

'Any idea where she is?' Fixx kept his voice so neutral he might have been discussing the weather, except no one was neutral where that was concerned, not with storms ripping apart buildings from Salzburg to the Atlantic coast.

'Darkside, maybe,' said Lady Clare. 'Or one of the burbs. If it was LunaWorld or Planetside, I'd have noticed.'

Fixx didn't actually ask his question but the woman answered it anyway. 'Reciprocal security treaty. Besides, she was tagged,' said Lady Clare, her voice defensive.

'But the trace was removed,' Fixx finished for her, running what data he had through his mind and adding in what his old minder Albrecht would have done. 'Probably got a cortex bomb too by now, if they bothered to keep her alive.'

Lady Clare looked at him and then shook her head. 'LizAlec is alive.'

'Yeah?' Fixx had no doubt she meant it, he just wasn't so sure she was right. Either that, or there was a lot she wasn't telling him. 'How do you know?'

'I just do,' said Lady Clare. 'Put it down to a mother's intuition.'

If she could call herself a mother, which was doubtful. But then Fixx still called himself a musician and five years had gone walkabout since he'd fixxed anything worth releasing, and even that had just been a tarted-up remix of *KrystalKrash*, featuring clips by Coppola and classic samples from Roni Size and Wagner.

Even so, the man was on the other edge of genius. An IQ of over

160 matched to the EQ of an amoral infant, Lady Clare knew that, or she did now. According to Fixx, what drove humanity wasn't the usual troika of lust, greed and fear, it was vacuum. Whether people knew it or not, everything they did was about hiding from the void.

It wasn't hipness that made artists gut the past for designer role models: fashion was really just another need to feed. All anyone had left to ransack for inspiration was history, and there was still plenty of that to go round.

Fixx didn't deny that it was cheap, cut-price nihilism or that outside half a dozen minor academics he was probably one of the few people alive who could tell you who Sartre, de Beauvoir and Camus had been. Certainly the only person who might care.

All the same, Lady Clare wasn't sure what to make of a man who'd had one leg blown off in an *organitskaya* car bomb explosion and then promptly had the other one surgically removed to ensure symmetry . . .

Chapter 13

CasaNegro

The bar sucked her in through its wide adobe door, the way CasaNegro always vacuumed up those with no place to go. Inside Jude's place, the music was stripHop/cheezy-listening, stuff LizAlec hadn't heard in years. Original edits, too, but the tunes went with the heat, the slight edge of sweat and the mix of unshaven locals and bare-armed, stained-top backpackers.

Over the bar itself was a neon sign advertising Electric Soup. It flashed two pictures, one of a bikini-clad cowgirl, the other of the same girl with her clothes off. LizAlec wasn't to know, but as an original and still-functioning bit of Dallas kitsch it was one of Fracture's best-known sights. LizAlec wasn't sure what the girl advertised but she ordered a couple anyway, stuffing ice-cold tubes into the side pocket of Laughing Boy's oversized jumpsuit. The problems only started when LizAlec offered the woman behind the bar her gold HKS card in payment.

It would be a lie to say *everyone froze*, LizAlec decided. But shoulders definitely stiffened all the way along the scuffed and cracked oak plank that made do as a bartop. Chinoed men who'd clocked her entrance began to watch more openly and one or two were actually grinning. Still, not an enhanced canine in sight, LizAlec realized with relief. Not a vampire, not a wolfBoy or sandrat. Just straight human, even if most of them did look like spares from *Fistful*, that opening bit where you got offed by a rug-wearing psycho if you insulted his mule.

As for the blonde woman behind the bar, she looked tougher

than most of the men. She was certainly taller. '¿*Tú tienes alguna cósa persona que puedes usar?*'

LizAlec looked blank.

'Nihon?'

The girl shook her head. St Lucius didn't teach Japanese, they taught Latin instead. She'd always thought it was a bloody stupid decision.

'Inglés?'

'Yes,' said LizAlec, smiling with relief. She could do English.

'Honey, you got anything anyone can actually use?' The woman was thirty going on three hundred and then some. Her blue eyes were washed out with enough background to plot-line a thousand newsfeed *novelas*.

'You don't take cards?' LizAlec looked startled. The holos promised HKS was universal, one of the ads even had a grizzled miner on Io or somewhere happily swiping an HKS gold through his belt in return for an improbably large opal. 'What do you use?'

'What you got?' A young boy in combats and a goth T-shirt crowded in at her shoulder. He looked about fourteen and had the most stupid haircut she'd ever seen. Fuck it, thought LizAlec. She needed some smart-arse kid like she needed killer PMS. Actually she needed gut-rot *more* than she needed the kid.

'*Yáyase,*' snapped the woman and the boy stepped back. But he didn't go away, and it didn't look like he intended to.

LizAlec glanced over to a table near the door hoping for back-up, only to find Lars wasn't there. Typical. Maybe she should have left the freak out at the base. But she couldn't. Not after what she'd seen in his head. All those empty tunnels, all that blood. No wonder he was . . .

Actually, LizAlec didn't know what he was, she was still trying to work it out. As for exactly what Lars lacked, she'd given up on that one after she'd ticked off two lungs, a normal human set of teeth and a spiralling list of other things starting with a basic knowledge of what it was to be normal.

At least, what LizAlec considered normal.

And anyway, leaving him wasn't an option. He had Lazlo's black ring, the one that kept her face from exploding. She couldn't wear the bloody thing herself, could she? Not without closing the circuit. Which meant keeping Lars close by her for company.

That hadn't been too difficult to date, because he'd been safely punch-drunk when she'd bundled him into the back of the buggy and still groggy when she'd dragged him after her into the bar. Maybe that was the problem, LizAlec decided. Dragging a staggering freak behind her was bound to draw attention.

'I'll take the bracelet,' the woman said, nodding to the silver band wound tight round LizAlec's wrist. 'And I'll even give you some change.' Without waiting for LizAlec's reply, the woman hit a key and pulled a couple of dead presidents from an old bell, lever and clockwork till. Rococo scrolls of gold fluttered up the side and 'Industrial Business Machines' was written in script over every flat surface. It looked original.

LizAlec shook her head. 'The bracelet won't come off, I've tried.' And that was true. LizAlec wasn't sure exactly when the bracelet had woken up, but in the last hour it had wound itself so tight onto her arm that her flesh had puffed up around it.

'No problems.' The kid in the combats dipped his hand into a knee pocket and came up with a vicious-looking pair of pliers. 'I don't think we'll have any trouble.'

The woman frowned, the shake of her head so slight that at first the boy didn't notice it – until he saw her stare over his shoulder and turned to find Lars standing behind him, a clutter of talismans round his thick neck, arms slung loosely at his side, mouth half open. The sandrat's balloon suit was open to the navel, the flesh below it maggot-white and hairless.

'How you do that?' He was talking to LizAlec, the boy and

the woman so far out of his interest they might as well not have existed. 'How?'

He meant how did she knock him out, she knew that. LizAlec shrugged. 'I don't know.'

'You must.'

She didn't. Ripping out someone's memories wasn't one of her regular party tricks. But then, no one had ever tried to rape her before, whatever Lady Clare might think. LizAlec watched the sandrat stare into her eyes and then saw him shiver. 'Drink,' he demanded, noticing where he was for the first time.

The woman nodded towards LizAlec. 'She already got *dos. Nada* money. Only an HKS. *Sweedak*?' She raised her eyes, inviting Lars to admit how dumb that was.

'Here.' Lars ripped a silicon square from the clutter of talismans around his neck and dumped it on the wooden bar. Reaching under the bar for a reader, the woman striped Lars's stolen chip through the slot and took the price of two tubes. It put the cashchip into negative, but not enough to argue about, at least not with a sandrat. With a sigh, the woman tossed the empty cashchip into a bucket under the bar.

LizAlec looked on, baffled. Not understanding why Lars's cashchip was good while her own swipe card had been rejected. But even if he understood her unspoken question, Lars didn't have words to explain that empty&fills were good because they were finite, while a card that drew a credit stream through a proper orbiting bank was no use to anyone operating on the edges of legal finance.

'Need to sit,' said Lars and pushed past the boy without looking at him. The sandrat stopped at an occupied table right next to an over-chromed Cadillac jukebox and stared pointedly at two backpackers sitting in front of almost empty bottles of Kirin. When the grocks didn't take his point, Lars up-ended their metal table with a crash, shattering glass.

Behind the bar, Jude sighed . . . It was going to be a long day. Reaching for her stun gun, the woman began to lift the flap.

But her presence wasn't needed. Lars was already helping the tourists through the door and out into noonday heat hot enough to disgrace a hyperactive sauna, if only there'd been an inkling of humidity to go with it. The backpackers left without protest.

Jude figured it was the open lock-knife that helped the sandrat clinch his argument: though it might have been his bared teeth or the blood clotted down his chin that convinced them to try another bar.

Lars glared at LizAlec. 'Drink,' he demanded, pulling the table upright.

Yeah, right. LizAlec passed him the tubes, watching as the sandrat ring-pulled both, ice crystallizing like frost down their silver sides. He killed one with a single gulp, then swallowed half the second tube before passing it back to the girl.

'Thanks,' LizAlec said sweetly, but it was sarcasm wasted.

LizAlec started to wipe the edge on Laughing Boy's battle-dress and then gave up. The cloth was probably as germ-infested as the can. Besides, she'd had shots for every virus and infection known on Luna. The school had insisted. It was just a pisser she hadn't taken that menstruation shot when it was offered: her gut was cramping so fast she didn't even want to think about it.

The electric soup was cold as glacier meltwater, and thick like syrup. Sweet, too, but with a chemical aftertaste that should have warned her. LizAlec was taking a second gulp when the effects of her first swallow cut in, flicking the light level up a couple of clicks and putting glass-hard edges to the blades of the ceiling fan rotating slowly overhead.

Lars grinned as he took the tube from LizAlec's unprotesting fingers and tipped the dregs down his own throat. *Wizz, pop and bang* – crystalMeth, seratonin and amyl nitrate. She didn't yet know the effects, but she would.

LizAlec gasped, watching the room flick in and out of focus before it settled back to a hard-edged glow. A couple more of those and she'd either stop fretting altogether or go out and kill someone.

'Need power.' Lars told her. 'For Ben . . .' The sandrat stood up, brushed matted brown hair out of his eyes and shambled for the door, metal lung banging noisily against his hip. Out of his tunnels, the sandrat was less fluid, less graceful than usual. As if he was only used to moving up surfaces rather than across them.

Lars was gone longer than she expected. And when he reappeared in the doorway his face was white under the dirt and dried blood, his brown eyes suddenly panicked.

'Ben . . .' He demanded loudly, then stopped. 'Ben . . . ?'

Not callous but genuinely puzzled, LizAlec started to shrug and then stopped herself, filtering his thoughts through her own memory to come up with a Matsui ice bucket. That was Ben. Or rather, what was in there was Ben. Except she'd never seen the bucket and she certainly hadn't brought it with her. She was still wondering how to tell Lars when the need passed. Even across the crowded bar, he could see the answer scripted in her face.

The sandrat howled. It was a genuine, animal howl that filled the whole of CasaNegro, bringing conversation to a halt. This time everything did stop. Except for the Cadillac jukebox that kept spitting out its sour/sweet words of loss and lament.

Strat was a walled village, a jumble of adobe houses balanced on the lower slopes of a vast gap-toothed puig. Three roads led in, each guarded by scrawny pi dogs. Some visitors the packs let through, others were turned away with low growls and bared teeth. No one knew the logic of their choice, the augmentation was coded too far back for anyone to remember. There were three bars and only two served outsiders: CasaNegro was the larger, less intimidating of those, and howling sandrats were not on the menu.

Too tatty to be right on the tourist trail, a little too close to the crater's entrance to be genuinely Sierra Mal, the CasaNegro's jukebox was the stuff of skewed memory, full of white clouds, galloping horses and sad sunsets. Ersatz homesickness for people who'd long since stopped calling Mexico, Central America and the southern US their home.

The UN immigration laws of forty years ago had seen to that, stripping citizenship from any person more than two generations removed from a valid Earth passport. LizAlec knew about it vaguely, but only as history.

'Kid,' Jude said, her hand gripping LizAlec's thin wrist. 'You'd better get him out of here. My customers don't like this.'

LizAlec didn't blame them. Lars had his hands round a doorpost and was trying to shake it loose, anguished grunts coming from low in his throat. The post was real enough but its purpose was fake. The door to CasaNegro was virus-grown, currently healthy: it didn't need props. But that still didn't mean Jude's regulars wanted the place destroyed.

'He's nothing to do with me,' LizAlec said.

Jude's eyes narrowed, though the smile stayed fixed to her tired face. 'You dragged him in, you drag him out again . . .'

LizAlec nodded. When it came down to it she didn't have any option. It wasn't as if she could just dump him and run, not while he wore that bloody ring. All the same, she couldn't stay in Strat or Fracture either, not long term. Come to that, she probably shouldn't even remain on the Moon.

The tall Frenchman wasn't going to know it was Lars who'd trashed Mickey and Laughing Boy. The man would send someone after her, no doubt about it.

'Can you use this?' LizAlec asked, pulling the Beretta that Laughing Boy had been carrying out of her pocket and sliding it across the table towards Jude. The woman covered it quickly with her hands, then glanced round the room. Everyone was still looking at Lars shaking and moaning over by the door.

'I thought you didn't have anything to trade,' Jude said, staring hard at LizAlec. In answer, the girl pushed her hands into the side pocket of Laughing Boy's balloon suit and pulled out a pack of shells, a second clip and the Zeiss nightspex he'd been wearing on his way down the corridor.

'That's the lot,' said LizAlec. 'They're yours if you can get me to Earth . . .'

'Just Earth?' Jude's voice was amused, the problem of Lars temporarily forgotten.

'Europe, Paris . . .'

'Honey,' the woman's expression was sympathetic. 'Don't you watch the newsfeeds? There *ain't* no shuttles to Europe. America maybe, you got the spread. But Europe – it's closed.' She said it like that was obvious, which it was when LizAlec thought about it. Five days from the New Year was what the Met office had reckoned it would take for the virus to sweep Western Europe and hit the Atlantic, and LizAlec knew her mother considered that optimistic. No one knew how long it would take to cross the water.

'I *have* to get away,' LizAlec insisted. It came out sounding more desperate than she intended, but then Jude didn't need words to work that out. Sitting on the wrong side of a bar gave you more than enough experience matching thoughts to expressions.

'Problems?' Jude asked.

LizAlec nodded.

'Men problems?'

LizAlec nodded again, thinking of the man in the Versace suit. 'Yeah, she said, 'men problems, mother problems and PMS bad enough to take your head off.'

'Okay, no promises.' The woman turned her head, shouting over her shoulder at the boy in the combats, 'Hey, Leon!' The boy wandered over, just slowly enough to irritate Jude who was scowling by the time he finally reached their table. The boy smiled back, blandly, his expression hovering on the edge of bored. But when he looked at LizAlec his brown eyes told another story.

Chapter 14

Killers under the Skin

Count Lazlo was upset, seriously cross – mostly with himself for underestimating Lady Clare. It hadn't occurred to him that she wouldn't break immediately. That she might actually be prepared to ditch her little bitch of a daughter.

And now the girl had gone and he had to clean up after her. Lazlo had been waiting all morning for the rain to stop and it wasn't going to happen: he was going to get wet on his way to the Tuileries. But there was something he needed to do first. Lazlo sighed, reached for a bottle of Evian and flipped open his Tosh. One minute thirty was what it took him to authorize the paperwork, falsify a few dates and leave a backdated trail of requisitions that hadn't been there before.

Lady Clare had just ordered the release of two clone-assassins from the bioWarfare complex at Marne, always assuming they still had power enough to work the finishing vats. The request went out under her official PGPz crypt key and the cost was billed direct to her office. Lazlo was pleased about that last touch. He wasn't stupid, he knew cost centres were an irrelevance with the Empire collapsing around him, but habit was something of which Lazlo approved and correct allocation of costs was the benchmark of a good executive.

The chance of someone actually back-checking those files was minimal. Paris would fall within a week, most likely days – certainly by the end of January. His beloved boss, her beloved Prince Imperial, both would be dead or on the run along with all their mindless, fawning officials. That was, if they didn't come round first.

Lazlo's original instinct had been to torture LizAlec on camera, not to death but enough to get Lady Clare's attention. And that was what he should have done. But by the time he'd sent someone local to do the job, the brat was gone and his goons were dead. It wasn't their demise that worried him – they were dead men walking, anyway – it was the timing. And quite how the little bitch had managed to bite out the throat of a man twice her size Lazlo didn't know, but it seemed she had. Maybe shit like that was what he should have expected from the daughter of Razz . . .

Now he was faced with sending in the cleaners, getting someone to run her down and sweep up the mess. That was where the clones came in. Both were to be *aptered* for tracking and close combat using MS/Skillsoft, but it was shallow programming only. Though not as shallow as their given identities. They had names, S3 diplomatic passports and were chipped for loyalty, that was enough. It would have to be. His big problem was time. Getting them to the Moon was going to take five days: three to reach Mexico by zeppelin, half a day for a coyote to run them across the US border and half a day to grab an illegal launch from the Free Texas Airforce. Which left one for the flight.

Count Lazlo hoped it was going to work. It bloody well should, given what the travel arrangements were costing him. On his way out of his office, Lazlo wondered if he should have stipulated that the clones should only capture LizAlec, then dismissed the idea. Killing her would simplify matters. And since Lady Clare didn't know LizAlec had escaped it shouldn't make the blindest bit of difference when Lazlo came to put the pressure on. At least, the Count hoped not.

Chapter 15

Last Supper at the Hôtel Sabatini

'Shiori?' Fixx demanded, picking a garlic-laden snail out of its shell with a Napoleon III snail fork, its two elongated prongs spearing into the mollusc's rubbery flesh.

Just thinking about chewing the thing made his jaw ache. Mind you, that wasn't surprising, given the purple bruise spread birthmark-like along one side of his face. Rubber hoses might not break major bones, but they ruptured flesh and split skin effortlessly. It was a pity that mending the damage wasn't as easy.

Three large medipedes stapled together the gash over his right eye, Lady Clare having jammed the 'pedes' jaws either side of the cut, breaking off each body in turn to let the insect's death-agony snap shut its jaws. Neat, efficient and cheap – all you could ask from combat surgery. She'd learnt the knack from the Auditor-General of the Church of Christ Geneticist, except he'd been only a simple priest back then.

It wasn't pretension or love for French tradition that made Clare serve snails. It was necessity. If she hadn't needed the medipedes for Fixx's face she'd probably have tried cooking them too. There was nothing in the city to eat, except a dwindling flock of pigeons and the odd especially cunning cat; even the rats were mostly gone. Lady Clare had found the snails in her small kitchen garden. While Fixx had found a tabby kitten on his way through the darkened courtyard, he just refused to hand it over for the pot.

'Shiori?' Fixx repeated, chewing heavily.

'Her street name,' Lady Clare explained, cutting herself the thinnest sliver of Mahon. The Spanish cheese was tallow-like with age and oxide-green around the rind but Lady Clare didn't mind: being anorexic didn't seem so strange when everyone else was starving too.

'She'll be waiting for me?' Fixx said, for about the fifth time.

Lady Clare sighed. 'She arrives Planetside ten hours before you do. She'll find you.'

'How do I recognize her?' Fixx demanded.

Clare looked at him in amazement. 'You won't need to,' she said heavily. 'Chances are she'll recognize you.' Lady Clare looked pointedly at his black arm. She didn't bother to mention the little dreadlocks, his legs or the unusual silver sheen to his eyes.

Fixx tugged the top off a bottle of Tuborg, crushing the cap between metal fingers. He downed the stubby in one gulp and added it to the miniature Carnac growing in front of him; a few more bottles and he'd be able to start on Stonehenge. The snails weren't great, Lady Clare was prepared to admit that, but she still didn't think they needed that much beer to wash them down . . .

Shiori was pulled off Lady Clare's Tosh database, filed under *ferryman* and cross-linked to *Charon*. Twenty-eight years old, twenty-four accredited kills, born on the thirty-second floor of a slum project. It was all numbers where Shiori was concerned. Even Lady Clare hadn't been able to pin a single emotional outburst on her. But then, you didn't get to work for General Que and top the field as a reflex-boosted ballerina if you had flaws.

Combat clones were all right, but they couldn't really think. C/clones just responded to programming. And bioroids were fine if you thought the ability to consider two million options in a single moment and reject all but one was the key to a good street samurai — but Lady Clare *didn't* think so. She'd rather go for a blade who intuited the correct response first time up without having to first discard the others.

Wiping greasy fingers on a cotton napkin, Lady Clare pushed back her chair and walked over to the fireplace. It was stacked with unlit wood and torn-out pages. The pages were ripped from a first edition of Tipler's *Physics of Immortality*, the wood a child's smashed-up oak desk she'd found in the attic.

The fire lit easily, first time. Lady Clare dropped her match into the rising flames and reached for an Italian jug of beaten silver. With its ivory handle and Sabatini crest, it should have been serving chilled wine in Umbria, but it was what she used to make coffee these days, not that she had much real Colombian left. About half a packet if her memory was correct.

Lady Clare tipped three spoons' worth of precious coffee into the silver jug, added rain water and thrust it into the centre of the flames. The ivory handle had discoloured with heat the first time she tried making coffee this way, but Lady Clare was past caring. Ruined ivory handles didn't feature high on her list of disasters. The entrance hall stank of wet rot. The vaulted cellars were already full of Seine water, rain was eating away the Hotel Sabatini's foundations. Without even going up there, Lady Clare knew the floor of the attic was turning brown with damp. It wouldn't be long before water crumbled the ceilings in the rooms below and the upper floors began to fall in. And once that happened . . .

'Coffee?' Lady Clare suggested and held the silver jug towards Fixx who shook his head, reaching instead for another Tuborg. Crumbs of Mahon had spilled down his shirt and stuck under his fingernails. He'd eaten most of the cheese and fed what was left of the mould-rich rind to his bloody kitten. So Lady Clare finished off the coffee herself, without milk. Her shaking fingers wrapped tight round the handle of a Sèvres cup.

If it wasn't for waiting on the kidnappers, she'd have been long gone, vanished into any one of a dozen pre-created ready-to-wear identities. At least, that was what Lady Clare told herself. But even as she thought it, Lady Clare knew it wasn't really true.

As long as Paris was home to the Prince Imperial this was where she would stay.

Stupid.

She didn't doubt it.

Deluded.

She didn't doubt that either. But the old man wouldn't leave, and nobody could make him; and besides, it was probably too late anyway. He'd be lynched if he tried to leave Paris and, even if he wasn't, he'd never get past the army of the Reich camped around the city's edge.

It was said that outside the *périphérique* Ishies and journalists outnumbered Reich officers two to one. Clare doubted it, but she didn't know for sure. The Third Section's central database was down, its RISC chips no longer parallel to anything, four terrabytes of hard sphere spun to a standstill for lack of power.

No, the old bastard would stay in the ruins of his capital. And all Lady Clare had to do was persuade him to surrender gracefully and LizAlec would be safe . . . but that wasn't going to happen, part of Lady Clare had already accepted that fact. She wanted to be out doing something dynamic – rebuilding the army, ripping up cobbles to build barricades – instead she was sitting in a thunder storm, in the huge dining room of her own house on the Ile St-Louis drinking the last of her Colombian coffee, while the man she'd spent the last three weeks wanting to kill sat at the other end of an original Napoleon III table, getting drunk on looted lager. There was no logic to life and even less justice.

'Ready to go?' Lady Clare demanded – and thrust back her chair without waiting for Fixx to answer.

It didn't matter to Lady Clare that the World Aviation Authority had banned all take-offs from Europe: she still had a Boeing shuttle waiting for her out at Les Tourelles. The last shuttle in Paris, the last in France for all she knew or cared.

'How long's this going to take?' Fixx asked crossly. Thirty

seconds of standing in the rain while Lady Clare locked her front door and already he was soaked through, icy water sticking his shirt to his back.

'To get to Luna?'

Fixx shook his dreadlocked head. He was keeping himself upright by holding onto the huge metal ring that acted as the door's knocker.

'You mean the shuttle?'

Yeah, he did.

'A hour, maybe two . . . I've got horses, though,' Lady Clare added, feeling ridiculously proud of herself. She had, too, a pair of huge dray-horses stabled out of the rain, off the cobbled courtyard in what had once been servant's quarters. Last time she'd looked in on them they'd been shitting dung straight onto mouldering Persian carpet, but what could she do? Her housekeeper was long gone and she'd shocked her bodyguard by sending him back to his family at Les Halles.

Rank sentimentality, Lady Clare knew that. All the same, she couldn't wipe from her mind the fact that he had a daughter the same age as LizAlec. He'd wanted advice on what the kid should do if the Black Hundreds did take the city. Lady Clare hadn't been able to give him any. Suggesting his daughter kick out her own teeth, then grease herself front and back, didn't seem appropriate . . .

It took longer than Lady Clare had allowed to get Fixx onto the horse, mainly because he refused to let go of his kitten. But then, as if to make up for his incompetence, Fixx kept his seat well and it took them less than an hour to reach Les Tourelles, riding through the sodden streets. Hailstones hit the back of her neck like handfuls of cold gravel and beneath her black slacks the leather saddle was as damp and cold as bad sex. Though Lady Clare had to go back to Count Lazlo just to remember what bad sex was like – or any sex, come to that.

To make matters worse, the horses stank, steam rising in heavy clouds from their wet skin as their hooves slid on the wet cobbles, splashing heavily as the animals edged their way through vast puddles.

Slung across his back, Fixx carried a S3-issue Colt Hunter, ceramic-barrelled and stocked in grey zytel: another weapon virus-proof by accident rather than design. From habit, Lady Clare carried a steel-barrelled HiPower, except now she wore it openly in the belt of her black Dior coat. Her Colt looked sound enough, but that meant nothing. These days you didn't know a weapon was infected until it blew to pieces in your hands. Lady Clare had no idea if hers would fire and was hoping she wouldn't have to find out.

She didn't. They saw no one – and if anybody saw them they wisely kept to the shadows. Not even the riot cops were out, which worried Lady Clare, given that regular patrols by Lazlo's *Compagnie Impériale de Sécurité* was the last thing to be agreed at that morning's summit.

The shuttle was waiting and so were her men. A fresh-faced lieutenant she vaguely recognized saluted smartly and stepped forward, his arm under her elbow as he moved to help Lady Clare down from her horse.

'Stop fussing . . .' Her words were clipped, cross; snapped out before she had time to consider then. The boy stepped back, stony-faced, and Lady Clare cursed herself. He'd been standing in the rain for what . . . ? Five hours minimum. And not even because she'd told him to, but because she'd instructed her deputy who'd ordered someone else who'd finally dumped the job on the boy in front of her.

The city was rotting around him, self-confessed/self-elected fascists were camped less than two miles away, it was raining in a deluge fit to drown them, and he was upset because she'd slighted his offer of help. The woman sighed. Here she was having a hard time getting her own head round the concept of duty while this kid took his for granted.

'I'm sorry, that was unfair,' said Lady Clare and then stopped, uncertain where to go from there. As far as she could remember she'd never apologized to a junior in living memory. She glanced up at the night sky, then looked quickly away as drops of water hammered into her tired eyes. 'It's this rain,' she said. 'Is the shuttle ready?'

'Yes, Ma'am.' He smiled uncertainly, keeping his face neutral. She could imagine what the Guard had been saying about her. Roughly what she'd have said about anyone stupid enough to offer up such an idiot plan. Launching a shuttle at night, with a hostile army only three klicks distant was bad enough. But to launch an old-model Boeing X3 from a city riddled with Azerbaijani virus to a destination that wasn't accepting incoming flights, at least not from Europe . . . The days that Lady Clare thought she was losing it were beginning to outnumber those when she thought she wasn't.

The young lieutenant had no way of knowing just how much of the shuttle's make-up was steel, but Lady Clare knew, more or less exactly. Not that she was going to tell him, or Fixx. According to stats from the S3 mainframe before it took its first nosedive, over half of the Boeing's shell was pre-cast polycrete, pressure-treated with super-critical CO_2, twenty-six per cent was organic polymer or optic fibre and thirteen per cent of the bloody thing was titanium/steel alloy – and most of that was structural.

The night before last, sleepless and wired on too much coffee, Lady Clare had developed a theory that the rain was holding the virus at bay. The nanites were like tiny insects blasted out of the sky by heavy droplets, unable to get started before they got washed off. She didn't know if she really believed it, in fact she was pretty sure she didn't, but it was her justification for the risk Fixx was about to take.

'Is it the Prince Imperial?' The lieutenant was at her side, his dark eyes fixed on the hunched man who was swaying gently from side to side, his head hidden beneath a huge woollen hood. It appeared to the lieutenant that the man had a tiny bedraggled kitten folded into the flaps of his cloak.

Lady Clare shook her head. 'No.' She said it sadly. 'His Highness is refusing to leave . . . This is . . .' Lady Clare hesitated and then caught herself; why not start a useful rumour? God knew, she could do with all the help she could get. 'This is a secret and important mission. One that could save the city. Secret and important . . .'

So fucking secret, thought Lady Clare, that even she didn't really know why she was doing whatever it was she was doing. Still, that applied to most of her recent life if she thought about it: which she didn't intend to, unless she couldn't help herself.

Lady Clare snorted, not knowing which she thought was worse. To fool yourself, justify yourself or just not care. Well, at least she still cared, more or less.

'Okay, let's go,' she told the rider and watched the swathed figure clamber clumsily down from his dray-horse. Lady Clare waited while Fixx looked at the lieutenant, then at the stubby silhouette of the Boeing, void-black against the darkness of the night sky. It had basic stealth capabilities, not to mention a prophylactic sheath of ferrite supposedly capable of rendering it radar-invisible by absorbing radio waves. Though how much of that was left was anybody's guess.

'This is it?' Fixx looked amused, suddenly alive, sober even. His silver eyes swept over the rain-stained hull, the pools of flood water building up round the ramp. 'Very . . .' he searched for the word, black cloak flung back to reveal the Extopian eye-candy of his metal arm and legs. He was performing, Lady Clare realized, and he was doing it well.

The take-off crew watched surreptitiously, while the lieutenant was more open about it, but all of them were looking at Fixx and it was obvious to Lady Clare that, even drenched and cold, the Fixxer had come awake, revelling in their attention.

'Well?' She said at last, giving Fixx his feed line.

'Very . . . retro.' Fixx smiled, nodded to Lady Clare and made for the ladder without looking back. He climbed it in huge, easy steps, his legs powering him effortlessly up wet rungs.

'A borg!' Behind her the lieutenant sounded impressed despite himself, and Clare nodded. Well, he was, sort of . . . And just because she hated the poisonous shit didn't meant she couldn't recognize a good performance when she saw one.

The hatch shut itself, the hiss of its hydraulics lost in the howling rain, and then the X3 began to count itself down, its voice an irritating whine. Water was trickling down her back, cold rivulets using her spine as a roadway before soaking into her waistband. Lady Clare'd always thought 'brain-freeze' was just another of LizAlec's clichés, but she was beginning to learn differently. Her neck burned with tension and both breasts ached with cold but it was Lady Clare's forehead that was the focus of real, concrete pain.

All the same, she stayed to watch the X3's lift-off and saw it rise almost silently into the night to be swallowed by dense rain cloud. No guns opened fire from out beyond the Bois, no G2A missiles ripped through the sky.

The bloody thing was launched and Fixx with it. Now he just had to prove he was as good at performing as he thought he was.

Chapter 16

TsujiGiri

'In between this moon and you . . .' Fixx hit a key, disliked what he heard and hit another, wiping his previous edit. He was enjoying himself, which was more than could be said for the kitten.

Ghost bounced into an old-fashioned plastic deck, accidentally trod on a pressure pad and the simulacrum of Ludwig Van Beethoven died mid-chord, replaced by an amphetamined-up Mozart who promptly changed both key and tempo. Fixx didn't mind too much: he just remixed one into the other and ran a long Ginger Baker drum fill under both.

Currently he had a seventeen-year-old Wolfgang Amadeus on keyboard – at least he did now, thanks to Ghost – Goldie was in there on vocals, $+N_2X$ was on korg and 303 and Fixx was thinking of using either Lennon and McCartney or the Gallaghers for backing vocals, except he couldn't find the right file.

Flicking fingers across the deck, Fixx keyed in echo-shredded birdsong and a CySat C3N sound-grab of a tank crushing a barricade in Tashkent. He riffed machine-gun fire with rolling static and looped the lot before Ginger Baker had even finished on snares.

Sweet as honey and with more bloody layers than an over-thick piece of baklava.

Beneath it all was static from deep space, laid over a click track of quasar pulses, and at its heart was coded a fractal equation that turned and twisted on itself, opening sounds out like the petals of a never-ending flower.

LISA was going to love it. Sure, it was five years since he'd had a thing going with LISA but her tastes couldn't have changed that much. That was the difference between AIs and humans: AIs didn't have the capacity to make themselves over or drop out of sight. Maybe somewhere an AI had walked out on its job or nipped out to get a six-pack and never come home, but if it had then Fixx had never heard of it.

Sound echoed out of every speaker around him, danced as exploding lines of light across the black glass of a sillyscope. At least, Fixx figured that was what it was before he ripped out its streamers and wired them to the deck's digital feed.

Back at Sony in the old days, he'd have added vision, something bittersweet lifted from a newsfeed, maybe thrown in some obscure scents, morphed up a tri-D Laura or two. But this wasn't Sony — it was some fucked-up, cramped, still-damp cabin of an out-of-date Boeing X3 shuttle. And he was running out of time.

'Shit, Ghost, what we going to do?'

The kitten said nothing, Fixx didn't expect it to. Black and scrawny as an empty purse, Ghost was going to be his good-luck talisman. Sure, anyone else would probably have eaten it, but Fixx prided himself on not being anyone else. That had been the whole basis of his magnesium-brief flash of fame.

Though, looking at the animal retching its guts out, Fixx wondered if it wouldn't have been kinder just to let Lady Clare cook it. He might be strapped in but the terrified kitten was making the trip in freefall and pellets of cat shit hung in the air like black bees. Having seen the result of doing it once, Fixx was managing to avoid the urge to swat them again.

Okay, party time. Popping his last bubble of paraDerm, Fixx scratched the underside of his good wrist and slapped the patch into position, feeling warmth spread up though his arm. Inside his head, dorphs flooded in, his limbic system kicked up a gear and he forgot completely about his bruised jaw. Bayer-Rochelle had designed the derm to work on unbroken skin, but Fixx

Jon Courtenay Grimwood

couldn't be bothered to wait around while the analgesic soaked through.

There were three things he needed to do and, as always when Fixx couldn't crack the priorities, he was busy doing none of them. If he'd been bothered enough, he could have downloaded an MS Routesoft walk-through for Planetside, checked out in advance where the grab happened. But the stop/start jumpiness of commercial VGR made him sick, so he was going to *apt* his memory instead. The only problem was, to get a current workable remembrance agent he needed access to LISA – and these days it seemed she had more hard armament slapped around her than Paris.

LizAlec was too young to remember black ice, but Fixx wasn't. It was just a fuck of a long time since he'd done anything about it except talk.

'Ain't that always the way?' The cat said nothing, just kept on looking sick. Fixx didn't blame it. Approaching them was the bright side of the Moon, thousands of miles of shit-coloured, pock-marked rock with the occasional crater domed over in water and glass or roofed with earth. It made Paris look good.

Music for LISA, an APTR link for him via a pair of wraparounds, and what for the X3 . . . ? Authorization, and quick.

'Up/L youse l/code . . . ization need now.' The voice from Planetside traffic control was tired and irritated, reassuringly human. *'Up/L youse l/code. . .'* Give it another thousand klicks and that voice would be swearing or shouting instructions to Planetside defence control to blow him out of the sky.

Fixx grinned. Fifteen thousand miles back, the voice had been an unheard digital bitstream between his shuttle and the traffic semiAI. Five thousand miles later the voice switched to audible bio. Bringing in a human had only just happened. Fixx could imagine the bio and the trafficAI being seriously hacked off.

He was being tracked, no doubt about it. Had Planetside known he was fresh up from Paris they'd have burnt him swifter than swatting a fly. Even then, with the X3 reconfigured

by a particle beam, chances were they'd be too late. For all
Fixx knew, viruses had been falling like dust off his X3 even
since it came into low orbit. Or maybe they all went belly-up
and froze in mid-space. How the fuck was he to know? Drugs
and music was his thing, not biologically grounded base-level
atomic assemblers.

What he *had* worked out, sitting with his spewing kitten and
the flight console he'd rewired as a mixing deck, was that if the
shuttle was infected then he was a plague carrier. It wasn't a
good feeling. On Earth, ferroconcrete buildings tumbled down
if they got infected. Up here, craters weren't going to fall, they
were going to blow open, crack apart.

Fucking darkness. Fucking cold.

Hollowed out.

How many ruptured airlocks would it take to gut every tourist
in LunaWorld? Fixx didn't know but he wondered about it, in
the bit of his cortex not worrying about bluffing the traffic AI or
wondering if LISA really would, after five years, forgive him in
return for a piece of baroque, self-writing North African trance.
And it was hard not to wonder if Lady Clare *really* understood
she risked condemning an entire arcology to death.

If the answer was *yes*, then Fixx decided the bitch had to be
even more ruthless than LizAlec made out. And suppose it was
no? That didn't make him feel any better.

Fixx came into landing orbit just as the cargo shuttle carrying
LizAlec and Lars started its drop to *The Arc*. They weren't
listed on the manifest. Unless they were on there as assorted
animals, because that's what the shuttle was carrying. At Jude's
suggestion, LizAlec had cropped her hair and wrapped her
head in a white cotton headscarf, wrapped tightly around her
head and half-covering her face. Unwrapped, she looked like a
rich-kid punk for Chrysler, but wearing the scarf LizAlec looked
like a tourist-stall Madonna, the kind with a light in the base.

LizAlec knew all about *The Arc*, she just didn't know that was where she was going. Leon, the smart-arse boy from CasaNegro who got them on board the Boeing X7, had promised the shuttle was Seattle-bound. He'd lied. But then, back at CasaNegro Jude had reckoned that if the little rich girl really wanted off Luna that badly, it didn't matter too much where she went. Besides which, the kid would probably do well at *The Arc*. From what Jude had heard, it was full of spoilt brats trying to simplify their lives.

'*L/code . . . L/code . . . .*' The voice at the other end had been reduced to a petulant monotone. Fixx could have called on his ship's digital intelligence for help with what was going to happen next, but the DI wasn't talking to him. Not after Fixx's five-minute rant to Ghost about how Europe had been corrupted by the greed of US-owned metaNationals.

Fixx hadn't known the X3 had a USAF biocore, an old fly-by-light hand who'd practically begged to be DI'd by Boeing. That had been thirty years before, and from what he gathered the snotty little data intelligence hadn't been that happy when the USAF sold the shuttle cheap to the French. Which was what happened if you decided to get digital without bothering to read the small print.

'Anyway,' Fixx told Ghost crossly, as the kitten floated past his face, 'the fucking fuck's probably too squeamish to help us anyway . . .' What came next was definitely illegal and bios were tied to some coded-in moral cut-off, or at least that was the theory.

'Input.'

Fingers flicked over the deck, pulling up blocks of code. Fixx could have used the floating focus on his wraparounds, but he liked the solidity of a screen, the way the blocks flashed into being, even though they only existed as pixels, ghost images of binary life.

Even the Chinese didn't have an up-front ice-breaker hard enough to crack open LISA. Fixx was trading through as a command and its echo. In the first split second of contact, LISA would reach out for the command and instantly unravel anything not recognized as legitimate, required code. The junk would be stripped out, unread, unaccessed, unravelled like strands of discarded digital DNA.

Not that Fixx wanted to turn the shit-kick rush of on-the-fly coding into the dry waste of some history lesson, but there'd been a time – way back – when the viruses came first and had to be cleaned out. When firewalls existed to limit outside access, not flame incoming viruses in some Web-based auto-da-fé.

There were kids back at Schrödinger's Kaff who reckoned they could hack anything from the Pentagon to HKS. Fixx had been around long enough to know that for the shit it was.

'And it is, you know,' Fixx told the bedraggled kitten. 'Complete fucking cack. And it misses the point . . .' Which was that the best way to hack a computer was to ask another computer to do it for you. Fixx just hoped LISA still loved him enough to help: and anyway, this wasn't hacking, it was almost legitimate, at least the second bit was.

Fingers still flicking, Fixx hit LISA's firewall, dumped the command he'd been constructing and watched the junk code inside it unravel into flashes on the screen. It would look better stacked up as graphics, but he couldn't afford the distraction.

And as a subset of a subset ate up his Trojan horse, Fixx tried a trick that S3 had bullied and bribed out of some scared, long-dead employee at Annapolis – and then saved until they needed it, which was now.

LISA might be an old US naval AI, fuzzy as all fuck in her logic and rigid in her control parameters, but somewhere down in her core – written over, upgraded, augmented with additional layers of logic until it was almost buried – was a basic BigRedSwitch. The kind that went, if *this*, then *that* . . .

So Fixx clicked it, using legal code, hot-keying himself through without trouble – LISA was that old. 'Sweet as pie,' said Fixx, his voice over-loud, but Ghost ignored him anyway so Fixx turned back to his deck. Sliding a series of reassurances in through the trapdoor. He had maybe five per cent of LISA's attention now. Keying open her trapdoor would have guaranteed that anyway, but he was using old naval commands to smooth the loop. They told the subset currently on watch that Fixx not only knew what he was doing, but that he had a right to do it.

On his screen, the subset patched up half a key and waited. It was happy to wait, anything was better than acting as second back-up to Planetside's temperature control, which was what it had been doing until called to trapdoor duty. Under the key, Fixx typed a second line, watching as both lines meshed to produce a third.

Fixx grinned.

'Welcome', said a voice that echoed tinnily out of the flatscreen's built-in speaker.

'Happy to be here,' Fixx typed back.

'Name?'

'Commander Bond,' typed Fixx. Nothing too senior, nothing too junior, that was the way to go. If the X3's bio had known what Fixx was doing, it would have hung itself, but it didn't. Fixx had ripped out its ribbons, cutting its links to the deck. And without that link, the DI was just some jerk's memory trapped in a box. And if trashing memories was murder, thought Fixx, then half his girlfriends should be behind bars.

'Susan,' announced the voice, introducing itself. *'Subset Using . . .'*

'Okay,' said Fixx as the software began reeling off its designation, he got the picture. The voice was American, middle-aged, slightly fussy. Just what Fixx would expect from a subset originally programmed to sell visiting dignitaries on the mythic delights of apple pie, Mom and naval intelligence.

'Can I ask your purpose?'

Fixx thought about it.

'Security,' he said at last, which covered most sins. If you took out politics, religion and commerce, what the fuck was left? Sex, maybe. 'Internal security,' Fixx elaborated. 'I need cloaking. Nothing elaborate. Just enough to put down at Planetside . . .'

If the subset could have nodded, Fixx swore it would have done then. Commanders, security, cloaking clandestine arrivals, that was what it had originally lived for. Not as a control routine for a civilian base. As well as temperature, it might monitor radiation, recycling resources and air pressure in the domes, but that didn't mean it liked the job.

'Cover following,' Fixx said, and a digital squirt carried his life story to Susan. It was heavily edited, obviously. There was the briefest of silences while Susan considered the glorious if unlikely past of Commander Bond. A silence Fixx hurriedly broke before Susan decided to do something stupid like double-check it.

'Please patch me though to LISA . . .'

'LISA?' The subset sounded doubtful.

'Now, please,' Fixx said firmly before the subset had time to refuse. 'I want to talk to Luna Intelligent Systems Analysis.'

'I'm sorry,' Susan said apologetically, 'I'm afraid . . .' The voice stopped. 'Oh yes,' it said brightly, 'we can patch you through from here.'

Fixx sighed. Give me a lever and I'll move the Earth: no statement was truer. Even if that Greek guy hadn't been talking about social engineering.

'This is LISA.' The voice was non-personal, efficient, not as he recalled her. And then Fixx remembered that she didn't know who he was. All the same, Fixx felt his stomach knot up and sweat break out under his arms. He hadn't felt like this since he was thirteen, waiting on the Ha'penny Bridge in Dublin for that girl who never showed up.

'That you, sweetie?' Fixx said, less calmly than he would have liked. Silence blossomed as absolute as any shutdown. Seconds later Fixx began to breathe again.

'Fixx?' LISA sounded somewhere between shocked and hopeful. At least she did to Fixx, though he feared he might be imagining it. That level of emotional nuance hadn't been programmed into language back when she was commissioned.

'Yeah,' said Fixx, looking at the screen. 'It's me and I need your help.'

LISA sighed, the kind of sigh that said, *What's new?*

'I need to land.'

'Then get clearance.' LISA sounded puzzled.

'Like I wouldn't if I could . . .'

LISA tutted. When she spoke again LISA sounded more maternal than romantic. 'I don't want to know where you've come from, do I?'

'No,' said Fixx firmly. 'You don't. What you want to do is get me down quietly, discreetly.'

'Really?' LISA's voice was amused. 'I can think of three good reasons why that's a bad idea.'

Fixx could think of a hundred but he wasn't going to tell her that.

'One, I don't know where you've been. Two, you're a shit. And three, if you can remember that court settlement, you shouldn't even be talking to me. In fact, I should stop this conversation now. Unless there's a good reason why not . . . ?'

So Fixx told LISA all about LizAlec, well, everything except the bits involving him. But she was smart enough to put those in for herself. And then just to sweeten the hook Fixx pumped through *StarGlazz*. Not honey-wrapped but as raw machine code. And then he fed through his famous fractal equation, the one he'd stumbled over as a fifteen-year-old deckjock, wired to fuck, hacking hell out of a Segasim mixer in a cellar club called Infinite Spiral at the back of Temple Bar. He'd gone from street kid to syndication on seven continents, three orbitals and most of Luna inside a year. No wonder he hadn't been able to hack the lifestyle.

'Well,' Fixx said, when he figured LISA had worked out that if she fed the music through the equation then *StarGlazz* might run for several years. 'Are you going to help me?'

LISA thought about it, ran through several thousand alternatives, reduced that to slightly less than a thousand and took the most unlikely. Fixx didn't even notice she'd been gone. 'Twenty-four hours,' Lisa said firmly. 'Then you leave, okay?'

Fixx grinned. 'Yeah,' he said. 'Twenty-four hours. I promise.'

Lisa didn't tell him she already knew where LizAlec had gone.

Chapter 17

If it bleeds/We can kill it

'Fixx Valmont?'

'You got it . . .'

A nervous courier gave Fixx the 1stVirtual platinum card on his way out of VIP Customs. There had been a time he'd owned not just platinum cards but his own orbiting bank, but then, go back fifteen years and his arrival at somewhere like Planetside Arrivals would have ground the place to a halt. CySat, C3N, all freelance Ishies not nailed down or wired into a feed recharging batteries would have been crawling up the walls to get a grab of him, quite literally. Hell, there'd been five versions of the Fixx Valmont doll, bending arms, working legs, each one chipped up to say 'You got it,' and a lot else beside.

Fixx took his 1stV card, sliding it effortlessly into the inside pocket of his swirling black cloak. It would be drawn against the US Navy's own Luna account. Somehow Fixx doubted if they even realized they still had one.

He'd been waved through Immigration, excused sonic cleaning because of the electronics in his arm, and had his cloak, cotton shirt and black leather trousers taken by an embarrassed young woman in uniform, who returned with them a few minutes later, already irradiated and freeze-pressed.

'I've also been told to give you this.' Head down, the courier handed Fixx a small neoprene-sheathed blade, her eyes looking everywhere except at his metal arm. Or it might have been the explosion of yellow bruises that embarrassed the courier. But then, short of sitting around in a decompression chamber waiting for hyperbaric oxygenation to force extra oxygen into his bloodstream, Fixx was stuck with the bruising for as long as it took his body to repair the damaged tissue.

'Thanks.' The musician's easy Dublin drawl was soft, miles from the rough Parisian street snarl he'd taken to using. Fuck knew what LISA had dumped into his records, but whatever it was, Fixx was enjoying the attention. It was like his early days of being on board with Sony, before being famous became hard work.

Fixx could almost believe he was up here to launch some new Sim. *StarGlazz*, maybe. Perhaps trying to screw over Bernie, his manager, in court hadn't been such a good idea after all . . .

'Is everything okay?' the courier asked.

'Sure is.' Fixx ran his thumb along the ice-tempered molybdenum/vandium blade, gently as he could, and blood beaded his skin, strung out in a line like little red pearls. 'In fact, it couldn't be better.' He nodded, tiny dreadlocks bobbing against the shaved sides of his head, tipped into slo/moby the one-sixth gravity. So far, that was the only thing he was having trouble with, the slight time lapse between physical action and reaction. Didn't look like Ghost was enjoying it much either.

The courier looked doubtfully at the kitten. 'Regulations don't . . .' But whatever she was about to say, she didn't bother. It wasn't her problem. Nodding quickly, the woman backed away.

Shit, thought Fixx, maybe LISA hadn't told them he was filthy rich and famous after all, maybe it was just contagious. He was still watching the scuttling courier when someone else materialized at his side. Understated grey suit, lead-weighted leather shoes, white cotton shirt and red tie, a very slight bulge under one arm.

'Rez Aziz,' the man announced, sticking out his hand.

Fixx shook, feeling the firm shake of a professional. Clear brown eyes were watching him, gauging something. From the close-cropped hair and heavy moustache to the trim gut that spoke of workouts in an artificial gravity gym, everything about the man said *police*.

If he found Fixx's cloak and leather trousers unusual, he didn't let it show. Instead he flipped a pastel from a plastic dispenser and sucked heavily. A scent of violets filled the air between them.

'We weren't expecting to see you again . . .'

'Surprise trip,' said Fixx.

The man looked at him, eyes narrowing as he examined the hasty repair job on Fixx's face. He looked like the kind of man who could tell you, to the last blow, just how long it would take to inflict damage of that level.

'All the same . . .' His words were was emotionless, unaccented. It was the kind of voice Fixx found impossible to pin down. Middle Eastern sometime back, when the designation still meant something. And the twist of Arabic script on his gold ring suggested he kept his family's faith. But the cologne and bland Seiko watch were as anonymous as his voice.

Five minutes after leaving him, Fixx knew he would find it impossible to remember the face, another five minutes and he'd probably have forgotten the clothes. And somehow Fixx got the feeling the man wanted it that way.

'Your luggage?' Mr Aziz looked round vaguely.

'I travel light,' said Fixx, nodding towards Ghost who was rubbing his neck against Fixx's ankle.

'Twenty-four hours,' the man said firmly.

Fixx looked blank.

'It is twenty-four hours, isn't it? Before you blast off for your new ring colony . . .'

So that *was* how LISA had swung it. Obscenely rich and just passing through. 'Yeah,' said Fixx, 'if you say so.' Hefting Ghost under one arm, Fixx turned for the door marked Exit. It opened before he was ten paces away, offering him a cheerful welcome in a language he didn't understand. Japanese from the sound of it, which said something about who usually used the VIP lounge.

'They didn't have time to change the program,' Rez Aziz said after him. He didn't sound apologetic, just matter-of-fact, as if reclusive, arrogant, by-law breaking CySat stars came through all the time, expecting to be humoured. But then, hell, maybe they did.

Outside the door was a walkway, perched high above the floor of Arrivals. And looking down, Fixx could see a swirling blue mosaic and below that wall-to-wall tourists, refugees and journalists. People were beginning to look up – first one or two, then dozens – attracted by the glint of light on his arm and the cloak that billowed behind him when it remembered.

Some of them, the older ones, recognized him and Fixx bowed, unable to resist the urge; but even as he did, part of him wondered where to buy clothes that were more anonymous, for when he needed to blend in, become invisible.

It was one thing to be famous, even once-famous. Quite another to find a kidnapped girl when every step you took advertised who you were. All Fixx had in his favour was that no one yet knew he was here to find LizAlec.

'Can I get a look down there?' Fixx asked a passing cleaner. The cleaner whirred, glass eyes swivelling towards Fixx, and it nodded reluctantly. Fixx took the slight bob of its head to mean he should use the lift.

A drop lift stood waiting to take passengers down to the marble floor below and Fixx carried Ghost into the Orvis. A button released the holding magnet and his own weight-plus-gravity took them slowly down. Another button blasted the lift back to its original position. The whole contraption was based on an ancient Victorian idea of using pneumatic power to send messages down tubes from one office to another.

The American woman who'd taken out the patent on the pneumatic lift was now Croesus-rich and holed up in Baja

California, her blood, kidneys and lungs wired into a Mitsubishi Extopian Special.

'Need any help?' the lift asked as its doors opened.

Fixx shook his head.

'Then enjoy your stay,' said the lift and was gone back to the VIP floor, leaving Fixx standing in the swirl of people crowding Arrivals Hall. The vast atrium stank of people, McDonald's soyburgers and recycled air. It was a smell Fixx had forgotten and one he was going to have to get used to – fast.

Every breath, every gulp of water taken on the Moon was endlessly recycled. Tears, sweat, piss, everything was collected or leached from the air and swallowed back into the system. Breathing someone else's stink was a fact of life. As locals never stopped telling the tourists, if they didn't like the air they could always try outside.

Plenty of people looked at Fixx. Men glancing away or defiantly meeting his silver eyes, the women smiling at Ghost and Fixx's ludicrous cloak, or frowning at his hair. Only kids watched the weird man with undisguised interest, stopping to nudge each other at the metal arm, leather trousers and kitten clutched like a baby in his arm.

Floor level at Planetside was logo hell and fly-post heaven. HoloAds for Coke jostled flashing neon bottles of Bud. Someone had staple-gunned a flickering faux-telex *It's cheaper with Mercury* over the top of Cablebox's flashing *Now phone home*. There were signs pointing you to God, LunaWorld and the nearest legalized brothel. What there wasn't was any sign of a Japanese ballerina.

LunaWorld's Man on the Moon Spacetel was themed to mid-twentieth-century America. At least, Fixx figured it was mid-twentieth from the bright clothes in the photographs and the big pink Cadillac with fins that stood in the foyer. He knew it was a Cadillac from the reverential little notice alongside.

Booking him into the MMS had to be LISA's idea of a joke,

but it wasn't one that amused the desk staff. Oh, they had his reservation, right enough. Made months back. They just didn't have a room to spare. Fixx shrugged and took a swig from his complimentary beer. After Paris anything was bliss.

Out of the bar window was a view of a huge white Saturn rocket taking off in a billowing cloud of smoke. It was convincing enough to fool a child, but Fixx noticed the slight jump where the tape was looped, to let the same rocket endlessly fire up its engines and vanish into an impossibly blue Cape Canaveral sky.

Ignoring the window was the sign of an old hand. Fixx realized that when he noticed that only he and a family of newly arrived South Africans were watching: everyone else was pointedly ignoring the thing. All the same, Fixx kept looking until the sequence had started over again.

Speaking personally, if he'd been fixxing the sequence he'd have done a *2001* with the colours, put an orange Saturn blasting into a purple shy, black flames belching from the afterburners. And he'd have put in some proper contemporaneous music. Maybe a little mid-period Jimi Hendrix, but hey . . . Fixx finished his beer and shrugged.

He didn't see what was so wrong with watching a fake window. It couldn't have been a real one anyway. Like all of LunaWorld except the actual dome, the MMS was dug into bedrock, sealed safely away from the sucking vacuum of the surface. It was easier, cheaper and faster to dig out the space you needed and let the overhead rock take the strain. You did away with the problems of radiation, too.

'Mr Valmont?' The thirty-something woman standing in front of him was Luna-born. Wasp-waisted from where low gravity kept her guts from pressing down into her abdomen and with pert breasts that would never know the need for a bra, but her arms were muscle-withered and her face puffy with water retention.

No amount of working out could help, unless you were rich

enough to afford weekly membership of an artificial-gravity gym, and that meant going orbital. Fixx knew, he'd seen the holoAds in the Arrivals Hall.

'Yeah, that's me.' Like it was going to be anyone else. She was desperate to tell him how difficult it had been to find him a room, Fixx could see that from her harassed face, but he didn't need telling. Half of Europe had fled into exile and credit alone wasn't enough to find you living space on Planetside, not these days. Whatever electronic strings LISA had tugged, it had impressed and irritated the hotel in equal amounts.

'I want to thank you,' said Fixx, looking into her grey eyes, and smiled. 'I know how impossible it must have been.' The woman waved away his thanks hurriedly, but blushed all the same. She was old enough to remember him when had been famous.

Leaving the South African family still trying to check in, Fixx followed the woman into a lift, dropping five floors to level minus five. His suite was vast but filthy. Grey dust frosted like chalk across a glass table in the centre of the main room and in the bedroom it covered the grey enamel bedside locker. The bed was themed, like the rest of the furniture in the suite. And while the puffed satin headboard was undeniably hideous it wasn't anything like as bad as the bedside lamp that had gold tassels that swung when brushed.

'It's great,' Fixx said warmly and the woman looked reassured.

'If there's anything you want,' she said, 'anything I can provide . . .' She stopped, realized how he might interpret that and blushed, backing for the door before Fixx had time to reassure her that he was fine. Listening to her steps in the corridor outside, Fixx shrugged. Okay, so his reputation had been bad, but that bad . . . ?

Hanging his cloak in a dark cupboard so that it would go to sleep, Fixx clicked on the screen and called up the LunaWorld shopping channel. The clothes on offer were dreadful but he didn't care, not once a lisping voice had assured him that they could be delivered direct to his hotel door.

In the corner of the room was a hotel minibar, the kind that said *Have a nice stay* everytime you shut the door and *Please shut me* every time you left it open for longer than ten seconds. Inside the minibar was a Snickers, a see-through bag of Hershey's Kisses, three packs of honey-roast protein and five different types of Coke. In the enamel locker a Gideon Bible was stacked on top of a copy of the Torah. On top of the Bible was a Koran. All were untouched.

'Protein,' Fixx suggested, offering Ghost the bag. The kitten licked one of the honey-roast lumps and sneezed, tripping off the edge of the bed. 'Hey, I'm sorry.' Fixx scooped the bundle of fur lightly off the floor and propped Ghost on a lacy pink pillow. He needed to find Ghost a shit tray and something cat-like to eat. Actually, he didn't, not when he thought about it. Fixx flicked the vidphone onto vox and called up room service.

Food for Ghost was no problem, but the hotel didn't have a real bar, at least not one that sold anything stronger than beer, so God knew what reception would do if he rang through and asked them to arrange a few rocks or a couple of lines of wizz. So he called up the desk again and asked for someone to catsit Ghost instead.

His new clothes weren't ready yet, so Fixx dug his cloak back out of the cupboard and checked out through LunaWorld's perimeter gate into Aldrin Square, Planetside's biggest space and a pedestrian-only zone. From ceiling to polished rock floor was maybe forty-feet, and from one side of Aldrin Square to the other was roughly half a mile. Alleys led off from the edge of the square in all directions and between the alley entrances were tourist shops cut into the rock. In the centre two rows of tired palms were turning yellow, despite strip lights set almost exactly overhead. Cleaning droids scuttled by and so did two English tourists, heads down as they scooted through on their way to a girlie bar. Down one of the nearby alleys was Washington Plaza, the heart of Planetside's red-light area. Except that everything in the Plaza was as packaged up and sanitized as London's Soho or 42nd Street and Times Square back in Manhattan.

It took no time at all to cross the square, though Fixx slid to a halt as a gang of bladers split in the middle, wheels hissing as the kids zipped around him, laughing. Things got darker in the miles that followed, once he'd turned off the square. Lights became less frequent and those that were there worked less often. People looked more and smiled less. From what Fixx remembered of the hotel map, he was nearing the Edge.

Every city has areas that don't make it into the Lonely Planet guides, except with warnings: for Luna it was the Edge. The Edge was where you went if you liked living dangerously or were just plain stupid. And Fixx had long ago worked out that he qualified on both counts. Besides, he wanted to check if LizAlec had come this way and LISA had said that when it came to getting out of Planetside, this was jump city.

Fixx liked that. It felt like an album title, or maybe a bad show, something that might manage one day's hang time in a minor gallery off André des Arts. Fifteen minutes after hitting hooker heaven Fixx stumbled on a crowded Swedish bar selling frozen Alborg and even colder blondes. Fixx tossed up in his head and settled for the Aquavit, his one or two stomach-settling shots ending up as five or six big ones that left his throat frozen and his lungs sodden with alcohol vapour. By the end of the evening, he was passing round his only picture of LizAlec, asking if anyone had seen his special friend.

They hadn't and from the sideways looks Fixx got it seemed like most of the clientele didn't think he should, either. Too bad. Grabbing back his tattered Kodak from a boy in combats, Fixx made it to the door and out into a small square, turning left, then left again and finally ending up in a narrow tunnel. It didn't matter that an illuminated panel set into the rock announced the alley as Mir Street. As far as Fixx was concerned, if it looked like a tunnel and smelt like a tunnel then it was a tunnel.

It was also a bit late to remember that if he'd brought floating-focus Zeiss he could have imprinted LISA's matrix over the top of his real surroundings. All the same, he remembered it anyway, and kept on remembering it until he walked slap into a wall and all his memory shut down for a while.

Halfway back to LunaWorld, Fixx threw up in a gutter, splashing soy meatballs and undigested alcohol across the grey rock floor. A Honda droid would have got around to cleaning it up just before dawn, but the droid wasn't needed because the rats got there first. By then Fixx was flopped on his bed beside Ghost, flicking through the twenty-four-hour newsfeeds. The passing through of Fixx Valmont, once a major CySat star, made a 'Hey, guess what' newsblip five minutes before the end of the hour-long show. Which was how Fixx got to be three-quarters down an obscenely expensive take-out bottle of Aquavit before Ghost got to watch a younger, thinner, less-lined version of his new owner perform on screen.

The next day Fixx spent sleeping, the one after that was spent nursing the hangover he should have had twenty-four hours earlier. Working on the half-baked basis that LizAlec was perfectly capable of abducting herself from St Lucius, Fixx took his hangover out to play at LunaWorld, just in case LizAlec had done what any intelligent kid on the lam might do, lose herself among all the others.

He left Ghost with reception and let them run a swipe off his platinum card in case the kitten needed anything serious, like medical attention. He didn't tell reception he might not be back for a while but he reckoned the kitten knew from the way it scowled at Fixx when he left. If Ghost had known they were both two days over their leave-by date, Fixx figured he'd be scowling even more.

Leaving MMS, Ghost and his guilt behind, Fixx went kid spotting. He rode the big rides, hung out in the Simbars, took the new Astral Tour to watch pre-packaged groups hyperboost their endorphin levels with statistically safe, sphincter-tightening pre-packaged danger. He ate bad ice-cream with the Space Pirates, drank Coke he didn't want at New York, New York. Looked over the kids and young girls until the LD security guards got nervous. But by the end of the afternoon he knew LizAlec wasn't there.

He saw no trace of her and none of the kids he struck up chance conversations with had any memory of her either. Somehow, given the way LizAlec stalked forward on the balls of her feet, the way she held her head, Fixx had a feeling the boys at least would remember if they'd seen her. Her tits alone were worth dying for. Well, they were in his opinion.

Right at the start LISA had told him that LizAlec was not registered at any Planetside hotel. The AI had checked that out as the X3 was coming in to land. And even using military-grade visual recognition software, a rapid scan of Planetside's m/wave cameras produced nothing. If Planetside was out then so was Chrysler: its very exclusivity made it too hermetic for strangers. Which left Islamabad, Voertrekker, half a dozen private craters and Fracture. Fixx didn't doubt that he'd find her, however impossible that seemed, it was just the slight matter of timing. If true genius was the ability to come up with *two* good ideas and also see both sides of any argument, then Fixx was off the scale. His whole life had always been connections, digital, social or neural.

Fixx shivered. He was standing in the queue for SpaceWarp again, late afternoon having slid into evening. Twenty-four-hour daylight was illegal on Planetside though at LunaWorld the rides still stayed open round the clock. But the overhead sky was dimming again to signify the start of late evening. If you were using melatonin to reset Circadian rhythms, now was the time to take it.

Next door to SpaceWarp was a long glass-fronted bar called the SanRat. It looked loathsome. Slide guitar slid from the wide doorway, its oily notes as thin as any kid's whining. Over the door was a sign in cracked enamel, riddled with fake bullet holes. The block letters announced that for the convenience of LunaWorld's patrons, alcohol wasn't on sale. And, in the window, adults who'd paid to sit there surrounded by tired and irritated kids looked like they hated every aspartamine-sweet minute of it.

Time to get a Bud and that meant going back to his hotel. Either that, or go find another bar. Fixx ducked under a barrier, ignoring the angry shout of a guard, and pushed his way out of the SpaceWarp queue. The kids were welcome to their ride. All he really wanted was a cold Bud, a bed that didn't have pink frills and maybe . . .

That woman over there.

Fixx stopped dead and took another look, but the badly dressed blonde had stopped watching him and was examining the poster for SpaceWarp as if she'd never seen a physical-reality ride before, as if listening to the poster took up all her attention. And then Fixx realized she wasn't listening at all, she was still busy watching his reflection . . .

Police?

It was possible, but then again, maybe not. Five-ten, maybe taller, mid-weight, badly-cut blonde hair: she didn't look neat enough to be brass, and he'd never have noticed her if she was street-level. Or maybe he would have, but not that easily. Unless, of course, she wanted him to notice her.

Fixx sighed. It was one thing for Lady Clare to say go find LizAlec, Fixx thought, pushing his way towards the woman, quite another for LISA to expect him to have been able to do it in twenty-four hours. He wasn't looking forward to the next time he had to talk to her. Three steps took Fixx to the still-burbling poster. 'Look,' Fixx said, 'you can't listen to the fucking thing for a fourth time. It's not that interesting . . .'

Washed-out blue eyes met his, held his gaze. Fixx was impressed. He was all in favour of first impressions and his was that this wasn't the kind of woman who slapped, she punched. Much like LizAlec really, except LizAlec didn't yet know it while this woman did. From the tiredness in her face, Fixx reckoned she was getting bored with living up to the mark.

Paper print dress, the kind without sleeves, unwashed hair, cheap make-up, she also didn't belong in LunaWorld and that much was obvious from the way guards were hovering, as if desperate to shepherd Fixx and the woman away from the rest of the ice-cream-eating, Coke-slurping queue.

'Out at the Edge you?' Her accent was so thick that Fixx could hardly grasp what she was asking, if it actually was a question.

'You? Two night back?'

Two nights . . . Yeah, Fixx had it, she was talking about that over-chromed brothel, the sinbin that offed him more dead presidents for a take-out bottle of Alborg than he usually had to live on for a month back in Paris. Fixx nodded. 'You got it.'

'Kodak?' the woman demanded.

Fixx handed over his tri-D of LizAlec, noticing that the blonde's nails were chipped and worn; and not even purple Candy could hide the half-circles of grime beneath.

'No water,' the woman said shortly, following his eyes. 'All goes to places like this. Sweedak?' She nodded around her, not bothering to keep the contempt from her voice. 'This your friend?' she asked, watching him carefully.

'Yeah, special friend.'

'An t'boy?'

'Boy?' Fixx said, surprised. For a second they glanced at each other, and then the hangover swallowed Fixx, leaving him staring blankly over her shoulder at a distant ride.

That LizAlec should have set up her own kidnap didn't surprise him. That she set it up with someone other than him . . . ? Fixx shrugged. He was too old and too ugly to worry about getting his feelings hurt, wasn't he . . . ?

Wasn't he?

Fixx shook his head. How come Lady Clare hadn't thought

this through? She'd watched the kid grow up. Why hadn't the snotty bitch reached the same conclusion, that it was a set-up, that LizAlec was on the lam . . . ? Lady Clare was bright, cynical. She must have got to this conclusion before him, so what made her reject it?

'A boy?' Fixx kept his voice neutral. Only his eyes betrayed what he was really thinking.

'San'rat,' said the woman.

'From the Moon?' Fixx asked in disbelief.

Jude smiled, not kindly. 'Honey, where else you get san'rats?'

'You've actually seen her . . .'

Jude began to nod and thought better of it. 'You her *special* friend?' There was a world of ironic emphasis on that *special*.

'I'm a friend of her mother's,' Fixx said, surprising himself.

Jude thought about it. 'She in bad trouble, t'girl?'

'Yeah, big trouble. People want her dead.' As lies went it wasn't inspired but the blonde woman had no way of knowing it wasn't true.

'Jude,' said Jude, thrusting out her hand. Fixx shook. 'I got a bar,' Jude said, 'in Strat, t'CasaNegro. You come see me sometime, we talk, maybe . . .' Dodging round an approaching guard, Jude was gone before Fixx even realized she was leaving.

'My Kodak,' Fixx demanded hastily.

Jude didn't answer him, but somehow Fixx didn't expect her to.

Chapter 18

Christ on Crutches

The ship stank. The kind of stink you get if you put twenty flea-bitten goats in a stainless-steel pen and then tie them down with neoprene mesh so they can't float away in free fall. Why even the Family would want to ship animals from Planetside to Seattle, fuck alone knew. But as to why they didn't take the Kobe option and put the goats in suspended animation, LizAlec knew that. The brotherhood didn't believe in recreational drugs, nanotechnology or extopian solutions and who was she to question the word of God?

LizAlec smiled sourly, remembering Fixx's insistence on an inverse link between IQ and absolute faith. *The more you believe the less you think.* Not surprisingly, that never got taught at St Lucius, either.

Briefly, LizAlec wondered what kind of crap the amulet-wearing Lars believed in, and then decided she didn't care enough to find out. She was bored with Lars and his creepy, clanky steel lung, bored with staring at goats, hungry too.

They were in an air vent hung over a hold, that much was obvious. And the hold had been walled off into three pens, two small pens divided between the goats and ten black, bristle-backed pigs. There was also a larger pen for six of the ugliest cows LizAlec had ever seen.

All the animals stank: the pigs less than the cows, surprisingly. At least, it surprised LizAlec, who'd assumed the cows would be the cleanest.

'Less animals, more shit,' Lars told her baldly, and he was

right. The leathery-skinned, thin-hipped cows in the pen next door were crusted in their own excrement, huge scabs of dung drying to cake on their hides. Only the pigs still looked vaguely pink. Every hour a woman with wide hips and protruding buttocks stamped into each pen in turn and vacuumed clean the air with a huge hose.

She didn't look happy with her job, but she never swore, not even when the DustBuster broke one time and spat everything out of the other end again, much like the animals.

'Family,' LizAlec told Lars, who just looked puzzled.

'Yours?' His voice sounded doubtful.

LizAlec grunted with frustration. Being trapped for hours in the hold of a filthy cargo shuttle with some slack-jawed retard had worn her patience so thin it was practically transparent.

No,' LizAlec said abruptly. '*Family*.' She said it like the retard should know what she was talking about, which she figured he should. 'Oh fuck . . . Forget it.' She crept forward and looked down through an air vent at the goats. She was sure one or two were looking back at her.

They'd started out in a cupboard, locked into a tiny side room by Leon, the combat kid, who only just remembered to click the oxygen/atmosphere on before jumping shuttle and heading back to Fracture. It was Lars who'd prised off the grille to a ventilation shaft in their original hiding place and wriggled up, leaving her trapped and almost crying until frustration slid into skin-slicked fear as LizAlec remembered the bioSemtex worm wrapped away inside her skull. Just how far Lars had to wander before he broke the connection and splattered her brains against the utility-green walls of the tiny cupboard wasn't something LizAlec liked to think about.

Two hours later, Lars reappeared. Not back down the shaft, but in through the cupboard door to find a hysterical LizAlec crouched behind it, clutching the door handle in a desperate attempt to stop herself floating away, one fist raised to protect herself. She'd tried to punch him anyway, slashing clumsily at his face, but Lars twisted out of reach with a zero-gravity grace LizAlec knew she'd never manage. One chop from Lars to her wrist and she'd let go of the door handle and gone spinning, straight into the cupboard's opposite wall.

Since then they'd been hiding in a ventilation shaft in the roof of the hold, keeping a safe distance from each other. Ten to eighteen hours was the usual shuttle time and LizAlec reckoned they were now way beyond that. The shuttle should be down, its livestock stashed in quarantine pods outside Seattle, and LizAlec should long since have worked out how to escape the shuttle without being seen, closely followed by discovering how to get that fucking bioSemtex worm out of her head, and finishing off with a call to her mother.

Make that Lady Clare, LizAlec corrected herself. She was looking forward to that bit least of all. But they weren't in Seattle, they weren't even in minimal enough gravity to suggest they might be getting close. They just seemed to be hanging around in space doing nothing.

'What's that noise?' Lars asked suddenly.

'What noise?' All LizAlec could hear was the snuffle of the goats and the steady thud of an oxygen unit that pushed a warm fug past her ear.

'Noise,' Lars insisted, head twisted slightly to one side. With his oversized head, lower canines and protruding jaw, he looked positively simian. One of the three monkeys from the ivory statue that stood on the desk in Lady Clare's study. The one LizAlec had in mind had its hands clamped over its mouth, except it was LizAlec not Lars who was trying not to throw up her guts from weightlessness.

'Someone,' said Lars and rammed his feet, hands and back against the walls of the vent until he was solid and still. Below them a door clanged open, startling the goats. Only this time it wasn't the wide-hipped woman with her industrial Hoover, it was a broad man with a greying beard and thin ponytail.

High-sided grey boots stuck him to the metal floor. Suction, thought LizAlec, but she was wrong. They were ReeGravs, magnetic sneakers with a diode on each heel that flashed red just before the man took a step and turned green each time his foot hit the floor. He made a two-part slapping noise as he walked, *slip/slop*, like the sound of an old man shuffling in slippers.

It wasn't the goats he was worried about. That much was obvious from the Moby in his hand. A small and neat one, but a Moby just the same. From where she crouched above him, LizAlec could see a spool of micro-thin monofilament wound tight behind the Moby's sharp electric dart. Taiwanese then, no one else still made harpoon tasers . . . At least, that was what Fixx had said that afternoon they curled up on his sofa to watch a rerun of *Death Patrol*.

LizAlec blushed and wrapped her arms tight around her knees, huddling herself. From the Crash&Burn, the hippest b/beat club in le Bastille, to this . . . She'd go up against the taser if she absolutely had to, but she wouldn't win. She knew that in advance. Even a street samurai couldn't take 50,000 volts in the chest and keep standing.

The grey-bearded man looked at the meshed-down goats, glanced round the pen and shrugged. 'Nothing here, Brother,' he said into a geek mike slung in front of his face. The ear bead squawked something back and the man nodded, shutting the goat pen behind him.

A clang in the next pen told LizAlec the man was checking there, too. Another clang followed a few seconds later and then he was gone, kicking free of the ground and pulling himself through free fall by grabbing at the red polymer handholds set neatly into the corridor wall.

'They know,' said Lars. The sandrat somersaulted slowly backwards, only just brushing the sides of the vent as he tumbled. Lars liked free fall even better than one-sixth G. He could move upwards and along with only the slightest effort, using splayed fingers as springs to bounce off walls or break his trajectory. Being on the ship was like being back in the tunnels, just easier.

He liked the animals too, dropping through a ventilation grille to pet the goats whenever he thought it was safe. The only thing Lars still wasn't happy about was having left the ice bucket behind. Ben would never come back if his head unfroze. Or if he did, he'd probably be just stupid or something.

'They know,' Lars said again, prodding LizAlec in the back to get her attention.

'No, they don't,' said the girl, not bothering to look around. She didn't know any such thing, but she didn't want the little freak to see she was worried.

Lars grunted and began to run his hands along the side of a large grille just over his head. The grille blocked him off from a tunnel above and Lars was feeling for screws, rivets, anything he could slide a blade under and snap off. The shuttle was old and its conversion to bulk carrier had been cheap. Most of the new panels were just sheet Duralumin staple-gunned at the edges and sprayed over with liquid polymer. The rest were compressed polycrete. Only the original fixtures were welded and Lars had been busy avoiding those.

'Go somewhere else,' he told LizAlec, pushing his broken blade under the edge of the overhead grille. Flakes of yellowing resin began to build up where he cut into epoxied polycrete. Up and down counted for little in zeroG — not that Lars had given them much attention even back on Luna — but he was squatting with his feet pushing down towards the goats, so maybe the tunnel he was trying to enter counted as up. If only he could break the epoxy . . .

Pushing the knife deeper into a gap, Lars twisted, feeling one corner of the grille crack free a second or so ahead of his own wrist reaching breaking point. LowG leached calcium from a body faster than it could take it in, even if you swore by Bayer-Rochelle's complete Traveller's Deep-Space Pac. And Lars hadn't even heard of Bayer-Rochelle.

Lars wasn't sure the narrow tunnel he crouched in counted as an air vent, since all of the hold was full of air. And although the air pushing toward them was warm it didn't really seem hot enough to count as heating. He'd asked LizAlec what she thought but she hadn't bothered to answer.

Maybe she didn't know, thought Lars. Or maybe she just didn't want to talk to him. Shaking his hair out of his eyes, Lars slid the point of his blade under another corner of the grille and pulled up. Nothing much happened, so Lars went back to worrying the tired epoxy that kept the ceramic mesh in place. Staying put made no sense to him, but then a tunnel with only two ways out made even less. Apart from his own tunnel below the Arrivals Hall, which was different because no one but him knew about it.

The shuttle crew knew about this one, though. How could they not? It hung square and box-like above their heads in the hold. They just didn't know that Lars and the girl were here, and Lars wasn't so sure about that, whatever she thought.

'Need to hide,' Lars insisted. The sandrat saw the slight, high scrape of his blade over polycrete as flashes, little purple sparks that vanished when the epoxy finally gave way. That was how Lars knew to move on.

'Move *now*,' said Lars, prising up the last corner with the edge of the blade and sliding his fingers under the mesh. He wanted to lever the grid away, but his arms weren't strong enough. The girl could do it, though.

'Help . . . ?' Lars suggested.

'Oh, fuck off, you freak . . .' LizAlec turned her back on him and got on with fretting about why the shuttle hadn't begun its descent yet. She was hungry, hungrier than she'd imagined possible: her gut was hollowed out with vomiting. She'd had to crap in sight of Lars, squatting at one end of the air vent while he watched her idly, wondering why she was so angry. And just to finish everything off, cramp was punching waves across her abdomen.

Jude had given her a packet of Coag and also some Tampax, in case LizAlec hadn't taken the Coag in time to stop her period and LizAlec wasn't yet sure she had. If she didn't get to a clean, decent bathroom soon she was going to end up killing the little shit. In fact, only the fact Lars wore that stupid ring stopped her doing it right now.

No, LizAlec caught herself, that wasn't true. She didn't have the guts to kill someone. Fixx did and so did her mothers, both of them. At least, thought LizAlec, tilting her head to one side, she'd always assumed Fixx did. The early levels of *Fixx Laughs Last* had certainly been bloody enough to rate the sim as 18R in the States and get it banned altogether in Britain, Iran and Saudi Arabia.

Five weeks it had taken her to find a copy. Even the tomb sites on the Web hadn't thought it worth including in their Retro Raves. She'd finally picked up a tatty pirate DVD-Rom on Rue Jean-Henri-Fabre, having already practically gutted the Marché Biron in her search. Another little trip out to the flea markets that Lady Clare didn't know about. That was back last summer when the Azerbaijani virus worked when it was still just something that happened to other people somewhere hot and Islamic.

LizAlec shook her head crossly and watched in surprise as a large pearl flipped over to the wall of the shaft and fragmented like glass. It took LizAlec at least two seconds to realize she was crying and then it didn't matter any more. Because the door below swung open and five people stamped in, ReeGravs *slip/slopping* and their soles stuck fast to the floor.

One was the goat woman, only this time she wasn't holding her Hoover. Beside her, looking sullen, was the short bearded man with the grey ponytail, and behind him was Jesus Christ, or maybe his clone. The central figure was tall, with long raven-dark hair and a close-cropped beard so casual it had to take at least two hours each morning. A brown homespun robe was belted with rope round his middle and fell full-length to the floor. (Which was either pretty remarkable, given it was a zeroG environment, or the hem was weighted in some way with electromagnets.)

Beneath the robe he might have been shod in leather sandals and be defying gravity by will-power alone, but LizAlec guessed he was probably wearing ReeGravs like the rest of them. Flanking him were two women, their T-shirts, jeans and skin all black. Both carried Mobys.

Jesus Christ had to be Californian. Even squinting down at him through a grille, LizAlec could tell that his face was perfect. A thin nose led down to full lips. His brown eyes were deep set and framed by high cheekbones and perfect eyebrows. Of course, it could have been genetic, either natural or engineered, but LizAlec knew it wasn't. She'd caught enough episodes of *Other People's Faces* to recognize the cosmetic genius of Heinsik Jacob when she saw it. And besides, she knew that face . . .

LizAlec finally accepted what she already knew, that she wasn't on a cargo shuttle bound for Seattle. The man nodded up towards the grille and it seemed to LizAlec that his eyes penetrated the gloom and looked straight at her.

'Come down,' he ordered, the sternness of his voice undercut with warmth, sincerity even. LizAlec was ripping up the grille almost before Brother Michael had finished speaking and was sliding through the narrow gap. She felt like a little girl caught searching her parents' room.

'No.' Lars grabbed at her collar but LizAlec was gone, momentum carrying her down to the floor, where she grabbed a rail while trying to wrap Jude's white cotton scarf round her shaven head.

Both guards moved in to grab her but Brother Michael quickly shook his head, one hand reaching out to take LizAlec's face, turning it so LizAlec had no option but to stare into eyes as deep as the Big Black. This was the man whose God's Family party held the balance in Congress. The Web evangelist who'd driven the last President out of the White House for an adultery committed fifteen years before she was even elected.

The man most Bible Belt Americans had believed would be their next President, until he announced he was renouncing the world, its temptations and sins. (He didn't mention also avoiding the IRS.) Instead he would create an ark in space to take the godly out to the gates of Heaven where they belonged.

Insane and dangerous, was Lady Clare's judgement: but then it would be, LizAlec decided, looking deep into his brown eyes. She was part of the ungodly that Brother Michael's family were renouncing.

'Child,' said Brother Michael, letting go her face. 'What are you doing here?'

'Following you,' LizAlec said as she wrapped the scarf still tighter round her head. She switched languages effortlessly, her accent obviously not US English but still rich with sincerity and echoes of old money.

Brother Michael smiled. 'And the other?' The man looked towards the air vent where Lars still hid.

'He's with me,' LizAlec said lightly. It was what Fixx said every time he took her to a bar in Bastille. And most times it worked except when fat and balding security men – and they were always both – got difficult about her age, but Fixx tended to avoid clubs where that happened.

'With you?' Brother Michael looked at LizAlec, his brown eyes assessing something. Whatever he was after, he found it, for the man nodded slightly. 'So be it . . . You, come down.'

Lars poked his head uncertainly over the edge of the grille and one of the goats immediately bleated, twisting round to get a better view. Lars smiled, pushing himself out of the vent to land near the goat, petting it back into silence.

'Interesting,' said Brother Michael. His eyes looked at Lars and then at the tied-down animals. 'You like my goats?' Lars nodded. The only animals he'd seen close-up before were rats. He liked those too, but the goats were more interesting.

'Good,' said Brother Michael. 'You can look after them, it's time Sister Rachel had a rest.' If the wide-hipped, olive-skinned woman had objections, she didn't voice them. In fact, LizAlec noticed, no one tried to interrupt when Brother Michael was speaking.

'So you want to follow me?'

LizAlec nodded, violet eyes downcast, face mostly hidden in her cotton scarf. It was time she accepted the shuttle wasn't going to Seattle. And looking at the tall man with his two bodyguards, LizAlec decided she could take a good guess where they *were* going — and she was a bit upset about it. It was just that . . . now didn't seem like a really good time to say so.

'Well,' said Brother Michael, 'if you're going to follow me I'd better know your name . . .'

'Que Anchee, Anchee Que,' said LizAlec pulling off her heavy silver bracelet and handing it to the preacher. 'My father owns Shanghai First Orbital. See? There's his mark.' Beside her, Lars's dark eyes widened with shock, impressed despite himself. But his expression was nothing to that which crossed the impossibly handsome face of Brother Michael as he turned Anchee's bracelet over in his hand and then pocketed it.

Chapter 19

Walking Wounded

Getting into Chrysler involved submitting to a DNA test, being screened for retroVirus and undergoing a total sonic clean. And that was just the medical side of the procedure: the financial tests were much worse. Fracture, on the other hand, was simplicity itself. You just slipped the guard a hundred dead presidents and joined the queue. They didn't even charge him entry for the cat.

Finding Strat wasn't difficult either. There was a bus leaving from the entrance gate and Fixx took it. He didn't even mind that it had wheels and a human driver. As the timetable told him at least three times, using a hover was antisocial in any closed ecosystem where the ground was composed mainly of dust. And anyway, hovers were useless at going up hills and if there was one thing Fracture wasn't short of it was little feldspar-rich mountain ranges.

Zeiss wraparounds secure over his eyes, Fixx found the CasaNegro without trouble. Well, if you could call three wrong turnings and a dead end no trouble. The raytrace overlay from Routesoft that LISA fed to his wraparounds was fifty years out of date. Some of the original alleys had been blocked off, little squares had been filled in with adobe buildings and, from what Fixx could work out, one whole street had gone over the edge of a cliff ten years back in a rock slide.

And as Fixx quickly discovered there was hot and then there was trying to walk up hills in Strat where the night-time temperatures dipped to thirty degrees Centigrade if everyone got lucky. But at least no one tried to mug him and he didn't get slapped when he walked slam into a *Policia Local* while rubber-necking up the Carrer Nou, checking out the Saturday afternoon market for everything from cheap bubblesuits to an obscure remix of *SonicNRG/OrthoriT.*

'CasaNegro?' The uniformed officer looked amused. 'Left up Sant Vincent into Sant Jossep.' He paused, looking at Fixx's new clothes: Timberland Maxx, new Levi 550s and a blue cotton shirt guaranteed to repel dirt. 'Where y'hear about CasaNegro?'

Fixx shrugged and shifted Ghost up onto his shoulders. 'It got mentioned.'

'It did?' The cop grinned. 'Get back safe.'

Turning up Sant Vincent, Fixx stepped off the narrow pavement to let a wizened woman in widow's weeds stalk past, her cane tapping noisily on the dusty ground. And then stood aside again as three girls in shorts and T-shirts came pounding down the hill, long legs scattering dust as they raced past him in a jumble of dark eyes, flowing hair and smiles that said *We belong here, you don't.* One of them glanced at him as she passed and Fixx looked away, embarrassed. He didn't hear what she said but it made the other girls laugh anyway.

The reason it felt like he was being watched was because he was, Fixx realised suddenly. LISA was keeping track, following his progress from a series of m/wave pods spidered onto Fracture's glass sky. They were way too high for him to see but that meant nothing. If she wanted to, LISA could probably do everything from a quick and dirty CT-scan of his cortex to recording the fingerprints of his one good hand. The sky looked infinitely distant, blue and hot, but only the last two were real. Fixx doubted if the gap from the crater floor to the cracked sky overhead was more than a mile. Less than the height of an Earth mountain.

He was also coming round to realizing that the clumsy way Routesoft changed resolution wasn't a bug in the code, it was LISA's attempts to feed him information she thought he needed.

The feeling was kind of creepy. Especially as until then he wasn't even sure LISA knew he was still on Luna. After all, his one great love had given him twenty-four hours to get out of her virtual hair and he was currently pushing the envelope at four days. Added to which, half of him reckoned her dues had been paid when she cloaked his shuttle to let it land and then blasted it off again for him, both without clearance.

It had been up to Fixx to find his own way off the Moon when the twenty-four hours were up. He hadn't done it but then maybe she'd never expected him to. What she did do for him, though, was get rid of his original shuttle. She blew it for him, 205,000 klicks out from Darkside. A brief fireball no one noticed. Now that *was* murder, but Fixx figured he owed it to Earth not to take the risk that the shuttle was infected. Besides, where was the bio going to land it?

Back in Paris?

He'd ripped out all the streamers, trickwired the console. That way he figured the digital intelligence wouldn't know it was getting dead until the last second. Maybe it never knew. Fixx shook his head, sliding in through the CasaNegro's bead curtain. He left those kind of questions to kids like LizAlec. Late thirties was way too old to still be dealing with that *why/what/who-are-we* shit. And, anyway, he was too tired. It was time to get a beer quick, before he decided he needed something stronger.

The CasaNegro was larger than he'd expected, cleaner too. Eight or nine tables and a long bar at the far end racked up behind with dust-covered bottles. The ones that got drunk were smudged with heavy fingerprints, the others were shrouded white with grit. Above them all was a dumb sign of a neon broad who did nothing but take her bikini off and then put it back on again.

Overhead a ceiling fan thudded loud as a copter blade but did little except shuffle the hot air around. *Drink first, then think* wasn't on the level of *I think therefore I am* but it was still one of his Da's maxims, along with *Paid his taxes, died broke* . . . The prison service should have etched that on his gravestone, except they cremated him out at Kilmainham Gaol in a job lot during a typhoid wave when Fixx was fourteen.

Fixx saw Jude before she saw him. She was behind the wooden bar, mopping down its battered surface with what looked like an old T-shirt. 'Beer,' Fixx said, leaning on the bar, his elbow resting heavily on a corner of her cloth. The woman looked up in irritation and then recognized him.

'Round here we say *please*,' Jude said loudly, 'Sweedak?'

Fixx glanced round at the silent regulars, smaller than him, most of them. Weaker, too, if the wasted muscles in their arms were any clue. But they looked drunker and besides, there were way more of them.

'That so?' Putting a nervous-looking Ghost on the bar, Fixx stepped back and sketched his trademark bow, the one that once had Sydney Opera House trashing chairs in delight. Then he picked up his kitten and smiled sweetly.

'A cold beer . . . please.'

In the corner a boy laughed and Jude slammed down a cold tube. Her eyes were flat with anger and a small tic pulled at the side of her mouth. He wasn't the only one who didn't like being mocked.

The beer was some Hispanic brand Fixx had never even heard of. He took it just the same, hooked his thumb under the top and pulled it up. Ice frosted the sides of the tube. 'Open a tab,' Fixx said, pouring cold sweet beer down his throat.

Jude pointed to the sign below the neon girl which read 'No tabs, no promises, definitely no credit.' Beneath it, someone had scrawled something obscene involving MickMouse dollars.

It was Fixx's turn to shrug.

They compromised. That involved Fixx putting his platinum HKS card behind the bar, even though Jude pointed out it was useless to her unless he wanted her to sell it on to some guy who could strip out the account and run up a strictly illegal credit debt. He didn't.

'Want a drink?' Fixx asked.

Jude shook her head, flashing him a cocktail smile: one part anger, two parts contempt. 'I ain't had a drink in years,' she said flatly, her accent even thicker than back at LunaWorld. Or maybe that was just memory.

'Why you bother me?'

'LizAlec,' Fixx reminded her.

'You want know 'bout that little girl?' Only someone like Jude could describe LizAlec as little, thought Fixx, looking at the woman's broad shoulders. Most bars he knew had a step up behind the counter, to give the bar staff delusions of grandeur and keep punters in their place. Behind Jude's bar a good foot had been hacked out of the tiled floor and crudely 'creted over. And still Jude towered over everyone but Fixx.

'Yeah,' said Jude, watching his eyes check behind the bar, 'Don't want to put them off spending their money. Now you tell me 'bout that girl, 'bout your *special* friend . . .'

Fixx thought about it.

'Her name's Lady Elizabeth Alexandra Fabio,' said Fixx, watching Jude's blue eyes. Nothing, not even a flicker of recognition, but then, no surprise either. 'She got kidnapped from Arrivals Hall nearly three weeks ago. It didn't make CySat/Luna?'

Jude jerked her chin towards a group of dark-haired boys clustered round a Sonysim. Above its surface a tiny, impossibly pneumatic American schoolgirl was stripping off her cheerleader's outfit and doing something with her baton the makers hadn't intended. It was LaLa from *PsychoPopsycles*. The gameware was ten years out of date and obviously corrupted.

'Honey, it look like t'watch the newsfeed?'

Fixx had to admit it didn't. He took the fresh tube Jude offered and flipped its top. When he put it down again a small plate of almonds had materialized at his elbow.

'Synth,' Jude said curtly. 'Still, better than t'shit they feed you up at LunaWorld.'

Fixx washed away the almonds' salt taste with another tube, then shook his head when Jude offered a fourth.

'You seen her?' Fixx asked. He tried to keep his voice casual, but he wasn't fooling either of them. If she hadn't seen LizAlec then Fixx wouldn't have been there. And if Jude really had seen LizAlec then the girl was in trouble. Bad trouble. LizAlec was many things, but spoilt was the big one. When she slummed it was for a reason and CasaNegro wasn't her style.

LizAlec liked the Crash&Burn back in Bastille for the black clothes and the anorexic amphetamined-out would-be Warhols who hung out there in silence, touting old Thai RomReaders loaded up with Rambeau. Where LizAlec was concerned, not even terminal irony could excuse CasaNegro's white-washed adobe walls, its chrome jukebox and kitsch neon stripper. Hacienda Hispanic definitely wasn't her thing. Nothing but dire need would have put LizAlec through that bead-curtained door.

Of course, the real irony was that, Bastille bars apart, LizAlec's concept of living dangerously probably ended where Jude's idea of normality began.

'And the boy . . . ?' Fixx said.

Jude smiled, sketched a height line just about level with her shoulders. 'So high, matted hair, dog jaw, smelt . . .' She racked her memory for other clues. 'One lung,' she said, finally.

Fixx just looked.

'One lung,' Jude repeated. 'And a steel bottle, 'bout here.' She sketched in an imaginary shape at her side, a little above her hip. 'Sandrat, see. One flesh lung for air, one bottle for empty tunnels . . .'

'Real san'rats all dead,' interrupted a boy in combats, leaning himself against Jude's bar. Jude frowned, but said nothing. 'They're all dead,' the boy told Fixx. 'That freak was just pretending. He had two good lungs.'

Imperceptibly, Jude shook her head, disagreeing.

'And the girl with him?' Fixx asked. 'You saw her?'

The boy grinned. 'Yeah, pretty, or would be if her face was mended.' He glanced knowingly at the bruises stained yellow down one side of Fixx's face.

Fixx shook his head. 'Police,' he said, lightly touching his cheek.

The boy nodded. That was something he understood. For a second he glanced at Jude, as if wondering how far he dared go. 'I saw police this morning,' he said hesitantly. 'Looking for her . . .'

Jude was wide awake now, her lazy boredom gone the way of the act it was. 'You didn't tell me,' she said crossly.

The boy shrugged. 'You didn't ask.' That was when Fixx finally realized that Jude was the combat kid's mother.

'What did they look like?' demanded Fixx, getting his question in before Jude and Leon could start quarrelling for real. 'Japanese?'

'Nah,' the boy helped himself to a handful of dried almonds from a saucer. 'Thin guys, weird voices, both wearing . . .' He ran his hand across his front, indicating lapels.

'A suit,' said Fixx.

'If you say so . . .' Leon shrugged. 'Nasty-looking people,' he added, scooping the rest of the nuts into his filthy palm. 'Not good. They had . . .' His hands indicated a bulge under one armpit. Fixx got the message.

Chapter 20

Running the Loop of Redemption

'. . . QueCorps,' LizAlec was saying, her head bowed as she walked beside Brother Michael, the scarf still wrapped round her head. On her feet she now wore a pair of ReeGravs, small electromagnets turning on and off with the flex of each foot.

She still clanked as she walked, which Brother Michael didn't, but it was less undignified than hauling herself round corridors in free fall, which was what she'd been doing until Brother Michael told someone to find her proper shoes.

The shuttle didn't have artificial gravity.

'The holding company for Shanghai Orbital and Ford eeAsia. My father also has shares in CySat Beijing, Petronas 2Towers in KL. Oh . . .' LizAlec said, tossing in something else she remembered Anchee saying, 'and he's planning to build a health spa on Io.'

Brother Michael kept silent, but LizAlec could tell by the way he kept his step in time with hers as she clanked slowly along the corridor that she had his full attention. 'We're going to *The Arc*, aren't we?' LizAlec said.

'Is that where you want to go?'

She nodded, enthusiastically. For the briefest second, she considered telling Brother Michael everything. About the kidnapping and beating. That all she really wanted to do was get back to Paris and Fixx. But instinct told her that wasn't what the priest wanted to hear.

And the best way to handle grown-ups was to give them what they wanted: then duck and weave before they could suss

out they'd been had. It worked with her mother. Actually . . .
LizAlec paused in her stride, thinking about it: no, it didn't.
Otherwise she wouldn't have ended up at St Lucius again.
She'd still be hanging out at the Crash&Burn or Schrödinger's
Kaff trying to scam her way into Fixx's bed.

LizAlec snorted. She didn't buy into Lady Clare's reasoning
that she was getting shipped out to the new St Lucius for her
own safety. It was for her mother's convenience – that and to
get her away from Fixx – and it didn't have to be the Moon
either, there was a perfectly good St Lucius in New York.

She could have got out on a Corps Noblique passport. True,
the Reich had been closing in but even they wouldn't have dared
arrest a young girl travelling under a safe pass. Not if it was done
in front of enough cameras.

Face it, no one had shot down the Paris-St Lucius shuttle, had
they? Not after C3N had pre-broadcast its launch, stressing it was
stuffed full of kids.

'Has Paris fallen?' LizAlec demanded without thinking, her
question out of her mouth before she realized. 'A friend at
school . . .' LizAlec said hurriedly. The rest of her sentence
trailed away into embarrassed silence.

'No, not yet.' The tall priest looked thoughtful, one arm
sliding sympathetically round the girl's thin shoulders. 'You
have family in Paris?'

LizAlec shook her head hastily. 'No, my father's in Shanghai.'

'And your mother?'

LizAlec froze, suddenly realizing she knew less than nothing
about Anchee's mother. Which, when LizAlec thought about it,
told her all she needed to know. 'I don't know my mother.'

Brother Michael's smile was compassionate. 'Such is the
world . . .'

From the way his voice trailed away, LizAlec wasn't sure if he
assumed her mother was dead or just divorced. Mind you, the
Family were fundamentalist, so to Brother Michael they were
probably interchangeable.

'The boy . . . ?' Brother Michael nodded over his shoulder at Lars, who was turning somersaults along the corridor ceiling and giggling to himself. He was dribbling, too, pearl-like drops of spittle strung out from his mouth.

'He's . . .' LizAlec shrugged. She was unwilling to commit to anything Lars might later contradict but, more than that, she didn't want Brother Michael separating the two of them, not while she had that bioSemtex worm curled up inside her face.

'Lars relies on me,' LizAlec said. It was meant to sound smooth, but it came out clumsy, childlike.

The tall priest shrugged. *The Arc* didn't really need a goat boy: every simple-minded Bible-belt fanatic in the US wanted a place on board. And even Brother Michael was shocked by the number of lottery tickets the Family had sold. Humbled was the word he used, but it translated the same.

Heiresses were something different. The primal couple might be chosen by lottery to go and reclaim Eden but there was always room for another suitable handmaiden. Though it obviously depended on how the trusts were set up. It was a waste of his time to fawn over some kid who couldn't buy a set of powerblades without getting written agreement from at least two trustees.

Maybe she was being too cynical, thought LizAlec, maybe the man really was after her soul: but given the way his fingers now rested lightly on the nape of her neck, she doubted it. Cash first, LizAlec decided, and then something rather more basic.

'If we could have cabins close together?'

'Cabins?' Brother Michael asked. Beyond his shoulder, LizAlec could see Sister Rachel smile sourly.

'This is a cargo shuttle,' Brother Michael said gently. 'We have two dormitories. Men to port, women starboard, just like Noah's ark. Though I have a small prayer room, just behind the cockpit. You could sleep there, for tonight only . . .'

Very softly, one of the bodyguards shook her head; so briefly that for a second LizAlec almost thought she was imagining it.

'No,' said LizAlec. 'I'll sleep in the dorm.'

'No special treatment.' Brother Michael nodded to himself. 'Perhaps that's for the boot.'

The Arc looked like nothing so much as a fat ring-doughnut with a pen pushed through the hole in the middle. Except that, instead of just hanging there, the doughnut was attached to the pen with four vast steel spars and the ten-klick-long pen was actually the *Arc*'s spindle, capped at the top end with a vast Gothic cathedral fashioned from glass and steel.

Far down at the other end of the spindle were the computing rooms of NilApocrypha, where every word of the Old Testament was to be referenced and cross-referenced by vast banks of parallel processors. Until God's certain opinion – on everything – could be had at the click of a key. The 'southern' end was also where the shuttle was to dock, swallowed whole by an iris-ringed door in the spar.

But that wasn't what was impressive.

What impressed the fuck out of LizAlec, though she wouldn't admit it, was the doughnut itself, a fat fifty-kilometre silver ring that spun twenty times an hour around the spindle, like a vast wheel rolling around a hub.

LizAlec decided to be impressed. Anchee would have been.

'It's incredible,' she said softly.

Beside her, Brother Michael smiled.

'No,' said Brother Michael, 'it's a miracle.' The bodyguard on the other side of him sighed slightly and LizAlec realized it wasn't the first time she'd heard that line. But that didn't mean it wasn't true. To build that . . .

'It's huge,' said LizAlec. None of the newsfeeds had done *The Arc* justice in their descriptions. God, if only she had a camera. LizAlec could just imagine what CySat would pay for on-site digital grabs of the finished colony. They had shots of the squat fat drones that would haul it out into deep space and they had long-range grabs of the outside seen from Earth, from the Moon, from passing shuttles. But shots of the actual inside . . . ?

'Fabulous,' LizAlec whispered to herself, almost shivering with excitement.

'God's purpose always is.'

'How many people?' asked LizAlec.

'Just ten of us,' Brother Michael said, sounding amused. 'Sister Aaron, myself, Brother Gerard, my two protectors and five handmaidens. We tend to our hope and the world.' Brother Michael gestured towards the distant ring. 'Once the new primal couple are in place the world will be left to look after itself. Well . . .' Brother Michael smiled. 'Perhaps with a little help.'

LizAlec nodded, watching the distant ring on one screen, while on another the cargo shuttle got closer and closer to the central spar. The man was barking, certifiably mad. 'What about the animals?' LizAlec asked.

'We loaded American reptiles last month, this month it's smaller African mammals. Of course . . .' His voice sounded sad, resigned . . . 'These days it's hard to find species that aren't geneered, which means it takes us longer.' He nodded towards the hold. 'That's why we ended up having to buy those beasts from the Voertrekkers. But then, we don't want sheep that produce human milk, or rice that cooks itself. We want what God intended . . .'

Which counted *her* out, LizAlec thought darkly. Though how right she was LizAlec didn't yet know. The product of an inactivated clone and frozen sperm, especially one whose cortex was overrun with bioClay symbiote, wasn't what the Family had in mind. As for being the daughter of Alex Gibson . . . The girl shivered and turned her attention back to the screen. However hard she tried, she couldn't take in the size of that spinning wheel.

'Here,' Brother Michael said. 'Let me.' He leant across, his shoulder just brushing her front as he opened a distant window. That is, he hit a key that activated a camera floating by itself in space, ten klicks distant. If LizAlec didn't know better, she'd have thought it part of some defence system.

She'd have liked to have seen *The Arc* for real, with her own eyes. But radiation was too much of a problem to allow random use of window glass, even the toughened stuff. And the other alternatives were too expensive for a mere shuttle.

'You can see the ring better from the cathedral,' Brother Michael told her. 'It has shielded glass.' His hands rested lightly on the console, tapping at an occasional key, but he wasn't actually docking the ship himself. A semi-AI was taking them in, LEDs on the deck lighting as retros fired in turn to slow the shuttle even further.

Ahead of the shuttle, a vast circle opened like an eye widening with surprise and the shuttle flew through it into darkness, lights immediately flicking on around them as booms moved out to steady and then hold the ship. That was what the apparently random splatter of diodes had been talking about.

Except the optics flashing like tiny electronic fireflies were anything but random. Fixx could have told LizAlec that . . . Look long enough and you'll always find the pattern. And even though it might be chaotic, fractal or crypted within itself, the pattern is always there.

Always.

Anchee, Que . . . Quiet, intelligent, polite . . . Outstanding SATS . . . Unquestionably rich in her own right . . . So far so good. What wasn't was the lack of visual confirmation that the girl he was holding was indeed the General's daughter.

Not one current tri-D, no digital grabs, no pix of any sort . . . Sitting in his darkened vestry, tucked away in a corner of the cathedral, Brother Michael decided he could cope with the irritating time/distance lag induced by accessing a cuts library in Los Angeles: it was the lack of photographs that was beginning to concern him.

Of course, had he been Anchee's father he'd have done exactly the same. Ring-fenced her from paparazzi, made sure no one knew what she looked like and let slip dark hints about what was likely to happen to Ishies who tried to find out. It was a sinful world, full of misguided people.

Something more concrete than threats were in place too, they'd have to be. Anchee's father would have bodyguards, self-covering contracts. Of course, the man would have a family clone somewhere on ice, but to need a clone was a sign of family failure and it didn't seem like the General would be happy with that idea.

Brother Michael shivered. It was *possible* that the girl had run away, but unlikely. And yet, if she hadn't run off what was she doing stowed away on an *Arc*-bound shuttle? The question was impossible to answer without more information, and nagging at the problem didn't make it better.

All recorded information was automatically out of date, that was obvious. The used-news value of information fell rapidly from gold dust to worthless. Only the word of God never corrupted. Even so, there should be news somewhere of Anchee's disappearance. Brother Michael was paying through the nose for a commercial search that was thorough, up to the minute and, most of all, breathtakingly discreet. And all the agency could come back with was nothing.

Europe he could have understood: after all, the Azerbaijani virus had more or less bombed it back to the Stone Age. But Shanghai produced no news and nor did Los Angeles, and the Web infrastructure was working fine for both. Brother Michael had had that checked, adding to his already astronomical bill.

So where were the rumours that Anchee had vanished? Or had her father locked down even conspiracy theories harder than ice? That might be possible: he owned large chunks of CySat eeAsia and a whole provider network in Western China.

Maybe it was stupid to expect to find news of Anchee's escape from school.

'Orange juice.' Brother Michael tossed the words out, as if to an angel at his shoulder, knowing it would be heard. One of the handmaidens would find the oranges, pulp them in the way he liked them pulped and then come creeping into the vestry to bring him a juice bladder and his straw. That was what the handmaidens were there for. Well, one of the things. With luck it would be Sarah. He liked the way she kept her pale eyes carefully lowered when she was around him. Or Anne maybe, little Annie Van Hoek, heir to the bioSemtex manufacturing arcology in Montana. She'd been a catch. No trustees, direct control of her own shares: without Annie Van Hoek and her explosives *The Arc* could never have been built.

It was strange, all those little rich girls with empty heads and aching voids where their souls should have been. So desperate a hunger for love and truth, so little need for the funds and platinum cards that saw them through the choppy waters of early adolescence.

All waiting, just for him. It was magnificent, but then God's will always was. Once, years back, Brother Michael had gone though torment trying to distinguish between divine intent and his own wishes. In fact, there had even been a time before that when his thirst for God had been a sham. A hollow vessel, all sound and fury signifying nothing. But then, in the overheated, stinking cell of a 4x6 lockdown at Rikers, he'd met the Padre, 200lb of oiled muscle and iron will.

No one touched the Padre. Not the Latino gangs, not the Chink data runners hooked into Rikers out of mah-jong dives on Chatham Square, not even the banged-up Viet street soldiers with their fussy haircuts and dragon tattoos. Even the sodding Aryan brotherhood didn't trouble the Padre. The only one to try had ended up with a shank rammed where God doesn't go. His own shank, all of it: crudely ground blade *and* handle fashioned from molten toothbrushes.

Locked down in a cell with the Padre, Michael Howell had two options: convert or get stamped. Brother Michael converted, taking the cheap paper Bible from the Padre's fat fingers. He read it, like he was told to, page by aching page.

There was nothing else it was good for. The pages were printed paper, nothing fancy like those nanite Korans that wrote the sacred words on each opening page. And the paper was polymer-coated, impregnated with nauseant. So there was no point ripping out the pages, even if he'd had any skag to roll in them, which he hadn't. No skag and no blow: the Padre had taxed his last little ball of resin the moment the screws pushed Michael through the door.

Besides, the Padre would have felt bad if Michael had defaced the word of God, no matter how cheaply printed. So Michael read the book, and as long as he was reading it the Padre let him be. He read it straight through, finger limping along the sentences, tongue stumbling over the odd names, the weird-shit families, the blinding strangeness of a world with no automobiles or CySatTV. Stumbling over the oddness of God's sense of humour.

And then Michael read it again, more slowly, following the twists in the plot, egging on the good guys. The guy writing it didn't do a good description of the weapons at the fall of Jericho, but Michael knew just what he was talking about. The warders had trashed Block 3 using a borrowed NVPD sonic gun, taking out the Islams. Half the ragheads in Rikers still had their eardrums blown.

The third time Michael picked up the book and started over on Genesis, the Padre took the holy book out of Michael's hands and made him kneel on the lockdown floor, right down there on the sticky tiles. When he stood up, Michael was a fully fledged member of the Brotherhood of God's Word in the Desert, licensed to perform marriage in five different states, eligible for zero tax rating (not that he'd ever paid tax, except city tax when he couldn't avoid it).

He was authorized to take handmaidens, too, young girls for whom suitable husbands could not be found. 'Suitable' meant devout, and devout was in short supply unless you included the Latinos with all their gold and fancy titles.

No, back then the Brotherhood was a simple religion, a poor religion. The Padre didn't like the incense and statues of the United Papacy, but he liked the Church of Christ Geneticist even less. The Messiah wasn't to be rushed into being by overpaid scientists: He'd come again when He was ready, in His own sweet time.

As for science itself, Michael found it was hard to argue with the Padre's belief that if God had wanted the world different then He'd have built it different.

But sometimes – of course – you had to compromise. Building big in space was next to impossible if you left nanetics out of the equation.

O'Neills and ring colonies needed to be grown, though no one had yet built a ring colony *quite* like this one. Dyson spheres would need growing too, when anyone hacked the maths, though Brother Michael wasn't too sure how he felt about throwing up a shell right around some sun to trap its light. That seemed like arrogance – for humanity to change the face of heaven, even if it was only to darken the light of one star.

Five and a half years now separated Brother Michael from Rikers Island. Sixty-six sweat-filled months in which he laboured to release the vision he'd seen the night D Block burnt to the ground. In the midst of a riot, while blood sluiced down half-gutters let into the white-tiled corridors and flames licked spray-gunned polymer off the walls, Brother Michael stood on the melting roof and dreamed his dream.

Life was corrupted. The howls of the Aryan Nation, the shrieks of screws as they were tipped over the edge and died on the net below: they all said the same. (The net was designed to catch anyone thrown into the stairwell, but the Padre had wired the net to an industrial generator to produce not so much an electric chair as a vast electric bed.)

The Earth was due to be cleansed. And he, Brother Michael,

was to build the new arc. No simple flood would be enough this time, it would have to be fire, Brother Michael was certain of it. Nothing else would have the cleansing power. But he would be gone before the conflagration started.

For a prison designed to withstand riot, siege and flame, Rikers Island burnt beautifully, flames licking round Brother Michael like a wall of fire. And when the NYPD lifted him off the burning roof, his eyes were turned not to his rescuers, brave though they were, but to the smoky heavens.

It wasn't Brother Michael's intention that his howl of prophecy should be caught by a circling CySat Sikorsky 'copter, or that CySatC3N bounced that grab of him naked and howling to every one of their US syndicated newsfeeds. By the time a NY Correctional Department official went Webside to stress that Brother Michael was insane, it was already too late. Thirty-two per cent of the US thought he was inspired directly by God.

Money poured in. In Seattle a fifth-generation silicon heiress donated her entire fortune. A bible-belt farmer with 200 draught-blasted acres donated his entire lottery win. Like it or not, *The Arc* was already a reality in most people's minds.

'Orange,' demanded Brother Michael crossly: he wasn't used to having to ask twice. In fact, it upset him more than was rational. But then, rationality was over-used and anyway was merely an adjunct of agnosticism. Pushing himself out of his chair, Brother Michael strode once round the small vestry and ended up at a simple wool-covered sofa, wrapping a belt over his lap to keep him in place. This would have to do . . .

A door clanged and he saw flickering strip lights stutter shadows on the white vestry walls. A wiring fault in the light outside, he'd have it seen to in the morning. It was Rachel, that much was obvious from the hesitant steps through the gloom towards him. Five months on *The Arc* and the stupid girl still couldn't get the hang of ReeGravs.

Sweet Jesus . . . Brother Michael clicked his fingers and all the lights came up but the olive-skinned girl didn't increase her speed. She was too afraid of tripping. Long black hair framed Rachel's face, reaching almost to her thin waist. Only the lumbering hips spoilt the promise of her waist and full breasts: something she'd always known, mainly because her father had never let her forget. In her hands she held a shimmering flask of silver fabric filled with pulped orange. At the bottom was a strip of velcro and from its top protruded a simple straw.

'I've brought fresh juice . . .' She watched Brother Michael bite back some unkind remark and instantly felt sick. If he'd shouted at her, that would have been good. If he'd raised his hand to her, that would have been better. She was used to that. It was his strained patience that Rachel couldn't stand.

'Come here,' Brother Michael patted the space beside him.

'I have tasks . . .' Rachel tried to make her voice sound firm, but she never managed it like the other girls did; her words just came out sounding sullen and petulant.

'Here.' Brother Michael patted the seat again, waiting for her to obey. His brown eyes stared at her, peering deep into Rachel's soul until the woman reddened and glanced hurriedly away.

'How are you?' Brother Michael asked.

'Fine . . .'

'Really?' The man nodded towards the arm of the woollen sofa, watching while Rachel pushed the flask into the cloth, velcro locking the flask safely into place. 'Are you sure? You seem uneasy.'

Uneasy! Rachel's mouth set into a thin line.

'We need to pray,' announced Brother Michael firmly, reaching out for her hand.

'Your juice . . .'

'God comes first,' said Brother Michael, looking serious. 'You know that.' And then, deciding his reply wasn't sufficient, he smiled his most winning smile, the one that had brought Rachel Cargassi to him in the first place. 'Besides,' he said, 'what's my thirst, compared to your happiness, compared to the health of your soul?'

There was no answer. There wasn't meant to be.

Rachel looked at her tormentor, at the silver dusting of age that touched his temples, at the deep egg-speckled eyes. The man was handsome, as silver-tongued as the devil and as over-powering as incense. Power oozed out of him the way that sour ghosts of fear oozed from everybody else on *The Arc*.

Even the skin of his instantly recognizable face was an elegant contradiction, soft but weather-beaten at the same time. Most people still had some cosmetic treatment, usually in the early teens when such things started to matter. Rachel knew all about that. Her hips were beyond rebuilding, a deep genetic flaw put there by her father's refusal to let her mother get the embryo tested.

As for her face, she'd tried five different clinics before she was happy. Four Bupex and finally one black clinic in Budapest that stripped off her old face and then reformatted it using fresh tissue. Rachel didn't know where her new face had come from: she didn't want to know. She just knew she liked it and had no intention of giving it back.

Brother Michael clicked his fingers again and the lights in the vestry dipped back into gloom. One elegantly manicured finger brushed over a datapad set into the arm of his sofa and the nearby window exploded into an array of pale blue as Sister Rachel looked out at the curve of the distant Earth. Space would be clear as ice and black beyond imagining once they had left the planets behind. That Brother Michael had promised her.

'Kneel,' Brother Michael demanded and Rachel knelt: not on both knees as she had been taught as a child but with one knee raised the way people prayed in zero gravity, so that a boot could remain flush with the floor, its sole locked to the deck.

Almost casually, Brother Michael gripped Rachel's narrow shoulders and repositioned her so that she knelt directly in front of him. His knees shut around her raised leg and his hands reached for her head.

Brother Michael's study was a zero-gravity habitat, but that wasn't why Rachel adopted that posture. It was the Brother-hood's trade mark, literally. Lawyers had tied it down on all seven continents, not to mention on Planetside, but then, every-thing was franchised or trademarked up there. Rachel should have known: through proxies she'd owned three of Luna's more valuable ad agencies before she'd bequeathed them to Brother Michael.

Prayer with Brother Michael was silent. Or rather, the congre-gation stayed silent while Brother Michael spoke: sometimes to them and sometimes to God, but mostly to himself.

Hands now rested on the sides of Rachel's head, fingers lightly caressing her long hair. When she'd arrived at *The Arc*, Rachel had wanted to crop her hair short but it hadn't been allowed. As Brother Michael had pointed out, her raven-black hair was the one really beautiful thing about her.

Rachel tried not to stiffen her shoulders as his fingers began to knead out their knots of muscle, all the while bending Rachel further, moving her head towards his robed lap. She could smell him through the rough cloth. An earth-like odour mixed with urine. All men were the same, she decided. At least, all the ones she'd met in her twenty-three years. But then, that wasn't many, as even Rachel was prepared to admit.

'Pray,' said Brother Michael, pressing on the back of her head.

She could feel him, swollen beneath the cloak, his hands pushing her face further into his lap. He'd keep pushing, too, until she did what he wanted, Rachel knew that. It was *her* choice, the other handmaidens had made that clear right at the start. She could almost suffocate against the cloth of his lap as Brother Michael prayed fiercely over her head. Or she could soothe him, the way David soothed the wild tumult of Saul.

Rachel did what Brother Michael wanted, accepting the inevi-table. She was getting good at that, Rachel told herself bitterly. She wouldn't cry, though. Not now, not ever . . .

Sliding Brother Michael's robe over his knees and up around

his waist, Rachel bent her head and prayed. Above her, Brother Michael groaned and began to pray even more fervently, his words spilling out into the silence of his starlit vestry.

The other handmaidens had tried to tell Rachel how to grip so he couldn't fill her mouth entirely. And how to use her tongue and sucking to speed up his release. Rachel tried: every time she was called to pray she tried to remember. And always she gave up, letting Brother Michael push her up and down into his lap.

His words were a litany now, a high complex song that spun up to the cold waiting stars. But Rachel couldn't hear any of it: she was trying to breathe. And then he was shouting, his hands tight around her head as he pumped wet salt into the back of her throat. Rachel swallowed. She had to, she wanted to breathe.

And then it was over, Brother Michael's hands lifting her head away from his lap to push his gown back into position. They stood after that, his hands on her shoulders as unsmiling eyes stared deep into her. Whatever he saw there he was satisfied.

Fear, probably, Rachel thought bitterly.

'Go with God.' He said it dismissively, fingers already flicking over the sofa's data panel, closing down the ice-cold array of heaven. Brother Michael waited until Rachel had reached the door before calling her back, pointing to his juice flask. 'Take that away. Oh . . .' He paused, watching her shoulders stiffen and seeing the tendons stand out at the back of her bowed head. There was, he had to admit, something about this one that brought out the worst in him.

'Bring me fresh juice before you go to your bed . . .'

Lars watched in disgust. Although it was disgust tinged with fascination. So this was Brother Michael, the new Noah. He smiled, not kindly, and shuffled backwards, then flipped himself round and ran on his hands and knees down an air vent. He loved being in zero G, it was even better than being on the Moon. But he was training himself to handle gravity, too.

Originally he'd been assigned to the men's dorm. But Brother

Robert was the only man there was and he didn't want Lars around, not with the sandrat's muttering and sour animal stink. So Lars bedded down in the goat pen.

Tomorrow the goats would be released into one of the Valleys – or so Rachel said – but tonight they provided him with warmth and company. And none of them complained when he unscrewed a panel and vanished for a few hours into the security of the tunnels.

The goat pen was all right, little more than ten paces by ten paces, but the dorm had horrified him, going on into the distance like a great circular emptiness. Nothing but echoing space and curved walls so big that the far side was almost a blur.

Lars didn't know it and he wasn't interested enough to find out, but the dorm was a roofed-off segment near the outer end of a four-kilometre spar, which gave the dorm its own gravity, though obviously not quite as much as in the ring itself. And it wasn't real gravity, of course. But centrifugal force gave a good-enough illusion of gravity to be gratefully accepted by the human mind.

The doughnut ring didn't need a central spindle. Why should it, when the ring just hung in space and there was nothing to stop it revolving around its own empty centre? In the same way, there was nothing to stop cargo shuttles docking alongside the ring instead of at the southern end of the spindle. At a speed of one revolution every twenty seconds, any decent pilot could dock without trouble; while to a semiAI or bio it would be less than nothing, a mere subset of a subroutine.

But Brother Michael had wanted a traditional wheel-of-life design. Or so Lars gathered, the way he gathered most news, by listening at grilles or hiding in air vents. The only problem for Lars was that the gravity on the station was fucked. Try as he might, Lars couldn't get a mental fix on what was *up* and what counted as *down*, mainly because it kept changing.

When he was in the spindle, then 'up' was North, towards the cathedral, and that was the way the lifts travelled. But if he was in one of the four spars that rotated around the spindle, then 'up' was towards the spindle and 'down' was towards the giant doughnut. At least, that was the way gravity worked, getting stronger the further down he went.

Lars hadn't been out to the doughnut yet, because it wasn't allowed. And besides, that was where the mad lady lived, except thatRachel'sfriendRuthsaidshewassleeping.Whenthedoughnutwas finished and the animals were all in place, it would be possible for them to start walking straight ahead and then keep going until they came back to where they'd started, two days later, having walked right round the whole *Arc*.

Lars wasn't sure he believed it. In fact, he wasn't going to believe it until he'd done it for himself. He didn't tell Ruth that, though. He liked her too much. At first, before he'd seen Brother Michael praying over Rachel, Lars had thought Ruth must be upset not to get called to pray as often as the others: but when he suggested that, Ruth just smiled sourly and flashed him a lopsided grin.

'No,' she'd said, patting Lars on the arm. 'I'm lousy at pray-ing. My teeth are too big and I'm clumsy, very clumsy.' Lars wasn't muddled by that any more. Not now, not any longer. He knew just what she was talking about. In fact, Lars reckoned that Brother Michael was a man who had his shit seriously together . . . To use the words of Ben, whose head was now probably just slop in a bucket of slime.

All the same, as Lars scuttled rat-like down the air vent back to the warmth and friendship of the goat pen he wondered what LizAlec would do when Brother Michael called on her to pray.

Chapter 21

Identity/Crisis

Letting the self-cleaning neoprene hose slide back into its mounting, Brother Michael adjusted his cassock and pulled down the panel that launched his office. He'd taken the Sunday-morning communion, presided at breakfast and confessed two of the handmaidens. He was exhausted.

Diodes winked as the flatscreen picked up where he'd left off the night before, pulling up a visual link to the now-empty women's dormitory. Angrily, the priest hit a key and broke the link. The whole *Arc* was wired for sight, both infrared and m/wave, but he didn't want the distraction.

Built into the flap was a neat fold-up keyboard. It had touch-sensitive keys, floating track ball and an input socket for Zeiss wraprounds in case the user was working on something too confidential to be accessed on open screen. The office had tri-D capacity, too – as well as a Sony neural link – and the whole thing had been bought by mail order from a Virgin MegaStore: only Brother Michael didn't approve of bioClay implants and unfortunately he'd never learned to use a deck, at least not properly. But this wasn't a message one of the girls could key-up for him.

He couldn't trust them not to talk.

The screen cleared and a tiny smiling bot asked Brother Michael if he wanted to create a new visual of himself or use the vActor file already in memory. He chose the file. An ex-MGM/UA programmer in Burbank had coded it for him – and it had to be one of the few vActors around that showed its proprietor as less attractive than he really was.

Early on, Brother Michael had discovered that while Central Asian zaibatsu khans liked ostentation, most Chinese zaibatsu grandees considered the West's obsession with mere surface to be shallow, which it was. (Bizarre as it seemed, *face* was actually about what went on under the skin.) He'd also realized that many West Coast Americans were only happy if they were physically the most attractive party in any deal. And so Brother Michael looked less good on screen than he did in life.

It saved him millions. For a start it meant the Californians he went up against weren't trying to screw him because of his good looks, and the Japanese and East Coast Chinese regarded him as more than a mere lightweight.

Which was good policy. At least, Brother Michael thought so. Not least because it had given rise to the myth of his personal magnetism. Every C3N journalist, every CySat power suit he'd come into direct contact with had gone away to spread stories about how magnetic, attractive and spiritually powerful Brother Michael was when you met him face to face.

Excellent surgery, a basic knowledge of the human psyche, Sister Aaron's side interest in pheromones and an understanding that to err might be human but that most people wanted someone to admire had taken Brother Michael from a forty-three-second picture grab to a role as the new Messiah.

Whether or not Sister Aaron and he would actually go with *The Arc* to act as angels was a question exercising every station from CySat's award-winning *MyGod* to the pirate evangelists of Mongolia. And Brother Michael had to say, quite honestly, that the real answer was – he hadn't the faintest . . . What he did know was that Sister Aaron was determined to travel with *The Arc* and letting her leave would be like losing part of himself. Besides, part of him wanted to leave behind the corrupted cities and launch into the cleansing vastness of space.

The priest smiled, watching his reflection in the screen like an overlay on the more homely vActor beneath. *Corrupted cities, the cleansing vastness of space* . . . He couldn't help it. The simple sentence constructions, the dramatic cadences of speech he'd once found so difficult now came to him like second nature.

There'd been a voice coach in Des Moines, but he was dead now. Come to that, so was the MGM coder who'd constructed the vActor. The guards who'd held him in lock-down at Rikers were also gone, those who'd survived the riot. Doing the Lord's work was sometimes a bloody and frightening business, but then, even the simplest reading of the Old Testament told you that.

Brother Michael couldn't say he liked the new girl. There was a darkness behind her violet eyes and she held her body awkwardly, as if she was unhappy with who she was. The way she hunched forward suggested her changing body made her uncomfortable, and not just physically. And as for that hand she kept folded across her stomach . . . There was a violence about her too, an ungodliness.

All in all, decided Brother Michael, she'd be difficult to integrate with the other handmaidens. Which left him with two choices: to drop her quietly into space, or return her to a sender who might or might not be pleased to get her back.

The bracelet was real enough, though. The five-clawed celestial dragon circling a poppy *mon* had been on the battle flags of the General's army. And now the bracelet circled Brother Michael's wrist, dark and ancient. It was too big, too heavy and it hit against the keyboard when Brother Michael tried to key in instructions, but he was still reluctant to take it off.

He would have to, though, and sooner than he wanted. Sister Aaron had woken up from one of her periodic beauty-enhancing naps in cryo and found out about the bracelet from *The Arc*'s AI. Now she wanted it for herself. He'd give it to Sister Aaron, too. At a price . . . And the price would be her. It always was.

Brother Michael pulled the heavy silver circle off his wrist and put it by the keyboard. He might be tired, but he was never too tired to take what Sister Aaron only ever offered reluctantly. All the same, he made a mental note to swallow

L'Argenine, sildenafil citrate and yohimbe before taking Sister Aaron the silver bracelet.

On Brother Michael's screen was a grab of Anchee Que's father, dressed in khaki uniform and staring hard at the cameraman, an Ishie probably. No one else would be insane enough to go after General Que. Brother Michael stared at the man's face but there was nothing there to indicate anything but fury at being caught on camera. Still, contacting him had to be worth a try.

Brother Michael would keep the mutant boy, though. It hadn't escaped Brother Michael's notice how well Lars handled the animals and how much better natured Rachel was when the boy was around. Rachel and a sandrat . . . Sweet Jesus, it hurt just to imagine what their offspring would look like. So much so, it was almost worth breeding them to find out.

In the end, Brother Michael cancelled his vActor and sent the message as ASCII text, pure and simple, tagging on a videograb of himself as a file attachment. He didn't bother to crypt the message, since there was no need to disguise where it came from. And he didn't bother to make himself less attractive. Let the old bastard realize the temptations his precious daughter faced. From what Brother Michael had heard about the grand Shanghai families he'd feel obliged to have her returned, even if he then stripped the skin off her back with a whip.

Brother Michael would have liked to have kept the girl himself. But she was too big, too dangerous a prize even for him. This way was better.

Besides, it wasn't a kidnapping and Brother Michael wasn't demanding a ransom for her return, merely suggesting a donation to the Brotherhood might be in order for the trouble they'd taken to ensure the girl's well-being.

It didn't reach the desk of Anchee's father, not at first and not for a while. Nothing did without first being filtered: And the semiTuring that plucked Brother Michael's message from the in-basket would tie up its not-too-sophisticated MS OfficeSoft neural net for half a day, trying to balance the contents of Brother Michael's message against St Lucius's weekly update that reported Anchee happy and healthy. At the end of twelve hours it passed the problem up one Turing level to Mencius, the General's house AI, and promptly forgot about the problem. The AI put out an all-points call for the General's pet ballerina and then promptly did the same.

Chapter 22

Nerves of Steel

Jude stank of dried sweat. Mind you, Fixx probably smelt too, the erstwhile media star reminded himself. Ghost certainly did, of God knew what but Fixx could smell the kitten from where he stood at a half-shuttered window, staring intently through its gap into the narrow dusty street beyond. On the house opposite a fat iridescent gecko was glued to the whitewashed wall, half in daylight, half hidden in shade. Every so often the lizard leant forward and tongue-whipped a fly stupid enough to get too close.

The kitten wanted the gecko: it just couldn't work out how to spring the trap.

'Handy for every occasion,' announced the box as Fixx grabbed another tissue. He tossed box and tissue into the bin. It had been two days since he'd last had a pressure shower and body wipes just didn't do the job, whatever they told you. What Fixx really wanted to do was clean himself off, but he didn't want to ask in case Jude couldn't spare the water.

Fixx smiled and stretched lazily. It was amazing what sex could do to improve a situation. He'd come into the CasaNegro prepared to nanchuk it up, if that's what it took to get the information he needed. Now he didn't even want to waste the woman's water. Not without paying, anyway.

'Hey,' said Fixx, turning back from the window to stare at Jude. 'You got a water shower that works?'

Jude rolled over and smiled, half happy, half mocking. 'Oh sweet honey. You t'k you finished . . . ?'

Fixx grinned and moved back to the wooden bed, hand reaching for a full breast, resting metal fingers softly on its dark nipple, feeling it swell and grow taut. Electric sensors beneath his organic polymer skin relayed sensations of softness back to his brain.

He rolled on top of her, and then laughed as she rolled on top of him. Her full breasts felt good to Fixx so he kept on caressing them and playing with her nipples, and then he did it some more.

'Hey,' Jude said sulkily, 'You going t'roll that between your fingers all day?' She took Fixx's wrist and moved his hand down her body until he could reach between her legs. She was big. Not fat, just big. Nipples thick as thumbs, heavy breasts that one hand alone had no hope of cupping. Strong arms and heavy fists that looked like they could crack heads the way other people opened eggs.

Her thighs and legs he knew all about. When they'd reached round him earlier it had been like being gripped by steel.

'Geneered,' said Jude as she watched him examine her body. 'Class geneering and a good full-gravity gym.'

Fixx nodded, looking up at her. Since he'd done a Tetsuo, he'd got so used to dwarfing his partners that it felt good to be fucking someone his own size, like he didn't have to hold back. Fixx slid his hand out from beneath Jude's legs and reached for a can of Electric Soup.

Jude laughed. But then she'd laughed back at the beginning when Fixx had pulled a can out of her fridge and began to check its label. And she'd laughed again when he had loaded twenty neon-hued tubes into a crate and lugged it to her bedroom at the back of the bar.

She'd listed the ingredients for Fixx. Not that he'd believed her, at least not to start with. He did now, though. One look at the luminous edges to her velvet breasts told Fixx that it wasn't just ethanol wreaking havoc with his synapses. And the problem was, stripped naked she looked like some vast Greek statue while he looked like some bit-part Tetsuo. Two false legs and one false arm grafted onto a body minced to gristle by a car bomb. Which all seemed cool with Jude, but didn't change the fact the Fixx had started to hate his own reflection.

She didn't mind that he was a patchwork quilt of hues and textures. That his legs and right arm were obviously, intentionally synthetic. That the black of their wafer-thin vat-grown skin clashed with the pale white of his chest and belly. In remaking himself to be seen on stage, dressed up in a cloak and surrounded by a swirling sublimating fog of liquid nitrogen, he'd been concentrating on what looked good on vid. And what looked slick as all shit on screen didn't necessarily look that hot up close.

Hell, he should have got clone-grown new limbs and had a traditional transplant, or just Soul Chipped himself and risked a total reclone. He could have afforded it, even without his 1stVirtual insurance policy. It was time he fucking faced facts. Getting Tetsuoed up had been a lousy long-term call.

Rolling himself on top, Fixx forgot all about clinics and bad decisions, letting one hand trail gently down her body. Jude was swollen, wet and beginning to get sore: after three bouts of full-on fucking she couldn't really be much else. Taking care, Fixx eased his index finger into her, curling his hand so that it cupped the top of her vulva, its heel pressing onto her hooded clitoris. He could feel it like a small bead, rolling beneath his touch. Slowly, very slowly, he moved the finger buried inside her, not in and out like some schoolboy, but side to side in slow rolls that pressed first one side and then the other.

Jude shut her eyes and groaned.

Fixx smiled to himself. At thirty-six it was ridiculous to still be so pleased when things worked out in bed, but that didn't mean he wasn't. Pulling back his hand, Fixx swapped wet finger for thumb, sliding that deep into Jude instead, feeling her muscles close tight around its base.

And then, with the freed finger, he reached down between

Jude's buttocks. The woman's eyes opened wide as Fixx found the swollen starfish of her anus. But Fixx just grinned and Jude shifted her hips to let his damp finger reach the ring of puckered muscle. Round and then stop, round and then stop, his thumb moving gently inside her all the time, feeling the puffy, sticky, swollen floor of her vagina.

'Hey, who you b'n practising this with?' Jude demanded, rocking her hips, vulva tightening round the base of his thumb every time his finger trailed gently over her anus.

Fixx grinned, kept quiet. The true answer was that he'd learnt it so far back he couldn't remember. Keeping his hand there, Fixx lifted his lips from her soft mouth and smoothed them down her body, stopping to bite softly into the underside of a breast, tasting sweat, before reaching round to close his teeth on her nipple.

Jude shuddered.

'And this you didn't learn with anyone either?' Her voice was warm, but something in it said she didn't believe him and she was right not to. That one he'd been taught by a woman twelve years older than him. She taught music at Juilliard and at twenty-eight she'd seemed so adult to Fixx he couldn't imagine ever getting that old. Couldn't imagine what it was like to be that grown up. Now he was older than she'd been then – and he still didn't know.

Slipping his mouth down from Jude's heavy breast, Fixx traced a line with his tongue back to her stomach and down between her opening legs. If there was one thing the music mistress at Juilliard had taught Fixx, it was to taste his partners full on, head buried deep between their thighs, not lap at them sideways like some nervous cat at the cream. That was what she'd told him and no one since had contradicted her. Shifting himself on Jude's vast wooden bed, he sunk his head between her thighs, pushing her knees back to open her out to him.

She tasted of salt, acid and alkaline at the same time – sex cocktail – her juices and his mixed from their earlier bouts.

Fixx used his tongue to trace up one side of her vulva, tongue just missing her swollen clitoris before tracing down through the sodden fur of the other lip. Jude pushed her hips up crossly, but Fixx kept the circle going, never quite touching her clitoris. He knew just what she wanted. It was what he wanted, too. To thrust his tongue deep inside her, so far that his jaw hurt and his lips got bruised as she ground up against him. But he wasn't going to, not yet.

Instead Fixx licked gently one more time around the outer lips and then used his tongue to peel aside her inner labia, finishing with the lightest flick of his tongue. Jude jumped and grabbed his head, pulling it hard against her. She was opened right out, vulva swollen with hunger.

Fixx sunk his finger deep into her anus. Jude stopped dead, so Fixx brushed his lower lip up across the exposed pink pearl of her clitoris and Jude jerked back into life again as Fixx sunk his thumb slowly into her cunt, squeezing the floor of her vagina against the walls of her anus, feeling the hard thud of her pulse in the flesh trapped between his finger and thumb.

'Sweet Jesus,' Jude said plaintively

Fixx smiled and then he was pulling finger and thumb out of her and kneeling between her knees and kissing her hard, all the while knowing she could taste herself on his lips. And as Jude's arms came up to lock round his shoulders, he sunk slowly into her and then pulled out. Going in again harder, for the pleasure of feeling her tighten.

Jude's legs snaked over the back of his legs, locking her hips against his. It was hard and vicious, her arms wrapped so tight around him that the pressure squashed her breasts almost flat as she rolled her full hips up into him, time and again. She was gasping with the effort, growling in his ear. And then she was done, tipped over the edge in a muffled groan, her vagina rippling in a long roll that tailed away into an after-echo of sudden jerks and tiny spasms.

'All done?' Fixx asked Jude as she unlocked her arms and

sprawled back on the bed's grey foam slab. The woman grinned, her face, breasts and stomach varnished with sweat. She stank of everything he liked. They should have used latex, but Fixx didn't have any spray and Jude hadn't volunteered any of her own.

'Yeah,' said Jude, looking up at him. 'I'm finished.' Her smile twisted slightly and the expression that crossed her wide face was half resigned, half sad. 'Now I s'pose you want to talk about where t'girl went . . . ?'

'No,' said Fixx, pulling out of Jude. 'Not yet, I got something to finish.'

He rolled Jude over so she lay face down on the mattress. Her blonde hair splayed forward on the bed, her breasts bulging taut at the side, light though her weight was in one-sixth G.

Pulling himself up on his arms, Fixx positioned himself above Jude's buttocks and reached down to guide himself. Jude went utterly still, gecko-like and watchful. She didn't push her bum up against him as he pushed gently against her, and she didn't twist away: she just waited. For a second, Fixx considered it and then decided not. After all, this was more or less a first date.

Shifting slightly, he slid himself into her vulva instead, feeling her buttocks push up to meet him. The force of his hips as they came down on her curved bottom rocked Jude forward on her bed, sending tiny shockwaves up the skin of her back. And then Fixx was pounding into her, all subtlety forgotten as he ploughed himself against her behind, driving Jude further and further up the mat, until at last she reached out her hands and pressed them flat against the wall, holding herself in place.

Fixx could feel his heartbeat spiral up over 120bpm, basic techno, as sweat ran down the inside of his arms. Reaching under her with both hands, Fixx worked his fingers between mattress and flesh until he rested on his knuckles, his fingers twisted hard around her soft nipples.

Blood pumped like thunder in his ears as Jude shook and moaned under his thrusts, her whole back stiff with shock each time he entered her. And then Fixx got lucky. Because it certainly wasn't judgement that timed his spasm just as he'd buried himself to the hilt in her sweat-slicked body. Hands that had been grasping her breasts ripped free and Fixx grabbed her shoulders tight, still pulling himself into her long after the spasms were gone.

'Honey,' Jude's voice was wondering, 'You sure did need that . . .'

Collapsed along her broad back, Fixx nodded. Yeah, he had, it was years, maybe even a decade since he'd had a straight-forward, no-holds-barred animal fuck. It wasn't bought, it wasn't earned and it certainly hadn't been down to who he was or even who he'd once been. It was just sex.

The first Fixx knew something was wrong was when Jude stiffened. Her face tightened and Fixx realized she was no longer there in the room with him. Every scrap of her attention was focused on the other side of that bar room door.

'What is it?' Fixx asked. He was whispering, without even knowing why.

'Listen,' said Jude and Fixx did, unable to hear anything. A split second later he realized that was the point, but by then Jude was already pulling a cotton dress over her head, smoothing the creased material down round her bare hips.

'Wait,' said Jude and was gone, shutting the door on Fixx before he had time to protest. He could hear her outside, giving someone heavy grief, and then there was silence. Not a shot, then silence. Nor a scream, then silence. Just silence, like she'd suddenly decided to stop talking.

Fixx jacked up his hearing, pulling on his jeans and pushing himself into a T-shirt. But even with his skull implant turned right up he could hear nothing but a little heavy breathing and the creak of a cheap polycrete chair as someone shifted uneasily in their seat.

Not even the Cadillac jukebox was working. That in itself would have worried Fixx if he'd known more about the

CasaNegro. Fixx quietly opened the heavy wooden door and tried to slip into the bar unnoticed, earning himself a few seconds' reaction time.

But that wasn't how things worked out.

A hand reached out to grab his throat, pulling Fixx through the door and tossing him into the centre of the room. Footsteps followed fast behind and then someone in a suit asked him a question.

'*WhoYou*?' The words were swallowed, elided together into a single wet hiss. Only Fixx didn't have time to notice the suit's strange diction. He was too busy concentrating on the gun thrust hard against his throat.

An old-fashioned floating-breech Colt, with thirteen-shot magazine and ceramic barrel. Built-in silencer and primitive laser sight. At least, that was what it looked like on first glance: it was difficult to tell for sure when all you could see was a bit of the breech and the top of the handle, where the suit's hand wasn't. It was an official-issue Colt, though. Even with the muzzle pushed hard into his larynx, Fixx could see that.

'Me? I'm Fixx,' Fixx Valmont said. There didn't seem much point in lying. Not that he needed to bother: the clone's dark eyes remained as impassive as when Fixx first looked into them.

'*YouSeenThisGirl*?'

Fixx found himself staring at a cheap tri-D of LizAlec with her school shirt undone, her white bra pushed down to show small bare breasts. Behind her head was a poster of Tranquillity and a strapline that read *Welcome to Planetside*. She was crying.

'No,' Fixx said firmly, but he couldn't drag his eyes from her face, not even when the gun was pushed even harder against his throat.

'*YouSureYouNotSeenHer*?'

Fixx shook his head, and then yelped as the Colt punched down on his temple, splitting skin.

'*AnswerMyQuestion*,' the wet voice hissed. '*YouKnowThisGirl*?'

'No,' said Fixx sadly, still looking at the tri-D, 'I don't know her at all.' Warm liquid ran sluggishly slow down his face, until he could taste blood, thick and salt, on his tongue. The gash would need a couple of instant stitches but he'd have settled for synthetic skin and a pack of paraDerm.

Behind the clone, Fixx saw Jude reach carefully under the bar, her fingers feeling along the underside of its surface. A taser velcroed into place maybe, or perhaps a little Browning snubPup, it depended how illegal her instincts were. But whatever it was, it wouldn't be enough.

Fixx could tell her that for free.

'Leave it,' Fixx insisted and Jude froze, a scowl on her face.

'*WiseManDeadOtherwise* . . .' the clone said wetly, nodding to a second suit who strode over to the bar and pushed Jude out of the way. He came up with a moby and a simple Ruger stungun. It seemed that for all CasaNegro's chic, Jude's taste in weapons wasn't that extreme after all.

Both clones wore classically cut spider's-silk Italian jackets, narrow lapels shimmering with black fluorescents strung into the cloth's warp and weft. The effect was flashy but still restrained. Only three social groups still wore such clothes: senior Japanese politicians, CySat executives and Fourth Reich hitmen. And they didn't look like executives or political animals to Fixx.

'*You*,' the first suit said softly, lifting Fixx so far upright he had to stand on tiptoe. '*WeKnowYouKnowThisGirl*.'

The clone hissed because his vocal chords weren't fully formed, any more than his skin was thick enough to retain moisture. Hang the bastard out in the sun and he'd dehydrate. Whoever had backed out the matrix of genes for this one hadn't gone for subtlety or form, the clone was designed for pure ruthlessness. Which meant it came out of some bioWarfare complex somewhere. And that made it strictly illegal. Clone soldiers had been banned under the fifth amendment to the European Constitution: and that had been back before Fixx was even born.

'No,' Fixx insisted heavily. 'Not biblically, not personally . . .' The handle of the Colt sent shock waves rocking across his cranial cavity, dropping Fixx to his knees. What he felt as blinding pain was his bruised cortex swelling against the inside of his skull. Too many more blows like that and Fixx wouldn't be around to not answer the man's questions: even Fixx realized that.

'Don't know her,' Fixx said again, adding, 'What a way to go.' But by then he was talking to himself. Blood ran between shaking fingers to drip like Rorschach blots onto the dusty floor. He looked at the drips and then he looked again, but nothing in the blots made any sense, they didn't even look like butterflies.

Jude had troubles of her own, Fixx realized sadly. The other clone had Jude's moby to her own throat, its two copper electrodes not quite touching her skin, but the little diode on the handle was lit red and Fixx could see the dancing sparks from where he knelt. Throat jobs were about as nasty as it got without getting obscene. One move from the clone and she'd be biting out her own tongue in a convulsing bundle on the floor.

Fixx could feel Jude's eyes on him, pale and blue. Shit, he could even see the impotent anger that burnt in them, but that wasn't going to help him none. Of course, he'd looked death in the face before. As a kid out on the estates, surrounded by cheap crumbling concrete and spavined nags tethered fifteen floors up on dung-covered balconies. And the ones that weren't on the balconies were hobbled with lengths of wire to keep them from wandering off the tissue-sided allotments.

Back then he'd nodded back to a Gardi who was toiling up a piss-stained stairwell in Adamshouse. That night, back of the bar, Crazy Liam put a gun to his head and pulled the trigger. Even Liam looked surprised when the gun misfired. The second time was later, in Paris, after lighting a candle for his dead mother in Sacré-Coeur. He'd just finished pushing his way through the tourists and had slid off down a side street when he'd been jumped by a mugger armed with molywire, but he'd never even got the lasso over Fixx's neck.

Two bullets later, the man's djellaba was stained red and his corpse was being rolled off the sidewalk by Fixx's irate bodyguard. Not that Fixx was there to see it. He'd already been bundled onto the back of a Honda Ultraglide, all bulletproof back seat and turbo-boosted engine.

That was the end of his being allowed to wander out on his own, at least until his contract with Sony went the same way as the bodyguard, the Ultraglide and unlimited studio time. But then that was life, or it was his anyway. Fingers gripped his hair and yanked, Fixx rose and kept rising until he was face to face with the same impassive eyes.

'*YouNoSeeThisGirl*?'

'No,' Fixx said crossly. '*NoSeeThisGirl* . . . Okay?'

It wasn't. The clone released Fixx and sank rigid fingers into Fixx's solar plexus, fingertips pushing up to shock the heart into silence mid-beat. Fixx looked around once, saw the petrified crowd and then crumpled, his knees hitting the floor before his head did, though it was a close-run thing. The world accelerated away from him down an endless tunnel; as if it had been the roof of a lift and someone had just cut the wire.

Chapter 23

Heart of Glass

What saved Fixx was a bio-augmentation he didn't even remember having fitted. But had he ever bothered to read the subframes of his now long-cancelled contract he'd have realized the bioAug was standard. A fingernail-sized generator stapled to his left collarbone kick-started his heart. It did so by firing a single electric shock along a thin wire that led from the defibrillator down a vein and into the chambers of his heart. When the sensor buried in the heart muscle failed to detect sufficient movement from the first shock, the tiny generator fired up again and then shut down as the heart resumed its beat.

But by then no one in the CasaNegro was watching Fixx. Not even Jude and certainly not the clone, who stood over Fixx's body blank-eyed and seemingly frozen as he stared at a Japanese woman who'd somehow materialized in the middle of the floor. Since neither bedroom door nor street curtain had been disturbed since Fixx had followed Jude out into the bar, the Japanese woman had to have been there all along. It was just that no one remembered seeing her.

Though it was hard to work out how Jude, Fixx or the clones could have failed to notice a waif-thin Japanese woman dressed in black and holding a long and very dangerous sword. The kind of sword that was all stealth-edged blade with a simple handle bound up in rope, the kind you usually only saw in Samurai tri-Ds.

She was *kunoichi*. One of the silent killers. And not getting noticed was her job. She'd been doing it for six days, trailing after Fixx like some shadow he thought he'd long since left behind. Only the rules had just changed and, as of now, Shiori was back working for the General.

It wasn't the deadly looking blade that caught Fixx's attention when he stuttered back to life, it was the odd way the woman was standing. Twisted round herself, the blade parallel to the ground, hilt held right-handed in front of her narrow face, her left hand pressed flat against the pommel. Danger radiated from her like potential energy from an over-wound spring.

'Stand away from the body,' she said quietly. She was talking about him, Fixx realized with shock. Nobody moved. Though Fixx sensed rather than saw the clone standing over him stiffen slightly.

'You hear me?' The girl spoke perfect English but with a mixed West Coast drawl and Japanese lilt that sounded utterly beautiful to Fixx's ears. Though he might just have liked her voice because she was busy saving his life. A Japanese ballerina with a stack of Japanese fighting techniques. He was too drunk, Fixx realized, too drunk, too wired and too battered to work it out: so he just lay there on the warm grit floor and watched the ballet unfold.

The real death waltz.

Jude was backing away now. Sliding to safety behind the bar. She glanced once at where Fixx lay curled into a foetal ball and then looked away. If the huge woman was surprised to find him still alive she didn't let it show; though she smiled and began cleaning up the top of the bar.

Stripped naked, Fixx looked like a bizarre toy – all metal legs, silver eyes and scarred-up body – but the man was a survivor, they both were. That's what made fucking him so good. All the same, Jude knew he'd be out of there eventually, off to find his pretty little rich girl.

Fuck it all . . .

Jude was surprised to find how much she minded. Amphetamine, ethanol and endorphin-boosters hit her gut as Jude did what she'd always promised herself she'd never do, take a gulp out of her own profits. The cold Electric Soup bit into the back of her throat like iced novocain, then expanded inside her temples as she hit brainfreeze. Hard edges crystallized around objects in the bar as the world came into hyperfocus.

And then Jude forgot about taking her second gulp as the first clone swivelled Jude's double-barrelled stungun once, fast-forward round his trigger finger cowboy style, and blasted the Japanese woman. Bottles exploded and ears popped as sound bounced in waves from whitewashed walls like sonic ricochet. Only, when everyone looked, the ballerina wasn't there any more. Instead there was just an ugly pile of shattered glass from the table behind her and a fat man on his knees, blood oozing slowly from one ear.

Mekuramashi, Fixx thought admiringly. He'd read about it, even coded it as a cheat into his sims, but he'd never seen *mekuramashi* in action. The art of distraction.

She was across the room now, balanced on her toes, blade still parallel to the floor, except this time she was crouched on top of a bottle-strewn table. All around her the table's occupants had frozen, shocked into sudden protective silence.

The clone standing over Fixx lifted his Colt, finger tightening round the trigger, thumb flicking the laser sights into action. And as a tiny diode lit to say the automatic was sighted in, Fixx grinned. The one thing you *could* say for prosthetic limbs was they meant never having to worry about muscles wasting . . .

His kick caught the clone on the side of his knee, popping its joint in a single tear of gristle. And then Fixx's metal fingers closed around the fallen clone's hand, crushing it against the handle of the Colt. Bones inside the hand cracked like twigs then twisted as ball-joints ruptured between palm and fingers, needle-like splinters of metacarpal pushing out through the clone's skin as Fixx shifted his grip, found the man's fingers and ground them to bloody pulp.

Fixx couldn't remember how long it had been since he'd last

enjoyed himself so much. Twisting the Colt out of the clone's bleeding hand, he rammed it into the shrieking open mouth. The clone stopped screaming.

Up on the table, the Japanese woman looked irritated. Brief annoyance twisted her lips into a sneer. Though Fixx didn't know if he or the clone was the target for her contempt. She flipped sideways off the table top, somersaulting over her own blade to land neatly on a deserted patch of floor.

She wasn't drawing fire away from the crowded table: Fixx could see from the hard certainty in her eyes that the woman didn't give a fuck about civilians. Why would she? As Fixx always said, 'There *are* no innocent bystanders. What were they doing there in the first place . . . ?'

The woman was clearing herself space to move, the fifteen or so people in the bar falling back, away from the woman and away from the stungun. When the gun fired again, she flipped neatly away from the sonic wave, covering her ears to shield herself from the blast. That she could do both in one-sixthG said she'd been trained for off-planet work, probably in a lowG or free-fall dojo. And what that suggested, Fixx wasn't too sure. Serious money, maybe.

The essence of *Kamui*-style was to clear the mind of every distraction: to concentrate only on matching, meeting and defeating each blow. Except Shiori was using basic *Kamui* mixed with West Coast Two Skies . . .

The stungun was useless now, both barrels already blown. Which left the suited man with the automatic, inconveniently tucked inside his shoulder holster, or with Jude's moby which was still clutched in his left hand. That might be enough against a bushido blade – if you were very, very good – but Fixx wouldn't want to bet on it, not if it was his life. Instead he concentrated on stuffing the barrel of his Colt further down the first clone's gurgling throat. Give the clone long enough, he'd learn to swallow the whole gun.

'Who sent you?' It was the girl, her words soft, sweetly

lilting. The moby-holding clone said nothing, but his head twitched as he hesitated between trying to free the other clone or going after the Japanese woman. He was the bio-equivalent of a point-and-kill missile, good for hitting one target, not made to amend code on the fly.

'Who sent you?'

Shiori needed to know. Reporting back information like that was usually worth a little extra, whoever her client was. But Shiori never got a chance to claim a bonus, because instead of answering the clone flipped up his hand and released the moby, its tiny electric harpoon dragging out a hair-thin strand of molywire in its wake.

Observation and perception are two separate things: so said Miyamoto Mushasi. And Shiori knew the *Water Scroll* by heart. Knew the whole of *Five Rings*, come to that.

She moved so fast that no one saw it happen. One second she was standing watching the dart race towards her heart, the next she'd spun sideways – matador-style – to let the dart flick by and bury itself in the adobe wall beyond, electricity flickering like blue fire along the molywire.

The woman smiled and flicked her blade in a lazy double circle, its razor-sharp tip tracing an effortless figure of eight through the air. She didn't even blink when the clone dropped the moby in disgust and finessed a narrow steel cylinder out of nowhere, yanking it apart to reveal two short metal handles joined by a thin chain.

Learn to see everything accurately, said the sixth number in the Earth Scroll. And she did, not consciously but clearly, deep down in the reptilian basement of her brain. Her dark eyes never faltered.

Both ballerina and clone were dancing now, moving round each other in cold silence. One end, then the other of the clone's nanchuku flowed in an arc and then flicked twice across his front in a blinding figure of eight. *Hachiji-Gaeshi.*

Flipping one handle over his shoulder, he caught it behind his back and whipped the handle out towards the woman, into a circle, and then caught it under his arm. *Waki-Basami.* Flick and catch, turning his body as he did so, building a flowing protective shield of shining steel.

He was good, Fixx realized, watching the clone hold the Japanese ballerina at bay. It had to be more than just basic neural programming that moved the nanchuku with such ease. And judging from the corpse-white hue to the clone's skin and the liquid gurgle of his voice, the man hadn't been hatched more than a week.

Upper position, lower position, middle position . . . Right-hand guard, left-hand guard. Shiori ran through all five without even knowing she had. Acting not by thought but on instinct, the blade an extension of her arm, her mind as sharp as its fractalled edge.

Neither had yet come close to touching the other: the tip of the silver sword never quite crossing the seamless arc of the nanchuku, the swirling steel handles never extending their arc far enough to clash with the blade.

It was a ballet of beautiful, complex physics; of laws of conservation of angular rotation. But the silent regulars didn't see it like that. They just saw a thin Japanese woman flick her sword from side to side while the suited man in front of her spun complex webs of flashing metal.

She didn't even seem to be watching the nanchuku. In fact, as far as Fixx could tell, her eyes never once moved from the clone's sullen, sweating face. She just made move and counter-move. It was Zen-fucking-perfect, a deadly poetry that went way beyond simple motion . . .

Without realizing it, Fixx began to put the lethal ballet to music, wrapping their motion around with swirls of sound. Battered, clinically concussed, wired on cheap amphetamines, Fixx was still grinning fit to burst as he threw in a backbeat and mixed in some temple drums somewhere inside his head. One hand kept the barrel of his Colt stuffed deep into the throat of the clone lying bitter-eyed beside him, the other began to tap out a ridiculously complex click track.

The rhythm tapped out by his right fingers got ever more ornate as Fixx tried to thread a second fractured backbeat into the mix, heel clicking against the ground, head jerking as he locked it all together in his head. Everyone in the bar was silent, except for the two fighters . . . and Fixx, who was providing the backing track, whether they like it or not. Even Jude was quiet, leaning against her own bar, a half-drunk tube of Electric Soup standing forgotten at her elbow.

It was time to thread in that third beat, Fixx decided. Inside his head, a graphic score was building up, so complex it looked purely random. Not that anything was ever completely random, or pure come to that. Not in this life . . .

'You, shithead, shut the fuck—'

Shiori never did get to finish her sentence, because the second she started speaking the clone's arm whipped down in a blur, the free end of his nanchuku whistling in towards her skull. By all the laws of physics the result should have been like hitting a soft-boiled egg with a hammer. But instead of throwing herself backward and letting the nanchuku drive white cranial splinters deep into the jelly of her cortex, Shiori stepped right into the blow, blade flicking up to the right to halt beside her head. She didn't even flinch when the wire wrapped itself down the left side of her face and round the back of her skull, the nanchuku's handle swinging in on itself to clang hard against her upright blade.

No one had time to marvel because the woman was already on the move, her blade severing the nanchuku's wire then sweeping down and back up in a single stroke that caught the clone in the groin and opened out his front from pubis to breastbone. Still moving, Shiori pivoted her blade in mid-air and swept its razor-like edge across the clone's throat, cutting a blood-fringed grin below his jaw.

Gurgling more wetly than ever, the suited man stepped forward and slipped on his own guts, falling to his knees. Lack of understanding was written across his shocked face, more powerful even than the agony that pulled his lips back into an animal snarl.

Shrugging, Shiori put her blade to the gash in his throat and slammed the sword's handle with the flat of her free hand, severing the man's spinal chord. It was her one kindness, though she doubted he knew that. In all probability he'd already passed understanding anything.

'Neat,' said Fixx, clambering to his feet. He kicked the first clone once in the gut for luck and went to meet his saviour. The other clone was where Shiori left him, gutted open on the bar floor, but victory wasn't enough to make her happy, not nearly. She shot Fixx the glare a snotty mongoose gives a third-rate cobra and started stalking towards him, only it didn't look like she wanted to shake hands.

'Hey, wait.' Fixx sounded worried, which was fair enough, he was . . . Anyone faced with a furious *kuniochi* wielding a naked sword had a right to be worried, in Fixx's opinion.

'You won,' he said desperately, backing away. 'What's your problem?' It turned out her problem was him.

'Shithead.' She punched Fixx hard with her left hand. Since her right held the sword, Fixx was glad for small mercies. And her accent might sound quaint but there was no mistaking the anger in her voice. To make doubly sure Fixx got the point, the Japanese woman grabbed him by the front of his shirt and hurled him into a wall. Adobe cracked and behind it 'creteblocks echoed hollowly.

Had he lain there, she'd probably just have kicked him and left it at that. But Fixx had other ideas. He always had other ideas, that had long been part of his problem.

Time to fight back, Fixx decided. And as her slender hand reached down to yank him off the floor, Fixx went slack and as Shiori stumbled under his unexpected weight, he jabbed his left hand in under her ribs hard, servo-motors running full tilt as his metal fingers punched into her liver.

Brown eyes widened first with pain, then shock. But as Fixx pulled back his hand to punch again, Shiori was already busy controlling her pain. And before Fixx could land a finishing blow, the Japanese woman beat him to it, whipping her hand down, driving the hilt of her sword into the nerves of his shoulder, freezing his metal arm mid-movement. A blow to the shoulder, a blow to the face. He hit the ground, flat on his back.

Any normal person would have given up but Fixx never had been normal, even he admitted that. And besides, he was drunk on Electric Soup, with his aggression levels wired to fuck, and she was still groggy. In reply, Fixx kicked up with the sole of his foot, his heel catching Shiori hard between the legs. Men weren't the only ones to have nerve endings there, Fixx reminded himself as he watched her body go rigid with shock.

Scrambling up, Fixx stepped away from her and dropped into a fighter's crouch, pulling reflexes out of memory. The only problem was that it was the memory of a series he'd been in briefly, maybe twenty years before. When it came to the real thing he was so far out of his depth he didn't even know he was swimming. Fixx was still thinking that one through when the razor-edged blade vanished from the Japanese woman's hand. Not got sheathed or folded away like some oversized *biente neube*. The blade just shrank before his eyes like a candle flame denied oxygen.

She was back in control and what little advantage Fixx's low blow had given him was gone, that much was obvious. Shiori feinted and Fixx jumped back, then back again as she kept coming. Two hands reached for his throat and threw Fixx backwards, into the wall behind him. Adobe shattered, polycrete blocks splintered and Fixx found himself on his back on a grit-strewn floor. Around him was a dark, dusty cupboard, three walls of bare 'creteblock and one of steel. The small room stank of damp, the air thick with microspore thrown up when Fixx landed in the dirt.

There were other smells as well, sweet putrefaction and something low-level and sour like escaped gas, but Fixx didn't have time to consider them. The Japanese girl was standing over him, raising her heel to stamp down on his chest. Rolling sideways, Fixx desperately hooked up his knee and caught the girl behind her ankle. For a second she staggered, and that gave Fixx time enough to clamber painfully to his feet, facing her.

He was tired, breath dragging noisily through his throat, but the tiredness was worse in his head than in his lactic-laden, oxygen-starved muscles. And worst of all, he was empty. The song he'd been weaving was gone, broken beyond repair into fragments of memory by her punches. All gone. Pulling the sound back together would take as long as starting the track afresh.

Not that he could be bothered. Blood still ran from his gashed head, falling in slo/mo into the dirt to congeal into pointless, meaningless Rorschach blots. And what was he meant to see in them anyway, what was he ever meant to have seen?

His wasted life?

His missing love?

LizAlec was a sweet kid . . . Actually scratch that, Lady Elizabeth Alexandra Fabio was a brittle, spoilt little brat, though she was still good to have around . . . All the same, Fixx was beginning to wonder what he was doing standing in a bar in Fracture, with a female ninja about to take his throat out. And try as he might, he couldn't come up with a good answer. Actually, he couldn't come up with any real answer at all.

'I'm going to kill you,' the Japanese girl said between gasps. The blade was growing in her hand again, only this time Fixx could see that it came from a bracelet around her right wrist, metal flowing through her grip to recreate the razor-edged sword.

Fixx shrugged. 'So get the fuck on with it,' he said and turned his back on her. No more than a second passed between turning his back and walking away, but all the while he could feel that cold edge waiting to cut. When it didn't, Fixx forced one leg in front of the other until he reached the shattered wall, ducking through it to reach the bar. Without looking back he pulled a Soup tube from Jude's Braun icebox.

'Honey, you had enough.'

Yeah, Fixx thought, looking at the tall woman who'd materialized at his elbow, her cheap cotton dress still not properly buttoned over heavy breasts: he'd had way more than enough.

'Thought you were going to die out there . . .'

Fixx nodded. Yeah, so did he. And the grip that instinct was meant to keep on survival was less than he'd imagined, less than he'd expected.

The Japanese girl was back in the bar now, her face turned ostentatiously away from Fixx. But she was watching him all the same, catching his reflection in the polished polyglass dome of the Cadillac jukebox.

'Here.' Jude slammed a first-aid box in front of him and pulled out a small stapler. Taking a half full bottle of Stoli out of an icebox, she tipped what was left of its contents down the side of his face and then wiped at the crusted blood with an old bar towel.

'Hey, you . . .' Jude's fingers closed on his jerking head, holding it immobile as she cleaned up the cut. 'Keep still.' It was all Fixx could do not to shout with pain, but he couldn't, not with Jude and the Japanese girl listening.

'Okay, here goes.' Jude pinched together the gash on Fixx's temple and stapled it fast, before he had time to protest.

It look four staples to close the gash and then Jude was done. The instant skin she stuck in strips *across* the gash, instead of along it as the manufacturers recommended. He didn't ask her why, though Fixx knew without looking in a glass that he was going to need a skin graft when he got home. Always assuming the Reich left him a home to return to.

'You?' Jude asked the Japanese woman, who shook her head. 'Suit yourself.' Jude turned back to Fixx, slipped her first-aid box under the bar and came up holding the tattered Kodak of LizAlec. She looked at Fixx, long and slow, and then she glanced down at the piece of card in her hand, pale blue eyes gazing at LizAlec's intense face staring back.

'You like the girl?'

Fixx nodded.

'You fuck her?'

They looked at each other and Fixx remembered Jude kneeling over him, her hips pushing down hard as she bit her own bottom lip in concentration. He shook his head.

'You tried?'

Fixx thought about answering. But there was a lot of shit swirling around in his head that couldn't stand too good a look. Why the fuck else did Jude think he spent as much time as he could going AWOL inside his head, skipping reality's bail bonds?

In the end he just shrugged.

Jude nodded, half to herself. 'That girl was real afraid.' She jerked her chin at the dead clone sliced open on her bar floor. 'You think that shit was what scared her?'

No, Fixx didn't. 'Fresh hatched,' he said, having thought about it. 'Couldn't even talk properly yet . . .' But why the fuck ask him? Fixx wondered crossly. He didn't know what the fuck had scared LizAlec, who the fuck was after her, and he certainly didn't know where the fuck she was.

Jude looked at Fixx. 'You heard of *The Arc*?'

The tall musician nodded – everyone had heard of *The Arc* – and then he realized exactly what Jude was trying to say. LizAlec was out at the—

'Honey,' said Jude crossly, 'that kid was real frightened. I had to send her somewhere she couldn't get into trouble.'

Jude gave Fixx the tri-D, passing it across reluctantly, turning it face down before she gave it to him. Fixx didn't bother to turn it face up again before slipping the Kodak of LizAlec into his back pocket.

'You see the kid, you give her that back, you understand?'

Fixx nodded. He was picking salted almonds out of a blue dish and swallowing them without really tasting. Eating from habit and embarrassment. They both knew it was dangerously close to goodbye.

Jude smiled wryly at Fixx and looked past his shoulder at the hole in the wall. Through the gap they could both see the metal wall and the door set into it. There was a panel of diodes, touch-sensitive switches and read-outs set in the middle of the wall, but it was so covered with dust that it just looked like a grey square. Above it was a larger grey square, which would turn into a triple-glazed glass window when anyone bothered to wipe it down. At the moment there was only a small smudge of black where one of the regulars had cleared off enough of the dust to peer through at the vast cavern behind.

'Ice,' Jude said. 'Not your kind, my kind. Water.' She looked at Fixx.' 'You got any idea how much that amount of fresh ice is worth?'

He didn't. He wasn't even enough of a tourist to know about the ice reserves that had supposedly been found back at the beginning. A few of the guides said the water was brought to the Moon, the rest said it was chemically manufactured. But street rumour, deep rumour said the water had always been there as ice, right from the very start. Hidden at the bottom of the deepest craters, protected by the shadows.

'The next time you come back here, Strat's going to be a rich town. We'll have a market, electrics, fresh water . . .' Jude's rough voice trailed away at the thought of the possibilities. 'You know, I could sell that and go Earthside. Live like a queen.'

She couldn't, of course. Her augmentations were for Luna, not Earth. And it didn't matter that she worked out regularly in a full-gravity gym. The permanent sixfold increase in Earth gravity would burn out her metabolism within months and grind her calcium-starved bones to fragments, starting at her hips. What credit she began with would be swallowed up by medical care.

But Fixx wasn't about to say that, and besides, he knew that Jude already knew.

'You see it all, when you come back. Sweedak?'

Fixx nodded again and Jude gave him her best twisted smile. She wasn't stupid and nor was he: both knew he had more chance of surviving naked in a vacuum than walking back through that door. All the same . . .

Fixx scooped the last of the almonds out of the bowl and turned to go.

'Hey, you . . .' Jude's voice was loud.

For a second, Fixx thought she was going to do something stupid like suggest he stay, but she didn't. Instead Jude just pointed to the first clone, slumped unconscious against a cracked polycrete table.

'Take your trash with you . . .'

Chapter 24

Shanghai

Gamblers need luck. General Que had it. Luck followed him like his own shadow: that was what his own officers had said – and they were right. But General Que worked hard for his luck, in ways so old that most Shanghai families had forgotten them . . .

Unlucky days were as important as lucky days, he knew that. When the gods smiled, he'd put his entire estate on one single turn of baccarat. On other days he wouldn't have bet the loose chips in his pocket on remembering his dead wife's name.

His house had exactly the right number of rooms, his site of fortune was placed where good *feng shui* demanded it should be: panelled walls had been taken down and others erected to make sure this was true. He never stayed in hotels that had a thirteenth floor and only took suites with names that were lucky. His limousine was red, with red leather seats and red carpet.

Not once in his life had he placed a bet in a room that contained an old-fashioned printed hardback. (In a different context, the word for book could also mean failure.)

Although the most important guest in Shanghai's Imperial Casino, he never walked brazenly in through the vast revolving glass doors at the front, preferring to slip in through a discreet side door from Upgrade Alley. He knew, just as his father before him had known, that sometimes ill luck will be hiding in the foyer, waiting to mug you . . .

And yet, despite the large blue china lion dogs that guarded his study, the gold lucky symbol hanging from his red-painted

wall and his elegant, perfectly carved chop seal made from
mutton-fat jade, General Que was having a bad-luck day. A
very, very bad-luck day.

In fact, the General hadn't had such a bad-luck day since two
very young, very scared military policemen had ransacked his
house three weeks before, looking for something they realized
soon enough wasn't there. It wasn't there because the General
had given the shrine to his daughter as security against just such
a visit. Both of the police officers had since killed themselves,
thus saving him the effort of arranging their deaths himself.
Though whether they had committed suicide out of fear of his
retribution or terror at having failed Beijing, the General didn't
know or even care.

The man sat at his desk and frowned at the tiny monitor in
front of him. These days he wasn't a general, of course. He was
Mr Que – owner not just of Shanghai, that Los Angeles of the
Pacific, but of most of the newly ploughed-over countryside
surrounding it. Still as thin as he'd been at eighteen and with
hair that was only just beginning to grey at the temples, he wore
sober suits cut from Thai silk and patterned on an illustration
he'd once seen in an American magazine. *Esquire* or *GQ*. He
wasn't good with foreign names.

Eighteen was how old he'd been when first conscripted. At
twenty-two he was a full colonel, alternating his dress between
the gold braid and white silk of ceremonial and a combat
suit of self-sealing, earth-hued Kevlar. By twenty-three he'd
commanded the Army of the East as senior general, brokering
its peace with the old men in Beijing.

Beijing would have made him a field marshal – one of theirs –
but the General was a gambler and, like all good gamblers, could
taste luck in the back of his throat. For three years it had been
rich and clear, almost oil-like in its smoothness. But in Beijing
his luck had developed a sour aftertaste, like a burgundy just
beginning to oxidize. From wine to vinegar was a single fall of
the dice . . . it always had been so.

The General turned down their offer. And so avoided responsibility for not preventing the Lhasa uprising that finally ripped Buddhism's navel out of China's body politic. The old men hated him for it, but there was nothing they could do. Que turned his back on the Forbidden City and the concrete wastes of Beijing that surrounded it and moved himself and his pregnant wife to Shanghai, buying the whole Flatiron building and taking the top floor for himself.

In the West, the rich might like to live at ground level and keep the poor in towers, but this was China. And besides, he needed to be able to see the sky.

'Replay the St Lucius e-vid . . .' General Que demanded.

Mencius, his house AI, knew exactly which e-vid the General meant. The man had watched it five times already that morning while most of Shanghai still slept, fucked or thought of breakfast. It showed the General talking to Ms Gwyneth.

The AI didn't feel guilty about not notifying the General about the original message. Mistakes it understood, logged and coded into its fractal web to avoid repetition, but guilt was something else. Programming guilt into an AI was technically possible, but wastefully self-destructive. The last thing any user needed was a machine that put every other task on hold while it considered the implications of its own actions.

All the same, Mencius had been worried enough to make contact with a conveniently placed ballerina. And one of the General's best, no less . . . In the circumstances, it seemed just as well. The General needed to know that Anchee was safe, and not just because Anchee was his daughter. His fortune, his history, the soul of his family rested in that little silver shrine, maybe even his luck.

'Pan in,' demanded the General crossly, wishing he could see the woman's eyes . . .

Mencius did as he asked, cropping out most of the face on screen until only eyes remained, framed top and bottom by an elegant brow and the start of an aquiline nose. The woman was lying, that the General didn't doubt. The only question was, about what?

Without knowing it, the General drummed out a repetitive three-beat rhythm with his index finger, his elegantly trimmed nail clicking softly against the top of a priceless desk. Its top was cut from a single slab of jade carved around the edges with tiny, intricate immortals. The original slab had been cut from a vast jade boulder found in Burma at the start of the nineteenth century, but the carving was late nineteenth, when the Manchu dynasty was in terminal decline and the Empress Tz'u Hi was already dying.

The General, like most of his ancestors, disliked the Manchu and their memory. And even two centuries after their final collapse, he still regarded them as little more than incoming barbarians. It was just one of the things that hadn't made him popular in Beijing.

The monitor on his desk was a new-model Samsung, so small it looked like an unrolled banknote until his voice called it awake. An S3e monitor might cost a week's salary for one of his houseboys, but the General still had a drawerful, rolled tight like scrolls and tied with red ribbon. He used each monitor once only and then had it destroyed. Not sold, deconstructed or recycled but burnt in a furnace in his basement.

It was the General's firm belief that whatever had once been fired onto the screen's pixels could be recalled like blast shadows on a wall, if the software artisan doing the recalling was skilled enough. There was no proof of this, no scientific evidence. But it was his unshakeable belief all the same.

So far he'd wasted half a dozen screens and three hours of Sunday morning trying to decide what was wrong with the picture in front of him. Apart from the fact Ms Gwyneth was lying. The lies showed in her eyes every time he replayed the download.

Part of General Que wanted to commandeer the next commercial flight to the Moon and go find out for himself. A Beretta pushed hard against the temples often had a way of freeing the truth. But he couldn't, there were no flights. None at all. At the first rumour that the Azerbaijani virus had reached Brazil, the Moon had been declared off-limits to all Earth traffic.

The General snorted in disgust. Skyscrapers collapsed in São Paulo all the time. If he'd had to bet on it, he'd place his money on bribed building inspectors or sub-quality concrete. But the rumours had been enough for Planetside to lock off the landing computer and declare a Luna-wide low-orbit exclusion zone.

Now he was in Shanghai and Anchee was up there, apparently unable to take his call. Oh, he'd seen his daughter right enough, asleep in her bed at St Lucius. Or rather asleep in a bed in the school sanatorium. She'd been lying there, tucked under a crisp cotton sheet and resting on a clean, brand-new polyfoam slab. Her breathing was slow and regular, and when the shot panned in on her face, her closed eyes had flickered and jumped with healthy – perfectly healthy – rapid eye movement.

'Anchee's being rested,' announced the headmistress, pointing to a tiny tube inserted into the girl's thin wrist. He'd been told why too. So Anchee's immune system could avoid stress while her white blood cells fought off a viral infection; one that his daughter must have caught at home in Shanghai. No one mentioned chicken flu, but the inference rested there between them.

The General was left in no doubt that he was somehow to blame.

'Let me talk to . . .' On screen, the General was fumbling for the name of the noisy foreign girl. That his quiet, dutiful daughter had nevertheless made friends with her while so many other Han attended St Lucius worried him, but Anchee had. Still frowning into the lens, the General pulled LizAlec's name from his memory.

On screen, the woman shook her head. 'Lady Elizabeth is away for a few days . . .'

Which meant what? General Que still didn't know.

'Then wake my daughter.' He'd been losing his temper by this point, irritation overcoming his usual manners.

'No,' said a woman he'd never seen before, 'that I can't allow . . .' The new woman had a wide face and firm but smiling eyes. Her black hair was scraped back into little snakes and trapped under a nurse's cap. 'She must rest, I insist.'

Absent-mindedly, the nurse smoothed the front of her uniform, which was as white and as crisp as Anchee's turned-back sheet. Everything about the scene was reassuringly normal. Much too normal, in the General's opinion.

If that nurse was a vActor then her coding was better than anything the General had met before – and in his late teens he'd dealt with the best. The Chinese Army prided itself on its coding brigades, fit-triggering black ice, instant firewalls, self-setting trapdoors, he'd seen them all.

And he hadn't walked away from the Army of the East empty-handed. Mencius retained military-strength crypt capabilities, not to mention grade one vActor-stripping software. But try as Mencius might, he couldn't break down that picture.

Time and again, each new Samsung screen refreshed the opening image and Mencius set about stripping the scene back to basics. Except the basics weren't there to be stripped back to. No skin peeled away, no flesh vanished, no crude polygonal-construct appeared in place of his daughter's skull. The nurse, the walls, the fresh flowers, even the little oil painting of Bruges, they all checked out as real.

Which meant that if the touching little scene was computer-ghosted, then it was the best he'd seen. Scarily good. In his head the General tried to balance the screen shot of his daughter sleeping peacefully in her bed with the thinly disguised ransom demand from Brother Michael and the worrying, gut-churning fact that Brother Michael had Anchee's bracelet on the desk beside him.

The General made no better a job of the problem than Mencius had done twelve hours earlier or than Mencius's pet semiTuring had done twelve hours before that. The facts didn't balance and that meant someone was lying. Which, as always, made the General want to reach for his gun.

General Que sighed. The greatest strategist of his century and he was unable to come up with a logical answer. . . Oh, he didn't doubt something was badly wrong: he just couldn't believe one of the most exclusive school franchises in existence could be implicated in trying to cover up the disappearance of one of its own pupils.

For a brief moment, he considered hiring mercenaries, launching his own raid on the St Lucius O'Neill, but the General dismissed the idea immediately. He was forty-three, for God's sake, and an outright attack on somewhere his daughter probably wasn't was the response of an angry child. What he needed to do was make contact with the parents of Anchee's foreign friend. Find out if she was missing too, see if they'd had a message from Brother Michael.

As the General flicked off the little screen and tossed it into a rattan bin ready for burning, he wondered idly what was happening with his pet ballerina.

Chapter 25

BarOut

Shiori's plan was to hijack a Niponshi shuttle, hold the clone's captured Colt to the captain's head and command him to approach *The Arc* on its blind side.

It was Fixx who pointed out that spaceships don't have a blind side, they have tri-D 360-degree vision. Not to mention electronic sensors that would put the most complex multi-lens fly's eye to shame.

Fracture was way behind them and they were both back in Planetside, more or less. They were in a crowded tourist bar this time, halfway between Aldrin Square and the Edge, sandwiched in at the counter by a fat New Yorker and her even fatter husband on one side and two French boys on the other, neither of whom could keep their eyes off Shiori's perfect breasts. Fixx knew how they felt. The Japanese woman might have the kind of legs that combined genetic luck with hard exercise and a gut that was not just flat but actually slightly concave, but it was her breasts . . .

Small, perfect . . .

Fixx shook his head.

'So what do you suggest?' Shiori demanded as she misread his gesture.

So far Fixx hadn't been able to come up with an alternative. All the same, Shiori's plan had zero subtlety and even less chance of success. And Fixx was shocked to discover he wasn't ready to commit suicide, which was a revelation in itself.

Fixx tipped back his iced Stripe, buying time.

What did he think? Since meeting the clones, as little as

possible, really. The gash on his temple was beginning to mend and Fixx had teased his blond hair out of the tiny dreadlocks so it flopped around his face. He didn't like wearing his hair like that but it hid as many of the bruises as possible.

On first glance, Fixx looked good, even to himself. It was only when you got in close you could see lines round his eyes like cracks in glass. Fixx knew that was true, because he was watching his reflection in a mirror behind the bar. He used to like profiling, now it just made him feel old.

'Fuck it.' Fixx slammed his Stripe down on the counter harder than he intended, certainly harder than he should have done. The fat woman from Brooklyn squawked noisily with shock, and for the first time that morning both French boys looked hurriedly away. It didn't help that he stank, Fixx knew that. And it didn't help that he'd put the loudest possible track on the jukebox. One of his own, as it happened. Well, a remix of a remix of it.

'Is there a problem?'

The barman was pretend English, his accent sliding all over the place, but his face was impassive and his eyes hard.

'Yeah,' said Fixx, 'I'm thirsty.' He pushed his empty can at the man and waited . . .

Hands on counter, the barman lent forward, bracing himself for confrontation. But he never got the chance to throw Fixx out of his bar.

'The problem,' Shiori said smoothly, 'is that my husband's just been mugged. By Sandrats . . .' It was neatly done, one delicate hand sliding out to move Fixx's empty tube into neutral space on the bar in front of her. One arm sliding up round Fixx's shoulders as if to comfort him.

Not drunk after all, but upset . . .

'Sandrats . . . ?' one of the French boys asked, sounding suddenly very young.

Fixx nodded heavily, wincing at the pain that rolled through his head. His response wasn't faked, either – real reaction, real pain. Sandrats wasn't what the barman wanted to hear. And from the ugly twist to his mouth, Fixx realized it wasn't something he wanted his customers to hear, either. Planetside had no street crime, that was one of its big selling points. It was cheap, tacky, out-of-date and beyond fashion, but you didn't get mugged. That was what made it suitable for worried families, small children . . .

'You want to come in the back,' he suggested.

Fixx looked blank.

'Tidy up, maybe? I can get you a real doctor, on the bar . . .'

Jesus. The man was worried. No one used medics any more, except the very rich. It was well known that forty-three per cent of the educated Western world preferred to rely on MS MediSoft: the fail rate was lower.

Fixx said 'No' just as Shiori said 'Yes'.

'We don't need a doctor,' said Shiori. 'But somewhere to clean up would be good.' Her voice was soft, her accent liltingly Japanese. If Fixx hadn't seen her slice open the first clone with one easy stroke, he'd have thought her a student, maybe a junior salariwoman. Only her slate-grey eyes gave her away.

The barman blinked, nodded and lifted the hatch on his bar, letting them through. Instinctively, his gaze flicked down the line of customers, checking their glasses were full, their plates weren't empty, and then he turned to a steel door, allowing Fixx and Shiori to walk ahead of him into a small office. A bank of flat screens showed every part of the bar, including inside each toilet cubicle.

'We record everything,' the man said without embarrassment. 'It helps with insurance claims.' He smiled sourly, 'About every six months, some hick gets trashed, falls over and breaks his neck – even in a sixth G. Then his wife blames some imaginary bump in the floor.' He gestured at the old-model Sony screen bank and the basic m/wave vidcorder. 'This is cheaper than paying out . . .'

'Not to mention more entertaining,' Fixx said bluntly, as one screen showed the fat New Yorker struggling to get slacks down over her hips.

The barman shrugged. 'You really get mugged?'

Shiori lifted Fixx's blond hair away from the side of his head, revealing a long gash. The man whistled and stepped in close, fingers touching the line of staples. 'Haven't seen a job that clean since . . .' The man thought about it. 'Don't think I've ever seen one this neat. How far out into the tunnels were you guys?'

'Far enough,' said Shiori.

'And they really were Sandrats?'

She nodded, her face serious.

'Sweet fuck,' the man said. 'I thought the real san'rats were all dead.'

'Yeah,' said Shiori, 'so did we.'

Fixx knew just why the Japanese woman was lying. Sandrats in Planetside were unlikely, but not as unlikely as a pair of shipped-in clones, so wet behind the ears their vocal cords weren't even properly grown. Besides, if he really thought they'd been jumped by a sandrat he wasn't going to start telling anybody anything . . . His concern was with the tourists and the last thing he needed was for them to start locking themselves in behind LunaWorld's electrified fence.

'Seems they're alive,' Fixx said, putting up one hand to touch the gash. His fingers came back dry, fragments of scab crusted beneath ceramic finger nails.

'Where are you staying?' the barman asked. But by then he wasn't really concentrating anyway, his attention concentrated on the main screen as he watched customers grow restless waiting for his return.

'We've got a room at LunaWorld,' said Fixx. 'If you just let us use your bathroom, we'll clean up a bit and then leave.

'Sure thing. If that's what you want.' The man breathed a sigh of relief. 'Bathroom's through there,' he said adding. 'It's a bit crude. But what isn't round here . . . ? You can let yourselves out through the fire door.'

And then he was gone, leaving them in his office. Not that he was taking much of a risk. There was nothing in the place worth stealing, even assuming they wanted to. On the central screen, Fixx watched the barman scoop up tubes of what might have been Electric Soup – if it hadn't been half the strength and four times the price of the cans in Jude's bar – and begin distributing them, having skimmed the line of restless punters with a single glance to work out who was making the loudest noise so that he could serve them first. All the same, the bar wasn't a clip joint. The tubes were still half the price they'd be in any of the cafés lining Aldrin Square.

'Okay,' said Shiori, glancing at the barman busy on screen. 'Let's go.'

'No.' Fixx shook his head and regretted it immediately. He could practically feel his brain rattling around inside its box. Besides, his scalp itched from crusted blood and he stank so bad even he wouldn't have stood downwind of himself.

'I need a shower,' Fixx said firmly. The Japanese woman looked irritated, but she didn't disagree. It wasn't just stale sweat that clung to his body. The sour reek of comedown stuck like oil to his skin. Crushed fresh garlic and molecular chains broke along with the flesh, releasing that familiar stink. It was the same with blue crystalMeth.

He could scrub the smell from his skin but it would be back, and it would keep returning until he took another hit or fought clean. Word on the street was that, years back, the stink had been some Seattle bioChemist's idea of a bad joke, but if so no one had ever managed to rewrite the formula. Fixx certainly hadn't.

They went through to the bathroom together. It might have been innocent on Shiori's part but it certainly wasn't where Fixx was concerned, not that it made any difference. Shiori stripped off her tight black T-shirt in a single motion, hands crossed over her front to grip the edge of her top, peeling it up and away in one clean sweep. Shiori almost had the body of a boy, Fixx decided, looking at her thin ribs, or she would have done if it hadn't been for those small, high breasts topped with wine-dark nipples. But for all the attention she paid to Fixx he might as well have not been in the room.

Bending, Shiori stepped out of her crumpled Levis and tossed them into the corner of the bathroom, next to her T-shirt and leather boots. Watching her tight buttocks as she walked three paces across the 'crete floor, pulled open a glass door and swung herself up into the sonic booth, Fixx realized he hadn't seen anyone with a body that honed since CySatNY commissioned a piece on Bohemian Paris eighteen months back. There'd been a journalist hanging round the Crash&Burn, a green-eyed exec name of Passion.

She'd been good, thighs like steel, arms like whipcord and a vulva so tight she had to have put in a lifetime's work on her pelvic floor muscles. But Shiori was younger, and Fixx was pretty sure Passion's whole body had been a rebuild: something expensive from an offshore black clinic.

She sure as hell knew how to use it, though, wherever her body came from. She'd throated him whole and come back for more, kneeling on a bed in a wild apartment CySat owned in Montparnasse, so that fucking Passion had been like being suspended naked in the Parisian skyline. Just thinking about it hurt to bursting.

Fixx was still looking down at his erection when Shiori stepped out of the shower. They looked at each other and Fixx could almost swear he saw the Japanese woman curl her lip, then realized she probably wouldn't do anything that obvious.

Shiori nodded at his groin. 'You got a problem, you deal with it,' she said abruptly and turned her back on him, pulling the black jeans up around her hips, fixing her flies and buckling her belt before she even bothered to reach for her top.

She looked good from the back. But hell, she looked pretty neat from the front too. Fixx stripped off his clothes and stepped up into the glass booth. He'd like to do the same: set the controls to sonic and let the dirt, dead cells, sweat and microbes be blasted from his skin in a single sweep, but he couldn't.

Brauhess marketed the cubicle as sonic, because the idea of laser cleaning still had people worried. It wasn't as if sound wasn't involved: it was, in three oscillating frequencies. But most of the cleaning was a rapid laser peel, so shallow that it zapped no more than the first few interlocking cells of the epidermis. What the Brauhess did was take a surface reading a nanosec ahead of the laser pulse, then take mere microns off the result.

There were rumours of pregnant women cooking their babies, fat men breathing out at the wrong time and finding their guts on the shower floor and children who forgot to close their eyes getting an involuntary corneal shave that changed their sight forever – but that was what they were, just rumours.

Urban myth had nothing to do with the reason Fixx didn't choose the sonic option. It was simple self-preservation. Both his legs and one arm were bio-encased electronics. No way was he going to risk frying the chips.

No, he was going to shower the old way. His prosthetics might not stand a laser burst but at least they were waterproof.

Fixx let the cold trickle down his torso, slicking through body hair flecked with grey, picking up blood, dust and grit as it went. By the time he'd been under the shower for thirty seconds, the puddle at his feet was already grey with dirt, not that he could feel anything resembling water with his toes.

If he could have had his legs back, he would have done, height drop and all. Oh, they'd got him publicity, that night at the St Petersburg Palace Theatre when he stalked out on stage, half-man/half-machine. The *tetsuos* had been out in force, ranked along the front of the stage, providing security, whether the Russian police had wanted it or not.

And then the fights had begun, spilling out of the Palace Theatre onto Neva Prospekt. Every fucking Ishie in the city trying to eyecam the chaos without getting clubbed by some overwired member of Russia's finest. By midnight the bells at the Armenian Church next to the theatre were being rung in descending order to announce the deaths. Fixx was finally world-famous and for more than his fifteen minutes. No one could number how many people downloaded his new sim: the Web counters just couldn't cope. Hell, he'd claimed so much fucking bandwidth that, even with the new backbone in place, getting to his site was like drowning in treacle.

No one really knew what that meant until the media punters stopped and really thought about it. Fixx hadn't known, not when they told him, hadn't understood the implications at all. It only began to make sense when the credit started rolling in, the fractions of dollars, yen and euros adding up faster than his mind could comprehend.

He was more than rich, for a year or two he was beyond money. A mythical figure like Midas or the Gates-Hertoz dynasty. Fenced round with bodyguards and PAs, the bedrock of his finances so hard, so solid that stock-market dives and currency fluctuations broke against it like overwrought brokers hitting the pavement. And that's how things should have stayed. That's where he should have stuck . . .

Rubbing blood out of his hair, Fixx knew that was true. That was definitely where he should have stuck, with a firewall of tame lawyers between himself and the world. But he was addicted to grand gestures: to walking out on love affairs that weren't entirely perfect; to throwing his cloak over puddles that nobody needed to cross. Between giving to charity, breaking his recording contract and trying to sue Bernie and his other managers for fraud, he'd spent everything he'd ever earned, moolah spiralling out of his account as fast as it had spiralled in. Half the world thought he was a long-dead saint, the other half just thought he was dead . . .

'You got a knife?' Fixx stuck his head round the cubicle door, watching Shiori lace and relace her boots, the old-fashioned way. He didn't believe in any of that shit. His boots might have metal buckles all the way up the front, but they still undid at the side with a self-sealing molecular zip.

'Why?' Her eyes were amused, like she thought he might kill himself in the cubicle while she hung around fiddling with her boots.

'You want me to try shaving with a molyknife?'

Shiori didn't even have to think about it. No one would be that stupid, not even a flake like Fixx. She flipped him her ceramic blade and Fixx caught it neatly in mid-air, by the hilt.

Shiori nodded, impressed despite herself.

Pure luck. Back inside the cubicle, Fixx considered running the ceramic edge razor-like over his skull, but that seemed a bit extreme for what he wanted. So instead he took the edge of Shiori's blade to his chin, scrapping it against wet skin, losing the bristles.

If Shiori was surprised at the cleaned-up version of Fixx she didn't let it show. 'We need to move,' the Japanese woman told him flatly. 'Now . . .'

Fixx picked up some new clothes in an alley that had been blocked off at one end and converted into a market. The man behind the third stall took his watch in payment. Shuffling the gold Patek Philippe from hand to hand, the trader had been busy congratulating Fixx on the quality of the fake, when he realized the watch was real.

For a second, it looked like the man was going to refuse to take it. If the timepiece had been reported stolen then it couldn't easily be offloaded. Not if the watch was logged with Customs as missing on the way out. But something in Shiori's eyes made the man decide to honour the trade.

'What are you looking for?' He asked looking doubtfully at Fixx.

Fixx examined the clothes on show. Levis, T-shirts, jackets. Most were two, maybe three seasons out of date. Some of them so old he didn't even recognize the designer they were meant to be ripping off. Nearly everything was synthetic, some kind of clone-cotton/Kevlar mix that shed dirt by itself without having to be told.

In the end, Fixx took a black Thai jumpsuit, riveted in copper at the stress point of every seam. To go under it Fixx chose a blue T-shirt. The jumpsuit had been night black once, a real light-swallower until someone washed it in water and most of its fluorescence went down the drain. Now it looked more slate-grey.

'I'll take these,' said Fixx and stripped off his own Levis before the man had time to argue. Clambering into the jumpsuit, Fixx did it up at the side.

'Looks good,' said Shiori.

Fixx glanced round in surprise.

'What I mean,' Shiori said carefully, 'is that in those clothes you look less obvious . . .'

'You mean I blend in?'

Shiori and the stallholder looked at each other. Which was enough. Fixx didn't need their reply. He wasn't going to blend in anywhere until he got rid of his metal hand and that wasn't going to happen this side of getting rich again. All the same, the jumpsuit would do when they came to grab a shuttle. If he looked like anything in the faded-out garment, at least it was more like a maintenance engineer than anything else.

'Where's the nearest CyKaff? Fixx demanded. He couldn't believe there wasn't one up here somewhere, here in franchise heaven. Actually, Fixx reminded himself, everywhere was franchise heaven these days.

'Back towards Aldrin Square,' said the man, pointing vaguely into the distance.

'Okay.' Fixx turned to Shiori. 'I'll see you later.'

'Where?' It was obvious from the way Shiori had her hands slung on her hips that she didn't appreciate having to ask. But that wasn't his problem.

'Planetside,' suggested Fixx.

'Arrivals or departures?'

'Well, what do you think . . . ?'

Fixx left her standing there in the small square, a young

Japanese woman with neat features and tidy hair, who just happened to have breasts to kill for . . . The kind of woman you saw in everyday *novelas* about a nice salariman family in Osaka. Except the world of nice families wasn't where Shiori came from. This was a woman who killed for a living – and what was more, she enjoyed it. Fixx reminded himself to remember that . . .

Chapter 26

LISA says

Two girls looked up when Fixx came through the door. But their eyes glazed over and all their attention had been turned back to the NinSim games machine in front of them before Fixx even reached the coffee-stained counter.

'Espresso,' he ordered, pulling out what was left of his loose change. Shit, with its idiot flag on one side and an idealized silhouette of LunaWorld on the other, it really *was* Mickey Mouse money.

He got something hot and wet, slammed carelessly down on the zinc by a ponytailed boy in a dirty red Nintendo sweatshirt. Espresso it wasn't. Or rather, it was as close to real Italian coffee as the raddled Pigalle whores were close to the innocent Parisian schoolgirls featured in the bright holocards they busily pushed under hover wipers.

'I'll take a machine,' said Fixx, looking round him. The place had that neon half-gloom that passes for slick when you're about thirteen and it stank of cheap scent and cheaper coffee. Just being there made him nostalgic.

'Lucifer's Dragon, Apocalypso or CloneSex?'

Click none of the above, thought Fixx. He had a heavy date with LISA, the only problem being he was over three days late and she hated to be stood up. The tall musician shook his head. 'No sims. I just want a link.'

The boy shrugged and flicked his fingers over a screen, not quite touching. 'Squid?'

'No.' Fixx shook his head and tapped the pocket of his new jumpsuit. 'Just the machine, I've got my own 'trodes.'

You could see *sad fuck* written in the guy's eyes but he didn't say it, just pointed across the filthy bar. 'That one in the corner . . .'

The box he pointed to was slate-grey, bolted to a table top and decorated with a peeling tri-D sticker of Stepping Razor and what was left of a SlickShack logo. The other half of the logo had been cracked off with a knife a long time back. Some kid trying to lift the thing to brand his own clone box: Fixx could remember doing the same.

The box didn't look much but it suited Fixx fine. Anonymous, unpretentious. He slipped a pair of 'trodes from his pocket, licking one of the ends to fix it to his temple. The most basic neural link possible, slow and not too secure if someone was sitting nearby with an axon recorder.

But the two girls kicking digital hell out of a kitten-sized dragon were so dusted out they didn't look like they could cope with their own thought patterns, never mind grabbing his. And the little CloneZone jerk behind the bar was leching over some Roricon holoporn while pretending to skim that day's *Enquirer* download. Fixx could probably strip naked in the middle of the room and they wouldn't notice.

Fixx tapped his way into an online editing demo and coded a quick burst of RaiTek, tying reds and purples to anything over 250 bpm, leaving greens and golds for the rolling thud of anything that came in at a speed less than that of a frenzied heartbeat. Without even knowing what it was he was coding, he put in the shattered fragments he could remember of Shiori's fight. The quiet double stamp of her feet, her slow circling and dangerous silences broken with moves that unrolled like a spring uncoiling, he slotted the lot over the top of the RaiTek backing. Not so much a wall of sound as a tsunami of noise. Then Fixx busted it through to LISA, crypt-tagging his signature onto the end as an afterthought. It wasn't enough.

'What the fuck do you think you've been doing?' The voice inside his head was loud, furious. Burning with all the irritating self-righteousness of a machine that knows she's right. And it wasn't even LISA: she was so cross she'd delegated the job of being angry to a subset. The avatar was a low-res 40Mb of polygonated, etiolated middle-aged woman in a tawdry brown uniform. He was being snubbed bigtime, patronized even. The woman was scowling, hands on hips. It was all Fixx could do not to scowl back.

Instead, he spoke subvoc, relying on a throat mike he'd slicked to his neck. 'There's been some trouble . . .'

'You're telling me. LunaWorld called in the PSPD after you went missing. They turned over your suite looking for clues. And then some three-striped shithead on the make noticed that sure, you had landing clearance Planetside. But what didn't you have? A record of clearance for leaving Earth. You any idea how fast we had to move to tidy that up?'

'No,' said Fixx. 'No idea.'

The AI said nothing. Just made its avatar scowl some more. Which didn't improve Fixx's temper any. The only problem was he needed LISA and he wasn't good with needing people. In fact, he had a nasty habit of cutting the ground from under them before they could chop the legs out from under him. It wasn't sensible but it was instinct. Apologizing wasn't, but he made himself try anyway.

'Look,' said Fixx, taking a deep breath. 'I screwed up, okay? LizAlec's camped out on that fucking *Arc*, I'm hooked up with some ninja, I haven't a fucking idea what the fuck's going on here and as for at home . . .' Fixx sighed: as apologies went it wasn't much, but it was better than he usually managed.

'Home?' the woman in brown asked and then winked out, leaving a vague after-image behind his eyes, all edges and black space. In her place Fixx got a voice, LISA's, sounding almost sympathetic. 'You mean Paris?'

Fixx nodded. Yeah, that was exactly what he meant. That first month when he'd landed from Chrysler he'd loathed the city and its arrogant, anal residents, its spindly trees and dead Sundays.

Now the thought of the Reich and the Black Hundreds ripping through the narrow streets of the Marais, the old Jewish district, ate Fixx up inside, until his misery felt like a snake sliding through his intestines.

'I don't know,' said LISA, 'not exactly. It's hard to tell.' Both of them knew just what an admission that was for her. Knowledge didn't just want to be free, it wanted to be known – scrambling its way through optic lines of information, spewing out in satellite sprays of information – and knowing it was what LISA was there for.

Oh, the optic fibre was still in place, satellites still hung in low orbit, modems must still be gurgling to themselves somewhere, even if only in Alaska, but many of the links were gone, broken. Iron was such a basic element not even LISA had thought what might happen if someone took it away.

For most of Europe there was no power. A horse was now worth more than the newest Seraphim four-track, a simple zydel blade worth more than any steel-barrelled Colt. The rains had come and so had the Reich. He was in the wrong place, at the wrong time. LizAlec was alive and probably safer where she was than in Paris. He, however . . . 'I need to get back,' Fixx told LISA firmly. 'Lady Clare's had her pound of flesh. I need to get back now . . .'

'Flights to Europe are banned,' the AI replied from habit. 'And even if they weren't, not even Niponshi would hire you a shuttle so you could turn it to worthless oxide. Besides, you're not really finished yet, are you . . . ?'

The voice in his head was soft, sympatheic. So sympathetic that Fixx was immediately suspicious. As he was right to be. Into his head came an image of LizAlec, looking brave but crying, tears leaving track marks down her cheeks as she chewed at one corner of her bottom lip.

This was a picture Fixx hadn't seen. He strongly suspected it was a Kodak from the Arrivals Hall, one she hadn't sent. LizAlec would have hated it: brave but tired and tearful wasn't how LizAlec thought of herself at all.

'How did you . . .' Fixx started to ask, and then realized how stupid he sounded. LISA controlled all of Luna's electronic data exchange. And what was a Kodak moment, if not data?

'Someone's busy trawling, started yesterday,' said LISA. 'Another AI. It has a picture – two girls, a head shot – and it's trying to match both girls against data from the Arrivals Hall. A subroutine woke me up when it eventually spotted what was happening . . .' LISA sounded cross but mildly impressed, which meant whoever it was must be very good indeed. Mind you, she had a whole other problem with Arrivals Hall data supposedly going missing but she wasn't about to go into that with Fixx.

'And you're not the only one who's come out here after that girl,' LISA added.

'Two clones,' Fixx said.

'Two . . .'

'One now,' said Fixx, cutting LISA off before she could get started. 'One got killed at a bar out in Fracture.' Fixx thought of Jude and smiled. 'Give you good odds that one's already been recycled. Last time I saw the other it was folded double, taped up and dumped in a left luggage depot at Planetside Departures. Probably pissed itself by now . . .'

'Cut its throat and then get out of here,' said LISA. 'Go get LizAlec and do it now, before the LDPD work out your sweet little butt hasn't been murdered.'

'I can't just kill someone in cold blood,' Fixx said, sounding offended.

LISA sighed heavily. Okay, so Fixx knew that sometime, way back when, an IBM coder had fed in two dozen human sighs and an emotional equation that allowed LISA to vary their use. But the sigh seemed real enough to him, probably because it sounded the way his old manager Bernie used to, every time Fixx announced that actually, no, he really wasn't quite ready to do this leg of the tour . . . But it wasn't Fixx she was sighing about, not really.

'You know what we've had in here in the last week or so, apart from you?'

Of course he didn't.

'Two clones aboard a shielded cargo carrier and before that a fourth-generation Xan fighter that vanished off the screen almost before it came in range.' So Shiori could pilot her own plane . . . Fixx nodded. He should have wondered how she was getting to Planetside.

'Fifty-eight years without a single black landing and then I suddenly get three of the fuckers, including you . . .' LISA sounded almost aggrieved. 'And you always were a shitload of trouble.'

'But you love me anyway,' said Fixx. LISA didn't even bother to answer that one, which was probably just as well. 'Look,' Fixx added hurriedly, 'it stands to reason. Put up a blockade and someone's bound to run it. That's inevitable . . .'

'Yeah,' said LISA, 'but when the Xan belongs to China's most powerful industrialist and the two clones travel on *cartes* issued to the Napoleonic corps noblique. Then you've . . .'

'The clones had *cartes*?' Fixx exclaimed, then bit back his words when one of the girls turned to stare at him. Clones were illegal on Planetside, and as for *cartes* . . . People with *cartes* didn't holiday at LunaWorld, not even as refugees. They flew out to Elysian in private shuttles.

'*Cartes Nobliques*?' Fixx took care to speak softly, letting his throat mike pick up the startled question. He was shocked, really shocked, the kick-in-the-guts kind. That Lady Clare should mistrust him made sense − he sure as hell didn't trust her − but that the bitch should sick clones on him . . .

But then maybe it wasn't Lady Clare. Fixx drummed his nails on the edge of the cheap plastic deck and thought about it. 'You know who sent the clones?' he asked finally. There was silence as LISA vanished, leaving a low hiss like wind in his ears and behind his eyes the pop and crackle of neural feedback. Fixx surfaced to take a quick peek at himself in a nearby screen and went back inside his head. It was less depressing.

The silence stretched out until Fixx thought LISA was gone entirely and then she was back. 'They came in ready-cleared. Apparently I didn't register the fact because I already knew.' She sounded irritated, even troubled, not that Fixx had time to notice. He was too busy fretting, unable to shake the feeling he'd been set up; that maybe he had never been meant to find LizAlec in the first place, that maybe he was the distraction, Lady Clare's sleight of hand . . . Either that, or he was just some sad fuck on the wrong side of crystalMeth comedown.

'Was it Lady Clare?' Fixx demanded.

'I don't know,' said LISA apologetically. 'There's no record of their landing, only echoes. Though given time I could collect the echoes, reconstruct the code sequences.'

'Then do it,' Fixx suggested crossly.

Inside his head, LISA shook hers. 'Not even for you, gorgeous. It's too dangerous.'

Fixx looked puzzled. Actually, he looked like shit. His eyes were as empty as some burnt-out tenement block, his cheekbones jutting out of grey skin, but he tried not to mind about that. 'Dangerous?' Fixx asked finally, turning his head sideways as he tried to work out if he looked any better in profile. The tall musician had a nasty feeling the answer was probably a big fat no.

'Who do you think keeps Planetside's Sabatier3 cells functioning?' LISA said, sounding resigned. 'You think CO_2 just combines with hydrogen by itself? That water just electrolyses for the hell of it?'

Fixx continued to look puzzled. He was getting good at that.

'We're crowded out with refugees,' said LISA. 'Or haven't you noticed? The whole Planetside system's going to implode if I don't come up with something soon.'

'You?' Fixx asked.

'Me, gorgeous . . . Who do you think fills the tunnels with oxygen? Those Sabatier3s had a ninety-nine-year working life. You know how old they are?'

Fixx shook his head.

'186 years. Half the time I don't know why I don't just pack up and let you all die. Life would be so much more peaceful.' The AI was beginning to sound seriously pissed.

'You'd get bored,' said Fixx, with absolute certainty. 'You'd get bored out of your skull. If you had one, that is.'

He was right, too. Urban myths of big AIs committing suicide did the rounds but Fixx was pretty sure they *were* only myths. He'd never come across an actual case and he'd bet LISA hadn't either. BioAIs, now they were different, but then Fixx wasn't too sure he'd have wanted to be condemned to eternity as the galactic equivalent of a fridge door either.

'You know what I think, gorgeous? I think you should ditch Shiori and get out of here. Take a hike. Go get LizAlec and if you won't do that go back to Chrysler. I'll square it. You know, take the locks off your door, wire you back into a feed . . . But get out of Planetside before the PSPD catch up with you, and ditch Shiori while you're at it.'

'I'll think about it,' said Fixx. But they both knew he wouldn't. No way was Fixx going to walk away from a woman with a body like that.

'You know what you are?' LISA said sadly.

Fixx didn't, but he knew she was going to tell him. She always did.

'You're a dumb fuck,' said LISA and then she was gone.

And he was, too, such a dumb fuck he didn't see the spike-haired boy in the black T-shirt and combat trousers who started following him the moment he left the bar. But Leon saw Fixx which was all that mattered. Well, it was to Leon. Help the *tetsuo* – but don't get into trouble. Jude's instructions had been clear. And for once Leon was trying to do what he was told.

Chapter 27

You must be out of your tiny mind

Fixx couldn't be bothered to wait for Shiori to find him, so he found her instead, holed up in a polyfoamed pod she'd hired in the RunNowFun hotel. It was as much a Ripongi fuck joint as LunaWorld's 49er was a real pioneer bar. For a start Fixx could almost stand up in the pod, which he never could have managed in a real love hotel.

But it did have a traditional grey Togo slab and a time-locked minibar stuffed with vacuum-packed *wasabe* crackers and tubes of iced Sapporo. It even featured torn strips of rustling paper taped round the air vent to sound like breeze-fingered leaves. Not to mention an assortment of foil-wrapped vibrators and an evil-looking surgical steel speculum in a pink fur-lined box.

There was a tiny toilet cubicle, too. But the clone occupied all of that, its black suit trousers rucked in a heap around its feet. Its ankles were strapped together with the missing belt from the trousers and its hands were fastened tightly behind its neck with a red silk tie. From the blood dripping from a split lower lip and the flowering bruises that covered the clone's ribs, Shiori and the clone had been in mid-conversation. One that had been about to get much more serious if the short ceramic blade in Shiori's hand meant anything.

The Japanese girl swung round from where she crouched in the lavatory door. Grey eyes raked over Fixx, giving less than nothing away. But the reptilian part of Fixx didn't need to look into her eyes to know what was going on or how much Shiori was enjoying it. Mixed in with the stale air of the tiny pod and the sickly-sweet smell of the clone's blood was something darker, muskier. It wasn't so much conversation he'd interrupted, Fixx realized, as Shiori's own private version of foreplay.

Hot though the pod was, the Japanese woman's nipples stood proud beneath her sweat-stained cotton vest and his mind finally caught up with what his body already knew. He'd got into trouble the last time that happened.

Lady Elizabeth Alexandra Fabio. Fixx hadn't believed Lady Clare at first. Hadn't believed that the kid with the kohl-rimmed eyes, wearing a crushed purple coat really was corps noblique. He should have known, of course, even back when he first met LizAlec. Her arrogant self-confidence was clue enough. But people assume artists are observers, when most are just self-reflective, self-obsessed . . .

Fixx had drained his glass of marc, feeling the cheap grape-pip brandy burn in his throat. Fifty people in a filthy bar in Bastille and, because of who he'd once been, all of them respected the cerebral exclusion zone he'd erected around himself. Except her.

There was blood on the ballerina's blade and this time when he looked Shiori was smiling, her eyes bright with expectation. Punching the button that shut the toilet door, Shiori crossed her hands over her front and in the same elegant move Fixx had watched earlier, stripped off her black vest in a single movement to bare small elegant breasts.

It was the opposite of a striptease, quick and clean, but all the raunchier for its bald matter-of-factness. Unclicking the wall cupboard marked *lovedrugs*, Fixx grabbed an ampoule of amylNite8 and snapped it under his nose, inhaling its sour chemical stink. Without waiting to be asked, Fixx broke another glass straw under the nostrils of the bare-breasted woman standing opposite him – and watched as her eyes exploded, pupils widening into black holes.

He wanted to suggest Shiori put down her knife, then decided not. The last thing Fixx wanted to do was ruin her mood. Instead he kicked off his boots and scrabbled at his buttons. Getting out of a jumpsuit wasn't elegant but at least it was fast.

She had the inner stillness of a predator, with eyes to match. And as the Japanese woman watched him, Fixx got the feeling she was putting a value on him. It wasn't a sensation he liked.

'You're not really here to find LizAlec, are you?' Fixx kept his voice steady, his eyes on her wide face.

Shiori shook her head, then shrugged. 'Maybe it's LizAlec, maybe it's someone else. I need to check.'

For a moment, Fixx wanted to take LISA's advice and walk out of there, do what he should have done instead of coming to find her. Taken a hike, got sensible. But his wasn't that kind of life and this wasn't that kind of sex. The twisted smile on her hungry face told him that. Most people needed ice to get that wired, but all Shiori needed was . . .

Fixx glanced at the ceramic blade still balanced in her narrow fingers and knew exactly what Shiori needed. Hell, just looking at the blade put him on edge. So instead of walking, Fixx reached for her belt and slowly undid the heavy buckle. Unpopping the waist button to her Levis, Fixx ran his fingers down her fly, releasing it.

The kid had been watching him all evening, again. Not out of the corner of her eye, but openly – until he frowned at her and she glanced away or pretended to be looking over his shoulder at one of the faded holoposters on the sand-blasted brick wall behind.

As if anyone would be interested in bands that had folded, circuses that had never been more than virtual, in the whole tired Nouveau Bastille theatre of cruelty. Fixx doubted if she even knew Artonin Artaud had existed, never mind which century he'd lived in. But, in the end, he'd sent a drink over, telling the sad-eyed little rent boy behind the bar to take her a bottle of marc.

* * *

Fixx slid Shiori's jeans and thong carefully down to her ankles, moving back to let her step lazily out of them. The Levis were lined with some kind of polymer micromesh bonded to the inner surface. It looked like the vat-grown fabric DuPont produced to bomb-proof hover windows.

'Where'd you train?' Shiori's question came out of nowhere. At least nowhere Fixx knew about.

'Juilliard, Lincoln Center Plaza,' said Fixx, remembering the best six months of his life. Not that he'd thought that back then.

It was Shiori's turn to look blank.

'Music school in New York.'

'You're not . . .'

'Trained in all this?' Fixx nodded towards the lavatory door that had been shut on the tortured clone, 'No,' said Fixx, 'strictly fucking amateur.'

Shiori was about to say something else but Fixx stepped in close to stop it and cupped his hand around her mons, his fingers closing over fine body hair. This was the point he loved most, always had done. The split second before his fingertips found her labia. He could feel Shiori go tense as she waited for his fingers to slide into her. She wanted to push forward, to hurry him, but wasn't going to allow herself the indulgence.

Leaning forward, Fixx gripped the back of Shiori's head with his free hand and pulled her face roughly towards him. As she twisted her mouth away, Fixx let his fingers find her clit. Shiori arched backwards, mouth opening, and Fixx kissed her hard.

That was when Shiori bit into his lower lip, breaking skin: blood and saliva mixing between them. It was enough to give any sexual-health assessor a heart attack, not that Fixx had health insurance these days: some risks were just not good.

Fixx grinned and slicked his wet fingers up over her body, finding one breast. It was swollen like ripe fruit, the nipple gorged and purple, but it was still smaller and more elegant than even LizAlec's breasts had been. Clutching Shiori's nipple between his fingers, Fixx tugged gently, watching the dark circle around it pucker and tighten.

There'd been a time when he'd been proud of his capacity for empty sex and pointless drugs, when staying wasted was an end in itself, something that required real ingenuity. And given the Sony-trained bodyguards, therapists and minders who had glued themselves to him like leeches, that wasn't even an understatement. There'd been a period back there when getting the wherewithal to get wasted had turned into a full-time job.

Fixx dipped his head, tugging again at Shiori's left nipple and curling his tongue around it. Slick with her own juices, her nipple tasted tart and sour. Sliding his hand back between her legs, Fixx opened the Japanese woman's swollen vulva with his fingers and then took his hand back to his mouth, sucking his fingers one after the other.

Not quite up there with crystalMeth, but close enough.

Fixx dropped his other hand and closed thumb and first finger over her full lips, squeezing until Shiori moaned through gritted teeth and closed her hand tight around his penis, so hard Fixx thought he'd burst.

It was a straight stand-off.

The girl was younger than he'd first thought. Fixx realized that as soon as he got close to her table. She was holding the bottle he'd sent over, looking doubtfully at a label etched into its bubble-blown green glass. Fixx didn't blame her. The contents described on the label were cheap enough as it was, and the bar they were in was notorious for refilling empty bottles with crude ethanol brewed up by étudiants from the Sorbonne nearby. He wouldn't have wanted to touch it at her age either.

She drank all the same. Twisting off the top and swallowing two huge gulps before her throat closed in protest. By the bar, the rent boy was grinning. Phillipe didn't like girls, especially not little rich ones who were out slumming.

As he thumped the girl between her thin shoulder blades, Fixx

*tossed the words 'rich' and 'slumming' around in his head. And
then he handed her his own glass.*

'Drink this.'

*'Water . . .' LizAlec sounded surprised, which marked her out
as a newcomer to the bar. Everyone else knew Fixx's routine,
even if most of the younger ones didn't know his name. Monday
drunk, Tuesday hung-over, Wednesday sober, Thursday drunk,
Friday hung-over, Saturday and Sunday sober. Fixx resented
having to stay sober over the whole weekend, but when God
designed the week he hadn't allowed for drunks running a
six-day cycle. Although maybe he had, when he let someone
discover freebase . . .*

'Shit,' said Fixx as the Japanese woman dropped to her knees.
Instinctively, Fixx tried to jerk backwards, remembered in time
where Shiori was holding him and fell on top of her instead.
They landed on the polyfoam in a tangle of limbs. Grabbing her
wrist, Fixx slammed it hard against the floor, knocking free her
blade which skittered out of reach.

Fixx held tight to her wrist as she scrabbled in vain for the
handle, slowly forcing her arms up over her head, until she was
stretched naked beneath him. Fear was what he should have felt
– but his brain was too busy being aroused by the way her tits
pushed up towards him.

He was out of his head, Fixx knew that, but she wasn't just out
of her skull on amyl, she was like some predator on heat.

Gripping Shiori by the wrists – his bloody mouth pressed
down hard on hers, not quite knowing who was doing the biting
and who was being bit – Fixx eased himself into her twisting
body, feeling her cunt open slowly around him. There was that
tiny familiar jerk as his glans cleared the muscles at her entrance
and then Fixx was into her, sliding slowly up inside. Pushing in
only slightly and then pulling out.

Ignoring Shiori's protest and the lurch of her hips as she thrust
up towards him, Fixx rested just outside her swollen vulva. And

then he slid back in, a little further, feeling her tighten around him, hot and ready.

Indescribable.

Very slowly, Fixx released her wrists, his eyes watching Shiori's face, seeing her bruised mouth twist into a slight smile. Balancing himself over her, Fixx smiled back and then drove into her, as hard as he could. Shiori gasped, half in surprise and half from having the breath knocked from her body; and then her legs locked over his ankles.

'LizAlec,' Lady Elizabeth Alexandra said, taking his offered hand. Fixx shook politely as behind LizAlec the rent boy sneered on his way to the restroom and a hooker with bleached-blonde hair slid off her barstool and hit the floor kneeling, ideally placed to vomit.

LizAlec looked bemused and a little sick herself. It might have been the marc, but most probably it was his handshake. She'd drunk from his water glass and now she'd touched his skin, unshielded. Another kid might have hit the restroom in search of a viralwipe, but LizAlec didn't. There was a price to being cool and LizAlec was just learning it.

Gently, incredibly gently Shiori raised her head to kiss his neck and Fixx shivered. Except that when she kissed his neck again he realized she wasn't kissing him at all, she was very gently lapping the blood that flowed from a bite in his throat he didn't even remember happening.

She kissed, he shivered. He shivered, she kissed and then her grey eyes flicked open just as orgasm hit, her pupils expanded with nitrate and blind as a kitten. 'Fuck . . . fuck . . . fuck . . .'

Fixx didn't know if she was pleading or swearing, but from the ferocious intensity of her face she was some place he'd never get to, not even wired right out of his skull.

Sixtieth woman he'd fucked, six hundredth? Fixx had lost count of the number of women he'd slept with. Not because it was so high . . . Well, not for a superannuated rock git with a bad ice habit, but because he'd finally got old enough to think that keeping count was kind of childish. Though that could just have been because his memory wasn't what it was.

'Beautiful,' Fixx muttered, looking down at Shiori's head on the pillow. He was still marvelling at how defenceless she looked sprawling back in the afterglow of sex when he noticed the blade, back in her hand and resting lightly between loose fingers.

All the time she'd been clutching him tight, like a sloth hung from a tree, she'd had that blade in her hand, Fixx just knew it. The very thought made his balls shrivel. Gently, so Shiori wouldn't take offence, Fixx lent forward and lifted the knife from her grip. She moued in protest but let Fixx skitter the blade right across the pod, towards the far corner this time. And without giving Shiori time to change her mind, Fixx kissed his way down the Japanese woman's body, between her slight breasts, over her perfect stomach and on down.

Fixx used his teeth to tug gently at the narrow strip of her pubic hair, just enough to make Shiori shudder and then, as his foot found her discarded blade and pushed it even further into the pod's corner, he buried his face gently between her waiting thighs.

Her eyes were violet, hidden under a mask of heavy make-up, her curling black hair was scraped tightly back flat to her head, as if she'd wanted to go for a crop and hadn't quite had the nerve. Not that the heavy black plait which disappeared under the collar of her velvet coat didn't look good. It did.

As for her body . . . Fixx knew the math, one human produces Xw of heat, cram twenty people into a small space and you get 20xXw – and no one could accuse the Crash&Burn of being over-large. But still the kid kept herself under wraps. Which meant she'd been infected in one of the recent anorexia pandemics.

*'He said you're famous . . .' The girl nodded towards the rent
boy who was sulking at the bar, wiping his nose on his sleeve.*
'You recognize me?' Fixx asked her.
LizAlec shook her head.
Fixx shrugged. 'Then how can I be . . . ?'

Shiori tasted of truffle, the expensive kind people like Lady
Clare grated over the top of their game soup. Dark and rich, like
wet earth. Fixx ran his mouth up the woman's perineum and
pushed his tongue into her cunt, feeling Shiori push back against
him. And then before she had a chance to grip him again with
her thighs, Fixx slid up slightly, fastening his teeth gently over
the hood of her clitoris. Shiori bucked against him, crushing
his bruised lips, and Fixx dug his hands into her hips to hold
the woman still, flicking his tongue over the pink nakedness of
her clit.

'Enough,' Shiori said.

'No, said Fixx, 'not nearly.' But he moved his mouth all
the same.

*'You got a home to go to?' Fixx asked, looking at the kid. LizAlec
just stared back blankly and Fixx cursed himself for sounding
so old. He couldn't help it, though, he was late thirties going on
forever. And she . . . hell, he'd probably been twice as old as this
kid was when he was still only half her age.*

*She didn't answer his first question, the one about having a
home. So Fixx ran down his list of usual questions: did she
fancy coming back to his studio? (No). What did she think of
Herbert Marcuse? (Herbert who?) Did she prefer crystalMeth to
sulphate? (She just looked blank.)*

*'How about a deck?' Fixx asked finally. He could just imagine
her fingers flicking across the keys, writing code or snapping
notes out of mid-air. She didn't have a deck. He could tell that
just by looking at her face. She was embarrassed, aware that
somehow she'd disappointed him, and so was he.*

Fixx was many things but fair had never been one of them.

Fixx had a problem and it wasn't the clone bleeding noisily to death in the tiny restroom or the fact the woman rubbing her crotch into his face had tried to kill him less than forty-eight hours before. His problem was 230,000 miles away and a year in the past.

Pulling his head from between Shiori's legs, Fixx crawled up her body and hooked his arms behind her legs, forcing them up towards her head. Looking down, Fixx could no longer see the Japanese ballerina: the eyes staring up at him belonged to a young girl.

Darkness swirled across the room as Fixx fought to focus his eyes and then decided not to bother, white light blazing as nitrate and orgasm combined. All the same, it wasn't Shiori's face on the pillow when his brain went overload. The face he saw belonged to a fifteen-year-old French schoolgirl he'd refused to sleep with, no matter how often she'd asked him. Fixx didn't know what that said about him, but he knew it wouldn't be good. Stuff like that never was.

Chapter 28

Exit Music

'Madame?'

Lady Clare said nothing, did nothing and kept doing both. She was hoping that if she kept it up for long enough the voice would eventually go away.

It was raining, which wasn't unusual. Maybe if the roof slates hadn't been drumming with raindrops the size of pigeons' eggs, and maybe if the Seine hadn't once again broken its banks to flood her courtyard, Lady Clare Fabio might have taken notice.

As it was, she rolled over in her vast Third Empire bed and tried to pull the chenille cover up round her ears, protecting herself from the staccato crash of the rain.

'Get up.' The voice that addressed her was insistent. Polite as all sin but irritating in its refusal to let her go back to sleep. Which was a pity, because Lady Clare could practically feel unmetabolized alcohol sloshing around in her veins. And she didn't need to look at the Courvoisier bottle on the bedside cabinet to know how much she'd drunk. The time lapse in her head between movement and pain told her that.

'Go away,' Clare muttered and pulled up the chenille throw over her head, curling herself up into a foetal ball.

'Madame, you have to get up . . .'

'There's no "have to" about it,' said Clare crossly. 'You know who I am? I'm the Minister of—'

'I know,' said the voice sadly. 'Minister of the Interior, aide to His Highness . . .' The words trailed away into exasperated silence. Exasperated because he was too polite to state the truth, that she was turning into a prematurely aged, drunken, terrified woman.

Surprised, Lady Clare poked her head over the edge of the covers. There couldn't be too many men left in Paris who'd bother about being polite to one of the Prince Imperial's disgraced lackeys.

Because that's what she was, or would be soon enough. The whole of the Third Empire to protect and she hadn't even been able to look after her own daughter. No wonder the city was holding its breath, waiting for the Prince Imperial to surrender. Focusing her pale blue eyes, Lady Clare blinked. The guards officer looked twelve, swathed in the folds of a khaki greatcoat.

Neatly cut soft brown hair flopped over a high forehead. He had the snub nose of a Gascon and clear brown eyes. He looked younger than LizAlec, which wasn't surprising: practically everyone looked younger than LizAlec except her.

'Turn around,' Lady Clare demanded.

The boy looked blank.

'I sleep naked,' Lady Clare announced flatly. 'And I may be older than your mother but that's not the point . . .'

Stammering an apology, the boy swung about and stared at a point on the far wall, his whole body rigid with embarrassment.

'I'm not offended,' said Lady Clare tiredly, climbing out of bed and looking round for her old Kenzo dressing gown. Giving up the search, Lady Clare pulled the chenille wrap around her shoulders and kicked open the French doors to the balcony of her bedroom, stepping out into the rain and tossing the wrap back inside.

No one could see her. The balcony faced into the courtyard, which was deserted like the rest of the house. Apart from the young guards officer she was the only person there, and he was still staring hard at the wall. Lady Clare didn't need to look behind her to tell that, she just knew. She recognized him now, from the shuttle launch the other night.

He had one of those wide-open faces and a dog-like innocence in his eyes. He'd throw himself under the hooves of a Black Hundred Cossack if she ordered it and not even know why. And she would do it too, Lady Clare realized with a shudder, she would sacrifice him if she had to.

Rain washed over her, freezing her body. God alone knew what was in the water but she was pretty much certain nanites would be there, tiny and invisible. Not that they could hurt her or the house. She was flesh and blood and nothing but, not a single implant. As for the Hôtel Sabatini, the walls were sandstone and the roof was raftered with old oak and covered with dark Brittany slate.

'What's the hurry?' Lady Clare shouted over her shoulder but could not make out the boy's muttered answer. 'Oh for God's sake,' she said crossly. 'Come here.' She pointed at a spot on the carpet, just inside the room and out of the splashing rain. 'Keep your eyes shut if it makes you feel better . . .'

She wasn't being fair to him but so what. And anyway, he'd keep his eyes shut, he was the type. Lady Clare shook her head fiercely, drops splashing around her like water from the coat of a spaniel. Lady Clare Fabio smiled and turned to find the boy watching her curiously.

Maybe he wasn't the type, after all.

'Your coat,' Lady Clare told him, holding out her hand. The cloth was soft, woven in fine wool and lined with Italian silk decorated with baroque flowers, the kind of pattern you found stuccoed to villa walls in Calabria. The boy's family had money or they'd had it once. The coat's cut might be military but the quality definitely wasn't, not even for the guards. It looked one thing, but was really another. Appearance and reality, the hobbled twins. She'd always lived between them both, preferring to hide in the gaps that S3's demimonde provided.

'So why are you here?' Lady Clare demanded struggling into a small black dress − Dior − one of dozens. Usually she also wore sheer nanopore stockings, not to cover up her skin but just to soft-focus the slight imperfections. But she was out of clean pairs. Actually, she was out of everything except black Dior dresses and matching footwear.

'The Prince Imperial . . .' The boy stopped and then struggled to start again. Whatever it was he wanted to say, he wasn't finding saying it easy.

Lady Clare lifted one foot and slipped on a black court shoe. It would be worse than useless within minutes, its wafer-thin leather disintegrated to misshapen rags, but it was what she had . . .

'Paris,' the boy said hesitantly, approaching the problem from a different direction.

'Paris is falling,' announced Lady Clare, saying the unthinkable for him. 'The Third Reich has run out of patience, the press are bored. Half of them have taken a night schooner to England to watch London get washed into the sea. Besides, C3N might have ceramic-cased vids with graphite hard spheres and built-in ComSat capabilities but they're fuck-all use if lightning storms stop their camerajocks from managing long uploads. If the Reich's going to take Paris, then it might as well make the push now . . .'

'Someone gave you the news?' The boy sounded surprised.

'No,' said Lady Clare sadly. 'It's been coming for days.'

Chapter 29

Passion in Shades

Passion never thought she'd say it – never mind actually mean it – but she'd fuck a dead hyena for an unbroken pair of Raybans. Passion didn't even want to think about what she'd do for a cold shower . . .

Desert sun blinded her, turning Passion's famous sea-green eyes into mere slits that squinted from a sweat-beaded face. Every inch of exposed skin was covered with sunblock factor thirty, but deserts reflected worse than water and still her skin burnt in the Megribian sunlight.

Perspiration trickled down her neck, interfering with the connection to her sub-voc throat bead. It dripped into the vee of her collarbone, then slid beneath the lapels of her filthy combat fatigues.

There was nothing to see and even less to film. But this was the big story, the news of the moment. And where history was happening you'd always find Passion di Orchi, though these days people knew her only by her first name. Passion: the person, the shows, the merchandise.

That was fame. People said her name and everyone knew exactly who they were talking about. Passion smiled, then remembered she was still on cam and pulled a solemn stare. Well, as solemn as she could manage while busy screwing up her eyes against the glare. Unlimited research budget and bleeding-edge tech and CySat still couldn't come up with a lightweight, sandproof vidcam that could film into bright sunlight without needing fill-in lights. Like she was going to have a power supply in the middle of the desert.

Well, actually she had just that . . . But like she was going to carry all the equipment? 'Yeah, right . . .' Passion said loud enough for the tiny Aerospatiale 182 to pick up, hesitated too long to run it into a coherent sentence and then swore, long and loud. Now she'd have to start the whole take again from the top. That was the big problem with her retro one-woman-brings-you-the-whole-world routine: everything had to be done in one clean take.

That was, if you didn't want some arsehole back in the studio to start doing a vocal cut-and-paste, and then before you knew it, you were up on screen with shit coming out of your mouth that you wouldn't be seen dead saying. No, Passion used a digital copyright lock on all her vidcopy. Try to fuck it over and you wouldn't see the pix for scattering digital dust. Sure, she had a cast-iron contract, but where the syndication department was concerned the motto was sell first, worry about illegal overdubs later. Passion should know: she was senior president of CySatNY.

If Ishies were the media hookers of life, then Passion was an expensive call girl, high class and gold card only, and that was the way it was going to stay . . .

'*The heat is on* . . ..' Passion said seriously. She was standing on a black rock so hot that it reduced the soles of her desert boots to the texture of melted cheese. '*But the stand-off continues. Inside the San Lorenzo complex, the auditor-general is still refusing to let naneticists of the UN Pax Force carry out their scheduled laboratory inspection, fuelling rumours that the Church Geneticist is hoarding a 'dote to the dreaded Azerbaijani virus now destroying Western Europe . . .*' Not to mention most of the Middle East, Passion added under her breath, but she knew her listeners weren't interested in that.

'*So tell me, Commander,*' said Passion, turning to a squat man whose bulky heat-controlled NBC combat clothing made him look squatter still. '*What do you say to the auditor-general's claim that the Geneticists have only ever been interested in biotek?*'

'Biotek, nanotek, what's the difference? It's all dangerous.' The man squinted at where he thought the spinning vidcam would be. *'If they're clean then let us in, show the UN they've got nothing to hide. Until then . . . Well, honey, you know my private opinion.'*

The squat man put his arm round Passion's shoulder and smiled grimly as Passion tried not to flinch. *'I think they're kooks. I don't care if they're Christian like us or not. Any raghead who lives underground in a desert and thinks he can bring Jesus back to life has got to be crazy. I think he's got the 'dote. Hell, personally I think the bastard probably invented the nanoVirus in the first place. He's nuts enough.'*

The General was working himself up for an attack, Passion realized. Covering his back on camera. Personally, she didn't believe for a minute that the Geneticists invented the virus any more than that they were hoarding a nanetic antidote. And as for the auditor general, he was about as out-of-control as a teetotal Wall Street broker. If the man had a 'dote, she'd have heard about it already – because the Geneticists would have been out there licensing it to every State desperate enough to sign on the dotted line.

And that meant all of them.

'Will Auditor-General Volublilis fight? Will he let the UN PaxForce down into the tunnels of the San Lorenzo complex? Or will he try to negotiate an altogether different deal? As yet, we don't know. But as soon as we do, you'll be the first to hear about it . . . This is Passion, outside the San Lorenzo Complex in Africa's Megribian Desert, bringing you the world as it happens . . . Until next time.'

Signing off with a long, serious gaze to the camera, Passion clicked her fingers and the tiny Aerospatiale 182 retracted its lens and flew into her hand. From there Passion downloaded the data to her belt, uploaded it to a local low-level satellite – and smiled.

Chapter 30

Inside the Gold Mine

'How good of you to come . . .' The comment wasn't ironic, the old man really meant it. Though Lady Clare didn't see how he could. The Prince Imperial was waiting for Lady Clare in his study, six of his other advisers standing around the room. They'd been waiting on her arrival.

'I'm sorry . . .'

The old man waved her apologies aside. 'Dry yourself,' he suggested.

A huge open fire burned in the grate, flames dancing against a carved fireback of Merovingian bees. What had once been a mahogany table burnt fiercely in the flames. What was left of the other legs was sawed into logs and stacked neatly against the wall. The old man didn't need the fire, she knew that. He might have been born too late to be grown to one of FffC's patented genetic templates, but he'd still undergone more viral rewirings than most exotics. Which was probably why he'd ended up banning both biotek and elective surgery against the advice of his own ministers. Nothing quite like a reformed junkie for banging on about the virtues of others staying clean.

All the same, Lady Clare was grateful for the warmth of the fire, for the normality of dancing flames; though she knew that was exactly why the fire was there. For the same reason fresh coffee now sat in a jug on the table and fresh croissants spilled over from a Sèvres plate . . . She knew her history as well as the Prince Imperial. When the *Titanic* sank a member of the Guggenheim family who'd been wearing an ordinary suit went to change into evening wear, so that he could meet death properly dressed.

Paris wasn't sinking, it was being drowned. And though God might not be in his heaven and all might not be right with the world, the Prince Imperial would never be impolite enough to point out the fact, at least not in public. His empire was built on such elaborate negations of reality. Most empires were. Augustus Caesar ruled over a republic, at least on paper. The Prince governed an empire without an emperor, on paper and in fact.

The Emperor's body would be in Switzerland, where it always was. To get into his crypt, sappers from the Fourth Reich would have to cut their way through slabs of titanium-reinforced concrete and then lance open a bombproof cocoon spun from alternate threads of boron mesh, graphite and tungsten alloy, laid at right angles to each other.

They wouldn't bother. If they ever got past HKS Zurich's automated defences, the Reich would just kill the juice to the Emperor's pod. The old bastard wouldn't know his body was dead, any more than he now knew it was alive. No thoughts could exist in that frozen neural wasteland of his. He'd been all but flatlining up in that satellite for years, the occasional flickers nothing but echoes and feedback . . .

She was crying without noticing it. Tears tumbled from Lady Clare's blue eyes to trickle down her tired face. No one in this room had ever known the Emperor, not even the Prince Imperial. The Prince had been a zygote suspended in liquid nitrogen when his father had had a stroke. All his talked-about memories of his beloved male parent were based on relentless watching of old vids.

'My dear . . .' Sitting in a straight-backed wooden chair, his hands gripping lion's paws carved from oak, the old man stared at her, waiting. They were all staring into the abyss and the abyss wasn't so much staring back as reaching out to grip them by the throat. But the Prince at least was keeping his dignity.

Shibui. Notions of personal restraint. It was one thing to espouse the idea in public, which the Prince did particularly when visiting Edo, quite another to suddenly decide you were going to live and die by it. Personally Lady Clare blamed the old man's long-dead tutor for drumming that crap into him. It wouldn't be allowed to happen these days, not if her departments had anything to do with it. Her departments . . . Lady Clare began crying again.

And then stopped dead when she realized just how much entertainment her tears were providing for Count Lazlo. No way was she going to be his amusement. Lady Clare shook her head crossly, a sudden wave of fury putting back the backbone as she pushed one thin knuckle into her own eye sockets. There were men she was prepared to cry in front of, but the newly promoted Minister for External Security wasn't one of them.

'Gentlemen . . .' Lazlo looked round at the four ministers standing near the Prince Imperial, then nodded ironically in Lady Clare's direction. 'And Lady Clare, of course . . .'

Lady Clare just stared back, as coldly as she could manage. Tears were still drying in tracks on her cheeks, her hair was uncombed, unbrushed and unwashed. Only the Dior dress gave her some confidence, that and the ridiculous shoes. Lady Clare looked down at the already disintegrating court shoes and smiled bitterly.

She should have been worrying desperately about the Empire. Except that even the Empire didn't really get a look in compared with what really filled her head: that she wasn't able to say a proper goodbye to her daughter. Memories of LizAlec's face looking sullen and cold flickered through Lady Clare's mind. All Lady Clare could remember was her daughter's contemptuous gaze and the rigid straightness of LizAlec's spine as she stalked towards the departure gate, never once looking back. Not even a silent nod to signal goodbye.

The girl would have cried on the shuttle, Lady Clare knew

that. But not at Charles de Gaulle, not in public, not in front of her. Lady Clare was like that, too. Well, she used to be . . .

'Are you with us?' The words were politeness itself, icily so. Lazlo stood in front of her, offering her a handwritten list of figures. Everyone else already had a set, including the Prince Imperial. Lady Clare looked at Lazlo's scrawl and knew instantly what it was. A numerical statement of the Third Empire's military strength. Row after row of figures about the *Garde Impériale*. That only the *Garde Impériale* was listed told Lady Clare that Lazlo had no faith in the other regiments holding to their oath of loyalty.

Only one regiment and not a single experienced human commander to lead them. Both the field marshal and the general were dead. Not that they'd had much real experience either, except at listening to their machines.

Maybe this was what war always came down to, a huddle of people taking critical decisions from a position of blind ignorance. There were still a few combatAIs, of course, and JCIT decks, but they were empty shells, nothing more: reduced to muttering in corners, those of them that hadn't been reduced to dust.

Not one person in the room could handle the necessary equations to fight an efficient war. Probably no one living could, not manually, unaided. And the Black Hundred didn't need to, they won by strength of numbers. Everyone in the room knew that too.

'It seems to me,' said Lazlo, 'that we don't have much choice.' Tapping the paper with the back of one lacquered nail, he selected figures at random. 'Outnumbered four to one . . . Number of *Garde Impériale* armed with ceramic rifles, twenty-eight per cent. Number armed with aquatic-issue subsonic assassination weapons, twelve per cent . . .'

'The rest?' That was the Prince Imperial asking what Lady Clare couldn't bring herself to ask.

'Unarmed,' said Lazlo. 'Our tanks and APVs are so much

scrap. There isn't a functioning battle hover in the entire city. The figures are all there.' Lazlo didn't bother to add *Your Highness* or *sir*. In fact, Clare realized, he hadn't used the conventional honorific once since the meeting began. Which told her what she wanted to know, but not yet as much as she needed.

'Totally unarmed . . . ?'

Lazlo just looked at her.

'Totally?' Lady Clare kept her voice calm. Repeating her question into the silence, as the others around them stopped talking and began watching instead.

'Glass knives, zytel blades, sharpened sticks . . .' Count Lazlo's voice was contemptuous, making it obvious he answered her only out of politeness.

Thin and bird-like, Lady Clare leant forward and Lazlo flinched as she prodded him once over his breastbone. 'Even a sharpened stick kills if it's stuck in the right place.' Lady Clare smiled grimly. 'Ask Vlad Tepes . . . Besides, there must be glass bottles, reserves of petrol, rags . . .' Lady Clare raised her chin slightly and pushed back her shoulders. So, this wasn't how she'd intended the confrontation to go. But she wasn't going to let Lazlo . . . Lady Clare stopped and caught her thoughts before they span out of control. Just what was she trying to save? That old man sitting smiling at her, the Third Empire itself, or the girl she'd given birth to? No one could protect all three, not even her.

So had she the guts to betray her country or the brains not to have to, Lady Clare asked herself. Maybe she'd have found it easier if LizAlec really had been her daughter – or maybe she wouldn't. Lady Clare knew exactly why she should save LizAlec, basic responsibility, but she had less than no idea why she should attempt to save a corrupt, rotting empire. Even assuming the Empire could be saved or she could do it.

'How noble that sounds,' Lazlo said lightly. 'Fighting the Reich with pointed sticks. But let's be less emotional about this, shall we?' He stopped, looked around the small study. 'I take it everyone agrees our first priority is to protect the Prince Imperial . . .'

His gaze halted when he reached Lady Clare.

What did he want from her?

Agreement?

'No,' said Lady Clare. 'I don't believe our first duty is to save His Highness.' Even the Prince looked surprised at that: but he kept silent, his pale grey eyes never once leaving her face as she stalked across to a side table, leaving them waiting. Keeping them waiting while she slowly poured herself coffee and then poured another cup, carrying it back to the Prince Imperial, meeting his quizzical smile.

After a life of indulgence, the Prince had been forbidden coffee, cigars and cocaine by his doctors, not to mention sexual activity and stress. But Lady Clare figured caffeine was the least of his vices and, besides, he was about to need all the comfort he could get.

'Our job isn't to save His Highness,' said Lady Clare. 'It's to save the Empire. And even if we were successful, to save the Empire means condemning Paris.' They all knew she told the truth. Every one of them had seen Gdansk: not a building left standing, not an oak or plane tree that wasn't uprooted.

Any army could wreak that kind of damage with a small fission device, just as a neutron burst could clear a city but leave its historic buildings untouched. But to destroy Gdansk with gunpowder, crowbars and ropes because the semiAI howitzers were virus-struck and there were no drones to deliver bombs, that took will. The blood-and-iron kind that drunken Cossacks always sang about.

Lady Clare glanced apologetically at the Prince Imperial, but he just stared back, almost as if knew what she was about to ask. 'The question,' said Lady Clare, 'isn't can we save the empire, but should we . . . Is our Byzantium worth saving?'

Wind rattled the wooden shutters and flames spat in the

grate but that was all the noise there was. 'We have a choice,' Lady Clare announced into the silence. 'A simple, very basic choice. To have any chance of keeping the Empire together we have to fight, with sharpened sticks if that's what it takes. Alternatively, we surrender now, which saves Paris. But then the Empire falls . . .' Lady Clare looked at the others, watching their faces. That she didn't recognize two of them told her all she needed to know about how well the government was holding together. Chief ministers had been fleeing like proverbial rats, their places taken by underlings.

In a way that was good, Lady Clare decided, because it meant the only people who really counted in that room were her and Lazlo. Plus the Prince Imperial, obviously . . .

'There's a third alternative,' Lazlo said loudly, much too loudly. Which was interesting in itself. Either the man could feel control slipping away or he was having trouble keeping his temper. Lady Clare couldn't decide which she considered most unlikely.

'Is there?' asked Lady Clare, interrupting just as Lazlo opened his mouth to speak again.

The tall man flushed. He was leaning forward on the balls of his feet, like an athlete on the starting block, as impatient as any runner. Too fast, Lady Clare thought disapprovingly. You're going at it too fast. A vein throbbed in his temple and a tic pulled at the corner of one eye. He was under much more pressure than she'd realized. Lady Clare just wondered why she was so certain it wasn't the same pressure as the rest of them were suffering.

'What's the third option?' she asked, cutting in again as Count Lazlo opened his mouth. Out of the corner of her eye, Lady Clare could see the Prince Imperial smother a grin.

'The Prince Imperial could rule under the protection of the Fourth Reich . . .' Lazlo said furiously.

'And for how long?' Lady Clare asked softly. 'Until the last of the Ishies ups camp and leaves? Until CySat C3N pull out their final vidman?'

'No,' Lazlo shook his head. 'Forever, until . . .' He fumbled with the words. 'For as long as the Prince Imperial wants,' Lazlo finished lamely. He couldn't very well say until the prince died, because everyone knew the old man didn't intend to.

'Rule under the Reich? No.' The old man leant forward in his chair so suddenly he slopped coffee into his Sèvres saucer. Putting the cup and saucer down carefully, he absent-mindedly dried his hand on the hem of his smoking jacket. 'No,' he said more firmly. 'I hope everyone agrees that is not an option . . .' Grey eyes swept the room like intelligent fire and Lady Clare found herself nodding along with everyone except Lazlo.

'Paris fights to the end and maybe, just maybe, the Empire decides to fight back, inspired by our example.' The old man smiled sardonically, as if he couldn't believe what he was saying. 'Or we save the city and . . .' The prince spread his hands theatrically. He was smiling.

He was fucking good at it, thought Lady Clare, surprised by her own crudity. The old man could have been standing in a ballroom addressing 500 of the Empire's richest movers and shakers, or talking over a newsfeed to 500,000,000 of his erstwhile subjects. No one listening blind would have known he was talking to five scared councillors.

The Prince Imperial looked at Lazlo and then nodded – but it was to himself. Whatever his decision was, there would be no point trying to argue him out of it. The Bonaparte stubbornness was legendary. He would surrender Paris rather than see it destroyed, decided Lady Clare. The man always had been an old-fashioned liberal at heart: it was one of his worst failings.

'I intend to retire to my study,' said the Prince Imperial, looking straight at Lady Clare. He could have been speaking to her alone and it seemed to Lady Clare that he was. Standing unsteadily, the old man walked shakily across the damp carpet, turning back to the entrance.

'This is not a decision I can make,' he said sadly. 'You must decide as you see fit . . . And when you have, you must let me know your decision.' One ringed hand went up to still Lady Clare's protest. 'You are my advisor, advise me . . .'

Lady Clare looked at Lazlo and smiled, coldly, pulling images out of her memory. Not of the night they had spent together, disgusting though she'd found that. But of a clone that Lazlo kept hidden at his stone hunting lodge high on the edge of the Lot Valley. The big-boned blonde-haired peasant girl didn't look like a Kyoko, but she was. Lady Clare had blackmailed Lazlo's doctor in Cahors to run a DNA scan on the girl's final double-X pair. It had picked up a Sabine Industries copyright tacked into the chromosome's sugar-phosphate backbone.

Coding for intelligence she could understand. She'd insisted on that for LizAlec, along with some more unconventional modifications, and coding for beauty, for good health, even for sweetness of disposition, those she could understand, just. But that didn't stop Lady Clare finding distasteful the idea of gene coding a sexual partner for stupidity.

'Well,' Lady Clare said. 'Shall we take that vote?'

They didn't, of course, not then. Lazlo wanted time to talk to the others, strike deals. Lady Clare knew that and she let him have it. Watching as the tall man moved round the other Ministers, glad-handing newly promoted underlings to whom he wouldn't have given the nod had he met them in the marble corridors of the Tuileries two months before.

Lady Clare did nothing, except check if the coffee in the silver pot was still warm. It wasn't, but she drank another cup anyway, without touching a bowl of vast crystals of amber-hued cane sugar from the Prince Imperial's own estates in St Lucia. Her legs were so tired that all Lady Clare really wanted to do was sit. But anything that showed she might be tired, hung-over and old wasn't appropriate with Lazlo present. So Lady Clare perched herself on the edge of a side table as if bored by the anxious groups that hung around Count Lazlo.

And while she was sitting being ostentatiously bored, Lady

Clare tried to work out in her head exactly what she *did* want, keeping it personal like her analyst had always told her, until she fired him for repetition. In order, her list ran:

LizAlec back.

Her house undamaged (and with it Paris).

Her job . . .

The list was both selfish and personal. But Lady Clare didn't have a problem with that. Global was out and she was learning to think small, or so she told herself. But still, she couldn't have it all. To save LizAlec meant voting for surrender, the kidnappers' warning had been unequivocal on that. Vote to fight and LizAlec died – if she wasn't already dead.

The decision got no easier for being worried at. And Lady Clare was beginning to understand that it wasn't that her head told her one thing and her heart another: she just didn't know. Prejudice was the worst possible motive for selecting a side, but stripped down to nothing, which was where she stood, prejudice was all Lady Clare had. That, and a silent, almost unstated belief that if genetics counted for anything then LizAlec was a lot more dangerous and capable than anyone yet realized.

Hard thoughts for a mother to handle, but Lady Clare could and would. If Lazlo was for surrender then she was against it. As for LizAlec . . . Statistical probability and basic common sense said she was already dead, but Lady Clare couldn't quite believe it, any more than she quite believed her daughter was still alive. Emotionally she hoped, but intellectually she was agnostic.

Her certainty had gone, hollowed out by hunger, by the loss of LizAlec and by the apparently endless storms. That wind had stripped resolve from her as brutally as it had ripped tiles from the roof of the Hôtel Sabatini. Like the city, she was drowning in mud, in debilitating indecision. But she would do what she had to: decide.

'We fight . . .'

It wasn't a suggestion: the words were her statement of intent. She still outranked everyone in the study, even if she only outranked Lazlo now by length of service. The decision was hers to take, though open statements weren't her usual style.

The room stilled.

'We fight,' Lady Clare said fiercely, 'because we don't have any alternative.' Staring round, Lady Clare could tell that the others weren't convinced, and she wasn't surprised. Fat, balding or weak, they were even less impressed by the thought of having to get out there and fight than they were by the idea of dying. And she didn't blame them. In their place she'd have felt the same.

Lazlo would always be beyond reach, but not the others and in memetic terms five was a very small number of minds to colonize. As always, Lady Clare started in hard: forcing unpalatable facts down their throats. Sugar syrup could come later.

'Whatever we do, most people in this room will die.' That got their attention. 'Listen,' said Lady Clare. 'We're ministers, sub-ministers, heads of sections. Why would the Reich let any of us live?'

'No, wait . . .' The woman flipped up her hand to still Lazlo. 'You can talk later.' One of the junior ministers smiled and then another. And Lady Clare breathed a tiny sigh of relief. Some of them at least were obviously enjoying the tall minister's discomfort. She could bring round the others yet, Lady Clare just knew it.

'I want to tell you one of the Prince Imperial's favourite stories,' announced Lady Clare. 'It happened in ancient Greece, or maybe it was Rome . . .'

'Terrific,' the young finance minister who'd smiled when she put down Lazlo groaned aloud, but his muttered aside was friendly, almost resigned. The Prince Imperial was known for his ability (if ability it was) to draw a classical allusion from any event. There were those, Lazlo among them, who believed the old man knew more about Gallia Lugdunensis,

Germania Libra and the Belgae than he did about what went on within the borders of his own empire.

Lady Clare wasn't fooled and hadn't been for a long time. Not since the old man had pulled three disparate facts together and suddenly asked her a simple but unanswerable question about the religious situation in M'Dina. That was when she'd realized he hid the mind of a tactician behind the clumsiness of a buffoon. His role model wasn't the original little Corsican corporal who'd risen from poverty to be the first Napoleon. It was the stuttering Roman emperor Clau-Clau-Claudius.

'A general wanted to storm a city,' said Lady Clare. She kept her words simple. One of the ministers in the room didn't even have French as his main language, having been born in *France Outre-mer*. And besides that, simplicity paid. 'But the city walls were high and the gates were strong. For weeks the general besieged the city, without success, until a treacherous slave came to him in the night and offered to open the gates from within in return for gold.'

Lady Clare let her gaze drift slowly across the room to settle on Lazlo: let the others make of that what they would, and they would . . .

'The general accepted and that night the slave opened a side gate to let the enemy slip in and kill people where they slept. The last person to be murdered was the city's ruler, his throat cut by the general in front of the king's slave.'

Lady Clare stopped, just long enough to check that everyone was listening. She had their attention right enough, every scrap of it. Even Lazlo had stopped peering at his nails and pretending to be bored. But then Lazlo knew what happened next, even if the others didn't. Lady Clare wasn't the only one to have heard the tale told by the Prince Imperial.

Lazlo could interrupt her now, of course. But that would only make the others all the more anxious to hear what happened. She had him and Lady Clare knew it. Pushing herself away from the table, Lady Clare stood to face them. Her voice dropped an octave, as she tried to sound as much like the Prince Imperial as she could, but most of them never even noticed.

'When the city was taken and the inhabitants dead, the general ordered the slave to the top of the city walls to receive his bag of gold. And then, having given the slave his gold and made him a free man, the general ordered two of his own slaves to toss the traitor to the streets below. Because, as the general told the traitor before he was thrown to his death, if his old master couldn't trust him, who could?'

'We're not slaves,' Lazlo said contemptuously.

'Everyone's a slave to something,' said Lady Clare.

The young finance minister nodded. 'Marcus Aurelius.'

Lady Clare gave the man her best half-smile. 'The point is, if we fight the Reich they'll kill us. And if we surrender Paris and give up the Prince Imperial, then they'll kill us anyway, eventually. They'll have no choice, we'll have shown we can't be trusted . . .'

She was talking direct to Lazlo now. '. . . Of course, if you think you can cut a deal for yourself, then go ahead and try. But I imagine any deal depends on delivering not just the city but also His Highness. And I don't think that's going to happen, do you?'

He didn't. She could see the doubt in his green eyes. And behind the doubt, something darker, more malicious, infinitely more personal. That was when Lady Clare finally understood what had happened to LizAlec and why.

Lazlo smiled.

'My daughter is dead.' Lady Clare stated it as a fact. If Lazlo had LizAlec still alive, he'd have let her see tapes, made Lady Clare listen to LizAlec plead. She knew Lazlo, he wouldn't have been able to resist.

'Oh no,' said the tall minister, stepping in close. 'She's very much alive.' He hoped it was true, not that it mattered. Either way, the woman in front of him didn't know if it was true or not. 'But all it takes is one simple call. And my dashing friends do have one comStation still active, you know.'

It wasn't true. From Winchester pulse/Rs to satellite dishes, everything had turned out to contain steel somewhere. Even the Reich's metal-free non-detectable anti-personnel mines turned out to have a tiny hair-thin steel spike right at its heart. Carbon-shielded against microwave detection and destruction, but made of metal and virus-vulnerable all the same.

'I don't believe you,' said Lady Clare. Everyone else was forgotten. All the woman could see in her head, all she could think about was Lazlo and LizAlec. She refused to think about the thing she wanted to think about and then she did anyway. Wondering just how LizAlec had died.

'Don't you want to know where she is?' Lazlo's voice stopped Lady Clare as she swept towards the door, head held high, hands grasped tight to prevent them shaking. She turned back, contempt written across her thin, once beautiful face.

'My daughter is dead.'

Lazlo laughed. 'Your daughter?' He stretched lazily like a cat and reached for a decanter, pouring cognac into a balloon glass. 'Take your time before talking to the Prince. Think things over properly.' His voice was easy and confident – and Lady Clare had never hated someone so much in her life.

'LizAlec is alive?' Lady Clare forced herself to ask the question.

'At the moment.'

'And you know where she is?' Lady Clare met Lazlo's cold grey eyes, cutting a rapid deal with herself. 'Because if you do know where to find her, I think we should talk.'

'Oh yes,' said Lazlo smiling. 'I know exactly where to find her.'

Chapter 31

Death Incarnate

LizAlec was lost. At least, she figured she was. She'd been tumbling very slowly through space, cocooned in the neoprene chair of a LockMart escape pod: which sounded much more dramatic than it was, since LizAlec had almost no sense of movement at all.

Until the pod stopped suddenly, of its own accord, retro boosters hissing like an angry swan. The stars that had looped around her as trails of light, like the neural axons that ran jewelled and glistening through bioClay, suddenly reappeared as pricks of light. Only to vanish back into a tight encirclement of threads as the pod began to spin along its axis.

But all that movement was outside the pod and LizAlec couldn't see the stars anyway. Not for herself. The pod was stub-winged, windowless, radiation-proof, relying for vision on bug-eyed cams mounted in a ring around its middle like a studded belt.

The AI controlling the pod was so moronic that LizAlec wasn't even sure it qualified as semi. It was a joke among hardware, not so much conscious, more driven: functioning on some cut-down digital version of instinct. LizAlec hoped to fuck it knew what it was doing, because she certainly didn't.

And now it had stopped moving altogether.

She was free-floating in space, trapped in a glorified coffin about the size of a MaBell vidbooth: not one of the head-only jobs, obviously, but a full-length one, like the box on the corner of André des Arts, the one with the imaginative holoporn stickers crawling all over the inside.

Hanging in space wasn't the safest she'd ever been but then, blasting herself away from the slow-spinning silver grandeur of *The Arc* back towards Earth hadn't exactly been a risk-free option, either. Even LizAlec could work the numbers on that. The pod was stabilizing now, no longer spinning. If LizAlec hadn't known it was too unlikely, she'd have thought the escape pod was slowly, methodically putting itself into reverse, with much disgusted digital sucking of teeth.

In front of LizAlec, the Earth showed large and clear on her screen, cameras scanning through thick cloud to the ground below. Some primitive bioSoft kept imposing national boundaries as fluorescent red lines over the far, far distant landscape and edging up the coastlines in blue.

Somewhere on the unmarked panel in front of her would be a hot key to turn off the fluorescent overlay, but LizAlec couldn't find it. Not that she'd tried too hard. Hitting strange keys at random in a stationary escape pod didn't have much to recommend it. Not even to a girl who prided herself on living dangerously.

'Shit.' LizAlec tried to brush something off her face and found she couldn't. Her hands had just thoughtfully been fastened to her side. It was a mediSoft spider, scrambling out of hiding to repair her face and making a neat job of it too, LizAlec realized, looking at the tiny arachnid reflected in her screen. Mind you, the pod's medical software was as sophisticated as the AI was basic. Military-grade full-capability stuff. The rapid scan it had given her battered body in those first few seconds after the blast had been as thorough as anything she'd ever had done in Paris.

The spider clung to her cheek while infinitely articulated metal legs sewed shut a cut below her eye and pricked rapidly into the bruising on her cheek to suck away tiny droplets of blood. Blood from the surface had already undergone cell-salvage and been recycled straight back into her body.

This was just a tidy-up operation. The big stuff had been

done right back at the beginning, when the girl had thought she was still going to die. Now she had an intravenous feed plugged direct into her wrist, feeding through a ceramic socket the mediSoft had punched into place before LizAlec even knew what the pod had in mind.

LizAlec suspected the glucose solution being dripped into her wrist contained high-level seratonin-uptake inhibitors. She certainly felt a hell of a lot more calm than she had any right to be. The pinpricks from a spider perched on her throat were small doses of erythropoietin blasted straight through her skin to boost her red cell count, but they were so minor and happened so infrequently, that LizAlec hardly noticed them.

The only bit of the deal LizAlec objected to was the colonics plug which the pod had inserted of its own accord. Now she had a strange gurgling in her stomach as liquid was trickled in and waste pumped out. LizAlec had a nasty feeling that the water flowing around her colon and the chilled tasteless water being offered every few minutes through a self-sealing straw weren't entirely separate.

She'd seen programmes about closed-loop life-support systems. If she didn't get to wherever the pod was attempting to take her real soon, the machine would probably shut her down to let mediSoft spiders insert thousands of tiny catheters through her skin to drain her faltering lymph system. LizAlec wasn't sure how she was going to stop the pod doing that, if it suddenly decided that shutting LizAlec down was the girl's most viable long-term option. Still, just being alive was pretty miraculous, which was fitting since she'd been standing in a cathedral when the Big Black came in.

LizAlec hadn't intended to make a run for it, of course, not at the beginning. She certainly hadn't intended to leave the freaky little sandrat behind either. But she'd been left with no other option. Not after Brother Michael had called her up to the vestry. The other girls had looked at her as she sat finishing her breakfast and muttered to themselves, though not one of them had tried to warn her. Not that she needed warning. She'd been able to work out what went on for herself. Sara's downcast eyes and shuffling walk would have told her, even if Rachel hadn't cried herself to sleep every night – or at least on those nights when she been called to Brother Michael's vestry to pray.

LizAlec hadn't been called up there to pray, though, whatever the others thought. LizAlec could replay that conversation in her head, word for fucking word, so perfect that her eidetic memory could have been verified in a court of law. But before all that she'd have to get there.

She'd reached the cathedral by taking the Otis, feeling sick as the lift blasted down from the women's dorm, losing gravity as it approached the centre of the hub. And then it had swung itself out of the arm – feeling almost in free fall as it jumped the gap into the spindle – and turned through ninety degrees to rise rapidly towards Brother Michael's yttrium-glass cathedral. There had been a hiss of air and then the door had slid back to reveal an aquarium-like gloom lit only by Earthlight below and the tallow brightness of the moon above.

Brother Michael was waiting for her, sitting in a huge steel chair below the altar. Steel pillars rose to a crystal ceiling and the whole dark sky was revealed above his head, so that from where she stood in the Otis doorway LizAlec could see all the way through to eternity. If eternity was what was really out there beyond the dust and the space junk. She left the crystalMeth-fuelled cosmic ramblings to Fixx.

'You wanted to see me?' LizAlec demanded, staring at the seated man. No way was she praying with him. She'd decided that before the lift even blasted off from her level.

The man didn't answer. Instead, he just clicked his fingers twice and the lift door shut behind her, vanishing down the spindle with a low hiss.

LizAlec shrugged. If that was meant to impress her, she wasn't impressed. She'd trained a fridge at school to open its ice-cream compartment automatically every time LizAlec picked up a teaspoon. And as for Anchee, she had a whole set of self-opening LV luggage. LizAlec waited in silence. Waiting in silence was something she was good at. In fact, she'd got silent waiting down to something of an art form.

But then the door of the Otis opened again behind her. Thumbs dug into the flesh of her inner arms, trapping a peripheral nerve, and LizAlec screamed, her hands flash-frozen as pain raced back along nerve paths to her brain. He hadn't wanted to pray with her anyway. She'd been set up.

Some people got off on fear, LizAlec knew that. She knew also she wasn't one of them. She didn't get off on pain either, though there'd been a time she'd thought maybe Fixx did, until she realized what Fixx really got off on was cerebral self-flagellation, which wasn't at all the same. But her relationship with pain and fear wasn't quite normal, she knew that too. They clarified things, like hunger did. Pain especially heightened her senses, tightened her thoughts. Most of all, it crystallized her mind.

There was no effect Fixx could ascribe to his chemicals that LizAlec couldn't pull up inside her head. The glass-edged clarity of meth. That sense of flash-vidding each moment so it imprinted forever on memory. She got that, and more . . .

Much to Fixx's jealous disgust. He reckoned she came naturally wired. Either that or sometime before her birth Sabine Industries had strung in extra dopamine enhancers, uptake inhibitors and the rest of the whole insane pharmacopoeia. And maybe bundled in some heightened reflexes for luck. It wasn't impossible.

'So,' said Brother Michael, pushing himself out of his metal chair. 'What do we have here? At least, what do we really have?' He stopped in front of LizAlec, his ReeGravs creaking on the floor. LizAlec could feel the seconds stretch out inside her head.

She was meant to break the silence. It was her role to ask what was wrong or maybe just 'fess to whatever it was – but she wasn't going to. If she'd learnt only one thing from Fixx

– other than that crystalMeth fucked you up – it was not to give away her leverage. Never confess, always fight back. It made for great sex and a lousy relationship.

Fixx could have got her out of going back to St Lucius. She would have done it, too, even if it meant cutting her ties with Lady Clare, but he never asked . . . Not once. *Lady Clare*, that was how she'd started to think of the woman now, as someone else, someone not her mother. When LizAlec got back, if she got back, finding out about Razz was going to come top of LizAlec's hit list. Not the myth, but the real stuff, what kind of CySat she had liked, what she ate, who she listened to.

Fuck it, maybe she'd collected sims by Fixx. That would be nicely ironic. Maybe that whole fucking Bastille kick of hers was Oedipal and the beat-meister was just some sad daddy-substitute. Maybe it was and maybe he knew. That could be why he kept refusing to fuck her.

'I know what you're thinking,' said Brother Michael.

I doubt it, thought LizAlec, but she didn't say that aloud. Instead she just scowled at the preacher, then cut him out of her thoughts . . . When LizAlec got back. No, make that *if*. *If* she got back she was going to find out about her dad, too. What was the point of being the daughter of a living god if you couldn't trade on it? Let's see Anchee try to top *that* at school.

'You're thinking, why is Brother Michael cross with me?'

'Like I give a fuck,' said LizAlec and yelped as the preacher backhanded her, hard enough to flip her head sideways.

'Fuck you, shithead . . .' LizAlec spun sideways and tried to grind her boot down the preacher's shin. But the person behind LizAlec just yanked her backwards and dug both thumbs even harder into her upper arm, so that her whole body shuddered with pain.

'Stop feeling my tits,' LizAlec's voice was raw with anger.

'I'm not doing . . .'

'Yes, you are,' LizAlec said savagely. 'If you're that fucking desperate to cop a feel,' she shot over her shoulder, 'go and play with the animals.'

Thumbs closed again on her arms, only this time an order from Brother Michael cut short the pain.

'Leonie, leave us.'

Leonie? LizAlec turned to find herself looking into the impassive face of one of Brother Michael's crop-haired bodyguards.

'I wasn't . . .' the woman began, staring at Brother Michael over LizAlec's shoulder. But the preacher just waved her away. The black woman thought better of protesting and went. Given the weird light that burned in Brother Michael's eyes it was probably a wise decision. Anyone who didn't know the brethren were teetotal drug abstainers might have thought the man was wired out of his skull.

'Wait,' demanded Brother Michael as the woman reached the lift door. He pointed at a smooth glass pulpit. 'Secure her first.' Viciously, the bodyguard did so, yanking first one and then the other of LizAlec's arms over her head, securing each wrist to a ring set high on the front of the pulpit. LizAlec had wondered what the rings were for.

The cuffs slid around her wrists like bindweed and tied her tightly to the glass rings. LizAlec didn't bother pulling against the cuffs: she'd watched enough episodes of *NYPD Extreme* to know how soft restraints worked.

Keeping her bulk between Brother Michael and LizAlec, the woman checked both cuffs one last time, then ran her hands down LizAlec's upstretched arms, heavy fingers smoothing briefly across the girl's pulled-up breasts.

LizAlec spat and enjoyed the blind fury that exploded across the woman's face. To hit LizAlec back was to admit what she'd been doing but to ignore LizAlec was to admit she'd won, at least briefly. Putting her hand over LizAlec's mouth, the woman sucker-punched LizAlec in the kidneys, keeping her fingers in place as the girl fought for breath.

'Finished?' Brother Michael asked. He had his back to the

pulpit, rustling through papers on a side table. An ornate Murano paperweight, inset with a tiny magnet and full of exploded blue and red flowers, rested on top of the pile to stop them floating away.

'I have now,' said the woman.

'What did you say your name was?' Brother Michael asked, his voice soft. He had LizAlec's face between his fingers, squeezing gently. His beard was oiled and trim, his mouth youthful and full, not yet thinned-down by age or slightly puffed-up at the edge with collagen enhancers. There were no worry lines anywhere on his forehead, and only the merest suggestion of crow's feet edged eyes that were the deepest brown. Staring at his face was like looking into a very beautiful vacuum.

Cold, dangerous, untrustworthy . . . Mind you, he didn't like her either. Not if the way his fingers kept tightening on her face was anything to go by. And where things went from here was anyone's guess.

She could keep to her original lie, try a new one or tell the truth, though the last option didn't really appeal to LizAlec. Telling the truth, the whole truth and nothing but the truth was a habit she'd ditched early on. Having Lady Clare Fabio as a mother didn't instil a strong desire to leave yourself vulnerable. A fact LizAlec had finally learnt to turn to her advantage when she realized her S3 shadow would be too worried about losing LizAlec to admit she'd flicked down some alley in the Marais and given him the slip.

Her bodyguard's fear of failure had worked for months. Until a half-yearly medical finally threw up bruising on LizAlec's thighs that her S3 shadow couldn't explain – and LizAlec wasn't prepared to. More than anything else, the girl was too embarrassed to admit the blotches were where Fixx's fingertips had dug into her. But she didn't have to.

The really scary thing was that Lady Clare knew exactly what the marks were: that much was clear from the ice-cold expression in her eyes. Though LizAlec was too naive and too young to recognize the expression not as anger but buried memory. Her shadow was gone that morning. Reassigned to some border that the Black Hundreds were due to cross on their unstoppable sweep west. LizAlec had felt guilty about that, briefly anyway.

His replacement was an S3 blackbird called Per, one of the Third Section's most handsome. The new shadow was as tall as Fixx, but with broad Scandinavian shoulders and hardened lizard-skin grafts that spread like speckled grey leather across his shoulders and down his spine. His hair was ash-blond and his eyes were light blue. Few heroes had nobler jaws or faces so perfect that LizAlec would have killed for their bone structure. But it was when Per announced that – like LizAlec – he scoured the flea markets for antique paperbacks that LizAlec knew she was meant to fall safely in love with him. But she didn't. Clean-cut and Aryan wasn't her type.

'Are you listening?' Brother Michael demanded furiously.

'Yeah, sure,' said LizAlec, smiling sweetly. Well, as sweetly as she could smile with Brother Michael's hands gripped round her jaw. She was listening, too, just not to him. LizAlec went back inside her head where she could listen to the hum of the air-scrubbers, the rustle of spiderplant leaves and the low thud of her heart. Somewhere down inside she was afraid, but not yet as afraid as she should be. The trouble was, she'd never had anything between blind panic and total indifference and just recently only the indifference ever reached her violet eyes. The cool exterior, the social armour fitted her body like a carapace: both kept her removed, which was the way she liked it.

Stepping back was a way not to get hurt. And if not getting hurt meant not getting involved either, then so be it. Her mother did that: signed away people's lives, ruined their careers, imposed cold order on warm chaos, but always smoothly, with no rough edges showing.

'Well? Brother Michael said.

'Well what?' LizAlec hadn't the remotest idea which question he wanted answered. Was it, was she listening? Or were they back to, who was she really? Was she listening LizAlec could handle, because the answer was, *Yeah, kind of . . .* But as to who she was, she needed notice of that question, it was way more difficult.

'Are you listening to me?' Brother Michael demanded.

'Oh, yeah,' said LizAlec, 'though I'm not hearing anything yet . . .'

Brother Michael frowned at that, as LizAlec knew he would. So she jutted her chin forward and tried to look dangerous. Pretty hard with your hands high up over your head and next to impossible when all you're wearing is a cotton smock that looks like a washed-out nightie, even if you don't have some maniac gripping your face and swinging it slowly from side to side like he was trying to check how much movement you had in your neck.

'You know who I am,' LizAlec hissed through gritted teeth, 'I told you when I arrived . . .'

'So you did,' said Brother Michael, releasing her face from his grip and running one finger softly down the side of her bruised cheek. 'But it wasn't true, was it? In fact, you told me a lie . . .' He slid his finger down her jaw and drew it slowly across her throat, just below her jaw line. It might have been a lover's caress, except it felt more like someone mimicking a knife blade.

Either way, LizAlec knew she was in deep shit.

Brother Michael nodded, pleased to have got a reaction. 'Time to turn off the cameras, I think,' he said lightly and clapped his hands twice. A tiny black K19 fell from the vaulted roof and landed on his lectern with a soft click. It had been so small and dark against the sky that LizAlec hadn't even known it was there.

And it couldn't have fallen, not really, because the cathedral had no gravity, which meant the vidSat was probably holding itself against the lectern by means of tiny retrorockets. Either that, or the lectern was metal and the camera could induce its own magnetic field.

'No cameras, no witnesses . . . But then, confession's a very private thing.' The tall preacher shrugged himself out of his long coat and threaded it through the back of his metal chair. Beneath the black coat he wore a white shirt, the kind with little pearl buttons up the front and no collar.

'So,' said Brother Michael, 'You're a liar and maybe a thief, but you're not Anchee . . . You know how I know you're not Anchee?'

LizAlec shook her head. She didn't mean to, in fact she meant not to, it just happened. Brother Michael sometimes had that effect on people.

'Because *this* is Anchee,' said Brother Michael, thrusting a paper printout in front of her face. It quivered in his hand, like seaweed under water.

It was Anchee, too. A bad, fuzzy long-distance camera grab. Even digitally enhanced and resampled, the scan had that tell-tale telephoto flatness and paparazzi blur. But, equally obviously, it wasn't LizAlec. The young girl in the picture was smaller, neater and much more obviously Chinese. Not that LizAlec was obviously anything much, she thought to herself bitterly.

'Yeah,' said LizAlec, shrugging. 'That's Anchee. Except these days she's got less teeth.'

The man suddenly looked interested. 'So you really know her, she's not just some name you grabbed from a rerun of *My Fortune*?'

LizAlec grinned, and if her hands hadn't been cuffed to the front of the pulpit she'd have spread them, street-style. 'Know Anchee? Hell, we're sisters . . .'

It wasn't what Brother Michael wanted to hear. He gripped LizAlec's face, fingers pressing hard into her left cheek, his thumb hooked so hard into her right cheekbone LizAlec thought her jaw would break.

'I want the truth,' demanded Brother Michael.

'Really,' hissed LizAlec. 'I thought you'd already settled for religion.' Brother Michael didn't like that one either, but then he wasn't meant to.

'You can tell me who you are,' said the preacher, 'or I can toss you out of an airlock. Do you know what happens in a vacuum?' His voice was cold and his brown eyes were glass-hard, glittering.

Insane, LizAlec decided suddenly, straightening up. Everything made sense once you accepted the man was insane. 'No,' LizAlec said coldly. 'I don't know. Why don't you step into the airlock and show me?' She nodded at a heavy glass door. Behind it was a titanium grid, then a space, then another grid and then a steel door. Beyond that was nothing but vacuum and blackness.

Why it was there and just who Brother Michael expected to turn up and hear him preach LizAlec didn't know: angels, probably. They looked at each other. LizAlec knew Brother Michael had the advantage. Pretty obvious, really, while she was chained to a pulpit like some . . . LizAlec finally remembered what being fastened there reminded her of – a vast painting in the Prince Imperial's bedroom, a picture that showed a fat girl chained naked to a windswept rock, waiting to be rescued. Except there was no way LizAlec carried that amount of weight and as for waiting to be rescued, no chance. She was going to have to get out of this herself. There was no one else around to do it for her.

'Lars,' Brother Michael barked suddenly, stepping away from her. What about the little freak, LizAlec wondered and then realized the preacher was talking into his button mike.

'Bring me a goat.'

Somewhere out in a spar, Lars answered, and asked his own question.

'No,' the preacher said heavily, 'I don't mind which one. Yes, that's fine, I'm sure Betty will do.' Brother Michael sighed and turned back to LizAlec. 'That boy's got the animal-empathy gene, you know. There were animals on the Moon, at first, but the tourists ate them.'

'Really? How interesting,' said LizAlec. 'How really fascinating.'

They waited in cold silence and LizAlec had a good idea what they were waiting for, which didn't improve her temper one little bit. Though what Brother Michael didn't appear to have realized was that the slack-tongued little sandrat was going to like his plan even less than she did.

LizAlec gave the cuffs the lightest tug but, light or not, they tightened all the same, closing around her wrists until flesh bulged either side of their undulating red surface. Another pull like that and she'd have them burrowed down to the bone. There was a simple code key to remove them, there was bound to be. LizAlec's problem was that she didn't yet know how she was going to get it out of Brother Michael.

But she had to get it, just as she had to ditch that bioSemtex worm at the same time. Only LizAlec liked that idea even less.

Sex was out as a lever. The preacher wasn't big on commitment. He'd no sooner fuck her than toss her aside, as he'd done with every other disciple. No, what she needed was to get under his skin, get unrestricted access to his mind. Up close and personal was what she had in mind. The only trouble was, getting there meant someone getting hurt and LizAlec just knew it was going to be her. Still, it *was* time to lose the worm.

'Hey, shit for brains,' LizAlec spat in Brother Michael's direction. At first the preacher looked like he couldn't believe what he'd just heard and then he looked like he believed it only too well.

'Yeah,' said LizAlec. 'I *was* talking to you.' She waited, watching. Her arms pulled up above her head, her body open, defenceless. Brother Michael wasn't going to pass up his chance to hurt her, he wasn't the type.

'Hey,' LizAlec demanded. 'You going to answer me, you dumb fuck?'

He did. The first slap caught her across the face, twisting her off to the side.

Sweet Jesus, LizAlec thought hazily, when she was back in a fit state to think anything. But it was too late to stop now.

'You're pathetic,' LizAlec told him, through a mouthful of blood. 'A pathetic, talentless . . .'

That was as far as she got before Brother Michael broke her nose with the palm of his hand and LizAlec almost blew everything by passing out with pain. Except she was Lady Elizabeth-fucking-Fabio, or maybe she wasn't, LizAlec wasn't sure, but whoever the fuck she was, she had built-in hyperfocus and it was on.

Fully functioning. Like her death wish.

LizAlec inhaled her own blood, as greedily as Fixx had ever sucked up the ice he kept offering her. She inhaled the warm liquid until it flooded her nasal cavity, almost choking as she tried to stop it backing up in her throat. Then she shook her head frantically from side to side and sucked in stale air through her mouth, pulling in dust, low-density sweat molecules, anything that would fill her lungs to bursting. And then, lungs full, she blew out hard, pushing blood and air through her swelling nose in a single snort, red liquid splattering across Brother Michael's white shirt like buckshot.

The bioSemtex wriggled like a crippled slow-worm as it tumbled slowly across the interior of the cathedral and ricocheted gently off the floor before bouncing off a far wall. Brother Michael had done that for her, shaken the monstrosity loose and filled its hiding place with blood until the worm could no longer keep its grip.

The girl wondered if Brother Michael knew that – as of now – she owed him her life . . . Not that LizAlec was going to point that out. Especially since she was going to kill the man. And she was, much sooner than he realized.

'Brother Michael,' said a shocked voice. It was Lars, standing in the doorway of the lift, a large nanny goat clutched firmly in his arms. The sandrat was doing his best to look anywhere except at LizAlec. When he finally did, LizAlec grinned at him and Lars went rapidly back to petting his goat, which had been hobbled with polymer wire to stop it struggling.

'You wanted to see Betty?' Lars held out the goat, then thought better of it and started slowly unwinding the wire. When that was finished, he held the goat out again but Brother Michael made no attempt to take the animal. In fact, he made no effort to go near the goat at all.

'Open hatch,' Brother Michael said crossly and the glass door to the airlock swung slowly back, opening until it could go no further. 'Grid,' Brother Michael demanded and the metal grille folded in on itself like the tendrils of a plant. Not sideways as LizAlec had expected, but from the bottom, folding up to almost nothing. So much for disapproving of nanetics.

'You,' Brother Michael said to Lars, 'Put the goat in the airlock . . .'

Lars just looked at him.

'The airlock,' said Brother Michael tiredly.

Lars did nothing.

'Is there a problem?' The tall preacher gave up trying to clean blood off his shirt and stared hard at the boy.

'That's an airlock,' Lars said.

'I know what it is,' said Brother Michael crossly.

'You want me to put Betty in there?' Lars sounded puzzled, as if he wasn't sure he'd heard the order correctly.

'Yes,' said Brother Michael. 'I want you to put the goat in the airlock.' He could have been giving instructions to an idiot. From the pained expression on Brother Michael's face it was obvious that was indeed how he saw it.

'Betty will die,' said Lars. 'Vacuums kill . . .' He said it as if, maybe, Brother Michael hadn't realized that. And in her head, LizAlec felt a blaze of eidetic memory. Lars and Ben. Vacuum. Death. The sandrat's own memories, stolen from him on Darkside that time he had tried to rape her.

Most people LizAlec could read but Lars was something else. Trying to second guess the sandrat was like looking into a paint-spattered screen: something was undoubtedly going on behind it but no one knew what.

'He wants to kill Betty,' LizAlec told Lars.

'Shut up,' Brother Michael ordered, but LizAlec didn't.

'He wants to put her in a vacuum . . . watch her eyes pop out. You wouldn't want him to do that, would you?'

'Shut it,' said Brother Michael, wrapping one huge hand over her mouth. But the damage was already done.

'You can't kill Betty,' Lars said suddenly. He stepped forward, looking intently at LizAlec's face for a second as she struggled against Brother Michael's grip, and then headed back towards the Otis, the goat wrapped protectively in his arms. 'I'm putting Betty back . . .'

'*You're what?*' Brother Michael was stunned. Not pretending, but the real thing. It was as though a lift door had turned round and answered him back.

'That's right,' said LizAlec quickly, getting her comment in before Brother Michael remembered he was supposed to be smothering her. She bit down hard on his thumb, earning herself another slap. Next time round, Brother Michael kept his fingers away from her teeth, manoeuvring his palm firmly over her swollen mouth, using its edge to block off her nostrils as well.

Behind Brother Michael, Lars was looking badly worried, but he wouldn't put down his bloody goat, he couldn't . . . There was nowhere to put it and Lars couldn't bring himself to let the animal float off in zero G, he knew goats hated that.

So instead he just looked on as Brother Michael slowly and certainly began to choke the life out of LizAlec. The man was smiling now, cold brown eyes hungrily staring into hers as he watched LizAlec go down into the rapidly approaching darkness.

'Shit,' LizAlec thought, as the glass cathedral around her began to fade. She was being murdered and there was nothing she could do to stop it happening. Nothing conscious.

Nothing human.

'He means it.'

LizAlec never knew exactly what woke her, but whatever it was she jerked awake to gulp down a breath that sank like melt water into her burning lungs. She could feel her heart kick-start into a steady reassuring beat as its right ventricle pumped sluggish blood to her lungs, where the blood took up oxygen and returned heartwards, haemoglobin-red, to be pumped through her arteries, releasing the gathered oxygen.

It was a beautiful, simple, inherently efficient system – and she was impressed. LizAlec didn't as yet understand the mechanics, any more than she really understood how an explosion of synaptic fire could translate into shock at still being alive.

She wasn't dead, that much was obvious, but LizAlec couldn't work out whether or not she had been. And if this was a standard near-death experience, where were the sympathetic angels and strange aliens? All that shit that qualified her to go on *Soulderado*? No. She was alive, watching Brother Michael walk towards Lars who was busily backing away, still holding his bloody goat. She was unquestionably alive. It was just that she wasn't expecting to be.

Her throat hurt.

That was so great an understatement that even Lady Clare would have been proud of her. Every breath burnt on the way down and then caught fire again on the way back up. Pain she could live with, it was how *much* pain she could live with that was beginning to surprise LizAlec. But what ripped her attention away from the hurt in her throat was not Brother

Michael's approach towards Lars but the steady chanting that started up in the back of her head.

Low, rhythmic. A chant so faint she couldn't hear the words. If LizAlec hadn't known better, she'd have thought it was someone muttering, but softly, under their breath.

Maybe she was having that fully fledged near-death experience after all. Either that, or she was mad. Whichever it was, there'd be a CySat show more than happy to talk to her. If she ever got back to safety, wherever the fuck that was.

'Who are you?' LizAlec demanded hoarsely, her own lips moving at the question, though she'd meant to ask it in her head.

Brother Michael spun round in disbelief. 'What the . . . ?'

And suddenly LizAlec saw herself as Brother Michael saw her. Chained to the base of the glass pulpit, hands pulled high above her head. She looked a wreck, No, more than that, she looked like death incarnate. Weird eyes burned out of a wide scowling face. She had good cheekbones and a strong jaw. What she could see of her skin was light brown, but her lip was split and her chin was black with dried blood.

'*Razz?*'

It was the voice in her head.

'No,' said LizAlec, 'Not Razz. Razz was my mother . . .'

'Your mother?' The voice smiled.

Impossible, LizAlec knew, but it happened just the same. An overwhelming sense of amusement, almost happiness swept through her mind. Brother Michael was watching her, slack-faced and frozen.

'You're doing that,' said the voice in her head. Inside its echo LizAlec got a sense of ghosts and howling wastelands that curled in on themselves, like folds in time or wormholes in space, except that no one had yet proved either of those existed.

'You're Elizabeth Alexandra?'

LizAlec nodded.

'Yeah, I heard you'd been born. At least I think I did. Maybe. It gets hard to remember . . .' The voice was soft as wind through an empty attic, as brittle as dried grass. LizAlec didn't yet know if the words were real or if she had imagined them. That both could be true hadn't yet occurred to her.

'Who are you?' LizAlec asked. And when the answer came the girl wondered if she'd always known, because she felt no sense of surprise.

'I'm Alex,' said the voice. 'Or maybe not. The real me is locked in a cell at San Lorenzo. The Church Geneticist will never let him go, you know . . . Not while he can spin DNA like that.'

'What are you really?' LizAlec asked.

The voice smiled again. 'You mean, am I a real ghost? Yes, I suppose so, in a ghost-like sort of way. Alex put me in here before you were born. Well, the neural framework, anyway. It's amazing what can be knitted out of little stretches of junk DNA.'

'The framework?' LizAlec said. 'What else is there?'

'Oh, a bit of naturally grown bioClay, a neat bridge between hemispheres, a little optic enhancement . . . Nothing clumsy enough to set off an m/wave sensor.'

LizAlec took a look inside her skull, seeing blood swirling through the Willis circle. There were more arteries and veins than she could ever imagine. Beneath and between were folds of tissue, rich with thread-like nerves. More stars fluoresced inside her head than LizAlec could see through the glass walls of the cathedral. The problem was, LizAlec didn't know what was meant to be there and what wasn't.

'Am I really looking inside myself?' LizAlec demanded.

For a second the voice seemed to hesitate. 'No, not really. But it's a perfect construct of exactly what you would see if you did.' There didn't seem to be much answer to that.

'No wonder I felt so odd,' LizAlec said bitterly, her voice loud enough to make Lars stop fussing over his goat and look up.

'The fury, the paranoia, that sense of standing outside looking in?'

LizAlec nodded.

'No,' said the voice. 'That's not odd, that's just the way it goes.'

'Yeah,' said LizAlec. 'Well, it's still shit.' She looked across to where Brother Michael stood frozen, then abruptly jerked herself out of his head. The preacher took two clanking steps towards her before she went back inside his mind and he froze as muscles knotted up and he almost stumbled sideways.

LizAlec pulled herself out of his head again and then went back in, repelled and fascinated. There were dark memories of other girls. On their knees or on their backs. A few were cuffed below the pulpit as she was, but unlike LizAlec they were naked. Some she knew, many she didn't. Unless she did and the change from fresh-faced disciple to silent shuffling slave was too great for even LizAlec to make the connection.

She was inside Brother Michael's head. Not physically among the blood and veins she'd found in her own skull, but feeding off dark memories remembered only as fixed neural patterns. He could feel her in there, pillaging his mind, and LizAlec was glad of it.

She thought pain and felt him stumble.

She told him to move and watched his disjointed steps.

'Key,' LizAlec demanded and Brother Michael winced, throwing up his hands to protect himself from something he couldn't see but could only feel.

She had her answer before Brother Michael could even get his fear-frozen lips to frame the code. LizAlec spoke the word aloud and felt the cuffs slither from her wrists and hang lifeless like laces over the rings fixed to the glass pulpit.

Two strides took LizAlec close enough to Brother Michael for her to be able to pull back her boot and kick him hard in the crotch. Which she did, enthusiastically. His scream echoed around the vast cathedral. LizAlec hadn't needed to kick him, she understood that. Any pain she wanted to inflict she could post straight through to his thalamus, jack up his limbic system. Pain only existed as electrical impulses anyway.

But LizAlec didn't want agony's simulacrum, at least not where Brother Michael was concerned. When you came down to it, she was an old-fashioned girl at heart. LizAlec took one last look at herself through his eyes. She looked insane. Maybe she was. Wild-eyed and staring, wired up on emotions even Fixx couldn't begin to imagine. Well, maybe he could, LizAlec admitted, but only with a little chemical help. And even then he couldn't do the things she could. Fixx needed music to make people do what he wanted: she just had to think about it.

LizAlec looked at the open airlock and then at Brother Michael.

'No . . .' The preacher was staring at her, aghast, his face weak with fear. He had his hands twisted together in front of him in a mockery of prayer. LizAlec didn't know if it was conscious or not, and she didn't care. She wasn't a believer anyway. It had taken three weeks of bullying from Lady Clare to get her to agree to get confirmed with all those other little *corps noblique* girls at Notre-Dame.

LizAlec fed Brother Michael back his own memories, Sarah again and then Rachel, sobbing for forgiveness, begging him to stop. LizAlec looped that memory and left it playing, an unending circle of blows and bitten-back moans.

'Get inside,' she told him and watched Brother Michael fight himself, then lose. Every sinew in his legs strained against her order, so tight that his knees were close to rupture, but still he put one foot in front of the other, like a dead man walking. Only stopping when he was inside the airlock.

'Please . . .' There were tears beading from his eyes like pearls that floated away into the stark empty beauty of the cathedral. He was shivering, begging, crying. LizAlec didn't bother to answer. There was nothing she wanted to say.

'You ever killed anyone before?' It was the neural construct of the father she'd never met and probably never would, the ghost in her head. She hadn't, and he knew she hadn't. There was nothing about her he didn't know.

But she answered all the same.

'You sure you want to do this?'

She was sure, but then LizAlec remembered why she couldn't. She didn't know how to operate an airlock. Fuck it. LizAlec cut off the endless loop inside Brother Michael's head and as he stopped, suddenly, blindly hopeful, LizAlec pulled out of his mind instructions on using the airlock, and then let him know exactly what she'd just taken.

It was enough to sink him back to his knees. Though it wasn't prayer that kept the preacher there but one gravity boot and abject fear. He was shivering like an injured animal, slipping between panic and his own approaching insanity, reaching for that refuge but never quite making it. LizAlec made damn sure of that. She didn't take kindly to having been killed and she wanted Brother Michael to know exactly what was happening to him, as it happened.

Every bursting vein, every ruptured internal organ.

LizAlec walked over to the gold eagle-winged lectern and waved her hand across its surface to awaken the keypad. Keys materialized on the surface, or rather the black glass reading surface swirled clear to show keys resting beneath. Brother Michael might claim not to approve of unfettered technology but he'd still bought the best deck Microsoft could supply.

Fingers flicking over the keys, never quite touching, LizAlec recreated the inner grille to the airlock, then closed the recessed door, checking its seal. Not that she needed to, the glass was machined to a four-micron tolerance. Even unbolted, it was designed to seal itself under pressure. And the opening servo couldn't kick in unless atmospheric pressure inside the lock stood at .52 and rising.

None of which was high on Brother Michael's worry list. With the door shut, LizAlec pulled herself from his mind, leaving him naked with terror. Now he was on the other side of the glass door, beating at the grille with his fists, his screams of abuse mixed with pleas for his life.

LizAlec shut down her mind and when that didn't work scrabbled at the keyboard until she found a way to kill the sound. Now he just looked like some character from a tri-D, one where the audio card had crashed.

'You really going to kill him?' It was the first thing Lars had said to her since he arrived with the goat. In fact, LizAlec had got round to wondering if he even recognized her. But of course he did. There weren't that many fifteen-year-olds aboard *The Arc* with English, African and Uzbek DNA in them, especially not ones he'd tried to rape.

'No,' said LizAlec, 'I'm going to blow him into space.' Like there was a difference . . .

Lars grunted and when she looked again he'd gone back to rubbing his chin in the fur of the goat's neck. The sandrat didn't even look up when she toggled the key to depress the chamber and open the airlock's space-side door. Brother Michael exploded into the Big Black on a rush of air, his arms and legs flailing like those of a puppet. His heart flared in blind panic, and his mouth opened as its final scream was ripped out of his lungs by the vacuum.

'Welcome to hell,' LizAlec said softly and those were the last words Brother Michael ever heard. Twelve to thirteen seconds is what it usually takes for a vacuum victim to black out. Though small children often only manage five. And there's a ninety-second window during which it's theoretically possible to pull someone back into a pressurized environment and revive them, with a medium-to-good chance they'll recover fully.

But there was no one to pull Brother Michael back – and there was no way LizAlec was going to let him die that quickly.

At plus thirteen seconds he was paralysed, but still conscious: the outward rush of water vapour was already freezing his nose and lips. Traumatic convulsions racked his body at plus-fifteen seconds and then paralysis set in again, seconds later. Inside the soft tissues of Brother Michael's flesh and inside his veins water vapour began to form, distorting his flesh. LizAlec couldn't have kept him alive beyond this, not even if she had wanted to. But she *was* going to keep him conscious until death. And that's what she did.

A spider's-silk overskin might have prevented embolism, but Brother Michael didn't have one, so instead water vapour pooled inside him until his skin distended to bursting. He was panic-stricken, beyond thought. Already his heart rate was in decline. At plus-forty seconds his blood pressure plummeted until pressure in his veins matched that of his arteries. Brother Michael's heart still tried desperately to beat, but blood could no longer flow.

LizAlec never felt Brother Michael rupture open, because that was the point she let go of his terrified, gibbering mind – and felt it scrabble gratefully out of existence.

Chapter 32

Welcome to Insanity

What did LizAlec believe in? She believed in herself: at least, she did now. Believed, too, in the voice, low and hollow in her head. The voice that told LizAlec justice wasn't always just, but it was dangerously satisfying.

Maybe even addictive.

'Get out of here,' LizAlec told Lars, but he just stared at her.

'Go,' she told the sandrat, her feet locked firmly to the steel floor of the cathedral. She could feel the electricity that worked the soles, sense the field emanating from the bottom of her shoes. Come to that, she could feel fields emanating from the lectern, from the altar lights, even from the black-glass pulpit.

The whole cathedral was a mess of shimmering EMFs that conflicted, overlapped, reacted with each other.

'Get out,' LizAlec insisted. 'Seal the safety doors on your spar, tell the others but don't tell the bodyguards, okay?'

The boy looked blank.

'If you don't lock the doors,' said LizAlec, 'the goat will get hurt . . .'

She should have realized that that was all it would take. Lars folded the bleating animal tightly in his arms and backed towards the Otis. He had no idea what LizAlec was planning to do, and he cared even less. She was a freak, all strange eyes and cropped hair. The girl's edges were too sharp, the colours around her flashing bright like the skin of an epileptic chameleon. Every time he looked at LizAlec, her outline had changed.

Lars preferred girls like Sara who kept her aura down to a few simple hues. Lars himself kept his Kirlian aura down to one colour only. He was rather proud of that. 'Be safe,' said the door and then Lars was gone, safe inside the pressurized Otis, on his way back to the goat pen. Tomorrow the mammals were going out to *The Arc* itself. Out to the ring where Sister Aaron was making a world for them full of fields, trees, small streams. Ants cleaned up the leaf litter and worms aerated the soil, all twelve feet of it. *The Arc* wasn't Eden, old or new, whatever CySat reported, but it was better than Planetside.

Face it, anything was better than that. *Time to go*, thought LizAlec.

Not that there was any point staying. The next cargo ship wasn't due for two months, according to the lectern. Paris could have fallen by then, Lady Clare might be dead, put up against a wall by the Black Hundreds. If that hadn't happened already. And as for Fixx, God only knew the trouble he'd be in.

LizAlec sucked her teeth, ran one shaking hand through the stubble of her hair and wondered about getting another boyfriend, one who wasn't so high-maintenance. It hurt her to think that Lady Clare might be right about anything, but she might be right about that.

'Escape pod,' LizAlec demanded.

'Situation normal,' announced the cathedral's bioAI, speaking through a tiny pair of bioVox speakers inset into the eagle's wings of the lectern. The voice had that irritating coded-by-number kindergarten tone LizAlec remembered from AIs at her first school.

'There *is* an escape pod?' LizAlec asked crossly and walked back to the lectern to skim frames of safety data, tilting the eagle's wings herself rather than waiting for the lectern to work out the best angle. Of course there was a pod: it was the bloody pulpit. LizAlec stared at the glass monstrosity rising like a block of black obsidian. She should have guessed from its size, not to mention the EMF field emanating from it.

Now all LizAlec needed was some skin. Not a full balloon suit or even a half-balloon, just some basic skin, the white spider's-silk kind.

'Pressure skin,' LizAlec demanded and waited while the bioAI weighed up her request. It could find no obvious reason to give her one, but then there seemed no obvious reason to refuse. The skin arrived in a vacuum-sealed foil package, etched with NASA's hologram and a shiny Tampertell copyright strap. No cheap Korean copies for the Brotherhood.

LizAlec stripped. Not easy in zero G wearing wrong-size ReeGravs, but she managed it, albeit somewhat clumsily. After peeling the cotton smock off over her head, LizAlec lobbed the garment into the air for the pleasure of watching its material balloon out and swirl like a jellyfish. The croptop Jude had thrust at her just over a week before had rotted under the arms with sweat and LizAlec tried not to imagine what she smelt like to others, not that Lars would have noticed. Even the goats smelt cleaner than he did.

Her knickers were vending-machine disposables and went the way of her croptop, into a waste tube. She didn't bother trying to take them off her over ReeGravs, just ripped them apart at the side seams.

To put on her second skin, LizAlec needed to take one foot out of her boot, push her foot hard into the tight elastic skin and get her foot back into the ReeGrav, all without overbalancing in zero G. Somehow, LizAlec didn't see how she was going to do it.

'Hold yourself to the floor,' said a voice.

LizAlec jumped, tried to cover herself and then remembered the voice was in her head. Alex couldn't really see her and even if he could, he was only a neural construct, nothing more.

'Good,' said Alex. 'You're getting a grip on it.'

Yeah, thought LizAlec . . . For a killer standing naked in a ring colony's vast glass-walled cathedral talking to the ghost of her father, she was doing brilliantly. It was just a shame Lady Clare wasn't there to be impressed.

Hold yourself to the floor.

LizAlec tried and failed, miserably. Every time she moved her unweighted leg, it tried floating upwards until she was almost tipped on her side. 'It's impossible,' said LizAlec, 'you can't defeat zero gravity, it's basic . . .'

'You reckon?'

LizAlec nodded. Yes, she did reckon.

'Throw that boot across the room,' said Alex.

LizAlec bent to pick up her spare ReeGrav and heard Alex sigh.

'Without touching it,' he insisted, sounding just like Lady Clare at her most patronizing.

Fucking terrific, now she had two of them on her case. Furiously, LizAlec catapulted the heavy boot across the cathedral and was watching it bounce off a grey steel pillar before she even realized what she'd just done.

Shit. She stopped the boot dead so it just hung there.

'Now,' said Alex, 'instead of flinging your shoe across the room, throw yourself at the floor, gently.'

LizAlec did and found she was standing steady, her bare unbooted foot planted firmly on the marble tiles. It wasn't gravity, not really, but it was a good imitation. All it took was, was what . . . ?

'The intelligence not to stand around naked looking for logic.' Alex sounded amused.

'Yeah, right.' LizAlec rolled on the first piece of skin, feeling the spider's silk tighten up her legs and over her stomach as molecular chains bound themselves around areas of potential stress. The suit fitted neatly up over her breasts and finished under her arms, sealing itself to her skin. The second piece went over her shoulders and down to her wrists, leaving LizAlec to thrust her fingers into gloves and roll them up until they sealed themselves tight.

All that was left was a two-part, full-head face mask, but there was no way LizAlec was going to use both bits, though she knew she should. She'd already suffocated once that morning. The thought of smart silk tightening over her mouth was more than LizAlec could handle. Stupid or not, some prices were too high to pay. In the end, LizAlec compromised with herself by struggling into the balaclava section without first fitting the underlag that sealed off nostrils and eyes.

She was done.

'Computer . . .'

The screen lit to show the bioAI was listening.

'The dome's about to blow out.'

Diodes flared all along the eagle's wing as the system ran emergency checks and came up with nothing. The bioAI was about to explain to LizAlec that she was in error, when LizAlec strode into the middle of the transept, stood below the pulpit and spread her arms.

Strung between metal pillars, the glass walls rose all around her and hung overhead in the ceiling vault of the vast cathedral. What they were built from was marketed as SlowGlass, but was really a radiation-resistant polymer designed to play back on one side anything it saw on the other. But LizAlec didn't know that – at least not consciously – and what she saw was so close to what there was outside it made no difference.

Besides, she was too busy concentrating.

Closing her violet eyes, LizAlec felt the crystal walls as sound, echo-locating her new senses against each constricting wall, feeling the walls hold solid as she pushed her mind against them. The cathedral was built to retain pressure far greater than the single atmosphere it now contained. Ribs of titanium alloy ran outside the glass walls, like fluid Art Nouveau pillars, as if Gaudi had started designing in liquid metal. Except the elegant metal tracery didn't hold the cathedral up, it held it in, safely containing the glass walls.

'Just do it,' said the voice of Alex. 'Don't think about it. Do it . . .'

Reaching up to grip the rings to which she'd been bound

only half an hour before, LizAlec did, punching out a harmonic so high that even she couldn't hear it, throwing the notes in all directions, feeling the internal lattice of the crystal walls scream under the vibration until cracks appeared and molecular bonds broke.

Vast sections of wall spun like oversized shrapnel into the void, almost taking LizAlec with them. All the warmth, all the air, everything that made space briefly human went in a single gulp as void and vacuum ripped out pews and prayer books, pulled the lectern from the floor. Banners, the simple altar, a fish tank, Brother Michael's metal chair, everything exploded away into space as the void tried and failed to pull LizAlec after them. Her shoulders burnt with agony as she clung to the rings. Sheer will power held her feet to the floor.

'Welcome to insanity,' said the voice in her head. 'You'll find it runs in the family.'

Bitter cold ripped warmth from LizAlec's body, a cold so absolute it was almost literally beyond her imagining. Breath was dragged from her lungs, her chest tightened in agony. LizAlec could feel Death waiting.

So she let go. Of the rings that held her to the pulpit, of her identity, of her mind.

For a second, as the dying wind pulled at her body, LizAlec thought she was about to join the vanishing detritus; but even as she was pulled off her feet, the pulpit cracked open and metal tentacles caught LizAlec and dragged her towards an opening pod.

Nine seconds from grab to go was the safety margin LockMart allowed, but the pod had her bundled into a chair and was sealing itself within two. By the time LizAlec's pod had cleared the shattered cathedral, another pod was already in position, rising from the floor. But there was no one else to rescue so it remained resolutely shut.

'*Heat*,' LizAlec told herself. That was what the sensors keyed in on, body heat. Set against the cold black of the vacuum she must have burned in their vision like a flame. All the same, she'd have liked to see how *The Arc*'s AI was going to assimilate *that* little episode to its learning curve. She was still wondering about it when the little metal spiders came and began cutting away the spider's skin covering most of her face.

Chapter 33

Shanghai Surprise

There were a number of things that Lady Clare Fabio expected to happen after she cut her deal with Lazlo. That Lazlo would send his goons after her anyway; that her beautiful Ile St-Louis house would soon be washed away by flood water; and that – deal or not – she'd probably still die without ever knowing if Lazlo had lied about LizAlec.

What she wasn't expecting was to find a Chinese general in her study, sitting at her *escritoire*, flipping though a leather-bound Mercurier atlas of Europe, *her* leather-bound Mercurier atlas of Europe. A book so valuable that Lady Clare kept it locked behind glass in a cupboard.

Lady Clare glanced across at the cupboard and was shocked to discover that the General had forced its tiny brass lock. Not crudely enough to damage the door's ivory inlay, but forced it all the same.

'That was Florentine,' Lady Clare protested, nodding towards the cupboard.

'Milanese,' the man corrected her, picking up a lit candelabra and walking over to look at the forced-open door. 'A post-*Risorgimento* copy, but not a bad one . . .'

For once in her life, Lady Clare was speechless. So General Que used the brief silence to introduce himself as Anchee's father. He took it for granted that she would already know him as a major industrialist. Standing in front of Lady Clare and bowing slightly before putting out his manicured hand, the man announced that he'd briefly been a warlord but was now a private citizen from Shanghai.

Lady Clare met his surprisingly gentle handshake and then sat quickly in her chair, before he had time to reclaim it. The General smiled.

'Are you hungry?'

It was such a stupid question that all Lady Clare could manage was a blank stare. Of course she was hungry. Everyone in Paris was starving, even the Prince Imperial. People didn't eat grass or tree bark unless there was no alternative. 'What do you think?'

'Then let's eat,' suggested the General. He took a packet of hard tack from the pocket of his trench coat and tore open the foil. 'Old rations,' he apologized, 'but they have a high protein/carbohydrate mix, plus six minerals and four vitamins. I designed the formula myself.'

The General took a biscuit and bit into it, catching the falling crumbs neatly in his upturned hand. Given the mildew that stained the wet floor, Lady Clare was surprised he bothered. But then, from the creases in his cavalry-twill trousers, she imagined the General was as meticulous about his table manners as he was about his dress. Old-fashioned, her own father would have called it. Though she was intelligent enough to accept that, even back then, others had regarded such behaviour as outdated, even obsessive or neurotic.

There was a time she'd been like that: it just seemed so long ago.

'Take one,' the General said, offering Lady Clare the packet.

She did. It was salt rather than sweet and crumbled against the roof of her mouth. The taste was good but the biscuit was still difficult to get down.

'Water,' suggested the General, dipping his hand into a poacher's pocket inside his coat and pulling out a plastic flask of Canadian Spring. After two months of making do with grime-flecked rain collected from her roof, Lady Clare was shocked at how clear the water looked.

By the time Lady Clare had drunk half the bottle and finished a second biscuit she felt exhausted.

'Long-term hunger does that,' said the General. 'Strips away the essential you. Not just your capacity to make decisions. Everything. Strength and alertness . . . your nerve. Why else are prisoners starved?' He spoke from experience, but she didn't know that.

When Lady Clare had eventually eaten a third biscuit and drunk all the water, she sat back in her Napoleon III desk chair and rested her elbows on its green-leather arms. For someone who'd spent more than half a lifetime intentionally trying to starve herself, Lady Clare found it ironic that getting three dry biscuits could make such a difference to her life. And then she realized the General's biscuits contained more than just minerals and vitamins. Something in there was neuronal, chosen to cause hyperpolarization of her post-synaptic neurons. All across her skull, carefully selected neurons *weren't* firing . . .

But she didn't have a problem with that.

'You flew in?'

The general nodded. 'Came in on the back of the storm. Sikorsky, full-stealth mode. Piloted it myself . . .' He was pleased with himself and tired enough to let it show.

'Which means you can't get out again,' said Lady Clare, sounding thoughtful.

Both knew it was true. Once inside the viral spread you couldn't get out again, not safely. There was a three-hour window once you hit the edge of viral airspace. Getting into trouble was never the problem, it was getting out again safely – same as it ever was. The man in front of Lady Clare didn't look like a risk taker, not to her – more Tao Mo than Kau Tze – and Lady Clare prided herself on her ability to sum up a person's character with one glance.

Prejudice, LizAlec called it.

The shrug he gave was almost embarrassed. 'Getting in was

very easy. How I get out depends on you. Actually . . .' the
General shrugged again, 'it's interesting how things happen.'

His voice was so quiet Lady Clare had to strain to hear him
over the hammering of rain on glass and wooden window
shutters. 'You once met the auditor-general,' said the man. 'Or
so I believe?'

'Volublilis?' Lady Clare nodded. 'He was a friend, for a
while.'

'A close friend?' The Church of Christ Geneticist might be
celibate, but there was no doubting what the General meant.

'Not like that,' said Lady Clare firmly. 'We played chess,
nothing more.' Without intending to she glanced towards ivory
figures laid out on a small table. Even buried under their patina
of dust, the carved chess pieces were still obviously of museum
quality. Almost everything in her study was.

'A clever man,' said the General. It was meant as a statement,
not a question, but Lady Clare nodded anyway. 'And an excellent negotiator,' added the General. 'You know the UN Pax Force
almost stormed San Lorenzo?'

She didn't. Lady Clare looked so shocked the General almost
laughed. 'It seems some idiot at the UN decided the Geneticists
had developed a 'dote. Of course, they hadn't.'

The man didn't say *I had*, but he thought it all the same. 'They
were going to fight their way into the complex . . .'

'So Volubilis negotiated a third-party inspection,' Lady Clare
said. 'With someone neutral like the Mufti of M'Dina. Got the
Mufti to sign a rock-solid confidentiality clause, with excep-
tionally punitive financial penalties for disclosure of any information not directly related to the Azerbaijani virus or its 'dote.
The Mufti indemnified the auditor-general, the UN indemnified
the Mufti, everyone saved face.'

It was the General's turn to looked surprised.

'He plays good chess,' said Lady Clare. 'And besides, that's
exactly what I'd have done.'

'I know,' said the General. 'I've been reading up on you.' He dropped his hand back into the poacher-pocket of his trench coat and produced not the hardcopy print of her life that Lady Clare had been half expecting, but a small Kodak tri-D that he put face down on the desk.

Poker, thought Lady Clare. The General was a natural poker player. He thought of it as a strength, but she'd never yet met a man whose strengths couldn't be turned into a weakness. Lady Clare didn't give General Que the satisfaction of reaching for the photograph since she guessed he wouldn't let her look at the Kodak, at least not yet. Never weaken your own hand, went the old motto. Though its corollary was, it's not necessary when there are always people around to do it for you.

Instead, Lady Clare sat back at her desk and waited. Strange generals didn't fly halfway round the planet because they wanted to deliver you biscuits. Somehow, somewhere she had something he wanted badly enough to compel him to leave home. And whatever it was, the General believed he had something to offer her in return. With food lining her gut and a litre of spring water now filtering through her overworked kidneys, she could afford to wait. Playing the long term had always been something she was good at, practised too.

The General smiled, sat back in his own chair. His brown eyes, thin lips, even the set of his narrow jaw gave nothing away at all. But Lady Clare didn't mind: just his being there gave her too much to think about as it was.

What did France have that could interest a Shanghai industrialist? A few ruined cities, a countryside stripped of crops and what little livestock there'd been. The freeways rubble, the ferroconcrete bridges collapsed in on themselves. And by next week, even Paris might not be hers to sell.

'My father ate his boots,' the General said suddenly. 'In Tibet, in the middle of a winter that took one of his feet and all of his fingers. He shot men for eating their dead comrades, but he ate his own boots while he still had hands to hold them.'

The man had been looking at her Dumas novels, Lady Clare

realized, and had seen the one with its leather cover ripped off. He'd known it for a sign of what it was. In that study she had five oil paintings, including one by Louis David, and a hundred times over in the last week she'd have swapped the lot, even the small Rodin bronze in the corner, for a scrap of bread and a glass of clean water.

She waited, watching him wait too. And then the General leant forward and took the tri-D from her desk. 'It's time we talked,' he said, turning the Kodak over so Lady Clare could finally see it.

LizAlec. Dressed in a white cotton smock and with her hair cropped down to her skull. She was still scowling.

'Two questions,' said the General. 'Do you know this girl?'

Lady Clare nodded. 'What's the other question?'

The General shrugged, almost apologetically. 'Do you want her back?'

Chapter 34

Escape Velocity

Shiori was coming in Moonside to *The Arc*, so she didn't get a distant scan of the pod as it screamed Earthwards. And besides, she wasn't looking for a pod, she was scanning for bodies and all she'd got so far was one, possibly *male*, very definitely *dead*.

LizAlec's pod, however, instantly identified the *Shockwave Rider* as a functioning cargo shuttle and recoded the pod's escape trajectory, beginning immediate procedures to bring it back on itself, abandoning the statistically less safe Earth trajectory.

The pod's semiAI could have used full retro, but it wasn't going to waste the fuel. Instead it gently began to slow the pod, chattering all the while to a sub-personality of the bioAI installed in the shuttle.

Shiori had started to scan for bodies after she saw the shattered cathedral, which was long before Fixx finally managed to drag himself away from the shuttle's battered Sony simbox. The cathedral looked like someone had cracked the top off a huge crystal egg and left the jagged shell sticking from a Gaudiesque eggcup.

'Sweet fuck,' was all Shiori said. Then she began to punch keys on a walkWear stuck to her belt, reading out its data from floating-focus fake Calvin wraprounds, Kwaloon-copies of last year's model.

No sign of life. Central spindle vacuumsucked.

'Hey,' said a voice, 'you didn't tell me there was going to be no war.' It was inner-city rough, street-smart but not as tough as its

owner wanted it to be. The combat kid would get there, though.
Anyone who could hotcard a cargo shuttle and only admit after
launch that he'd never actually piloted anything bigger than a
landskimmer was going to make it, in Fixx's view. If he didn't
end up dead first.

And if he did end up on ice, Shiori was going to be the one
to put him there. Leon and Shiori didn't like each other. In
fact, Shiori hadn't liked Leon from the moment Fixx and she
had stumbled out of the love hotel and found Leon waiting for
them, slouched over the rails outside. And she was wasting a
lot of Fixx's time letting him know.

Leon was keeping track of Fixx for Jude, only Fixx didn't
know that and nor did Leon, not really. Jude had sent Leon
to stay with his uncle for a week and told the boy to keep an
eye out for the tall musician and help him if at all possible. It
was just Jude's bad luck that the first thing Fixx asked the boy
was if he knew where they could acquire a shuttle . . .

The original idea had been that Leon would find them a
shuttle and Fixx and Shiroi would bribe the captain, using an
HKS goldcard Fixx had LISA top up for him. That was until
Leon discovered how much Fixx was intending to offer.

'Jesus fuck, you could *buy* a shuttle for that,' the kid protested.

'Fine,' said Fixx. 'Then buy us one.'

And that's how it had happened. According to Leon he
had an uncle who worked in the repair depot, who had a
friend whose cousin . . . It was a primitive familial version of
a firewall. Though the chances were there was no cousin. When
it came down to it, the crate had probably been 'borrowed'
by Leon's uncle, or the beer-gutted slob who passed for him.
Not that the *Shockwave Rider* was going to be missed. The
jerkhead who usually piloted it was sleeping off a drunk in
the cells at PSPD – that was the story Leon stuck to, anyway.

By the time Fixx had unhooked his violin from the shuttle's

simbox, the *Shockwave Rider* was hanging 200 metres off the edge of the shattered cathedral and Leon was running his own diagnostic, using the shuttle's infrared scan. A closed flask of hot sweet chocolate was clutched in one hand, straw stuck firmly in his mouth. The silver flask was stamped *US Marines*, but Fixx knew a fake when he saw one.

Leon had the data reading out on screen so Fixx could see it too. Except there was nothing to see. After the third abortive scan, Fixx accepted the inevitable: from the smashed-open cathedral at the top to the vast library at the bottom, the central spindle had been sucked dry. If anything had started out alive down there, it sure as hell wasn't any longer.

'Christ,' said Fixx, his voice raw. He was staring at the screen, looking in disbelief at the wreckage below. It looked like a blow-out, a bad one. What if LizAlec was . . .

What if . . .

Fixx shut his silver eyes and counted backwards from ten, so slowly that Shiori was already leaning over to check he was okay by the time he opened them again. She stepped quickly back, leaving him to stare blindly up at the screen. Whatever he was seeing wasn't out there.

'This girl means a lot to you . . . ?' Leon made it obvious he thought the idea of Fixx and LizAlec completely absurd. And somewhere at the back of his head, a fragment of Fixx's mind was beginning to agree.

'I owe her,' said Fixx. Just what it was he owed her, Fixx wasn't sure. She'd got him arrested as a terrorist, his studio smashed up, his legs ripped off. He'd been beaten, tortured, used by Lady Clare . . . But it wasn't that simple. If it wasn't for Fixx she wouldn't have been in trouble with Lady Clare in the first place. Or maybe she would, but not over him: which meant she wouldn't have been sent out to Planetside when St Lucius relocated . . .

No, Fixx told himself, she'd be stuck in Paris, starving. Waiting for the Black Hundreds to take the city, after which she'd be face down in flood water, throat cut, every orifice raped to a bloody pulp. Fixx shook his head.

'I want to take a look,' he said as calmly as he could.

'At that?' Leon demanded, nodding abruptly at the blown-out cathedral. 'I mean, you want me to set you down there . . . ?' His whole body language said, *We're fucked if you do, but I'll try it anyway.* And he would too, Fixx thought approvingly. Leon handled the battered shuttle as only a skate kid could, throwing unnecessary loops and tight trajectories. Hitting the boosters and then slamming on the retros.

'No,' said Shiori, without checking with Fixx. 'The whole spindle's dead. Take us out to the ring.' It was nothing personal, she was just busy focusing on data Fixx couldn't see, the stuff scrolling past her eyes.

Leon shrugged and threw a left to slide the shuttle down the length of the spindle, its surface whistling by beneath them. It was like skimming sideways along the crest of an impossibly long silver hill. Slipping down the spindle, Leon aimed towards a gap between two of the radial spars.

'Sure you don't want to check the bottom dome?' Leon asked Shiori. After her last order, he took it for granted that she was in charge and Fixx couldn't be arsed to argue. He was too busy thinking about LizAlec.

'No,' said Shiori. 'Take us out to the ring.'

Leon obediently flicked his fingers over a floating trackball and the *Shockwave Rider* suddenly slid away at a right angle to the central spindle, flipping over to skim low and tight along one of the radial spars that held the ring in place. At the last second, Leon flipped the shuttle up the approaching silver slope and down the other side, stopping dead as the outside edge of the ring flicked by below.

'Take it down and find a hatch,' Shiori said without looking up. She seemed to be basing all her decisions on whatever data scrolled up her Calvin wraprounds. Fixx got a burning desire to ask Shiori what she was really after. She'd been shocked by the shattered dome but not panicked. If he thought his boss's daughter was down there he'd have been shitting bricks. Hell, he still was . . .

He'd had her original reason – LizAlec – and back at the love hotel he'd had her revised reason, Anchee. He just didn't believe either of them. But he didn't ask: if there was one thing Fixx was still good at, it was timing . . .

'Hold her steady,' ordered Shiori as Leon matched the speed of the shuttle with the speed of the outside edge of the ring, until both seemed to come to a sudden halt. Whether they were above *The Arc* or *The Arc* was above them was impossible to say. But they now rested ten metres from the ring's outer edge, keeping pace, holding tight to the ring's revolution as steadily as any ramora clinging to its shark.

Shiori clicked her fingers blindly across a tiny keyboard on her wrist, pulling up figures, sliding into the ray-traced heart of the space station below her. It wasn't the missing girl the General's AI had sent her after, it wasn't even the Brother-hood's infamous smear list of dirt on every politician who'd ever expressed doubt in Brother Michael and Sister Aaron's God-given mission. Though no doubt the General would find a use for the list, should Shiori stumble across it.

No, what she wanted was not the General's daughter who Shiori now knew from the General was in bed, unconscious but unhurt, at St Lucius. And certainly not whatever the little tart was called that Fixx wanted found, not for herself anyway. What Shiori wanted, what the General needed finding, were his missing ancestors. And, from what Shiori had been told, they'd arrived on *The Arc* wrapped round the French girl's wrist.

And since Shiori hadn't got a read-out on the missing shrine from the ice-cold spindle, they had got be somewhere out in the ring. Now all she had to do was get in there and find them. That, and persuade Fixx or Leon that they wanted to help her unscrew a vacuum-sealed service hatch in the skin of *The Arc* down below. Pick the wrong hatch and it would chop you in half as it blew out into space, to say nothing of decompressing the entire ring. Leon would know that instinctively and even Fixx might work it out eventually, if she gave him enough time.

But Shiori wouldn't pick the wrong hatch. Not now, not ever, that was why the General employed her. Shiori shrugged and reached for a balloon suit. Her gut might be blade-scarred, her heart as cold as her reflexes were augmented but she got results. Precisely because she didn't care how she got them. Shanghai was full of ancestor-worshipping would-bes who lived in fear of the General. She didn't give a shit about all that, any more than she cared who ruled in Beijing.

As for her own immediate ancestors, Shiori hoped to hell they were out there howling somewhere in the void. Because you didn't get to be like Shiori without having had some help, and Shiori had certainly had plenty.

Chapter 35

One over the Nine

Two hours after LizAlec realized her pod was taking her back the way she'd come the over-priced silver coffin dumped her back at *The Arc*. Only, when she checked the screen, there was a cargo shuttle parked between the pod and Sister Aaron's spinning silver promise of a new Eden.

A shuttle wasn't due for six weeks, she'd checked that herself. Fuck it, LizAlec was certain she had. There was no way one was due . . . Which didn't alter the fact that a battered black Harland & Wolff was tethered to the outer edge of the ring. Whoever was piloting the thing had just parked up and tied off, like they were leaving a horse at a hitching post. LizAlec knew all about *equus*. Girls from St Lucius/Paris rode every Saturday morning in the Bois de Boulogne. Or at least they did back when the Parisian franchise of St Lucius was still located in the Sixth Arrondissement and the Bois had not yet been chopped down for firewood or shelter. The horses, of course, had gone the way of cats and rats, straight down the throats of hungry Parisians, just a lot faster.

Focusing in with her screen, LizAlec had to admit the shuttle hadn't just been tied off. Someone had flash-welded a ring to the outer skin of the arc and clipped on a bounty cable made from spun monofilament.

Wreckers maybe, or truckers . . . They were the only highrisers who used bounty cables, at least they were on tri-D. But no trucker would choose *The Arc* as a stop-off, wreckers neither, now LizAlec came to think about it.

LizAlec sucked at her teeth. Like she needed to be back at *The Arc* when she'd been safely on her way to Earth. Though how she landed and avoided burn-up had both crossed her mind, so maybe the pod's AI wasn't as stupid as she thought.

LizAlec searched the screen in front of her face, searching for some icon that might activate a transmitter. She was blindside to the cargo shuttle, so just maybe *The Arc* didn't know she was there. But the cargo ship must do.

She watched helplessly as modems whirred and diodes lit in syncopated dances across the console in front of her. LizAlec knew the two vessels were communicating frantically, she just didn't know what they were saying, though it sounded like something Fixx might dream up, the dance of suicidal fireflies remixed with the sound of dolphins reading aloud.

Only the main screen remained blank and none of the surrounding icons looked remotely like the international sign for vidmail, voicemail or synaptic link. In fact most of the screen was icon-less, just keys labelled in Hebrew, a script LizAlec had never seen before.

'Shit.' LizAlec drummed her fingers on the pale yellow fascia of the console. The last thing she needed to do was hit the wrong key, but still she had to do something.

She wanted out of there.

The ceramic wrist implant was almost perfectly healed round its edges, the porous matrix of the implant's lip melding seamlessly with her flesh. The spiders had done a neat job, it was just a pity she had to ruin it.

LizAlec gripped the end of the tube feeding her wrist and yanked, pulling free the pastel blue tube. Warm liquid kept dripping across LizAlec's fingers until she tied the tube into a half hitch. Reaching down between her legs, LizAlec found the catheter that drained her bladder and pulled, slowly. Removing it stung, but the pale pink tube came free. The designers obviously liked pastels, LizAlec decided. Some LokMart focus group must have told them pastel hues were soothing.

That left ... Well, LizAlec didn't like to think what that left ...

The restraining bodyweb was woven neoprene with velcro fastenings. As an original touch, the designers had made the belt a reassuring grey and coloured the velcro buckle bright red, probably so you couldn't loose the fastening in an accident. LizAlec peeled back the velcro and instantly every alarm in the pod went off at once.

The fucking belt had a smart buckle, which should have been obvious, though why the moronic AI should object to her loosing the gravity-web when it hadn't minded her shedding the catheters, LizAlec didn't know.

She hurriedly refastened her buckle.

'Listen,' she told the AI. 'I want to get out, okay?'

Nothing. Just the odd blip from a diode.

She was going to have to do it the hard way. Of course, she'd seen Sophie Thorland crash her way out of a burning escape pod in *Alien Empire III*, but that had been on Fixx's tatty tri-D recorder, the CD-ROM had been ancient and all LizAlec remembered was that Sophie got turned inside out by a vacuum long before she reached the rescue ship. (Having been turned inside out fifteen minutes earlier by the hero. It was one of those parts.)

Okay, so check the door. If you could call the upper half of the pod a door. LizAlec checked it anyway, looking for an emergency release. Everything might be smart but doors still had to be fitted with a protected manual override. It was in the NASA standard.

A recessed T-bar handle rested under a clear polymer cover to the right of her knee, its cover held in place around its edge by a row of tiny glueseals. Which took care of that one. Now *all* she needed was a bubble suit or an oxygen mask, any oX/m would do, but preferably the type you bit between your teeth.

There wasn't one.

LizAlec even prised away the plastic moulding behind her head but there wasn't a mask. At least not one that she could find. LizAlec was going to have to do it cold, literally.

Gripping the polymer cover, LizAlec applied steady pressure and slid it to one side. She was so impressed with herself that she slid the cover back into place and did it all over again. Jerk at it, knock it with her knee, and the cover stayed where it was, push on it with a steady conscious push and the glue liquidized. Which was neat, but tough luck on anyone who was in there panicking, which she wasn't — at least not yet.

Time to go.

Yanking up the red T-bar, LizAlec felt rather than saw the half-pod in front of her blast free to bounce into the cargo shuttle in front of it, then spin away like a maniacally tumbling surfboard. Retros on her half of the pod fired up, holding the pod to gyroscopic steadiness.

Nine seconds and counting.

In her right hand she held the emergency anchor and wrapped into her left she held its handle, her fingers pushed through its central slot to grip a dead-man's handle, her thumb tucked in over the top. Still strapped into her chair, LizAlec hurled the anchor and saw it fasten to the skin of the shuttle, next to an airlock. Without thinking, LizAlec squeezed hard on the line-adjust and almost dislocated her shoulder as the handle automatically reeled in any slack and then some.

Light line monofilament, with a b/s of five thousand Kg and impervious to cold down to absolute zero. Wind in any further and her shoulder would pop long before the line did. Keeping tight hold of the handle, LizAlec reached quickly down with her other hand and unbuckled her gravity web. This time the pod didn't complain. One squeeze on the anchor handle and LizAlec catapulted out of the pod towards the *Shockwave Rider*, only just managing to bring up her feet as she slammed into its surface. Then she was there, crouched to one side of the airlock, ripping off the cover to its emergency handle.

Thank God for NASA standards.

A steel door swung in, crashing on its hinges, and LizAlec went scrabbling hand over hand into the small airlock, pulling herself along on the airlock's luminous emergency rail. At the far end was a yellow handle that LizAlec slammed down as hard as she could. Behind her, the outer door began to shut slowly in a hiss of hydraulics. *Faster. Faster.* The girl would have been sobbing but her lungs were sucked dry, her arm muscles in spasm from toxin overload. Water vapour was being pulled up her throat in a steady hiss that flash-burnt her lips as it exited.

She was over the nine, LizAlec just knew she had to be. Black shadows raced in like clouds towards the edge of her vision, her cheeks were stretching, distorting. Her mouth was stiff, fingers cryo-cold, capillaries shrunk to invisible threads as her core temperature plummeted and LizAlec's body stole blood from her arms and legs. It was no good, she wasn't going to . . .

'You ever thought of using the door?' The kid crouching in front of LizAlec wore a stained Voidoids3 T-shirt and baggy combats. A glass blade was taped ostentatiously to his ankle and he had a silver crucifix round his neck, a real one with the tortured man on. She recognized him from somewhere. And if she hadn't been on her side vomiting her guts out, LizAlec might have remembered it was from the CasaNegro in Fracture. But instead she just noted she knew him, maybe.

Up close and personal, the boy looked street-rough, with a Luna accent to break glass. And he was staring at her with an odd, half-ironic expression. Like he couldn't believe what he'd just caught. As it was, LizAlec merely moved her head and spewed again onto the steel floor of the airlock, a string of yellow bile that burnt her throat before bubbling into little yellow marbles that hit the floor and floated gently away.

'Here,' said the boy, climbing over her to wipe LizAlec's frost-burned lips with his hand. He thrust an oxygen mask over her face, not asking whether or not she wanted it. She did. LizAlec pulled pure oxygen deep into her aching lungs. Inside her head, synapses relit and neuro-chemicals began to stabilize: it was like watching a city's lights come on after a blackout. She was still sucking oxygen from the mask harder than a baby pulling at a teat when Leon jabbed an SB hypo against her neck and hit the trigger. Endorphins blasted into her bloodstream and then the boy slammed open the hypo and slid in another slug. Glucose and *hypericum* followed.

'Like, you know . . . My uncle taught me,' the boy said by way of explanation. 'That smart skin's a real neat trick,' he added longingly, as he ran his finger down her arm. 'Never seen a real one before, too expensive.'

LizAlec shivered.

That was when she realized she was more or less naked, the spider's silk pulled in so tight against her body she could practically see the goose bumps on her inner thigh. And if she could see that, then LizAlec had a pretty good idea why the boy was still gawking at her.

Pulling LizAlec to her feet, Leon grinned, holding her while both her ReeGravs found the deck and locked onto it. LizAlec was about to shake off his hand but then she changed her mind: she needed all the help she could get.

'Through here,' Leon told her and together they limped into the hold of the *Shockwave Rider*, Leon closing the airlock's inner door behind him. He took her across the small hold and stopped at a door marked *Danger, Radiation, Keep Out*, opening it with a smart card hung on the same chain as his silver crucifix.

Inside the tiny room, white noise blared from every speaker, loud enough to blow out your eardrums. Voidoids3, LizAlec decided. Not that she could tell one Luna noise band from another. The area had started out as storage space and ended up as someone's bolt-hole, at least that was how it looked to LizAlec.

The place was wall-to-wall mess, empty McDonald's containers floating through the air, not even recycled or even netted down in a rubbish bag . . . But the bank of tek bolted to the steel floor was real enough. A Segasim, two Nintendos, a standard grey box and something square and black that had bits of crystal RAM sprouting from it like digital cancer. The walls were cluttered with cheap flickering flatscreens, epoxied or staple-gunned into place. Every single one of them was on. 197 channels and LizAlec didn't know which one to watch.

'Here.' Leon lifted a silver flask to her lips. Warm sweet chocolate slid down her throat, so thick and synthetic it could have been melted plastic. LizAlec pulled a face, but then reached for the flask as warmth began to spread through her body, radiating out from her gut.

'You want that lifeboat?' Leon asked, clapping his hands to lower the volume. For a second, LizAlec looked blank and then realized the boy was talking about her pod. No, she didn't want it. In fact, she hoped never to see the thing again.

'You mind if I have it?'

LizAlec shrugged. 'Sure,' she said glibly, 'it's yours.'

The boy nodded and walked over to the nearest flatscreen. Running his fingers over its flickering surface he woke an icon called *lasso* and watched as a cartoon drone navigated slow circles around a cartoon dustbin, wrapping it in monofilament.

'Salvage,' the boy explained. 'Space junk. You'd be 'mazed how much there is out here.' Leon knew, it was his ship. Well, seventeen per cent of it was and the figure was rising. Jude had put up the guarantee, but then that was what mothers were for, and he'd never missed a payment. Didn't intend to, either.

All that other shit was just stuff he'd told the other two. Fixx he could handle, provided Leon left his ma out of that equation, but the Japanese woman. Now that was someone he didn't trust . . .

On a bigger screen the real drone had finished trussing LizAlec's half-pod in a cocoon of monofilament, so the boy tapped a winch icon and the cargo doors opened to let the pod be pulled inside.

'Worth more than carrying people,' said Leon, without looking round. 'Less grief too, especially that pair.' He jerked his thumb downwards towards where *The Arc* must be. 'Should have seen the two of them. Bitched at each other the whole way out. Need locking up . . .'

Who needed locking up? LizAlec wondered, feeling puzzled. Mind you, she was getting expert at that. Maybe it was oxygen starvation, or perhaps she just didn't know what the fuck was going on any more.

'Locking up,' said Leon, 'and fed slop through a slit in the door. So they can blade each other to death or else fuck, whichever takes their fancy. Wouldn't put my cache on the one with metal legs, though . . .'

'What?' LizAlec looked startled.

'Too old,' explained Leon, 'too dopey. Came out to Strat looking for you and then fucked up, but Chink's a real professional, I've seen people like her before.' He didn't say it was on tri-D.

'Fixx?' LizAlec demanded, grabbing Leon by the arm. 'Fixx is here?' She practically shook Leon off balance in her excitement.

'Tall guy, metal legs and arm, silver eyes . . . ?'

The girl didn't need the list, she already knew it was Fixx. Jeeeez. Well, she thought, better late than never. Fixx had actually got off his arse and launched a rescue mission. LizAlec was grinning like a lunatic, but she didn't care. Swinging neatly on her heel, LizAlec let go of Leon's arm and stamped for the door, ReeGravs ringing like bells on the metal floor.

'Where you going?' Leon demanded. He had his head cocked to one side and for once he was looking only at her face. Whatever Leon saw there, it interested him. Mind you, great tits, narrow hips and killer scowl, the whole girl interested him. You didn't get too many of her type for your money in Fracture or Planetside. At least, not in the places he went anyway.

'I'm going to find Fixx,' said LizAlec as if it should be obvious.

'You and this guy. . .' For a second, Leon searched for a tactful way to ask but couldn't think of one, and fell back on what he knew. Tact wasn't in high demand in Strat or the salvage business. 'You know, like, you guys fuck?'

LizAlec just looked at him.

'Just asking,' said Leon. 'Because they had, you know? Didn't much like each other but, well . . .' Leon spread his hands. 'When has that ever stopped anybody?'

It wasn't the bile, but her throat suddenly felt sour and her gut was so hollow it hurt, like he'd just sucker-punched her under the heart.

'Fixx wouldn't,' said LizAlec. 'I don't believe you.' But they both knew she did.

After that, Leon concentrated on getting her pod safely stashed in the back of the cargo bay, making more adjustment to speed and angle than the job needed, until the ship's semiAI was having to compensate for logistical problems that shouldn't have been there in the first place.

When he'd done all he could to organize the cargo capture, Leon began adjusting the speaker sequence, ripping Voidoid3 white noise from one side of his cabin to the other in a cascade. After a while, even that grew boring.

'There's a spare balloon suit in that locker behind you,' Leon told LizAlec without looking up from his controls. The suit wasn't her size and it was none too clean, but that was what Leon had. She was welcome to use his suit if she wanted.

LizAlec didn't. She didn't want anything to do with Leon, but she couldn't stay as she was, dressed in an almost translucent second skin that was ripped in all the wrong places. 'You got a coat?' LizAlec demanded.

Leon shook his head. 'T-shirt,' he offered. 'In the sack in the corner.' He nodded towards a black bag, etched round with what looked like Togo stripes until LizAlec got close enough to see the holostrips were fake. The lock was uncoded, and the bag opened for her as soon as she knelt over it. A T-shirt in there, all right. What's more it was clean, and obviously enough it was black.

She took it and she took a pair of black Diesels too, without bothering to ask. It wasn't like she'd ever expected Fixx to be faithful. Actually, it wasn't like she'd ever expected much of Fixx, period. But LizAlec still couldn't help the tears welling up in her eyes.

'How do I get over to *The Arc*?' she asked Leon, pulling his Diesel jeans up round her narrow hips.

You don't, thought Leon. *Not unless you've got a death wish.* The boy considered not answering, his fingers over the icon that locked the cargo doors, and then he turned to face her anyway. If he saw the hurt in her eyes, he didn't let it show.

'You could wait until they get back,' he suggested. 'I mean,' he checked the time tattoo on his wrist, 'They said they'd be back, like, now.'

'What you mean,' said LizAlec, 'is they're already late.'

Leon nodded.

They'd gone in after her and now she was going in after them, that was fine, LizAlec didn't have a problem with symmetry. 'Can you get me close to the hatch?' LizAlec asked.

Did *La Papa* shit in the woods?

LizAlec felt the *Shockwave Rider* lurch slightly, engines humming. Whatever Leon was doing over at a screen, it was bringing the shuttle close into the ring. 'I'll erect a tunnel,' said Leon, 'leave the outer lock already open, tie her to that thing's skin.' He nodded his chin at an on-screen grab of *The Arc*. The boy could have been talking to himself and for all LizAlec knew, he was.

'Yeah,' he said, turning to her. 'I can get you in.' Leon grinned. 'But you'd better know what you're getting into. That bitch was armed and dancing – knife, molyblade, hotkeys, grenades . . . You don't tool out with stuff like that if you don't intend to use it.' Leon's smile was getting wider by the second.

'You know the first law of salvage?' Leon asked LizAlec.

LizAlec shook her head: of course she didn't. Thermodynamics, primogeniture, negative capability, yes . . . Even Salic law. But salvage?

'The first ship on the scene claims the lot.'

Looking at him, LizAlec could almost see Leon try to work out how much *The Arc* was worth as scrap.

Chapter 36

Carthage Burns

'Tell Lazlo I want a meeting . . .'

Lady Clare was standing in her study, leaning against its vast
carved overmantle, swaddled in a vast black coat that had once
belonged to Prince Sabatini. She was still frozen to the bone and
probably beyond. A black teak Buddha, two wooden doves from
a gilded Thai temple carving and a copy of *Twenty Years After*
now burned fitfully in the grate, flames dancing like unwilling
ghosts then fading as smoke backed up in the sodden chimney.

Her mahogany chess table and Prince Sabatini's battered
Jacobean stool had already been sacrificed that morning to
the ash. Lady Clare would have used just the books, but they
refused to burn properly, merely smouldering like badly dried
slabs of peat.

So instead she'd started breaking up the Hôtel Sabatini's
priceless collection of wooden furniture. Later, if there was a
later, history would hold their destruction against her, no doubt
along with greater crimes. Not that it mattered now . . . Money
had no value when there was nothing worthwhile to buy. And all
Lady Clare really wanted was to stay warm, that and keep up her
faltering courage. Because what came next would not be easy.

The General had gone, though Lady Clare didn't remember
where. He'd told her but she'd forgotten: her attention span as
brittle as her bird-boned body, which trembled every time it
moved. How the half-starved boy standing in front of her managed to stay at attention, Lady Clare didn't know. She couldn't
have managed it.

It was the same Imperial Guard who'd woken her two days earlier and before that had been waiting for Fixx and her at the shuttle. That was, what . . . ? Lady Clare tried to count back but got lost. It seemed forever ago, but it probably wasn't really that long.

She had food left and if she were kind . . .

'Here,' Lady Clare said, pushing one trembling hand into the coat's pocket. She extracted one of the General's biscuits. 'Eat it slowly.'

The gratitude in his eyes gave way to suspicion. If she had one biscuit, how many others did she have? Maybe she had a houseful of food? Maybe all the Imperial Ministers did . . .

'I had two left,' Lady Clare told him. 'Now I have one.'

She didn't mention that she was saving her last biscuit for her meeting with Lazlo. That it was her tiny reserve of strength and courage. God help her.

'Tell Count Lazlo I wish to discuss surrender,' said Lady Clare bleakly. 'Go now, tell him to meet me at the Tuileries.' She hunched forward, pushing frozen fingers further into her pockets, trying to ignore the chill that slid in through the rotting window frames. Half-decent glazing could have reduced the invading cold to nothing. But it was too late now, and besides, Lady Clare had spent nearly eighteen years restoring the Hôtel Sabatini to its original glory, wood sash-windows and all.

If she'd wanted comfort, she'd have lived in a purpose-built total-control complex somewhere like Lille. But she didn't want comfort. All Lady Clare had ever been after was elegance and everyone knew nothing came colder.

The boy was disappointed in her. He'd been expecting Lady Clare to fight, to die: somewhere inside his empty head he'd probably seen himself standing guard over her fallen body as he fought hand-to-hand with Black Cossacks. And now she was ordering a lieutenant of the *Garde Impériale* to help her betray His Highness.

'Do it,' she told the boy firmly, some of the old fire coming back into her voice. If the flame didn't reach her eyes that didn't matter, he was looking at the floor anyway. Saluting coldly, the boy stamped out of the room and slammed the study door behind him. Lady Clare smiled: that was probably going to be the one truly defiant gesture of his short life, poor child.

It was time to see Count Lazlo. On her way out of the study Lady Clare paused at a marble-topped table to pick up a tiny model of a cavalry sabre that rested on top of a pile of damp papers. Hand-written data she'd calmly ignored ever since it had arrived a week before. At a certain point of catastrophe, additional information no longer made a difference. Memoranda become the irrelevance they were. The idea had a certain appeal. Particularly if your job was to leave no traces.

Lady Clare held the paperweight lightly in her fingers, testing its balance. The blade curved in traditional cavalry fashion and the handle was bound with gold wire. Before it had been Lady Clare's, it had belonged to a minister called Pierre Nexus, and before him it had been the property of the Prince Imperial himself. A perfect copy of a sabre worn by Napoleon the First during his Cisalpine campaign, back in the days when he was a simple general.

Slipping the tiny sabre into her coat pocket, Lady Clare double-checked the wooden shutters and locked her study door against possible looters. The wide marble steps down to the entrance hall were black with dirty footprints and slick with condensation, but Lady Clare made her way safely, one frail hand clutching at the stone balustrade, her other holding a battered army-issue hurricane lamp. The whole Hôtel Sabatini felt as empty and lifeless as a restaurant that had gone out of fashion and seen its patrons go elsewhere.

The city was black, buried under darkness. No stars could break through the heavy layer of cloud, few lights showed, and when they did it was as flickering shards through closed shutters and tightly drawn curtains. Firelight or lamplight, not electricity, not for days now. Passing over the pedestrian-only Pont St-Louis, Lady Clare entered L'Ile de la Cité and tramped her way through the mud of what had once been a huge rose garden. Even the spider's-leg flying buttresses on the south side of Notre-Dame were almost lost to Lady Clare in the rain as she turned into the Place du ParvisND, edging nervously round the granite plinth of Charlemagne.

Puddles had spread to the size of small lakes, the river changed to a swollen slug of black water. Lady Clare navigated by instinct, stepping where years of being Parisian told her that roads, bridges and pavements should be, cutting between l'Hôtel Dieu and the Préfecture to reach the Quai de l'Horloge and finally Pont Neuf, the oldest bridge in the city.

She ducked at the thunder like some Stone Age primitive, counting off the seconds until lightning flared as she tried to work out how far away the storm was. Not far enough. Not nearly far enough away for the Ishies to upload what they were seeing. Alsatians didn't bark from inside the locked *préfecture de police*. Sodden feral cats didn't crouch spitting beneath deserted police trucks, there wasn't even the slightest scuttle of a swimming rat or the heavy flap of a grey owl's wings as it swooped low over the quai. It was as though only humans were left – and not too many of them, judging from the rain-soaked silence . . .

Lady Clare bent her head into the wind and headed west towards the Tuileries. She'd been protected from the worst of the storm by the buildings, more or less, but now she was face on to the howling wind, alone among the darkened deserted colonnades of the Rue de Rivoli. No one else was stupid enough to be out.

There were guards at the gate of the Palais Impériale, though. Tall boys wrapped tightly in sodden military-issue oilskins that did nothing to keep out the rain. One of them carried a Browning, held barrel-up to the open sky.

'Reverse it,' she told the startled boy, stepping out of the darkness of the Place de Palais. While he was still deciding whether to challenge her, Lady Clare leant forward and grabbed his rifle, swivelling it round until its barrel pointed at the cobbles. By the light of his single hurricane lamp, the boy could see water trickle from the muzzle and spread in an oily rainbow over the puddle at his feet.

'We don't need guns that explode in people's hands,' Lady Clare said tartly. 'We've got problems enough already . . .'

The boy recognized her then, snapping to attention and saluting fiercely.

'Madame, I'm sorry . . .'

So was she. For much more than the child could begin to imagine.

Lady Clare patted his arm in passing, and took herself inside to the Prince Imperial's study. She'd remembered where she was meant to meet the General. It was here, but there were things she needed to do first.

'My dear.' The Prince rose from his leather chair and clasped Lady Clare's hands. She had the fingers of a corpse, Lady Clare realized, looking down at them. As cold and as grey as those of any drowned woman.

She was only a quarter of the way into his room and already she'd left a trail of mud across a Persian carpet. Water was gathering in the hem of her coat and then splashing into a puddle on the floor. Her shoes were rotted, her short hair was an unruly halo of dark spikes. Rain had even gathered in what was left of her plucked eyebrows, dripping like tears onto her cheeks.

Over the old man's shoulder, backed by two bodyguards, Lady Clare could see the new Minister for External Security dressed immaculately in a suit cut from black Florentine wool. A balloon of pale liquid was clutched in one hand, though God knew how he'd found cognac in this city. She'd thought the Prince had drunk it all. Lazlo looked at Lady Clare and smiled, softly.

He was good, Lady Clare had no trouble admitting that. The man wasn't gloating – at least not obviously – and he wasn't pushing himself forward to take control, not yet. But his gaze let her know that Lazlo realized the depth of her defeat and savoured it. And it was a defeat, just being in the same room as Lazlo was proof of that.

'Minister,' the Minister for External Security bowed slightly. 'Can I offer you some Courvoisier . . . ?'

Instinct made Lady Clare almost refuse, but instead she nodded and tried to smile, watching Lazlo tip up the broad-shouldered bottle. The brandy stuck to the side of the glass as Lady Clare swirled it round to release its scent, pulling alcohol vapour deep into her lungs until welcome fire spread through her sodden body.

For a second, with the huge glass in her hand, watching Lazlo swirl and sniff his own cognac, Lady Clare could almost imagine the world was the same as it ever had been, but inside her head Lady Clare knew the world was anything but.

'What terms can we get?' Lady Clare asked Count Lazlo. The Prince put up one hand in protest but Lady Clare made herself ignore the bleak-eyed old man and kept her gaze firmly on the Minister for External Security.

Count Lazlo glanced towards his hired thugs. With their black tunics, cropped hair and practised scowls they looked like members of the Black Hundreds, or as alike as it was possible to get without wearing the enamel triple-headed eagle. Lady Clare wondered just how many more of them there were, men like those, waiting in her city.

'Guard the main door,' said Lazlo abruptly and waited while they stamped out into the hall, taking up position just inside the entrance, leaving the rain and darkness to the boys still standing outside.

Lazlo didn't want the main door guarded at all, Lady Clare realized. He just didn't want his men to overhear what he was about to say. She found it reassuring somehow that Lazlo was still a duplicitous bastard, even when it came to dealing with his own side.

'You agree Paris should surrender, then?' Lazlo said once the study door had swung safely shut again.

'Do we have an option?' Lady Clare wanted his answer. More than that, she *needed* his answer and needed it badly. Without it she would never be able to give a shape back to her life.

No trusted servant from the secretariat sat in the corner of the study, fingers flying. No tiny Aerospatiale K11 spun up near the ceiling, recording every word, duplicating with voiceType what was already being taken down on the keyboard.

But Lady Clare still wanted Lazlo's position on record, at least inside her head.

'No,' said Lazlo, 'we ran out of options a week ago.'

'So you think we should surrender?'

'Of course I do. You know what I think. Surrender's the only way to ensure the city's health. That's been my view since the start.'

'And now the Ishies are drifting away,' said Lady Clare. 'CySat packed up camp last night. The whole fucking circus is on the move. What's left of the world got bored with us. We're over, we're no longer news, we're history . . .' She put anger into her voice. Not that she wasn't angry for real, but she couldn't use up that real anger, not now, not yet. It was too fragile.

'I mean,' Lady Clare shrugged, 'what makes you think the Reich will deal with us?'

Count Lazlo smiled and shot the cuffs of his suit, revealing expensive cornelian cuff links. 'There've been talks already,' Lazlo said smugly.

'So,' said Lady Clare. 'It's agreed? We surrender Paris in return for safe passage for those of us who wish to leave.' Head down, Lady Clare's muffled voice made it clear she didn't include Lazlo in that list. She was hunting through a desk drawer, looking for ink cartridges. Fountain pens weren't items anyone had needed until recently. Most of those that still existed were in museums.

'Perhaps the old man knows where one is,' said Lazlo smoothly.

The Prince Imperial didn't say anything.

'Your Highness?' Lady Clare kept her voice polite but neutral.

The old man shrugged. 'Try inside the secretaire, middle drawer on the right.'

'You'll sign whatever Lazlo writes?' Lady Clare asked as she pulled out an antique Mont Blanc and unscrewed its barrel to check that there was a cartridge in place. There was.

'If that's what you advise.'

'You write it,' said Lady Clare and Lazlo took the pen from her fingers, manoeuvring her aside without quite touching her. Not that she had any objection to stepping away, stepping back. That was what she needed to do for what came next. All the same, she'd have liked to have known if the Count imagined his friends would honour the surrender and give the Prince Imperial safe passage. But she knew she'd never know.

With Count Lazlo bent over the open secretaire tapping the pen nib impatiently against a sheet of damp paper, Lady Clare slid one trembling hand into her pocket and found the handle of her paper knife. If that notice of surrender was ever delivered it would mean the end of Paris, probably of France. The Black Hundreds would have done the Reich's bidding and imposed a new order from the Urals to the Atlantic.

More than that, Lazlo would have won. She couldn't, wouldn't let that happen . . .

Pulling the tiny sabre from its black-leather scabbard, Lady Clare took the knife out of her pocket and held it blade down towards the ground and close to the side of her leg. It was critical the Prince Imperial couldn't see and didn't know what she intended to do. The old man had to be unimplicated, blameless.

'This is where it finishes,' Lady Clare told Count Lazlo, jerking her chin towards the paper.

The man nodded.

'And it finishes now,' said Lady Clare – and sank the curved

blade up under his rib cage, punching it in through his diaphragm. Inside Lazlo, the blade slit open the purple surface
of his liver, sliced through the pericardial sac and came to rest
against his heart. Lady Clare could feel it beating.

Lazlo opened his mouth to scream and Lady Clare pushed hard
on the hilt of the paperknife, forcing its point through muscle.
Lazlo's eyes widened with shock and then – much too late –
blanked into rising fear. He was dead before the full horror ever
hit him, leaving Lady Clare feeling cheated.

She struggled under Lazlo's sinking weight like a woman fielding
an unsavoury waltz partner and then the Prince Imperial stepped
forward, reached under the arms of the corpse and lifted it away
from Lady Clare. Together they laid Lazlo on the carpet.

Kneeling by the body, the Prince Imperial reached for the small
handle and pulled the paperknife from Lazlo's chest, wiping the
blade on the dead Minister's white cotton shirt before offering
the tiny sabre, hilt first, to Lady Clare.

He smiled. 'I really thought you were going to surrender.'

'So did I,' said Lady Clare, sounding empty.

She took another glass of cognac at the old man's insistence,
though she hardly touched it as she told the Prince Imperial
about LizAlec, about the kidnapping, about Anchee and General Que.

The old man said nothing, just listened as she explained what
the General wanted and what it would cost France. Which was
more than they could afford but less than losing an empire.
General Que got the contract to rebuild the whole of Paris, in
exchange the Prince Imperial got enough gold to bribe the regular
army into coming out against the Reich.

'But we have no food. How can the army . . .'

There would be a food drop within thirty-six hours, coming
east over the Atlantic. An airlift involving Niponshi drones.
Passion too was to be flown in especially to cover the conflict.
The UN was to be informed that there was an antidote to the
Azerbaijani virus but that its formula was known to the Prince

Imperial alone. And that the Prince Imperial would be staying in Paris.

All the General wanted in return was to be given Gibraltar.

'Gibraltar?' The Prince Imperial sounded bemused, as well he might. Lady Clare started to explain and then decided not to bother. There would be time later to go into the General's plans, which were either constructs of fiscal genius or the work of a madman, albeit a rich one.

'Are you prepared to sign an order to fight?'

'Is that what you advise?'

Lady Clare nodded.

The Prince Imperial reached for the Mont Blanc and tore the flyleaf from his own moth-eaten leather-bound copy of *Cyrano*. He was still writing the order when Lady Clare left the room, turning left into a marble-floored corridor. In a small armoury at the far end, amid walls covered with virus-eaten swords and halberds, the General sat reading by the light of a hurricane lamp. He'd found himself another atlas.

'We have a deal?'

'Yes,' said Lady Clare looking down at him. 'We have a deal. All we have to do now is rid ourselves of Lazlo's two goons guarding the main door.'

General Que picked up a buffalo-horn-handled, silver-bladed kukri once owned by the King of Nepal and weighed it in his hand. He was swinging it lightly from side to side as he made for the door.

Chapter 37

RingCycle

Swallows skimmed in low over the blue lake like combat aircraft, their tails spread in perfect vees as they slammed through hatching pupae, intercepting struggling mayfly before the insects had time to pull free from the surface tension of the water and begin their first precarious flight.

Fat bulrushes grew at the water's edge, thin stems rising up to bulbous heads the texture and hue of rotting brown velvet. There was damp meadow grass underfoot and shimmering pink cranberry flowers that looked delicate when set against the tougher white of common daisies. Only the fact that the small lake curved up towards the horizon told Fixx that he stood within the ring.

The grass felt good beneath his feet, springy and pressing up hard. Somewhere around five-sixths G, Fixx reckoned, though it was hard to tell. After a couple of weeks off-planet it was only too easy to forget what real Earth gravity felt like.

Beneath him was rock and soil, about two metres' worth. And buried under that were stunted tunnels filled with fat snakes of fibreoptix and long black powerlines. The metal floors of the tunnel had rung beneath their boots like a steel drum beaten with sticks. But looking at the lake, Fixx found it hard to believe he wasn't back on Earth, in some rich untroubled place like Norway. Only, that horizon . . .

'Move it,' Shiori ordered, standing up from the water's edge and flipping down the top on a bubble flask. Until a minute before her flask had been a flat strip of silver polymer, rolled tight and stuck to the belt of her chameleon suit. Now it bulged like the swim bladder of some fish, supplies for the trip ahead.

'Here,' she said, tossing Fixx the flask. 'You carry it.'

Fixx fumbled his catch on purpose and watched the shimmering silver bladder bounce football-like across the grass. It didn't burst or leak but then, organically woven polymer was designed to be tough.

To say Shiori had been getting on his nerves was a serious understatement. Of course, Fixx was an understated kind of guy in an overstated sort of way, but even he was getting close to saying something. All that stopped him was cowardice. Well, the hard cold expression on her face, which amounted to the same thing. That and the way Shiori kept stopping to read-off data from her Walkwear. As if the little grey box taped to her hip contained all of life's answers.

Maybe it did, but somehow Fixx doubted it.

Their relationship would have been easier if Shiori had bothered to tell him what was going on. But the Japanese woman no longer seemed even to hear his questions, as if somewhere inside her head a switch had been thrown.

Fixx was beginning to wonder if Shiori was entirely human. She obviously wasn't a straight off-the-peg clone, but there *was* something unnatural about the way she moved shadow-like across the rough grass, balanced on the balls of her feet, like a . . .

Fixx sighed. Like a fucking *ballerina* – where did he think that term came from?

Picking up Shiori's flask, Fixx took a long look round him. It was daylight up ahead and daylight behind, but there had to be night at some point to let all this vegetation breathe out and he couldn't see from where night might come. Unless some central AI just clicked off the overhead luminescent strip and shut down the whole *Arc* at one go . . .

He'd come into the ring maybe ten miles back, trailing after Shiori through an airlock. A long claustrophobic crawl on hands and knees through a service duct had led them to a dust-strewn polycrete bunker, where Shiori had casually slid in a wafer-thin *knocker* and blown the plastic door out of its frame, leaving Fixx half deaf with concussion. On the other side of the blown door was a narrow cave and beyond that daylight, or what passed for daylight on *The Arc.*

And now he was following Shiori's flickering migraine-inducing camouflage suit around the fringes of a lake, skirting the lower slopes of a small mountain. Though up ahead some design program had dictated that the lake's marshy edge should give way to small cliffs . . .

It was an illusion, but a clever one. Cut *The Arc* anywhere through its huge silver doughnut and you got a circle: the half-circle at the bottom was a valley, rising up to mountains on both sides, and the half-circle above was sky, painted electric blue . . . Except that the need to simulate gravity meant the landlocked *bottom* of the circle was actually the *Arc's* outer edge. It was better not to think about it.

Stamping after the Japanese woman, Fixx didn't notice at first that the vegetation was changing. But when *maquis* and blue-leafed hyssop began to replace meadow grass the change became impossible to ignore, even for Fixx. The fauna was different, too. Wild hopi called from rough-barked cork and stunted wild oak while feral cats pressed themselves to the ground, ears back as Shiori and Fixx strode by. There were twisted olive trunks, so fat and so badly split with age it was hard not to believe the trees had been there for hundreds of years.

The green slopes were giving way to endless tiny terraces cut into the olive-grey hillside and held in place by drystone walls. There were even dark wells, circled by pumice-hued brick and covered with flat roofs made from rough planks. Though Fixx knew that, on the lower slopes at least, the well shafts couldn't go down more than three or four metres at the most.

Fixx saw the goat boy, loping down a slope. Shiori didn't. Shiori was too busy staring moodily into the distance, following the floating-focus map that unrolled in front of her grey eyes. Both Walkwear and wraprounds were so hot from overuse they stank of burning electrics but she didn't even notice. Discomfort was something Shiori regarded as a luxury, her nervous system viral-rewired so that most pain didn't even register until it hit the middle reaches.

Pain was a distraction for working ballerinas. Most things were.

Shiori sighed and kept climbing across scrub, edging round a granite bolder flecked with mica. The huge stone was probably treated polycrete unless Sister Aaron had found a way to crystallize stone, and where that bitch was concerned anything was possible.

Shiori wasn't worried about meeting Sister Aaron: *iga*-training ensured her heart beat stayed at a steady sixty-five and her blood pressure kept to a balanced 100/80, but somewhere at the back of her mind, banished beyond consciousness, Shiori still allowed herself to be aware of the other woman's reputation.

Psionics was a dangerous art, not least because a part of Shiori's mind refused to admit it had a right to exist. The General needed his shrine back and it was Shiori's job to get it – swiftly, cleanly, neatly. The only problem so far was that the shrine wasn't showing up clearly on her screen – though it was here all right, she was getting a positive on that. But then, most of what was on file for Sister Aaron had be the product of trickery, so maybe she was keeping it hidden.

Sleight of hand and hypnotism . . . *mekuramashi* and *kawarimi*, both of those Shiori respected, they were core to the *kunoichi* tradition. Her tradition. But what the General kept on file for Sister Aaron wasn't sleight of hand, at least it didn't seem so. And so, if not actually worried, Shiori wasn't as rested as she would have liked.

'Keep up,' Shiori snapped over her shoulder, but Fixx just muttered something offensive.

Had she looked back, Shiori would have seen Fixx come face to face with the goat boy, who slid to a halt on the scree, scrawny goats jostling round his bare legs like dogs round their master. Though it was the boy who looked dog-like, his heavy jaw protruding from below a slack mouth.

'Hi,' said Fixx.

The boy just looked at him. Brown eyes flicked between Fixx and the shadow that still strode on, waist-deep in scrub, muttering to itself.

'These your goats?'

All Fixx got was a suspicious nod.

'They look really happy,' said Fixx. 'They must like you.'

The boy smiled, showing sharp canines.

Fixx sketched a line level with his shoulder. 'You seen a girl, 'bout this high, wavy black hair and weird violet eyes? She can be . . .' Fixx searched for the right word and gave up. LizAlec could be a fucking pain in the arse, but as descriptions went that didn't seem appropriate.

The goat boy had seen her. Fixx could see it in his wide face and Fixx didn't know what LizAlec had done to him, but the goat boy wasn't happy with her. Except it turned out that it wasn't what she'd done that had upset Lars, it was where LizAlec had gone.

'Girl not here,' he said simply. 'Brother Michael not here either.' The goat boy wiped his forehead with the back of his hand, sweat smearing into dirt. Fixx offered him the bubble flask and Lars took a pull, gathering his thoughts. 'Gone,' he said at last. 'Brother Michael dead, girl gone . . .'

'Shiori,' Fixx shouted and the shadow stopped climbing, one grey hand reaching up towards a grey boulder, her weight taken on her left leg, the right already raised to find a new foothold. A human climbing machine, Fixx thought. Though she had a great arse, he reminded himself: even if it was impossible to see properly now she was wearing that bloody chameleon suit.

'Down here,' Fixx shouted.

She came back down the slope, mouth hard, eyes hidden behind the wraprounds.

'This better be good.'

Fixx turned to Lars but the boy was gone and the goats with him. All Fixx could hear was the distant tinkle of bells behind a ridge in the distance. 'There was a dogboy,' Fixx began . . .

'Yeah,' said Shiori as she looked at the trodden-down scrub and pellet-like goat droppings. 'LizAlec's sandrat. Something was said about it . . . That fat woman in the bar. Remember?'

Fixx did, vaguely. As much as he was likely to remember anything through the haze of long-vanished Electric Soup and the trauma of nearly having his skull cracked open by a clone. Yeah, sometime after Fixx had got truly mashed, Jude had been saying something about some sandrat . . . Fixx didn't like Shiori calling Jude fat, though.

'Brother Michael's dead,' said Fixx and stopped . . . Half of Shiori's expression swung between pity and amusement, the rest just registered open contempt.

'Of course he's dead,' Shiori said shortly, 'You saw his cathedral. No one survives being vacuum-trashed. Not even self-proclaimed little Christian messiahs.'

Fixx nodded and raised his hand to wipe his lips. Which was when he realized the vanishing goat boy had taken not just his animals but the silver water flask too. More or less guaranteed to piss Shiori off, except Fixx was getting to the point where he no longer cared what the Japanese woman thought. Bigger problems were crowding in.

'If Brother Michael's dead . . .'

'Then maybe LizAlec is, too,' Shiori finished for him. 'Well done.' Her voice was so brittle, so bleakly ironic that Fixx had clenched his metal hand before he realized. Only Fixx never got near to throwing the punch. Shiori just stepped in close, one hand flicking up towards his chin. The razor-sharp point of her *biente-neube* slid a quarter of an inch into his flesh and then stopped dead as blood beaded around the tiny wound.

'Next time . . .'

There were threats and there were promises, and Fixx knew the difference. She would kill him too and without hesitation if it came to it, if he got in the way. Maybe Shiori didn't trash colleagues unless forced, but Fixx wasn't non-com anymore than she was, not up here on *The Arc*. Shiori needed that shrine and she intended to get it. Impatiently, the Japanese woman tapped the Sony Walkwear on her belt with the fingers of her left hand, the butterfly knife in her other hand never leaving Fixx's throat.

Sweet Jesus, thought Fixx. When am I going to learn that just because I've fucked some woman it doesn't mean she isn't still dangerous? I mean, I could type up a list . . . Still, the waves from this one were going to splatter the surface of a dozen lives like buckshot. There was Lady Clare, Anchee, kids at that stupid school, then there was him. Inside his head, Fixx was already lighting a candle for LizAlec before he remembered he wasn't Catholic. And there was another thought, coming at him out of the back of his head. If Shiori already knew LizAlec was dead, then what the fuck was she looking for as she scrambled about like a fool inside *The Arc*?

The kid's body?

Or maybe he was the one who was a fool . . . For a start, he was here, wasn't he? And he'd been the one getting beaten up, patronized and ignored while he chased around Strat and Planetside, and then hightailed it out to *The Arc* to trudge some toy wilderness, looking for a girl Shiori took for granted might already be dead.

Purple *maquis* gave way to desert scrub as cliffs edging a second lake shrunk until they were just shingle banks. The lake turned to mud shallows and then dried up altogether. Rough earth turned to grit and pebbles beneath his feet.

Fixx shook his head crossly. Shedding tears in this heat was just a waste of body water and he was losing enough of that in sweat. Gravel crunched under his feet as he concentrated on following Shiori's track. She'd moved ahead of Fixx about five minutes back, fed up with his stumbling walk and his muttered litany of curses that no amount of her threats could stop. The slab-grown skin on his ankles was coming away in strips, trailing behind him like tattered ribbon as he walked, but that wasn't what he was swearing about. He just couldn't believe LizAlec could fuck off and die like that, not this far down the line.

The only animals Fixx had seen in the last two hours were a pack of chattering meerkats, which he recognized from the way they stood high on their back legs. The cliffs he'd seen earlier had been there to separate temperate wildlife from Mediterranean, Fixx realized, but no physical boundary was needed to keep wildlife out of the desert. The blistering overhead light was enough to do that.

From what he could remember, given *The Arc*'s radius, it should take no more than two days to walk right round the ring. Which was fine as a theory, except it didn't take into account that the ground wasn't level. Instead the desert rose and fell in sweeping crescent-shaped dunes.

Up ahead, Shiori had stopped. Though all Fixx could see was the shimmering changing outline of her chameleon suit. Fixx kept his pace steady, concentrating on putting one foot in front of the other. If Shiori was waiting for him to catch up with her, then she could do just that: wait.

He was tired and hot and fucked-off, and most of his attention was taken up with thoughts of LizAlec, memories peeling back inside his mind like layers of dermis being stripped from a twitching body. Chemical self-abuse he could handle, this self-torture was something else. If he'd wanted shit like this, Fixx thought in disgust, he'd have swopped places with his old guitarist Lenny Sacher-Masoch.

And the stupid thing was, he'd never told LizAlec he loved her, not even back at the beginning when maybe he had. Oh, he'd talked about being proud of her, sure. Respecting her arrogance. Even wanting her until he was hollow-eyed with lust, but never love, not really. He wasn't big on admitting to love, and besides, they were too alike. One of him was enough.

But he was missing her already. In a warped kind of way.

Grit crunched underfoot as Fixx pushed his human hand into the pocket of his jumpsuit and, for the tenth time, dragged his nail around the seam looking for wizz he already knew wasn't there. All Fixx scraped up was cotton fluff, but he sucked at it anyway, just in case. But the grey fluff was just that, no more. There was no crunch as tiny crystals fractured along fault lines, no matching spark of neurons igniting in his brain. He was on his own, chemically speaking, stuck in a toytown Planet Earth theme park with some Japanese psychopath.

He'd blown it bigtime, as a successful musician, as a lover, even as a human . . . Maybe especially as a human. It was time he accepted the fact. Hell, it was time he accepted a dozen facts: he just wasn't very good at recognising the big picture. That writ from Sony had been his very own Galileo, the instrument that ripped him from the centre of the firmament and broke the old astrolabe, so no amount of spin could put him back in balance.

Fame wasn't just about banking credit, it was about holding back what passed for the real world while pretending that was where you came from. Banking street value without the effort of being street real. Fixx shook his head. Even as a kid he'd wanted to get away from the concrete, dog shit and more concrete. The hollow-chested horses kept on tower block rooftops and distempered guard dogs chained up on thirteenth-floor balconies.

He'd come from that world, but he'd never really belonged, not even when that was all he had. Not even when he was running with a gang and getting by in one of the Adamstown estates north of Dublin, one of those up-ended crumbling coffins where even life in the soaps looked glamorous. The kind of place where the loan shark knew more about you than your ma did. Where no victim ever went to the gardaí, but dobbing you in for a punishment beating counted as community spirit.

Everyone who could get out, got out. Coming up out of

Adamstown had been part of the Fixx Valmont mystique. To tell the truth, he'd been embarrassed by his beginnings but the publicist assigned to him had loved it. All that shit leaked to the pirate newsfeeds about Fixx leaning back against the office wall, cleaning his nails with a pearl-handled switchblade while Bernie, his new manager, argued his first contract.

Jesus fuck, no way would he have carried a blade back in Adamstown: just owning a gravity knife was worth two broken knees. Bernie had handed Fixx the switchblade just before they both went to meet the suits.

And besides, no one got heavy around Sony: it wasn't worth the grief.

Fixx wasn't tough, or pretty, or even that bright, not like LizAlec. He was a fixer, just a kid who mended broken tek and could bypass the utilities to get you power for free. ReMix was something he did on the side, a safeguard: the smartboys looked kindly if you mixed hard, got them drunk and pumped up and crying, if you scratched deck or played electric fiddle at their births, weddings or wakes. Other kids in the gang cooked up chemicals or did banks the hard way, with shotguns. He mixed and remixed. And later he got to be a rhythm doctor. If you had a fucked-up tune his bedroom studio was where you took it to get a fixx.

He wouldn't mind getting back to all that. In fact, if he ever got out of there he was going to pick up a deck and maybe go back to the CasaNegro to see if Jude needed a little regular help round the bar. No, Fixx shook his head. Make that *maybe* a *definitely*. He had to go back, the woman still had his bloody cat.

Shiori was right ahead of him now, down on one knee, blended into the crest of a dune. Even so, by squinting Fixx could see she had one hand up, shading her eyes against the brightness overhead. Fixx clambered up the steep dune behind her and stopped dead, shock clearing his head when he saw what the ballerina was looking at.

The desert ended.

Not turned into jungle or savannah, just ended. They were standing on the last dune and ahead of them the desert fell away not to bedrock but to shimmering metal overlaid with polycrete ducts and corridors. The metal curved up into the distance and vanished away into a rising smoke-grey horizon that eventually faded into blue. That was when Fixx noticed a satellite, tiny and distant, hanging silently in the air.

'Hey . . ..'

'Seen it,' Shiori snapped. 'K11, non-combat model, unknown modifications. It's been with us since we arrived.'

Now she tells me, Fixx thought crossly. He squinted hard at the spinning globe and wondered what it showed. A couple of exhausted deadbeats, probably. Great, his last recorded performance and he looked like shit . . . Still, as Bernie used to say, why change the habits of a lifetime?

'So what do we do now?' Fixx asked. His voice was dry as dust and so was the twist to his mouth.

'*We* do nothing,' Shiori said. '*You* go that way.' She pointed straight down the slope towards the bare metal. 'I'm going . . . well, somewhere else.' Shiori didn't bother to mention that, as she'd been operating in stealth mode, the tiny eyeSat had only got a clear view of Fixx. If Fixx couldn't work that out for himself, well that was his problem.

'We'll meet up later,' said Shiori, already walking away from him.

Yeah, right . . .

He didn't go the way Shiori said, but he didn't follow her, not at first. And it was letting Shiori go ahead that saved Fixx's life, though the musician didn't realize it until much later. He watched the blurred nothingness of her suit move away from him and saw the not-there shadow flick nimbly down the gravel slope in five easy jumps to land on a rock slab. He was meant to be keeping to the middle of the valley but he didn't. *The Arc* was bad enough without being on his own. He might not like Shiori.

No, wipe that, she might be an untrustworthy, psychotic little shit, but that didn't mean he was going to let her go off without him.

Apart from anything else, he didn't trust her not to hunt down whatever she was really up here for and make a run for the *Shockwave Rider*. The last thing Fixx needed was to be trapped on a two-thirds-finished ring colony with a goat boy, half a dozen chattering meerkats and a psychotic transsexual drug-designer named Sister Aaron who might, or might not, be in cold storage.

Three hours later, Fixx gave up skulking between long strips of shoulder-high polycrete that spliced into each other like wormcasts and decided to catch up with Shiori. But he never got the chance. Luck got in his way.

Ahead of him, the polycrete ducts had begun to be buried beneath a rising tide of black rock that rose rapidly and kept climbing until it became the slopes of a small mountain. Fist-sized gaps showed in the rock where bubbles had popped and it was obvious that the whole mountain was made of expanded 'crete, pressure-treated to increase its surface density.

The fist-sized pockmarks occurred every few yards up to where the ground level would be. Above that Fixx saw none at all, just the perfect sheen of black basalt. Everything was grown, Fixx realized suddenly. The wormcast service tunnels, this half-finished mountain, even the shimmering metal of the Ring's skin, it was all grown to order.

So much for the Brotherhood's hatred of nanetics.

Ahead of him, Shiori slipped out of sight as she reached the top, clambering hand over hand with easy confidence as Fixx struggled unseen behind her to find each grip. And as Shiori launched herself over the edge, the sky winked out and every siren in the ring sounded.

'Sweet fuck!' Fixx made it to the top faster than he'd thought possible, his human hand scraped raw from the effort. Rolling over the top in a breathless heap, Fixx heard a low whine and the sky relit, miles of central filament igniting at once.

'Holy shit.' Fixx crouched low, watching Shiori. The Japanese woman looked worried and Fixx didn't blame her. In Shiori's place he'd have been bricking it.

Standing in front of Shiori, dressed in a simple white sarong, was the most beautiful woman who'd ever lived. Behind the woman stood a vast block of obsidian that rippled lightly across its clean-cut surface as if little wavelets were running over a black-glass mirror. Ash-white hair flowed across perfect shoulders. Full breasts nuzzled against the silk of her sarong which stopped above her knee to reveal flawless legs.

Fixx took a deep breath.

'Ah,' said Sister Aaron happily, 'this must be your partner . . .'

Shiori turned slightly, saw Fixx and scowled.

'Now,' said Sister Aaron, 'that's not nice, is it?' She had the smile of an angel and the body of one, too. They went with her voice. Almost sadly, the woman shook her head at Shiori and then smiled again at Fixx, showing perfectly white, perfectly formed teeth.

Completely fucking barking, Fixx realized as he looked deep into her clear blue eyes. Absolutely off the scale.

'You shouldn't be here, you know . . .' Sister Aaron spoke only to Shiori, as if Fixx wasn't really there. Or rather, as if he existed for her only when she was staring directly at him. Fixx wasn't big on being ignored, but looking again into the burning clarity of her eyes Fixx decided he could live with it just this once.

'I don't have it,' Sister Aaron said lightly.

'Have what?' The words were out of Fixx's mouth before he remembered he was planning to stay silent.

'Whatever she's looking for,' said Sister Aaron. 'I'd ask if one of you killed my brother, but there's no point. Neither of you killed Michael, did you? You're just the hired help . . .' Her blue eyes were ice-cold, inhuman.

Behind her the obsidian slab bubbled and roiled across its surface. She turned towards it as it opened to reveal steps leading down into darkness. *Nanetics*, Fixx told himself hurriedly, nothing more.

'Wait,' Shiori demanded, moving purposefully towards the ash-haired woman, 'Tell me where Brother Michael hid the shrine.'

'Shrine?' The two women looked at each other, Fixx already forgotten, which was fine with him. 'I don't have your shrine and nor did my brother,' said Sister Aaron but Shiori just kept moving forwards on the balls of her feet, backing Sister Aaron towards the steps.

It was a bad move.

Noise exploded inside Fixx's skull and, as he buckled, he saw Shiori struggle to stay upright as she desperately tried to protect her ears with her hands. She was exposed, vulnerable, completely open, everything a ballerina was meant not to be.

Fixx didn't see the kick coming but then nor did Shiori or it wouldn't have broken her neck. Spinning to a stop, Sister Aaron looked down at the Japanese woman's twitching body and frowned.

'That was just too easy,' she said sadly. Bending over Shiori's body, Sister Aaron twisted the woman's head until it was straight again. Her hands rippled as they touched Shiori's skin and then Sister Aaron reached deep inside Shiori's flesh, clicking vertebrae back into place.

Fixx vomited.

Ignoring him, Sister Aaron pulled the Japanese girl upright and stepped back, leaving Shiori standing there, arms hanging loose at her side. 'Let's try that again,' said Sister Aaron, 'shall we?'

The pale woman moved in a circle around Shiori, silent and impassive, coming in close and then dancing back but never quite touching the Japanese ballerina. She moved like this until Shiori finally stopped trembling and began to concentrate, dropping into a fighter's crouch. Beginning to turn, not circling in the same way as Sister Aaron, but counter-clockwise so that she spun slowly in the opposite direction.

As she turned, Shiori bent slightly at the knees, alternately pushing her shoulders forward and then pulling them back, gathering power. Not letting herself attack until her mind was empty of all emotion. When Shiori's attack came it was breathtakingly fast, a flip that took the Japanese woman high over Sister Aaron's head and then *kusumigiri* as Shiori fell, the sword slash the ballerina had made her own.

Except there was no sword and Sister Aaron still stood, smiling happily.

Staring first at Sister Aaron and then at her own wrist, Shiori's disbelief slid into horror as she realized the bracelet on her wrist had remained just that, a narrow black bracelet, no more. For the first time since she moved up from street samurai to ballerina, *kusumigiri* had failed. She'd lost without striking a single blow.

Sister Aaron spun once, fingers flicking out to stroke Shiori's shoulder. A six-inch gash opened up in Shiori's combat suit as its top streaked with a vivid red that owed nothing to environment-sensitive spider's silk.

Before Shiori could react, Sister Aaron was moving again, a slight frown catching her empty, impossibly beautiful face. For a second, feeling Fixx's horrified gaze, Sister Aaron stopped dead, her frown dissolving as she gave Fixx her sweetest smile. And then she went back to tormenting Shiori.

She was hardwired, Fixx realized, her reaction times virally chopped, her nerves pulled taut on some methamphet derivative. But there was more to it than that. If he hadn't known better, he'd have said the woman was reading Shiori's moves ahead of the Japanese woman making them. The bitch was scanning Shiori's cortex and his, pulling out whatever amused her. That she could do both and fend off Shiori at the same time was what made it really frightening.

'Oh,' said Sister Aaron sourly, 'this is nothing.' Her left hand flicked forward, forcing Shiori to throw up a guard. And as Shiori blocked the move, Sister Aaron reached out with her right hand, touching Shiori. It looked briefly like Sister Aaron was trying to fondle the Japanese woman's breast. But when Sister Aaron took her fingers away, her nails were covered with blood and Shiori was staggering backwards, red oozing from a semicircular cut that gaped to show sick white flashes of naked rib.

'Children today,' Sister Aaron said crossly. 'You know,' she almost spat the words at Shiori, 'it's a bad mistake to rely on just one weapon. Particularly when it doesn't work.'

The Japanese woman was breathing heavily, pulling sour gasps through her open mouth. One hand held shut the gash in her right shoulder, the other was trying to staunch blood flowing from beneath her heart. Shiori still kept to her fighter's crouch, and she still turned in a slow circle, claiming space around her; but her grey eyes were bleak and her bottom lip jutted forward slightly in a child's pout.

Defeat clung to Shiori's overheated body like sweat. Even Fixx could smell it. She'd been the best because she'd never met anyone better. Wasn't it always the way? Horrified, Fixx sucked at his teeth, watching Sister Aaron move in for the kill.

The final cut was rapid and deep, starting above Shiori's left hip and sweeping in a semicircle across her gut, flesh peeling open under Sister Aaron's fingers. Shiori toppled forwards, hands scrabbling at her stomach as she tried to shovel her own pulsing, twitching intestines back inside her body.

Chapter 38

White light/White heat

'You could always kill her,' Sister Aaron told Fixx. 'If you think that would be kind.'

The woman reached down and ripped free a standard-issue combat knife taped to Shiori's ankle. The one Shiori had never even come close to using on her.

'Or you could always kill me instead. If you think you can . . .' The blonde woman tossed Fixx the lethal zytel blade, smiling as Fixx fumbled the catch and almost sliced his own fingers. 'Alternatively, we could think of something else . . .'

Blue eyes held his and Fixx almost heard the waterfall-roar as blood rushed through his body and inside his head synapses exploded, firing and re-firing as they completed a fluorescent and familiar web of addiction. Waves of absolute need rolled over him . . . Sister Aaron nodded to herself, quietly amused. 'So tell me,' she said, 'what *do* you want to do?'

'*Fuck you, probably*,' said a girl's voice behind her. '*Fixx always did think with his dick.*'

In that brief silent second before Sister Aaron turned round – while her eyes were still locked to those of Fixx – the musician saw real shock cross her face. And then the shock was gone, along with all other emotions, as Sister Aaron's perfect Helen-of-Troy mask slid safely back into place.

'Blind-sided,' said LizAlec contemptuously, from her position high on the obsidian block. She was breathing heavily from the climb, but her words were confident. 'You should learn to concentrate.'

Jumping down, she landed in a crouch, not even looking at Fixx. And if LizAlec noticed Shiori's blood drying like glazed black enamel on the parched ground then she didn't let it show.

Someone else slid out onto the edge of the obsidian block, looking a lot less certain than LizAlec. But he jumped down anyway to stand beside the girl. Leon still wore a black T-shirt and stupid hair, but a fractal blade was held firm in his hand like he knew how to use it. And, looking at the way the boy flicked the blade from side to side, Fixx decided that maybe he did. Except that even the sharpest mono-molecular edge was going to be no use against Sister Aaron. Fixx could have told them that for free.

'You want to do it now?' LizAlec asked Sister Aaron, casually waving the boy to one side. Leon almost refused to move but then shuffled sideways, his eyes suddenly dark . . . Oh, the anger of youth, thought Fixx enviously. On a good day he could still remember what that felt like.

'Well, do you?' LizAlec demanded.

The ash-blonde woman remained silent, almost unmoving.

'No,' said LizAlec, 'I didn't think so.' She stepped neatly round Sister Aaron's frozen form and knelt by Shiori. It looked, for a second, as if LizAlec intended to comfort the Japanese woman. But all LizAlec did was reach down and touch the black bracelet on Shiori's wrist.

Sister Aaron winced.

There's a point just before lead melts when it swells outwards and then splits through its own papery skin. That's what Shiori's bracelet did, coalescing into mirrored liquid that flowed up around LizAlec's wrist, solidifying into a heavy bangle. And then, as LizAlec emptied her mind, she knew what Shiori's bracelet was and how much more important the other one must be.

How much Anchee's bracelet might offer.

LizAlec smiled sourly. 'You know, if I hadn't met your other half I wouldn't know how to do that.' There was something about the way she said it that made Fixx's skin crawl.

'You're the little rich kid,' Sister Aaron said. It wasn't a question.

'And you're the clone Brother Michael had made with cells from his own rib. So he could fuck himself. Only you didn't like sex, did you?' LizAlec looked at the woman's unnerving perfection and shrugged. 'You must have been such a disappointment.'

Pain flared inside LizAlec's head, growing like cancer. But the waves never had time to overwhelm her. Wrapping her thoughts round with a stuttering barrier of noise, LizAlec pushed the other woman out of her head and pumped up the volume until white noise, white heat echoed round the inside of her skull.

Leon would be proud of her, LizAlec decided with a grin. And, despite herself, she glanced at the boy, taking in his serious scowl and black Voidoid3 T-shirt but most of all the blade held rock-steady in his hand. He'd insisted on coming along to cover her back. Except LizAlec didn't know who Leon might have to guard it against, apart from Sister Aaron. And LizAlec intended to take care of Sister Aaron herself.

She could do it, too. LizAlec was increasingly certain of that. Put LizAlec's life in danger and she had the power. At least, she did now . . . It came from being dead. That's how the girl thought of it. She'd been killed up there in the cathedral, Brother Michael's hands squeezing the life out of her as certainly as she now breathed.

Though I walk through the valley of the shadow of death . . .

LizAlec grinned. She was made flesh again. Only now, somewhere inside her head howled the ghost hordes of her father. . . She'd thought, while she was cached up in the pod, that maybe that whole incident was brief insanity brought on by oxygen starvation. But that wasn't it. She hadn't met angels or even the One True King, may he rock forever. She'd met herself.

'Meet yourself again,' suggested Sister Aaron inside her head and stepped forward, reaching for LizAlec's wrist. Before Leon could move or LizAlec even scream, the woman threw her against the obsidian block, *wing chun*-style. Only all LizAlec felt was cold wind on her face as she rolled blindly through the rock and fell headlong into blackness.

She screamed but there was no echo, her howl swallowed by the dark.

Stars flicked around her except she wasn't in space: deep space had no significant gravity and she was definitely falling, hard and fast. Landing even harder, as her feet caught on something and her legs buckled upwards to punch LizAlec violently in the chest, winding her.

Stars swung crazily from side to side. And then LizAlec realized the stars themselves weren't moving, it was the ground beneath her that was lurching backwards and forwards, creaking as it did. Dragging in a breath, LizAlec crawled across ice-cold metal only to hit a surface straight ahead that was hard and flat. It too was speckled with stars.

Glass, thought LizAlec as she brushed a finger across its cold surface. Without even knowing she'd done it, LizAlec retuned her optic nerves, running through infrared and m/wave, rejecting both and finally retuning the 120m rod cells in her retina. The trade-off shift to mute pastels and greys was the price of seeing clearly. It took just long enough for LizAlec to feel it happen and then she was suddenly looking at herself in a vast mirror that just hung there. Between the mirror and the steel grating on which she knelt was a two-feet-wide gap.

Through the gap LizAlec could see a space so vast it would have been impossible to contain within *The Arc* had it been real. But it wasn't. Distances multiplied and space doubled and then doubled again as LizAlec looked round at the wilderness of hanging mirrors.

Beside her, behind her, in front . . .

A thousand frightened, wide-eyed LizAlecs stared back, endlessly reflected. She looked shit, every single one of her. The T-shirt she'd borrowed from Leon was grit-smeared and stained, her cropped hair slick black with sweat. Ugly sweat circles stood out endlessly under her arms and down her gut.

Shit on wheels, no one could be expected to look at themselves looking like that, it was time she got out of there.

LizAlec gripped two freezing rails and slid down a long run of metal stairs, feet not touching the steps. Somewhere down below would be Sister Aaron's own little clone-zone. And if luck was good that's where she'd find the shrine everyone seemed to be after, including the lunatic in her head.

The next flight was single rail so she couldn't slide. Instead, LizAlec took it at a run. Screeching to a halt at the bottom she almost cannoned head-first into herself, the walkway rocking drunkenly from side to side. Glass again . . . LizAlec edged sideways along the mirror, trying to ignore her reflection as it did the same. Both reaching round the edge of the mirror to look at the back, except there was no back.

The floating glass reflected on both sides. They all did. And the mirrors weren't floating either, no matter what it looked like. Hair-thin threads of monofilament rose into the blackness up towards the distant ceiling, each one as taut as the string to any violin.

LizAlec reached out and tapped one of the threads, pulling back in shock as the wire sliced into her fingertip. Not monofilament but molywire. Behind LizAlec someone laughed.

'Sharp things cut,' said a voice.

LizAlec spun round and saw only herself reflected in a mirror off to the side.

'It's a maze,' said Sister Aaron.

'I know that,' LizAlec muttered bitterly, her eyes searching steps and runways, looking for Sister Aaron. 'Multi-level 3D.'

'Oh no,' the voice sounded genuinely amused. 'Not triD, it's very definitely *quad* . . .'

LizAlec was still trying to track down the voice when her own reflection swirled and faded in every glass LizAlec could see. She felt like someone had kicked her feet out from under her. Staring back was her own face but younger. The hair was neat and tied back into a plait, the violet eyes less hard, more hurt. Her mouth was petulant, over-glossed with black *shu uemura*.

As for the clothes . . . embroidered trousers, velvet shirt with pearl buttons: she wouldn't be seen dead wearing them, not now. But LizAlec recognized herself right enough. That night at the Crash&Burn in Bastille, when Fixx sent her over undrinkable brandy.

'Not far back enough?'

LizAlec swung round but there was no one standing there behind her. The only thing that had changed was the girl in the mirror. It was still LizAlec, looking younger still, more haunted. Ghost-ridden. In place of the sullen fourteen-year-old in a velvet shirt was a naked twelve-year-old, hands crossed tight over her hollow gut, shoulders hunched forward to hide tiny breasts. She was sitting on the edge of a bed, tears streaming down her anguished face, dark shadow hiding her thighs like a swirl of blood.

She could have been the model for Edvard Munch's *Puberty*.

Or for Felician Rops's engraving of *Don Juan's Greatest Conquest*.

But she was neither.

And the old man in the background struggling into a dressing gown woven from silk genetically engineered to contain pure gold was not an artist. LizAlec knew his face, every child did. It was the face on all the medals, on the holograms used to emboss *cartes blanches* and *nobliques*. The Prince Imperial looked thoughtful, even slightly sad, but there was no regret in his smoke-grey eyes.

No remorse.

No uncertainty.

'You owe Lady Clare nothing,' said a voice. And this time when LizAlec turned round, Sister Aaron was standing right behind her. 'Lady Clare's not even your real mother. You're a clone like me. And not even her clone.'

'No,' LizAlec shook her head frantically. She'd have known if she was a clone, LizAlec was certain of it.

'You belong here,' Sister Aaron said and the child in the mirror vanished as Sister Aaron gave LizAlec back her reflection. Except now they both knew exactly what flaws were hidden inside. Which didn't make LizAlec feel good about herself – and it didn't make LizAlec feel good about Sister Aaron, either.

Emotional manipulation, the girl thought bitterly, that's all this was. Nothing more. She stopped looking at the mirrors and stared instead at the woman in front of her. In most ways Sister Aaron was way too exotic for LizAlec to understand, but in one way she wasn't . . . LizAlec figured Sister Aaron had to have the same circuitry inside her head. Apparently that was something she shouldn't have thought.

'Make your choice,' said Sister Aaron abruptly, and every mirror around LizAlec reverted to the crying child. 'Be this, or be us. While you still can . . .' Her voice was cold and contemptuous, as if LizAlec had failed some test.

Maybe I have, LizAlec thought, but that changed nothing. Looking at Sister Aaron, LizAlec knew just what she intended to do. She was going to take back Anchee's shrine, even if she had to kill Sister Aaron to get it. And then, when she got back to Paris, she was going to face down the bitch she'd thought was her mother and ask the questions no child was meant to ask.

Why?

Who gave you the right?

Why me?

The two women stared at each other, a hand's breadth apart. And then LizAlec moved, spinning not at Sister Aaron but towards a mirror, hands flicking out in front of her. Shiori's razor-sharp katana was in LizAlec's hand before she was even conscious of it, metal flowing from between her fingers into a black blade that swung in a dazzling arc.

Katana hit molywire but it was the wire that snapped, whipping roofwards to smash another mirror on its way. A second stroke and another mirror broke free, falling a hundred metres to smash against the steel floor below.

I love the sound of breaking—

That was Fixx for you, still polluting her head with soundbites even when she was trying to save his life. Actually, if Alex Gibson was right, it was everybody's life, more or less. Lady-fucking-Clare included.

'Last chance,' said Sister Aaron.

LizAlec shook her head. No, her last chance was long gone. 'Give me Anchee's shrine,' LizAlec demanded and Sister Aaron laughed. Sharp as broken glass and cold as wind through an attic.

Bringing up the blade of her katana, LizAlec swirled towards another mirror and high-tension molywire ricocheted up into the distance as another sobbing child crashed to fragments on a walkway three levels beneath. Suddenly, there were mirrors everywhere, what looked like thousands of them, edging walkways at every level, reflecting LizAlec back at herself until she was being buried under her own memories.

LizAlec swung the blade in a clumsy arc around her head and turned to face Sister Aaron. 'Stop it,' said LizAlec. 'Stop it now.'

The face that smiled back was more beautiful than any LizAlec had seen, more beautiful even than Anchee. But the curve to her perfect lips was cold in the way that a Big Black was cold and her blue eyes were hard, inhuman.

'Walk away,' Sister Aaron offered. 'Leave *The Arc*. Take that ship and your *friends* . . .' For a second LizAlec saw Fixx and Leon through the eyes of Sister Aaron. A washed-up, has-been *tetsuo* and a would-be street punk. 'Take them and go.'

'No,' said LizAlec and knew she was saying the word three years too late and that no one would have listened to her back then anyway. But that wasn't the point. Even late can be better than never learning to say it at all.

'Get out of my head.'

LizAlec made her blade sweep an infinity spiral in front of her, tracing its figure of eight faster than human eye could see. Both LizAlec's feet were placed correctly, one forward for advance, one back and half turned to balance LizAlec on the rocking walkway . . . It wouldn't convince the St Lucius *sensai* but it still felt pretty neat to LizAlec.

Something about it didn't convince Sister Aaron either. Instead of backing away she stepped straight into the path of the blade, instinct making LizAlec throw wide her blow. Sister Aaron smiled.

'Sweet, aren't you?' The voice had gone back to being amused. Elegant fingers reached out to caress LizAlec's smooth cheek and the girl screamed. When Sister Aaron stepped back her immaculate fingers were lacquered in blood.

Sister Aaron moved in again. Only this time LizAlec stepped back and swung her blade hard at Sister Aaron's face, blinking as the woman spun effortlessly away. Fight or flight? There was no contest really. LizAlec turned tail and fled, sliding down to the next walkway, slamming into the bottom so hard that mirrors around the walkway rang like wind chimes.

Three directions, out to each side and straight ahead – and she didn't have the faintest which one to choose. LizAlec went ahead – it was easier than trying to throw a turn on a walkway that rocked like a badly-built house of cards.

Ice dragged at her throat as LizAlec pulled frozen air into her lungs and jumped another flight of steps, hanging a right because that was all there was. She jumped again and instinct saved her – pure, animal, unmissable – as she threw up her sword in front of her and promptly catapulted onto her back as her blade slammed into molywire strung throat-high across the walkway.

Scrambling to her feet, LizAlec hacked at the molywire, severing it in a flash of sparks. She took the next landing at a lope, sword in front of her this time. In one way, every walkway she reached was the same. Mirrors overlapped mirrors, everywhere, in all directions, and all of them showed her . . .

There were gaps between the mirrors, spaces a body might

slide through to reach walkways behind. But there was no way for LizAlec to find the gaps, short of running her hands over the face of every mirror she met, looking for where it ended and space began.

So instead LizAlec cut down her reflections, shattering the memories she'd worked so hard to forget. LizAlec as a small child, crying on her first day at the Lycée; the morning she lost her best friend; the Imperial ball, LizAlec sitting on a gilded chair on the edge while the Prince Imperial's bastard son Louis danced with someone else; that first time Fixx got drunk at the club and walked out on her. Small hurts and bigger ones, all ripped out of her head.

LizAlec slammed the razor-edged katana into molywire, sending memory after memory crashing into shards onto the walkways below. However many mirrors she cut there were always more behind, more walkways, more steps . . . LizAlec took the next flight at a run, blade in front of her – no wires – and slid right to find herself face to face with Sister Aaron.

LizAlec's blade swung for the woman's throat and glass shattered.

'You can run, but you can't hide . . .' Framed in another mirror, the ash-blonde woman adjusted her hair. Not a strand of it was out of place: no sweat patches stained her white sarong, the bitch's hairline wasn't even damp.

LizAlec shattered that mirror too and behind her Sister Aaron laughed, the real Sister Aaron this time.

'God, I love this game,' she told a breathless LizAlec. 'I can't tell you when I last had this much fun.' Fingers reached for LizAlec's face and the girl ducked back, sword flicked up in front of her.

'Back off,' LizAlec hissed, really meaning it, and swung, hard as hell, straight at Sister Aaron's head. But the woman just stepped sideways, elusive on her feet. 'Temper, temper . . .'

LizAlec attacked again, swinging viciously towards Sister Aaron's head and when that missed, she cut down hard towards the woman's bare legs. Let her walk on stumps . . . Neither blow came close.

'*Honey,*' snapped a voice deep inside her, '*Don't waste your energy.*' LizAlec froze, then jerked back as Sister Aaron's hooked fingers whistled past her eyes, so close that LizAlec could feel the breeze.

'Alex?'

'*Alex!*' Outrage filled LizAlec's head. '*You know what Alex-fucking-Gibson knows about close combat? Fuck all . . . Get down,*' snapped the voice and LizAlec did, Sister Aaron's clawed nails whistling over her head. '*Rule one, don't let the bitch make you fight on her territory.*' The voice sighed. '*Well, you've blown that. Rule two, find solid ground . . .*'

LizAlec hesitated.

'*That means fucking jump,*' the voice said irritably so LizAlec did, clearing a short run of steps and stumbling on the walkway below. '*Jump again,*' snapped the voice. And LizAlec ran straight into a mirror.

'*Sweet fucking Nazarene. Can't you do anything right?*'

'No,' LizAlec shook her head and pulled herself unsteadily to her feet. It seemed she couldn't, not properly.

'*All right, let's try this . . .*' Neurons exploded within LizAlec's cortex, burning into a double matrix of endlessly swirling impulses as axons and dendritic nerves sparked off each other, hollow as ghost fire. All LizAlec felt was a lurch in perception, no stronger than the beginning of an ice run, and then someone else was looking out through her eyes.

'*Don't worry,*' the someone said, using LizAlec's voice. '*Everyone's more than one person.*'

'Speak for yourself, darling,' said Sister Aaron, climbing up the stairs that LizAlec had been intending to go down. She still wore the white silk sarong fastened under her arms, her legs were still bare and her face was as empty and beautiful as ever, but that wasn't what LizAlec noticed. In Sister Aaron's hand was a sword, black with a silver cutting edge and a gently curving blade.

The woman swung the blade lightly in front of her and inside her mind LizAlec felt the ghost grow suddenly tense. Then the tension seeped away to leave nothing but whistling waste-like emptiness.

'*Close down*,' whispered the voice in her head. LizAlec tried, but didn't know what she was trying to do.

'*Think hollow*,' said the voice.

Sister Aaron smiled, still swinging the blade lazily. 'Relying on the hired help again, are we, darlings?' The woman's wrist flicked lightly sideways and her blade skimmed up towards LizAlec's unprotected throat.

It never came close to connecting. Inside the same split second, LizAlec blocked the incoming blade in a crash of sparks and pivoted her own sword around Sister Aaron's, pushing it to one side. Without stopping, LizAlec sliced sideways at waist level to open a rip in the blonde woman's white sarong that beaded with blood along its edges.

'Little bitch.'

The mind pushing at the outside edge of LizAlec's faded slightly as Sister Aaron drew back into herself, fingers touching the cut on her hip, as if she couldn't believe the wound was there.

'*Okay*,' said the voice, sounding tentatively relieved. As if what it had feared would happen just maybe wasn't going to. The walkway still rocked below LizAlec's feet as she circled Sister Aaron, but this time LizAlec had no trouble keeping her balance. She had the blade held in front of her, angled off-centre, ready to block any slice Sister Aaron might throw.

Left.

Right.

The tall woman's sword curved in, only to thud into LizAlec's silver blade, sparks flying, shock waves numbing the nerves in both their arms. Block, cut, block – fighting got easier once you got the empty rhythm of the moves.

'*Finish her*,' said the voice in LizAlec's head, but the girl only stepped back, raised her blade and began to circle again. She could do block and parry, at least she could now. Doing death was something else again. LizAlec didn't do death. She'd never even killed an insect, except by accident.

'*What about Brother Michael?*' The voice in her head sounded exasperated.

That was different. Anyway, she hadn't killed him, that had been left to the Big Black.

'*Get real,*' the voice told her. LizAlec didn't want to. She very seriously, very definitely didn't want to get real at all. She was just about coping with the idea that this wasn't real, that maybe she was merely insane.

'*Honey,*' said the voice. '*If we don't fucking finish this, she will . . .*'

And that looked to be true, too. Sister Aaron was closing in, pushing LizAlec back towards a glass behind her, until the girl had no more room to retreat.

'*Fall,*' the voice snapped and LizAlec fell, hearing Sister Aaron's sword explode into the glass above, showering LizAlec with razor-sharp splinters. In front of LizAlec, her own sword was changing shape, its blade shrinking down to dagger length.

'*Now. Roll,*' said the voice and LizAlec rolled in through Sister Aaron's legs, stabbing upwards as she did, hearing a wet sucking sound as metal severed flesh and then ground noisily against bone.

LizAlec didn't need the second blow, the one that would reach back and snap the hamstring of Sister Aaron's left ankle because the woman's bowels were already voiding, but LizAlec cut the hamstring anyway and the screaming woman buckled sideways, blue eyes already blank with shock, her blade retracting into itself, melting to a silver puddle next to her twitching hand.

'*Finish it, honey,*' demanded the voice. '*You have to.*'

Unfortunately for LizAlec that was true. Kneeling over Sister Aaron, LizAlec felt for the woman's heart and found its beat erratic and weak beneath one perfectly defined breast. Closing her own eyes, the girl positioned her blade between two thin ribs and pushed.

'*Now get that fucking shrine and get out of here, okay? No tears, no hanging about, no shit.*'

Not even bothering to take one last look at the corpse behind her, LizAlec flipped down some stairs with speed she didn't know she had, rolled into the gap between a mirror and the walkway and dropped into space, landing lightly twenty feet below. She was moving again almost before she was aware she'd landed, spinning sideways, cutting a wire she didn't even know she'd seen and then taking the next flight of steps at a single jump.

If she stopped now she'd never start again. LizAlec didn't know how she knew, she just did. Or maybe she didn't. Maybe it was the person looking out of her eyes who knew. Landing with another roll, LizAlec came face to face with herself in the mirror and saw a half-naked silver exotic looking back. Shark cartilage overlaid with lizard skin protected her shoulders, her eyes were silver and her fingers flexed and unflexed to show wicked molyglass nails that sprang out and retracted like those of a cat. Her exotic's top was covered with an open silver Issaki Mashui quilted jacket but from the hips down she was bare, her body hair depilated, pudenda sealed with three gold labia rings.

'What the . . .'

'*Razz,*' said Razz, and LizAlec felt herself flip sideways, then run for another flight of stairs. '*See me while you can.*'

'My mother.'

'*If you say so, honey.*' The voice sounded surprised but cool about it all the same. LizAlec needed to stop, to slow down and talk but the presence behind her eyes wouldn't let up, hurrying her ruthlessly down towards ground level. Making LizAlec ignore her mirrored reflection that changed with each drop, each new walkway. She'd long since ditched her own past, bleak though scraps of it were, and traded up to worse possibilities. The mirrors gave form to fears LizAlec had fought to keep nameless. All that had been locked inside her head was reflected endlessly in the surrounding, suffocating reflections. Infinity and horror stuffed into boxes.

'*Okay, honey, this is it . . .*'

LizAlec skidded to a halt on the final walkway and looked around. It was a shit move. The face staring back had its lips pulled up into a rictus snarl. She was stripped naked, not bare but flayed, her epidermis stripped back to reveal pulpy, blood-sweating flesh. Just looking at it hurt.

As LizAlec watched, horrified, her flayed skin shrivelled away like melting wax to reveal yellow fat-pustuled layers of hypodermis beneath. And, beneath that, striated muscle and tapeworm-like strips of tendon, and a pulsing, crawling pink-and-purple web of arteries and veins.

'*Honey, get up.*'

LizAlec was on her knees despite the shouting in her head. She needed to move, but she couldn't. She was coming apart in front of her own eyes. Shock-frozen as the upper muscle layer of her face flayed back, the jaw-closing bands of purple muscle rotting away to reveal her bare skull. Not white – as she somehow imagined – but glistening a tallow-wax yellow. Lidless pain-wrecked eyeballs stared at her from hollow sockets and then glazed over, like the eyes of a bludgeoned fish.

LizAlec vomited, spewing Leon's chocolate onto the metal floor.

'*Move, fuck it.*' The voice in her head was loud, vicious: pain blossoming through LizAlec's skull until she fought to stand upright just to make it go away. Standing took more will than LizAlec knew she had. To move away from that last glass took even more. But LizAlec did it, glancing back only once, to see the flesh on her chest and shoulders flay down to the bone.

'*Not bad, honey. Not bad at all . . .*' The words were softer, amused, almost impressed. And for the first time in days, LizAlec smiled as she walked towards a polycrete prefab thrown up in the middle of a vast curving floor littered with smashed glass.

High above her, like corrupted raytracing, walkways and stairs floated in frozen darkness, held in place by strands of molywire so thin as to be invisible. All around those, like antique circuit boards slotted into transparent mountings, hung endless mirrors suspended in mid-air. The whole structure still swayed slightly with the after-effects of her passing. LizAlec had just completed the Brotherhood's highest mystery, without ever intending to.

LizAlec opened the door of the prefab, fingers sticking briefly to the frozen handle, and then she found herself inside a simple windowless laboratory lit by halogen lights. It looked like something from St Lucius. Elements were stored down one wall, arranged according to the periodic table, radioactive materials clearly marked. On the opposite wall, racked in a cryo unit, were embryos and freeze-dried amino acids. There was a black Drexler Box in one corner and next to the matter compiler was a semi-AI fume cupboard. A greybox stuffed with parallel RISC processors sat on the floor, stripped back to its frame, lumps of oily bioClay stuck to it like cancer. Above it, a vast Tosh flatscreen was running endlessly through some fractal sequence.

At one end of a long plastic table sat a DNA polymerase reactor *cum* enzyme cutter, at the other an IBM nanite coder was on standby: between them was a molybdenum flask, a clay pot planted with valerian and a half-empty glass of water. Discarded by the plant was a simple silver bangle.

'*Get the shrine*,' said the voice in her head. '*And then let's get out of here.*'

LizAlec did.

Chapter 39

20/20 Hindsight

Air compacting in front of it, the magLev bullet train sped over the top of Gibraltar Dam, breaking a flickering ribbon of holotape. Djellaba-clad adults cheered and beautiful, wide-eyed children released balloons, but they were added post-production, backed up in ranks on the screen behind Passion until even CySat/Maroc's flamboyant on-site editor thought the effect was overdone.

Security was airtight, Sikorskys thudding low overhead, their gunpods outnumbered only by registered Aerospatiale drones fielding under-slung vidcams. The Ishies were pushed back behind an electric fence. The real public was hemmed in by a fence behind that. Even if the General had been willing to let the crowds get in close – and he wasn't – it was an absolute condition that Lady Clare didn't let the Prince Imperial appear in public without shutting down all risk.

The old man was in full dress as commander of the *Grenadiers à Cheval de la Garde Impériale*, gold braid rolling in cavalry loops across his blue jacket. At his side hung an antique sabre recently presented to him by the local Iman. The Bonapartes had managed to stay on good terms with the Islamic faith for over 300 years: the old man wasn't about to blow it now.

He was mounted on a magnificent Arab stallion that had been shot up with enough ketamine to sedate the horse but not enough to ruin the proud way the animal held its head. And if you didn't know, you wouldn't have been able to tell that horse and rider stood rigid inside a complex lattice of laser, protection against all but the most determined sniper.

From where she stood, Lady Clare could watch sand flies vaporize as they met the circle, but no one else was close enough to see. And it wouldn't show up on camera, laser lattices never did.

The old man hated the lattice, mostly because he refused to believe anyone might want to kill him. But Lady Clare had insisted, reeling off a list that began with the Antiguan Absolutists and ended with Zebediah Nouveau. Mind you, he didn't hate standing inside that circle as much as he hated being there at all.

But Lady Clare had insisted on that as well. Keeping her good side to the main CySat camera, Lady Clare smiled. It was amazing how much clout you carried when you'd linked data credits to gold reserves to keep the senior officers loyal, welcomed the UN Pax Force with open arms, arranged for Paris to be the first European city overflown with the new 'dote and put some backbone into the Prince Imperial. This was the General's payback, and as far as Lady Clare was concerned it was a small price.

As for *her* reward . . . The new Princess Imperial looked around her, eyes stopping briefly as they touched on a tired young Imperial Guard. Despite the thermal cooling built into his ornate uniform he looked hot and hollow-eyed.

For the briefest moment, Lady Clare felt almost guilty and then she shrugged. Good sex was a new experience for her. The boy could catch up on his sleep when this charade was over. Feeling the Prince Imperial catch her eye, the elegant woman hastily looked forward, concentrating on the speeding bullet train as it shot into the distance on its first run from Tromso to CapeCity.

She couldn't afford a scandal, not yet. And after years of discreetly rewriting society's moral code from behind the scenes, Clare was finding it tough to remember that CySat now had a vidcam permanently on her.

She'd have to get used to that. Have to do something about LizAlec and Leon too, but that can of worms could wait. Beside her stood the General, neat and spruce, brown eyes gleaming as he watched his train. But that wasn't his real reward. They were standing on that: atop a vast ferroconcrete dam that now divided the Mediterranean from the Atlantic. The water level in the inland sea was already 200 metres lower than in the outer ocean, and it was falling daily as high summer approached and sea water evaporated.

Solar energy and wave power were fine in their place. And no doubt, affordable fission would be too when some metaNational finally cracked it. But until then the General controlled the greatest source of hydroelectric power in Europe. His daughter was back, seemingly unharmed by the fact her mind had taken a four-week holiday wrapped around somebody else's wrist. His biotects were recreating Paris in perfect replica, coding each fallen building into an exact double grown from polycrete. Just shells at the moment, glass would come later.

As for the Fourth Reich, it was dust, from politics to history in twenty-four hours. After his elite team had taken out the high-ranking officers and key NCOs the Parisians had slaughtered the Black Hundreds, flooding to the battered, rubble-strewn outskirts of the city, driven by sudden patriotism and the thought of all that horsemeat. The Americans had done the rest, flying in UN battalions as soon as Langley confirmed that a 'dote definitely existed and it was up for licence. But that came later, two days later, which was how long Langley took to process the General's message that, actually, he and not the Prince Imperial knew the formula for the 'dote. He didn't, of course. Only old men inside the shrine knew the formula but he wasn't going to tell Langley that.

Making the fight for Paris about horsemeat was Lady Clare's idea, and like most of her ideas it was a good one. She was worth every bit of the twenty per cent holding in the Dam which the General had helped her hide behind shell companies. And

that was before she became Princess Imperial. Now she'd want more . . . and he'd pay it, eventually. General Que smiled, teeth drawn back over yellowing fangs.

It was going to be an interesting few years.